PRAISE FOR TERRI PARLATO AND
ALL THE DARK PLACES

"*All the Dark Places* by Terri Parlato is a must read for anyone who loves a good mystery! The suspense was spine-tingling, and the characters were interesting but believable. I loved this book and had to force myself to lay it aside at night. Seriously, a must read!"
—Lisa Jackson, # 1 *New York Times* bestselling author

"A creepy debut most notable for the nightmares it finds beneath apparently untroubled surfaces."
—*Kirkus Reviews*

"A moody, atmospheric thriller perfectly crafted with just enough clues dropped along the way to keep the reader guessing and hopelessly addicted. I know I was."
—Charlie Donlea, *USA Today* bestselling author of *Twenty Years Later*

"Gripping. . . . Tension builds as the action alternates between the first-person narratives of Rita and Molly. Assured pacing matches accomplished characterizations. Parlato is off to a strong start."
—*Publishers Weekly*

"Hooks you immediately. Sharp characters and a plot full of twists kept the pages turning to the last. Fantastic read!"
—Mary Burton, *New York Times* bestselling author

"*All the Dark Places* checks all the right boxes for domestic suspense fans. This chilling whodunnit hooked me on the first page and kept me guessing to the last."
—Wendy Corsi Staub, *New York Times* bestselling author

Books by Terri Parlato

ALL THE DARK PLACES

WHAT WAITS IN THE WOODS

Published by Kensington Publishing Corp.

TERRI PARLATO

ALL THE DARK PLACES

KENSINGTON
PUBLISHING CORP.

www.kensingtonbooks.com

KENSINGTON BOOKS are published by

Kensington Publishing Corp.
119 West 40th Street
New York, NY 10018

All Kensington titles, imprints, and distributed lines are available at special quantity discounts for bulk purchases for sales promotion, premiums, fund-raising, educational, or institutional use.

Special book excerpts or customized printings can also be created to fit specific needs. For details, write or phone the office of the Kensington Special Sales Manager: Attn. Special Sales Department, Kensington Publishing Corp, 119 West 40th Street, New York, NY 10018. Phone: 1-800-221-2647.

The K with book logo Reg US Pat. & TM Off.

ISBN: 978-1-4967-3857-8
First Kensington Hardcover Edition: January 2023
First Kensington Trade Edition: December 2023

ISBN: 978-1-4967-3858-5 (ebook)

10 9 8 7 6 5 4 3 2 1

Printed in the United States of America

For my husband and children with all my love.

Acknowledgments

I am so grateful for all the people who helped bring *All the Dark Places* to life. To my writers group members, Tacey Derenzy, R. H. Buffington and Sandra Erni, thank you for your hard work, insight, and encouragement. Your contributions to my story are boundless. I hope I have satisfied your calls for "more Rita." And Sandra, thank you for the twenty-five plus years of writing, reading and laughter!

And to Charlotte Smallwood, thank you for your eagerness to read more. Readers like you push me to do my best every day and I hope that I live up to your expectations.

To my wonderful editor, John Scognamiglio, a huge thank-you for saying yes to my manuscript and your enthusiasm for this story. Your suggestions made my novel so much better than I could have hoped. And thank-you to all the amazing people at Kensington who did such great work on this book.

To my incredible agent, Marlene Stringer, thank you so much for taking a chance on me. Among a million other things, you deftly handle my anxiety when it rears its ugly head. I can't thank you enough.

A heartfelt thank-you to my children, Brittany, Becca and Nick. You are amazing people, and I am so proud of you. You inspire me to always follow my dreams. And your support means the world to me. And lastly, thank you to my husband, Fred, for not batting an eyelash when I told you I wanted to quit my teaching job to write full-time. I never could have gotten to this place without your steadfast support and hard work to ensure that the household stayed afloat. I am forever grateful for you and our beautiful family.

Chapter 1

Molly

Sometimes I want to capture a happy moment to keep forever. Not like a picture or a video, but a feeling. A feeling that I want to relive for the rest of my life. (Why is it that nightmares insist on the same treatment?) I shudder and move away from the dark hallway and into the light of the living room, where my husband stands in front of the blazing fireplace while he relates a funny story to our friends. They've gathered for his birthday celebration and laugh with honest mirth. Everyone loves Jay. No one more than me.

The first week in January isn't a great time to have a birthday, but since we have no choice in the matter, I've done my best to make everything light and festive. Jay's fortieth is going to be one to remember if I can help it. The Christmas tree still shimmers in the corner, and white candles glow across the mantel, setting the photos there alight. Jay and I smiling and posing, the pictures illustrating our happy three-year marriage.

There's a sharp contrast between inside and out. Dark falls early in New England in the winter. It's been as black as coal dust outside the windows for over an hour. Only the glow of a single streetlight across the road illuminates our snow-shrouded neighborhood. We've been in the house not quite a year, yet it feels like home. It's an older place, almost historic, and the nooks and crannies and gleaming woodwork appealed to me right away. Inside, the house is bright, alive with friends and my perfect husband. I feel safe here.

The cake is a work of art and sits boxed in the fridge, hidden until the big moment. Jay didn't want a huge bash, just our best friends, good wine, and food. It should be a wonderful night. *Should* being the operative word. I'm praying I don't spoil it.

I stand at the granite counter, arrange the finger foods I'd ordered from our favorite café on the square. Everything looks delicious, if only I had an appetite. Instead, I pick up my wine, a rich Malbec we picked up on a trip to California last summer, and take a sip. Jay comes up behind me and wraps me in his arms, rests his chin on the top of my head. I love his touch, his strong arms that make me feel safe and grounded, the smell of his woodsy cologne. I sigh, and a tear escapes and runs down my cheek.

"Hey." He turns me to face him and wipes it away with his thumb. "None of that, okay? We've got this."

I nod, sniff. "Sorry."

"Don't be." He crushes me in his arms and skims his lips half on my mouth, half on my chin, a light reassuring kiss. "Everything's going to be fine, Molly."

At six-thirty, our friends started arriving, bringing winter air and a few stray snowflakes with them through the front door. There were hugs and kisses, presents, although I told everyone Jay didn't want any.

Kim, my best friend since second grade, and her husband, Josh, an old friend of Jay's, sit on the sofa. We introduced them shortly after Jay and I started dating. Kim is petite, dark-haired, with big brown eyes, a former cheerleader. She's as extroverted as I am quiet, but we complement one another.

Cal, Jay's hockey buddy, and his wife, Laken, a tall, beautiful blonde, sit in dining room chairs carried in to provide more seating. Laken owns a day spa in town, and at the door, she'd pressed a thick, cream-colored envelope into Jay's hand. A massage gift certificate, no doubt. Laken and I've gotten to be good friends too.

And Elise and Scott. Dr. Elise Westmore is Jay's partner in a family therapy practice, and they round out our group. The Westmores are older than we are, both in their early fifties. Jay met Elise in grad school, and they hit it off. He calls her the big sister he never had.

"Who wants what?" Jay asks, the Malbec bottle in his hand. Glasses are raised, and he pours, then slips behind the bar for a second bottle. "Cal, you want a beer instead? I just made a Trillium run."

Cal smiles and stands. "You know me, my friend. I'll get it." He turns to Scott, who sits next to Elise like an elder statesman. "You want a beer?"

"That would be great," Scott replies.

There's an easy rapport among the eight of us, and I smile as I carry a tray of mushroom and Gruyère crostini and place it on the coffee table. I refill my glass and try to enjoy the wine and the focus on Jay. I admire his total comfort with people. I guess that's why he's such a good psychologist. People trust him, know that they can. His easy smile and kind green eyes don't hurt either.

We've had a few drinks, eaten through half the food. The conversation has moved past the "What's new?" phase when Laken leans back in her chair, her long legs extending to the edge of the coffee table.

"So, Jay, how's the book coming?"

He takes a deep breath. "It's coming, slowly." His gaze shifts to the fireplace, where the flames snap and flare.

Jay's writing a book based on one of his grad-school papers. He doesn't talk about it, or his work, much really. That's all part of his boring, stuffy side, he says.

"Isn't it about some pretty creepy stuff? Abnormal psychology and gruesome crimes?" Laken asks.

Jay grimaces. "Some of it's pretty intense."

Elise straightens in her chair, eyes on Laken. "Abnormal psychology encompasses a wide range of behaviors, not all of them violent or particularly disturbing." A momentary tension crackles in the room. Barely there, but I feel it as I look from face to face. Kim leans forward and fills the silence.

"I had an aunt," she says, swallowing a sip of her drink, "who kept the fur she brushed out of all her dogs in a bag in the hall closet. My brother and I found it when we were kids. Scared the shit out of us. It had been there for like thirty years. Six dogs worth."

That makes Jay laugh. Kim is good at that. "The mind is a curious thing," he says and stands, picks up the nearly empty tray. "We need more food!" Something in Jay's voice has me on alert again. Something's been on his mind all week, but whenever I asked him about it, he brushed me off with a smile and said he was fine. I follow him into the kitchen, wander to the door, and look out across the backyard.

"The light's on in your office," I say, gazing at the old structure. The detached garage sits in the snow at the end of the driveway. No cars inside, just Jay's desk, a space heater, and other things he needs to furnish his home office.

"Must've left it on when I was working earlier." He uncorks another bottle of red. "I'll get it later. I might do a little more work after everyone leaves," he says, eyes on the wine as he refills his glass.

"Tonight?"

"For a little bit. I was in the middle of something when I had to come in and get ready for the party. Shouldn't take me long."

I move over to the counter, put a steadying hand on the edge. I finish my wine and hold out my glass to Jay. His eyes meet mine, and I smile, reassure him. "I'm fine, really."

He fills my glass, sets it on the table, and wraps his arms around me. "I have everything I need right here," he says.

Cal and Josh walk into the kitchen. Josh raises his empty glass. "What's the holdup?" He laughs. "Can't keep their hands off each other," he says to Cal.

"Do you blame me?" Jay says, brushing my long hair back over my shoulder.

I pull myself free and walk to the fridge. "Time for this, birthday boy." I set the box on the counter, lift the cake out. It's a canvas of sky-blue fondant with a garden of glistening orange and yellow flowers.

"Whoa. That's incredible. Be a shame to cut it," Jay says.

"They do a great job at André's," I say, removing a knife from the cutlery drawer.

"Chocolate or vanilla?" Cal asks.

Laken walks into the room. "God, Cal. It's *Jay*. Chocolate!"

Cal shrugs. "Maybe he got adventurous." The kitchen fills up with the rest of our friends, and I reach for the birthday candles.

Jay grabs my hand. "It would be a shame to ruin that beautiful cake with those!" But he's smiling. "What the hell? You only turn forty once, right?"

I know there is something wrong when I open my eyes and don't smell coffee. Jay isn't beside me in our king-size bed. He usually wakes before I do, but there's always the aroma of his favorite drink permeating the house. Jay's one of those people who sleeps only four or five hours a night. An inveterate coffee drinker, he downs five or six cups a day, enough to give most people a serious case of the jitters, but he thrives on it. I've gotten conditioned to that morning scent filling the house and my lids popping open, like clockwork.

The kitchen is cold, coffeepot sitting on the counter, empty and untouched.

"Jay?" I call, my voice echoing through the house. My heartbeat kicks up. I walk to the back door, peer outside. The door to

Jay's office is wide open. I fly down the porch steps and across the yard, my bare feet churning through the snow.

I stumble across the threshold. He isn't here.

"Jay?"

No answer. I move farther into the room, past the desk and space heater. Then I see him, lying on the floor, blood spattered on the wall and in a pool around his head. I drop to my knees, grab his hand. "Jay!"

But it's no use. He can't hear me. He's cold, lifeless. His neck gapes open beneath his stubbled chin. He's still dressed in the clothes he was wearing last night. His eyes are half-shut, and his dark hair is soaked in the puddle surrounding him. I fall back against the filing cabinet, screams erupting from someplace deep in my soul.

Cops swarm through the house as I sit in a kitchen chair. My sister, Corrine, is on her way. Someone brought me my robe from upstairs and helped me into it. It was that young officer, I think. The first one who arrived and escorted me back to the house. It was nice of her, but I'm still numb, my feet, my whole body.

The house is a wreck. I peek up and look out into the living room. Beer bottles and wineglasses litter every end table, even the fireplace mantel. Leftover dips and finger foods are spread across the counter, congealing, a disgusting mess. But who'd have thought anyone would be here before I'd had time to clear it all away? Who'd have thought my husband would be lying dead in his office the morning after his party? I cry into my fleecy sleeve. Who would do this to Jay? My life is collapsing around me, and I feel like I've fallen into a dark pit.

I hear Corrine's low, Lauren Bacall–like voice as she comes through the front door. She's talking to one of the cops. Then she's beside me, leaning over my shoulder, her perfume filling my nostrils. But it doesn't displace the smell of blood.

"What the hell happened, Molly?" She pulls me to standing and squeezes me in her arms.

I bury my face in her woolly coat.

"Ma'am, we need to ask you a few questions," a man's voice emanates from behind her.

Corrine turns to the cop and demands, "What's happened here?"

"That's what we're trying to figure out. Let's sit, okay?"

Somehow Corrine and I are sitting side by side while the husky, uniformed officer takes the chair across from us.

"I'm Sergeant Simmons," he says, and lays a notepad on the table. "Mrs. Bradley?"

I clear my throat, swipe a tissue under my nose. "Yes?"

"I need you to tell me what happened."

I try to breathe through my tears, try to pull a breath down into my chest. "Okay," I squeak, and think back to when I woke up, try to put disjointed pieces together. "I got up this morning, and my husband wasn't there, in bed. He's an early riser . . . There wasn't any coffee." I start to cry again, and the cop leans back in his chair.

Corrine drums the table with her fingers. "Is this necessary right now? She's distraught."

"I'm sorry, but we've got a dead man . . . You are?"

"Corrine Alworth. Her sister."

He nods. "Okay. Mrs. Bradley, so you woke up this morning, what time?"

I'm at a loss. My head is throbbing. I have no idea, so I look at the time on the microwave and try to figure it out. "Uh." It's ten-fifteen now. "Nine o'clock, maybe a little after."

"But you're not sure?"

"No."

He glances around the room, at the mess. "Had a party last night?"

"My husband's birthday." I duck my head, lean against Corrine. I want to disappear.

"Were you here, Ms. Alworth?"

"No. I wasn't," she says.

Is she angry? I can't always tell that about my big sister. She sounds angry a lot of the time. But she'd had other plans. I clutch my left forearm and work my fingers over my sleeve.

"Okay, Mrs. Bradley. You got up. Your husband wasn't in bed. Then what did you do?"

"I came downstairs, and I saw the office door was open. He said last night that he was going to do some work after everybody left."

"So he went out there last night?"

"Yes. That's what he said he was going to do."

"What time was that?" Sergeant Simmons's round, moon-like face is slack, patient, and I want to answer his questions. I want to be helpful, but anguished thoughts skitter through my brain like birds I can't catch.

"I don't know. Late."

"He always work late at night?"

"Yes, actually, he does."

"Okay. Did you lock the doors when you went to bed?"

I honestly don't know. My recollection is cloudy. We'd really had too much to drink. *I'd* had too much to drink. I barely remember walking up the stairs, and I'm suddenly cognizant of clumpy mascara sticking my lashes together, the gummy, unpleasant taste in my mouth. I hadn't even washed for bed.

I choke on a sob, clear my throat. "I think Jay did."

"But you don't know?"

Sergeant Simmons tries to catch my gaze, but I can't look at him. I don't want him here. I don't want my house filled with police officers touching our things, writing reports. I want Jay at the stove, flipping pancakes. Me beside him, frying bacon. I want to go back to yesterday. I shake my head, wipe my face with a tear-stained tissue.

"So you woke up this morning. Saw your husband wasn't in bed. Went downstairs to investigate and saw the office door open? Then what?"

"I ran across the yard to look for him." Corrine places a box in front of me, and I grab a fresh clump of tissues. I'm all snot and tears, as though I'm dissolving.

"Take your time, Mrs. Bradley."

I draw a deep breath. "I went into the office and saw Jay on the floor. His neck . . . he was dead." I drop my head to my chest and cry. Corrine's arm tightens around my shoulders.

I hear the buzz of voices. Other cops talking to Simmons. Then they move off.

"We're almost done, Mrs. Bradley. We'll need a list of everyone who was here at the party last night, okay?"

I try to meet his eyes and nod. *Jesus.* Do they think one of our friends did this? *That's not possible.*

Corrine rubs my shoulder. "We'll work on it, Officer. I'd like to get my sister something to drink. And she needs to get into some warm clothes."

"Take your time." He rises from the table. "We've got a forensics team on the way." He calls a female officer over. "Connors here will help you guys out, so you don't touch anything that might be important."

I nod and shuffle to my feet.

"Oh," he calls after me, "we need the clothes you were wearing last night." He shoots a glance at Officer Connors.

I choke out a breath. "Okay." *Does he think I had something to do with Jay's death?* The thought nearly buckles my knees.

CHAPTER 2

Rita

The first week of January, and we've already got a homicide. Times are definitely changing in our little Boston suburb. What a way to start a new year. And working a homicide is always an arduous task, the pinnacle of suffering and heartbreak for all involved. I blow out a breath, my hands gripping the wheel of my old van.

Simmons took the widow's statement, and then she left to stay with her sister. The forensics team is still on scene, and my partner, Detective Chase Fuller, and I are on our way over there.

Chase has a holiday hangover, still jazzed about Christmas with his wife and young son, gushing about all the cool toys the little guy got from Santa. This makes me think of Christmases when I was a kid. There were so many of us jostling to get close to the tree. Ma would yell and try to rein us in with threats of sending us to our rooms and canceling Christmas altogether. And there were only two gifts apiece, one from Ma and Dad and one from Santa. Money was tight, and since there were nine of us kids to provide for, there wasn't a lot to go around. But we had fun those Christmases until Ricky left for Vietnam and Jimmy got sick. That was the year everything went south for the McMahons.

"How did Sarah like the necklace?" I ask, slowing my van as

we approach the Bradley residence. I pull up behind a police cruiser.

"She loved it." He grins. "This was the first time I was able to give her something nice, you know?"

"Something without a cord?"

"Yeah." Chase has been a detective for less than a year, and while we don't make a buttload of money, he's making more than he did as a patrol cop. I like working with the young detectives. It can sometimes take the edge off a difficult case because you're in that teaching mode and you have that focus. Even after so many years, it's easy to get lost in the pain and evil we witness.

I glance in the rearview mirror. A media van is pulling up behind us. *Great.* "Let's head inside," I say. Time to get to work.

We jump out into the cold, my boots sinking into a pile of slush at the curb, and we move quickly up the walk to an impressive two-story. The neighborhood is older, the lots bigger than most of these new subdivisions with their nearly identical houses and tiny trimmed yards. Simmons said the vic was killed in a detached garage, but we head inside the house first.

The ME is leaning on the kitchen island, writing in her notebook. She drops her pen and looks up. "Hey, Rita."

I glance around. "Pretty messy," I say. Chase trails behind me, taking in the scene.

"Yeah. The wife said they had a party last night. The husband's birthday."

I wince. Killed after your own birthday party. That sucks. "That's too bad. He out in the garage?"

"Follow me." Susan Gaines and I have been in this line of work over thirty years. We both fought our way through our rookie days when law enforcement was basically a boys' club. Then she left for medical school, only to return to work in the criminal justice system. She and I get together occasionally for a beer and laugh about the old days and try to forget about the struggles.

The team is working the scene, and we weave around them and their equipment. I shout a hello here and there as we pass. They've taped off a path of well-trodden snow that leads across the yard. The sun's shining, and their evidence is literally melting before their eyes, so they work quickly. There's a side door in the building that had been described as a garage, but there are no cars in here. Chase and I pull on gloves and booties. The little building has all the appearance of a home office. Big desk covered in folders. A calendar with a mountain snow scene tacked on the wall, open to January. A dirty window that lets in weak sunlight. A coffee mug next to a Keurig that sits atop a filing cabinet next to the desk. Blood is drying in a big dark puddle around the body that used to be Dr. Jay Bradley.

"They find the murder weapon?" I ask Susan.

"Don't think so. There was nothing in here, but they've bagged up all the knives in the house."

I step over to the vic and drop down on my haunches. His head was nearly severed. The wound is wide and ugly. I peer up at Susan. "He was killed here, right?" Blood spatter from his severed artery decorates a nearby wall. Chase is coughing and clearing his throat behind me. "Check the desk," I tell him, and he moves back and away from the body.

"Yeah. Looks like." Susan drops down next to me. "The wound would've been quickly fatal." She points with her pen. "No defensive wounds apparent. But I'll know more after I get him back to the lab." She stands and heads outside.

I walk through the room, circle back to the filing cabinet. One drawer is pulled halfway out, and there are bloody smears near the handles. It looks like the perp wore gloves. There are also scratches near the lock. I pull out my phone and snap pictures. "The lock has been jimmied."

"What?" Chase says.

"The lock on the cabinet is broken." The first drawer yields what looks like research notes, old school-type papers. I lean over and check the bottom drawer. It's also crammed with odds and ends, news clippings and articles cut from magazines.

The desk drawers are also half-open and in disarray, as if someone had rifled through them. But a laptop sits on the desk, seemingly untouched. "He was looking for something," I say. Chase turns around from the far end of the room, where packing boxes are neatly stacked. "But left the computer."

"Not a robbery then," Chase says.

I shake my head. "He was looking for something specific." I draw a deep breath, turn to Chase. "Tell the team to take the filing cabinet to the lab." It'll be easier to sort through it there.

"Will do."

I check the floor for shoe prints, but don't find any. The perp must've been very careful not to step in the blood. I head outside, shade my eyes from the sun, and examine the snowy path. There are lots of shoe prints and footprints. Susan said the wife ran out this morning in her bare feet, but there are other prints, layered over each other and melting together. The snow is also churned up from the driveway to the office door. Chase is leaning against the side of the building and looks a little green. The smell in the garage was starting to get ripe.

He joins me, and we walk back across the yard.

"Sorry," he says.

"For what?"

"I never got used to it. The smell of blood. As a patrol officer, I always did my job, then stepped away as quickly as I could."

"No biggie. For some people, it never becomes routine."

We walk through the open kitchen door. Simmons stands by the sink, and he waves to flag me down. He and I confer, and he hands me his report, notes from his interview with Mrs. Bradley. Chase and I will head out to talk to her as soon as we're done here. But first I want to walk through the living room one more time. It's here that the Bradleys and their guests would have gathered. Laughed, talked, but maybe everything wasn't so friendly.

The mantel is covered with pictures and a couple of wine-glasses. The largest photo is of the Bradleys, I assume, decked out in their wedding finery. They're a handsome couple. He was dark-haired with a nice, confident smile. She's fine-featured, long red hair in an updo topped with a tiara.

I grab my notebook out of my satchel and flip to a new page. I quickly sketch my impressions of the scene, empty wine and beer glasses. Too many? I'll have to see the guest list, talk to the Mrs. Were people drinking too much? Was there something sinister simmering beneath the good cheer? Or was the house a happy cocoon with a murderer lurking in the garage, a beast waiting for his prey?

"Rita?" Chase calls.

"Yeah. Just a minute." I close my eyes and breathe deeply. Ma was a strict Catholic, but she believed in "feelings." Intuition, most people would call it. Not sure I buy into that, but I don't discount it either. I've trusted my gut over the course of my career, and it doesn't usually let me down, but I don't feel anything at the moment, only the sadness of the situation. A life lost, loved ones forever changed. I blow out a breath and glance out the window. Susan is standing in the backyard, directing her team as they load Dr. Bradley onto a stretcher and wheel him away.

I take a last look around. Who would want a young, handsome doctor dead?

CHAPTER 3

Molly

The police allowed me to change my clothes and pack a bag before leaving with Corrine. My home is now a crime scene, and I'm banished, at least for a little while. It pains me to leave, as though I'm turning my back on Jay and our life together. When I return, even his body will be gone, and I'll be alone again, an idea that shakes me to my core.

My sister and her husband, Rich, live in a tony apartment building in Boston. They'd moved there last year after their son left for college. Corrine was never the domestic type, and the less square footage to keep up, the better. Besides, she and Rich both work downtown in tall office buildings. The urban life suits them.

I changed out of my sweats when I got here, took a shower in the perfectly appointed guest bathroom, and dressed in leggings and a long blue sweater. Sergeant Simmons told me to expect a visit from the detectives.

I sit on my sister's expensive off-white sofa with a cup of tea she made and shoved into my icy hands. I can't seem to warm up but don't want to ask her to turn the heat up again. The view is beautiful, Boston Harbor in the distance, dark and still, and I try to make out the details of the boats anchored there, anything to keep from thinking about Jay. I'm beyond traumatized, temporarily emptied of tears, numb. I'm on autopilot. I know how to do this—function, don't think, and definitely don't feel.

Rich is away at a conference, so it'll be just my sister and me and our parents when they get here from Maynard. I really want to see Kim and Laken. I was able to call them and Elise quickly while my house was being searched, but then the cops asked for my phone, telling me they'd have it back as soon as possible. I guess I could've said no, but I don't want to hinder the investigation. Don't know what they think they'll find on it, but they assured me it was routine.

The bell chimes, and Corrine leads a man and an older woman into the living room. The woman is slim, has dark hair, with a light smattering of gray, pulled up in a bun, and light blue eyes that seem to take in everything around her. She's dressed in dark pants and a white, collared, button-up shirt, a jacket draped over her arm. The younger detective is bundled up in an overcoat and scarf. He carries a briefcase, and she drops a battered leather satchel on the floor next to the armchair. They introduce themselves as Detectives Myers and Fuller, Graybridge PD.

"We're sorry for your loss, Mrs. Bradley," Detective Myers says as she settles back in the chair.

I nod. It sounds so inadequate, as though my handbag went missing. But it's what people say in times like this.

Corrine appears from the kitchen. "Can I get anyone tea, coffee?"

They politely decline, and she heads back to the other room while I set my cup on the end table.

"Mind if I tape our conversation?" Detective Myers asks.

I shake my head, and she places her phone on the coffee table on top of a shiny art book. She has me state my name and the date before she dives into questions, scrawling in a little notebook as if the recording won't be enough.

"We've read the statement you gave to Sergeant Simmons. But we need to ask you to clarify a few things." Her eyes sweep over papers in a file folder. "How old are you, Mrs. Bradley?"

"Thirty-five." Why is that relevant?

"And your line of work?"

"I'm a sales associate at Graybridge Books." My gaze meets hers. "I have a college degree, English." That always comes out defensively.

"Okay. Your husband was forty? A psychologist in private practice?"

"Yes." I choke on my tears. The mention of Jay wipes away the numbness that had temporarily set in. I feel a gurgling in my chest as if my pain were a living thing clawing to get out.

"No children?"

That stings and I lower my eyes. "No."

"How long were you married?"

"Three years."

"Happy years?"

Detective Myers's eyes meet mine, and I push a clump of tissues under my nose. "*Yes.*"

"You and your husband weren't having problems?"

"No!" I gasp.

"How are your finances?"

I take a deep breath and shake my head. "Fine. Jay made a good living. We weren't having money trouble, if that's what you mean." I feel a flash of anger in my chest. "What are you doing to find my husband's killer, Detective? Who could've done this? Everybody loved Jay!" A sob erupts from deep inside me.

Detective Fuller leans forward, his dark eyes meet mine. "We're going to do everything we can to find his killer, Mrs. Bradley."

Detective Myers taps her pencil against her notebook. "We need to get all the details first, no matter how trivial they seem. Would you walk us through yesterday?"

Yesterday? Will I go through that day forever in my mind? Like a precious holiday never to be forgotten, but instead of family and fun, it's filled with pain and unimaginable sorrow. I don't want to recount it for these two strangers. It's mine, and I don't want to share my last day with Jay. Their request that I "walk through it" for them seems somehow obscene.

"Mrs. Bradley?"

"Okay." I guess I have no choice if I want Jay to be avenged, and I do. "It was a typical Saturday, except that it was Jay's birthday. We spent the morning running errands, groceries, post office, that sort of thing."

"Both of you?"

I nod and sniff. There's no more "both of us." "Then we stopped at André's on the square, and I ran in alone to pick up the cake and the party food." Detective Myers stops writing a moment, looks up. "I didn't want Jay to see the cake before the party. One of the guys who works there helped me carry everything to the car."

"Then what?"

"We went home. Had lunch. Jay went out to his office to work while I cleaned the house, got ready for the party."

Detective Myers leans back in her chair, trains her eyes on me. "Your husband has an office in town, right?"

"Yes. He and another therapist share space in the Tackler Building."

"Why does he need a home office in the garage?"

"A lot of people have a home office."

"Does he treat patients there?"

"Of course not. He just . . ." I take a deep breath. I'm rarely in

Jay's office. It's his intellectual equivalent of a man cave. "He researches. He writes. But he definitely doesn't see any patients out there."

"What's he writing?"

"A book about psychology. Scholarly stuff. He really doesn't talk too much about his work."

"Does he keep anything out there in the filing cabinet or his desk that someone might want?"

"I have no idea. I doubt it." But I remember the office had been in disarray. One of the filing cabinet drawers was open. Jay wouldn't have left it that way. "Do you think it was a robbery?"

"We don't know," Detective Myers says. She flips through papers in her folder. "You made a list of all the people at the party last night?"

"Yes. Our friends. Three couples."

"What time did they leave?"

I take a deep breath. I have no idea. "I'm not sure. I went up to bed, and Jay was still downstairs."

"You went to bed with your guests still there?"

I brush my hand through my damp hair. "No. I mean, everyone was getting ready to leave. Jay was walking them out."

"If you had to guess the time?"

"I don't know. Eleven-thirty maybe?"

The detective's eyes sweep over papers in her folder. "Any of your husband's patients giving him any cause for concern?"

"No. I don't think so. He doesn't discuss them with me except in vague terms on occasion."

"He wasn't worried about anyone, anything lately?"

I glance over her shoulder back out to the harbor and follow an expensive cabin cruiser as it motors slowly out to sea. "Not that he told me, but he was a little quiet this week. Something was on his mind, I think."

"Uh huh. But nothing you can pinpoint?"

"No." My gaze falls to my lap, where I've twisted a clump of tissues into a damp, fibrous mess. I want to help, but I really have no idea what was bothering Jay. I take a shuddering, teary breath. I should've pressed him. Why didn't I insist he tell me? I rub my hand over my eyes. It's my fault for being so needy, for being so focused on my own problems, never thinking that other people have troubles too. And now Jay's dead.

"Mrs. Bradley, are you sure you don't know what was on his mind?"

I try to weed through the last few days, remember our conversations, but nothing emerges that explains Jay's preoccupied mood. I shake my head. "I don't know what was bothering him, Detective," I say, feeling like a total failure.

"Okay. You hear anything after you went to bed? Raised voices? A scuffle?"

I was passed out. I can't even remember putting on my pajamas. "No. I didn't hear anything."

Detective Myers lifts a piece of notebook paper, looks it over through black-rimmed reading glasses. "So you had three couples at your house for the party. What can you tell me about them?"

I describe our friends and wonder what the detectives are thinking. Are they looking for trouble among our little group? From my perspective, that seems a waste of time. Whoever did this to Jay has to be a monster. No one who knew him would've hurt him. But maybe a patient, someone so disturbed that he or she shifted their animus onto Jay, made him the bad guy. I'm sure there's a psychological term for that.

Detective Myers nods as I talk. She writes in her notebook, her pencil scratching across the page, and I notice she's drawing, sketching a picture of me.

I look up and catch her gaze, and she snaps her notebook shut.

My cheeks are wet with tears, and I lean back into the sofa and wipe my face with my sleeve.

"Thank you, Mrs. Bradley," Detective Myers says. "That's all for now."

They stand, and Corrine pops up and walks them out. I wander to the window and glance down at the busy street below. I see cars, traffic, but no media, thank God. Not yet. I squeeze my eyes shut and pray they don't find me.

CHAPTER 4

Rita

Dr. Westmore answers her phone on the first ring. She and her husband are home, so we head back to Graybridge. The house is a massive three-story a few blocks from the Bradley residence. It sits back from the main road, obviously built a hundred years ago or more, with a big wraparound porch and gingerbread trim. We park in the long driveway, head up the walkway.

The door swings open, and we're greeted by a thin woman with shoulder-length brown hair and swooping bangs. She's dressed like she's going to work, even though it's Sunday. Neat beige trousers, a white blouse, green print scarf around her neck. She's older than Mrs. Bradley by at least a decade.

"Come in, Detectives," she says after we introduce ourselves. She leads us down a dark, polished hardwood hallway. A large tabby cat darts from a side room, quiet as a prowler. It scampers after her and escorts us into an antiques-laden parlor.

Dr. Westmore sits demurely in a carved and padded wooden chair, while Chase and I get settled on a stiff settee facing her.

"Is your husband here?" I ask.

"In the garden. Should I get him?"

I fish my notebook out of my satchel. "We'll talk to you first."

She nods, and her red-rimmed blue eyes take a furtive glance at a pack of cigarettes sitting next to an ashtray on the end table.

"I'm sorry about your friend," I say.

She tips her chin up toward the wedding cake of a ceiling and blows out a breath. "I can't believe it. Jay was . . ." She shakes her head. "He was a peach of a man. Smart, compassionate. A terrific psychologist." Her voice catches. "How could this have happened?" A tear slips down her cheek, and she wipes it away with a blood-red manicured fingernail.

"It's a puzzle right now, Dr. Westmore. Would you walk us through last night?"

She grabs a tissue from a box next to the ashtray. "Of course. We arrived at the Bradleys' house at around six-thirty. Kim and Josh were already there. Jay was Jay. Happy, pouring drinks."

"What'd you have?"

She smiles. "Wine. Malbec. Jay has a wonderful wine cellar."

I nod. A man after my own heart. "You guys do a lot of drinking?"

She tips her head. "Over the course of the evening, I suppose. Molly had a nice spread too, from André's. The food was terrific."

This I know. André is my neighbor, and he and his partner, Collin, provide me with dinner a few times a week from their café and catering business. They moved into the apartment above mine three years ago and gave me an expensive bottle of merlot as a get-to-know-you gesture. I hadn't been much of a wine drinker, but they explained that red wine was heart-healthy, and that was enough for me, although I'm careful to limit myself to two glasses on a work night. I'm too old to get shit-faced and function the next day.

"Was anyone drinking too much?" I ask.

It takes her a minute. She reaches down to stroke the cat, who's plopped down on her suede flats, licking its paws. "Maybe a little."

"Who?"

"I couldn't say, Detective. We were all just having a good time."

"How long have you known Dr. Bradley?" I ask, pencil poised.

She whooshes out a breath. "Gee, well. We met in grad school, so a long time. I was older than Jay. I'd gone back to school. Fifteen years, I'd say."

"You know anyone who would want to do him harm?"

She shakes her head firmly. "Absolutely not."

"Not a disgruntled patient, maybe?"

"Not that he told me. And he would've if he'd been worried."

"Does he confide in you, Dr. Westmore?"

She takes a minute, wipes away another tear. "Yes. He and I are close. He doesn't have much family."

"He didn't say anything or anyone was bothering him lately?"

"No. I wish . . ." Her gaze shifts to the window.

"What?"

"He did seem a little preoccupied last week."

"You didn't ask what was on his mind?"

She shrugs. "I figured he'd tell me when he was ready."

"Uh huh. So you have no idea what was bugging him?"

"No."

"What time did you and your husband leave?"

She picks up the cat and settles him on her lap. "I'm not positive. Before midnight, though. The floor clock was striking the hour when we got home."

"When you left, did anyone stay behind?"

"No. We all left at the same time." The cat's purrs fill the room with a gentle, throbbing hum. "Detective, you're not saying that one of us would've . . . hurt Jay?"

"Not saying that at all. Just trying to put together a timeline."

A man appears in the arched doorway.

"Scott, these are the detectives who called."

He's tall, thin but well-muscled, wearing jeans and a faded work shirt. His big hands are dirt stained, his hair cut short and graying. "Let me get cleaned up. I was out back working." He looks at his hands, then looks me in the eye. "I can't believe it about Jay." He turns on his heel and heads down the hall.

Dr. Westmore lowers her voice. "That's how he copes. Scott works. Some people cry. Others rage. Everyone has his or her own way of grieving."

"Uh huh. Kind of cold to be digging in the garden, isn't it?"

"He's a landscaper. He owns the business but likes to get his hands dirty. He doesn't mind the cold, and I think he's just been cleaning out the planters on the back porch."

"Hmmm. So there was no tension last night between anybody?" I shoot a glance at Chase, who's head down over his phone, taking notes.

"No. It was a delightful evening." She draws a deep breath and dabs at her eyes with a tissue. "We'll need to notify his patients," she says to herself.

Mr. Westmore returns. He's changed his clothes, washed his hands.

Dr. Westmore rises. "I'll be out front if you need me," she says, setting the cat on the floor and reaching for the cigarettes. The cat trots after her as she leaves the room. Her husband sits in the chair she vacated. He looks out of place in the fussy living room.

"Mr. Westmore," I begin, "would you tell us about last night?" He gives us the quick and dirty version. No frills. He seems like that kind of guy. Nothing he says deviates from his wife's account of the birthday party.

"How long have you known Dr. Bradley?" I ask.

He scratches the gray stubble on his chin with a callused finger. "As long as Elise has. She met him in grad school. We'd been married for a few years when she went back to school to finish her degree. He used to come over to the apartment sometimes." He smiles slightly at the memory. "We had a tiny little place downtown." He clasps his hands in front of him, rests his elbows on his knees, and drops his head. "Jay was a nice person."

"You think of anyone who wanted to hurt him?" The heat rumbles on loudly, like it does in some old houses.

Mr. Westmore waits until the noise subsides. "No. It doesn't make any sense."

"Why not?"

"He was just a good guy, that's all."

"You spend much time with him?" Through the bay window, I see Dr. Westmore pacing the porch, a cigarette clamped between her lips, smoke twirling in her wake.

"We went fishing occasionally."

"When was the last time?"

Mr. Westmore sits back, takes a deep breath. "Last fall. October, before it got real cold."

"He say anything at all that seemed unusual, troubling, in the last few days?"

"Not to me." He takes a deep breath, glances out the window, where his wife leans against the porch railing, her back to the house. "But I hope you find the bastard who killed him."

CHAPTER 5

Molly

Corrine's apartment is smothering me. I can't seem to take a deep breath, to pull air down deep into my lungs. I feel trapped here. I want to go home. That's where I want to be, home with Jay.

The doorbell chimes, and someone raps on the door as well. It has to be my parents. My mother is impatient in the best of times. I sigh and drag myself to standing.

Mother and Dad sweep into the apartment, brush by Corrine, and Mom pulls me into her arms. "Sweetheart, we just can't believe it. We can't believe Jay's gone." She stands back, her hands squeezing my arms, and looks me up and down. "But you're all right?"

I nod, my gaze on the floor.

"Thank God!" Her short brown hair is neatly combed, her glasses gleam. She looks every inch the math professor she is, organized and logical.

Dad nudges her aside and hugs me. "What did the cops say, Moll?" His chin wobbles just a little.

"I'll put coffee on," Corrine calls from the kitchen.

I clasp my arms across my chest. "They don't know anything yet."

"But someone *killed* him? Who in their right mind would do such a thing?" Mom clutches her hand over her mouth. But I see it in her eyes, a vague accusation as if this is my fault. *Trouble seems to find me* was her mantra when I was growing up.

I shake my head. I have no answers.

"It must've been some low-lifer on dope, don't you think?" Mom says. "You live in a pretty expensive neighborhood, Molly. I can't believe you two don't have a security system in that big place. Even Dad and I have ADT. And you, especially, should know better after . . ." She doesn't finish that thought. She doesn't have to.

I turn away, heat rising to my face. "It was on our list." It was one of the things we hadn't gotten around to since moving in last spring. The house had fallen into some disrepair when we bought it. There'd been a lot to do. Now, of course, I'm full of regrets. Refinishing the hardwood floors and updating the master bath seem irrelevant. And besides, Jay made me feel safe, untouchable, which is ridiculous in hindsight.

Mom's phone rings from her huge open purse. "It's been non-stop," she says, as she fishes the phone out and disappears into the powder room.

"You're okay, kid?" Dad asks. He looks utterly lost and hugs me again.

"Yeah. I'm okay." I tear up and start to walk over to the window, change direction, and swing into the kitchen. Corrine is standing at the counter, assembling a platter of snacks. "Can I borrow your phone. The cops have mine."

"What? Sure." She tips her head toward the table. "In my purse."

Phone in hand, I head to the guest room. I hear my mother talking in the powder room as I walk down the hall. Her loud nasal voice cuts through my head. I close the guest room door and drop down on the bed.

Kim answers right away. "Corrine?"

"No, Kimmie. It's me."

"Molly! I've left you about a dozen messages."

"The cops took my phone. I'm at my sister's."

"Oh my God, are you okay?" Her breath hitches, and she stifles a sob. "I didn't even get a chance to ask you this morning."

"I had to be quick. The cops needed to talk to me." I start crying. *Again.* I barely remember our conversation from this morning, just a teary "Jay's dead. Someone killed him last night. The cops are here."

"I can't believe it. Josh and I are devastated. Did someone break in? You could've been hurt too!"

"I'm fine. I didn't hear a thing. No one knows what happened." My voice comes out like a robot's. "I found him, Kim, in the office. Someone slit his throat."

"Oh my God." The line goes quiet. Kim coughs and blows her nose. "You're staying with Corrine?"

"Yes. I can't go home until the police are finished with the house."

"Do you even *want* to go back?" she asks tentatively.

My first thought is, I never want to set foot there again. Yet it's my home. Jay and I were so happy there. It's the first place I felt totally at ease, settled. Like an adult at long last. "I honestly don't know, but I'm not going to stay with my parents, and Corrine's place is too small."

"You can stay with us."

"Thanks, but you guys don't need me underfoot. Willow needs you." Kim and Josh's daughter is only four. She was born seven weeks premature and suffers from developmental delays that have her in therapy twice a week, so Kim's got her hands full.

"Willow's fine. You know you're her favorite person."

"I don't want her to see me like this. I'm okay here for now."

"Do you want us to come over?"

I sniff back tears, nod, though she can't see me. "Can you?"

"Of course. We'll drop Willow off at my mom's."

"Thanks, Kim." We hang up, and I dial Laken.

"Hello?"

"Laken, it's Molly."

"Oh my God, Moll." She sniffles. "How are you holding up?"

"I'm okay. I was pretty out of it this morning. I don't even know what I told you."

"Someone *killed* Jay? How can that have happened? I can't believe it." Laken takes a big teary breath, mumbles something to, I assume, her husband. "We can't believe it. Cal's been a basket case since you called this morning."

"I can't believe it either," I say. "We were just all together."

"Do you want us to come over?"

"Please. Kim and Josh are coming too."

"Of course. We'll be over as soon as we can. But we got a call from a *detective*. They're coming here to talk to us. We'll come after that. Okay?" I hear her blow her nose. "Poor Jay," she mumbles. "God, I can't believe it."

"Oh, I'm at Corrine's, by the way. My house is a crime scene." I drop my head in my hand.

"Did someone break in after we left?"

"I don't know. The door to the office was open when I came downstairs."

Laken sniffs, lets go a deep breath. "Did it happen this morning, do you think?"

"I don't *know*." I run my hand through my hair and glance around at the green pastel walls with their expensive artwork. It seems strange that Corrine's apartment is just the same. Everything is the same except my house and my life. And I don't even know why.

I hear noise in the background of the call. A doorbell. "Wait a sec," Laken says. A minute ticks by. "Those detectives are here," she whispers. "We'll come over as soon as they leave."

CHAPTER 6

Rita

The Ferrises sit side by side on a gray sectional. Mrs. Ferris is tall, with long straight blond hair, makeup perfect, glamorous even on a Sunday when her friend's husband has been murdered. Calvin Ferris is also tall, dark-haired, and wears scholarly-looking glasses, a handsome man but in a studious, serious way. They don't look like they ought to be together, like someone got their wires crossed on a dating app.

She's crying softly into a clump of tissues, while he pats her back and looks utterly confused as if he'd just heard aliens had landed at Fenway.

Chase and I sit across from them. I pull out my notebook. Chase, as usual, is taking notes on his phone, which even after months together, I find strange. Most of the younger cops use their phones for this purpose now. But for me, I like the heft of my notebook, the relative permanence of it, and it allows me to make sketches.

"Mr. Ferris, you and Dr. Bradley are friends?" I ask.

"Yes."

"Anything bothering him lately?"

He shakes his head. "No. I don't think so."

Mrs. Ferris leans forward. "Do you think one of his patients did it? When we left last night, everything was fine!" she half yells at us.

"Could be," I say. "You have any reason to believe it was one of his patients?"

She retreats into the couch. "No. Jay doesn't discuss his work with us."

Mr. Ferris nods in agreement. "But it could be, right?"

Two little boys skid into the room in their stocking feet. I don't know much about kids, but these two must be twins, carbon copies. Mrs. Ferris jumps up.

"Did you finish your lunch?" She herds them back into the kitchen. "You can each have one brownie. Come on."

When they leave the room, Mr. Ferris drops his head in his hands. "Jay was my friend," he says dejectedly, working his fingers through his thick hair. He glances up and meets my eyes. "How's Molly? Is she okay?"

"Doing as well as can be expected," I say.

His phone rings, and he reaches into his pocket and shuts it off. When Mrs. Ferris returns, we have them walk us through the previous evening, and it jibes with what Dr. Westmore and her husband told us. Everyone was having a good time. Nothing out of the ordinary. They all left before midnight. No one had been out in the office.

Chase and I head back to the station. I want to check in with Dr. Gaines and the tech guys. See what they've come up with.

My office is freezing cold. For some reason, Sundays are particularly cold at the station, as though law enforcement stops on the weekend. Chase is out in the squad room at his desk, and I sit and spread out my notes.

We still need to talk to the Pearsons. Neither of them has answered their phones, so I left messages. But I'm assuming they'll have the same story—everyone was having a good time, no sign of trouble.

My phone vibrates and rings on my blotter. It's the ME returning my call. She has nothing pertinent to add to the investigation at this point. The autopsy's scheduled for tomorrow morning, ten a.m., if I want to be there. I glance out my open door. Maybe I'll see if Chase wants to go. I've seen enough people cut up over the years, and my time's better spent elsewhere. We'll see.

By five p.m., I'm ready to close up for the day. Tomorrow will be busy.

Inside my apartment, I push up the thermostat, stick my feet into my slippers, and search the fridge for leftovers. I'm settled on the couch with a deli container of potato salad and a glass of cabernet when there's a knock on my door.

Shit. I'm tired and really don't feel like talking to anyone.

"Rita?" He calls through the door. "It's Collin. You home?"

He knows I'm home. My van is parked in its usual spot right out front. That's okay, I don't mind him. Collin and I've gotten close in the three years he's lived in the apartment above mine. He's the son I never had, he says, and he's not half wrong.

"Come on in. You want a glass?" I ask as he comes through the door. I tip my head in the direction of the wine bottle on the counter.

"No, I'm good. Thanks." He's wearing a navy-blue sweater and skinny jeans.

"What's up?" I ask as we flop on the couch.

"I was watching the news and heard about that man who was murdered."

"Uh huh."

"They showed a picture of his wife, and I *recognized* her." His eyes are wide, and a light smattering of freckles make him look younger than his twenty-nine years.

"Yeah?"

He leans forward, runs his hand through his bangs, pushes them back into his thick dark hair. "I think she's the lady who came into the café Saturday. André did a birthday cake for a Dr. Bradley, and I put together finger foods. That's them, right?"

Their names have been released, so I can confirm that to Collin. "Yes. You or André talk to her when she picked up everything?"

"I did. André wasn't there. I helped her put the order in the back of her Mercedes." Collin claps a hand over his mouth. "I can't believe it, Rita. Just think, André made that man's last birthday cake. Can you imagine? What would it be like if you were celebrating your birthday and you knew it was your last, the end."

"I don't think he had any idea, Collin."

I swallow a sip of wine, glance out the darkening window. Life can be cruel, as the cliché goes. Sometimes people *do* know. My brother Jimmy, along with our brother Danny, was my closest playmate growing up. Jimmy died of leukemia when he was eleven. And even as young as he was, he knew it was a death sentence back then. His last Christmas, he gave us each a gift, something of his to remember him by. I still have the Dick Tracy comic book he gave me. I try to stifle a sigh.

Collin raises his palms. "It's just so eerie." He often asks me about my work, but this is the first time since he and André moved into the building that he's had any contact with anyone I was investigating. He draws a deep breath. "She seemed like a nice woman. She told me to put the stuff in the trunk so her husband wouldn't see the cake. She wanted it to be a surprise."

"Did you talk to him at all?"

"No. He was just sitting in the car."

"She say anything other than the usual, 'Gee, nice job on the cake, how much do I owe you?'"

"No." He shakes his head. Then his gaze catches mine. "Will I have to go down to the police station and give a statement?"

I smile and sip my wine. "I don't think so, hon. But I'll let you know."

CHAPTER 7

Molly

The sun has set, ushering in a dreary winter evening. Corrine's apartment is bursting with noise, my parents in the living room with the TV turned up to accommodate Mom's encroaching hearing loss. Corrine on her phone, pacing the hall, taking care of all the concerned friends and relatives. I should be glad my phone is with the cops. I can't deal with Aunt Ellen or Cousin Shirley and the rest right now.

Corrine swings open the front door, expecting the delivery man. She'd ordered Chinese since it was getting on to dinnertime and my parents expect to be fed between five-thirty and six o'clock, like at home, so they can take their medicine. Nothing stops their routine. But it's Kim and Laken and their husbands. They wrap me in their arms, and we cry together. I clear my throat and lead them into the living room.

Cal and Josh sit side by side on the sofa, holding mugs of coffee that Corrine has passed around. They hang their heads, stunned, not knowing what to do, while my mother yammers on, intent on discussing every possible scenario, as though she's working out a math word problem. If the murderer arrived at midnight and the victim . . . The evening news blares on TV, and I'm anxious to get away. I don't want to see Jay on the news. I shudder and catch

Kim's and Laken's gaze, tip my head, and we head down the hall to the guest room.

I shut the door behind us, glad to be out of the noise. Kim's usual chirpy self is absent, her dark eyes tear-stained. She plops on the bed and pulls her legs up under her. Laken leans back in the only chair in the room as I pace between them.

"So what the hell happened?" Laken asks.

I shake my head. "I don't know. I have no idea who would want to hurt Jay." I swing to face them. "But it's all my fault." Sobs burst through my clamped lips.

Kim sits up at attention. "What? No, Molly. How could it be your fault?"

I wipe tears from my cheeks. "I was drinking too much. I just about passed out in our bed." My gaze meets first Kim, then Laken. "I don't even remember you guys leaving. I didn't know what to say when the detectives asked me about it."

"You *were* pretty trashed—"

Kim's mouth pops open. "Lake!"

"I didn't mean to imply it was her fault. That's not what I meant."

I shake my head. "It's all right. But if I hadn't been drinking, I might've heard something. I might've been able to help Jay, at least call 911." I drop my arms to my sides. "I slept through my husband's murder. I'll never forgive myself." I walk to the window, lean on the sill, and look down on the gray evening, watch the traffic crawl by under the streetlights. The story of my life, letting people down.

Kim's arm steals around my waist. "You got your period?" she asks quietly.

"Right before the party. Jay found me crying in the bathroom." I take a deep breath.

"We figured," Laken says as she stands on my other side, rests a hand on my shoulder. "We knew you wouldn't be drinking so much if there was a chance."

"Another twelve thousand dollars down the drain," I say. Then it dawns on me that Jay and I will never raise a child together. We'll never have another chance. We'd been in our third cycle of IVF, and we were so hopeful. "Jay gave me everything, and I couldn't even do the one thing he really wanted."

My friends lead me back to the bed, and we sit on the side.

"Oh, Molly, that wasn't your fault. Jay never blamed you, you know that," Kim says.

I nod, wipe my sleeve over my eyes. No, he didn't. Jay understood everything. Knew everything about me and loved me anyway. And now he's gone.

Chapter 8

Rita

Monday morning, Chief Bob Murphy assembles the team in the conference room. We're like those proverbial sardines in here as this is a complicated case, lots of forensics involved. At least we'll stay warm. And someone, thank God, has seen fit to bring in takeout coffee and pastries instead of the usual station coffee and vending machine fare. Chase and I stand against the back wall, hot paper cups in hand, while the chief and a couple of uniforms are busy at the front of the room.

"You want to attend the autopsy?" I whisper to Chase. "Susan said it was at ten. We should be out of here by then."

Chase swallows, eyes on his coffee. "If you want me to."

I shrug. "It'd be good if one of us was there. Since I've seen my share, thought you might like the experience."

"*Like* the experience?"

"You know what I mean. It's not that bad. You'll be okay."

Shit, Rita, I think to myself. Didn't he just tell me yesterday that blood made him woozy? I sigh. Well, he's in the wrong line of work. He'll have to get over it. Still. I adjust my shirt collar. "I can go," I say.

"No." He clears his throat. "I'll do it."

"Great. I want to run by Dr. Westmore's office after this. Then we can both go and see if Mrs. Bradley's neighbor is home."

Chase pulls on his tie knot. "Yeah. Okay."

The chief's looking a little gray this morning. He and I go back a long way, back to being rookies with the Boston PD. It was tough back in the day. There weren't a lot of women in the department who weren't secretaries. But Bob was one of the good guys. He treated me like any other officer, and that was what I was looking for. Our shared history and friendship included his wife, Deb, and my ex-husband, Ed. Bob still sees Ed now and then. They'll meet for a beer or go to a Red Sox game together. Then I have to hear all about it from Bob until I have to tell him to shut his big mouth. Ed and I have been divorced for years after a three-year marriage that didn't suit either of us. Deb died of breast cancer right after Bob took the job out here in Graybridge. Six months later, he asked me if I was interested in making a change, and I jumped at the chance to be a detective in a smaller department where there wasn't so much jostling for advancement. Besides, the grind of the city was starting to wear on me, and a new challenge was just what I needed.

Bob clears his throat, looks down at an open folder. He's been tired lately, and it looks like he's gained some weight over the holidays, which he doesn't need. I don't feel as old as Bob looks. Really. And I know I look a helluva lot younger. People are surprised when they find out we're nearly the same age. Makes me worry about him.

"Okay, people," he says, and wipes his mouth with his hand. "We've got a lot to go over." He runs through department business but leaves the Bradley case to me. "Rita?"

I set my coffee on the table and walk to the front of the room.

CHAPTER 9

Molly

It's morning, and Jay isn't here, will never be here again. I didn't sleep all night, just rested in bed listening to the sounds of the city and crying until my pillow was a soggy mess. I'm still wearing the leggings and sweater I put on yesterday to talk to the detectives.

I decide to get in the shower, not that I care so much about what I look like, but to warm up. Although the heat is on in the apartment, I'm freezing cold. I grab some clean clothes out of my suitcase and head down the hall. The smell of coffee hits me, and my throat closes up. Will it always remind me of Jay?

I run the water until steam fills the room and step under the spray. I wash slowly, using Corrine's expensive shampoo and soap until the heady scent of lavender and sage fills my nostrils, drowning out the coffee. Reluctantly, I finish, turn off the water, and get dressed.

Corrine convinced our parents to go home last night. She'd had enough of them and knew I needed some quiet. She's in the kitchen with Rich, eating sliced cantaloupe and yogurt. I didn't hear him come home this morning. He's like Corrine's twin, both blond, although his hair has run to gray. They work out, eat healthfully, are well-dressed and cosmopolitan. He rises and gives me a hug.

"How are you holding up?" he asks in a whisper, as though we're in church.

"I'm okay." My voice is raw, throaty.

"Have some breakfast," Corrine offers.

"In a little bit," I say, bypass the coffee machine and put the kettle on.

"I'm working from home today," Corrine says.

"You don't need to do that. I'm fine here."

Corrine rinses her bowl and places it in the dishwasher. "Nonsense. I'm not leaving you here alone. I work from home at least once a week these days anyway."

"She does," Rich adds as if I don't believe his wife.

I take my tea into the living room and stand in front of the window, watching the boats in the harbor. The sun's out, and what's left of the snow seems to have disappeared except for slush along the curbs.

I need to call my boss, Hayes Branch. He might have heard about Jay on the news by now. He'll be frantic to get in touch, and since I don't have my phone, he won't be able to reach me.

When I graduated from college with my English degree, I got a job writing for a small travel magazine. For four years, I scraped by, sharing an apartment with a pharmacy student whom I rarely saw. When the magazine folded, I got a job as an editor for an academic publishing house but was barely making enough to cover my bills, so I got a part-time job at Graybridge Books. Located on the square in a historic brick building, the bookstore has a cozy charm, and I'd spent many hours there when I was young. It was my favorite place and working there was like a balm to my soul, so when the publisher cut staff, and Hayes hired me full-time, I was happy, if not making a lot of money.

Owned by heiress Phyllis Branch, the store benefits from her devotion to the written word and her deep pockets. Among her many interests, Phyllis sees herself as a romance writer, and we proudly display her six self-published tomes on our shelves. Her son, Hayes, manages the store, and he and I have become friends over the years.

I borrow Corrine's phone again and walk into the kitchen. Corrine is in her office now, and I hear her clicking at her computer.

I tap in Hayes's number.

"Molly? *Thank God.* I've been trying to reach you. I heard about Jay." He draws a deep breath, and I picture him pushing his hipster glasses up the bridge of his nose. "I was so shocked. And so sorry." His voice breaks. He was friends with Jay too and only missed the party because of a previous commitment. "How are you?"

"As well as can be expected."

"What can I do to help?"

"Nothing really, Hayes. But it's nice to hear your voice."

"I just can't believe it. Have the police found who did it?"

"Not yet. They have no idea. Who would want to hurt Jay? I just can't figure it out." I start to cry.

"Do you want me to come over?"

"I'm at Corrine's. But I should be able to go home soon, I hope. I'll call you."

He takes a deep breath. "It'll be okay, Molly. We're here for you."

"Thanks," I mumble, and blow my nose.

Hayes clears his throat. "When is the service? Alice and I will be there, of course."

The service? Right. I'll have to do something about a funeral. *Jesus. Is this my life?* "Nothing's planned yet, but I'll let you know."

"Alice was very upset when I told her," Hayes whispers. I picture his eleven-year-old daughter sitting in the shop's window seat, reading her annotated *Little Women* book, crying over Beth March's death. She's very sensitive. Knowing her father's friend was murdered would be greatly disturbing to her.

"She's sweet, but tell her I'm okay and I'll see you both soon."

"Will do, Molly. Please let us know what we can do to help."

We hang up, and I place the phone on the granite countertop. I probably should try to eat something, so I peruse the fridge, but find nothing that appeals to me. So I pace the apartment instead. I need to get out of here for a while. But where can I go to avoid thinking of Jay? Nowhere.

CHAPTER 10

Rita

The Tackler Building sits in downtown Graybridge, two blocks off the square. It houses a pediatric practice, a law office, a couple of nondescript businesses, and Graybridge Family Therapy. There's a small but comfy waiting room that's empty at the moment and a counter where a young woman with sleek brown hair sits. She's on the phone and has a smooth, practiced, sympathetic voice. Her dark eyes shoot up to acknowledge me as I walk up to the counter.

"We'll see you on Thursday," she says into the phone, ends her call, and smiles up at me. "May I help you?"

"Yes. I'm here to see Dr. Westmore."

"Is she expecting you?"

"Yes. Detective Myers."

Her expression changes, eyes dart toward Dr. Bradley's closed door, but before she can pick up the phone, Elise Westmore walks into the waiting room. "Hello, come on in."

Her office is pristine but cluttered. Framed photos of what look like exotic vacations cover cherry-red walls. Books line floor-to-ceiling shelves, and there's a cozy seating area off to the side, a plump couch across from an armchair, a table between them with a box of tissues and a dish of wrapped mints on it. There's a soothing bubbling noise coming from somewhere.

"Please, have a seat."

She takes the armchair, so I have to sit on the couch, which makes me slightly uncomfortable, as if she can read my thoughts and discern my deep, dark secrets. The last place I want to be is on a shrink's couch.

I was there once, years ago. When I was thirty-two, still with the Boston force, my partner and I were called to a robbery in progress. When we got on scene, the suspect had already killed the liquor store clerk, who lay bleeding out behind the counter. The gunman swiveled, perspiration running down the sides of his face, and shot my partner in the shoulder, dropping him to the floor. Then the kid turned in my direction. Time seemed to stand still as he leveled his pistol at me. I don't remember shooting him. All I remember is his face. Young and scared. I was on desk duty, per department policy while it was sorted out. And I had to go see the department therapist, again required protocol. I didn't like it. I don't have anything against people seeking help when they need it. I'm all for that. But for me, it ate away at something inside. Maybe the way I was raised. Don't know, but I like to keep my own counsel. Not saying that kid's face doesn't show up at night sometimes when I'm sleeping. I guess it always will, along with my brothers Ricky and Jimmy and others I've lost along the way. But I don't need a shrink to analyze my nightmares. I get it.

Dr. Westmore leans back in her chair, tents her fingers. "What can I do for you, Detective?"

"I just have a few more questions about Dr. Bradley. You seem to know him as well as anybody."

She heaves a sigh. "Yes. As I said, Jay and I were close."

"What do you know about his family?" My eyes follow a bright blue fish as it swims in an aquarium on a credenza behind Dr. Westmore. The source of the bubbling.

"His mother died in a car accident when Jay was a little boy, nine, ten years old."

"That's too bad."

"Yes. He told me he was pretty much left on his own. No siblings. His father worked all the time." She glances out the window. "Jay became pretty introverted."

"He get in any trouble that you know about? A boy left to himself."

She shakes her head. "Jay's a real straight arrow. He says he spent most of his time in the library."

"Smart guy?"

"Brilliant." She smiles.

"Why would anyone want to kill a guy like that?"

Dr. Westmore reaches for a tissue, takes her time. "I have no idea."

The fish stops swimming and looks straight at me, its gills and fins flapping. "Do you think it's possible a patient might have been angry for some reason?"

She clears her throat and reaches for a mint. "I don't think so. It's possible, I suppose."

"But Dr. Bradley didn't mention anyone in particular to you?" I doodle in the margin of my notebook, drawing the blue fish.

"No. I have no idea how this could've happened."

"You still don't have any idea what was on his mind? Anything occur to you since we spoke yesterday?"

"Nothing." She shakes her head.

"Okay." I shut my notebook. "You mind showing me his office?"

We stand, and I follow her back across the waiting room. Dr. Bradley's office is sparsely decorated in cool greens and blues but has the same couch-chair setup off to the side.

"Molly called me," Dr. Westmore says. "She said to give you access to anything of Jay's."

"Yes. I spoke to her earlier today."

I pull latex gloves from my pocket, snap them on. "There anything in particular you think I should look at?" I'm walking around, trying desk drawers and filing cabinets, but they're all locked. Dr. Westmore removes a key ring from her pocket and shakes out a small key and hands it to me.

"I can't think of anything," she says.

I unlock the desk and start sifting through drawers. I take out a red leather-bound notebook. It looks like an appointment calendar, with last year stamped in gold on the front. I skim through the pages. "This looks like personal stuff."

"Probably. Candace keeps track of patient appointments."

"I'd like a printout of those appointments going back six months. We'll need to talk to his patients."

"We'll need a warrant, Detective. We can't hand over patient information without it."

"You'll have it." I take an evidence bag out of my satchel and slide the planner inside. I notice an identical planner in the corner of the desktop underneath a file folder. Looks brand-new and, since we're only a week into the new year, doesn't look like there's much written there, but I take it too.

"Has Dr. Bradley been in since December?"

"We've been closed for the holidays until today, but he was here last week doing paperwork. He brought that fern in." She walks over to the window, looks at the plant like she can't figure out what to do with it. "Molly told him he ought to have a few plants in the office."

"Uh huh."

I hunt around a little more while Dr. Westmore looks on, but I don't see anything else of note. I take one more turn around the room, pause in front of a framed picture of the Bradleys taken in front of the Louvre. "He and the Mrs. were happy?"

"Over the moon. He adored Molly."

"What's Dr. Bradley got going on in his home office?"

"I have no idea. Why?"

"His wife said he's writing a book. You know anything about that?"

"Jay has talked to me about it."

"About what?"

"Abnormal psychology and the criminal mind, as a matter of fact."

"Interesting. Any reason why?"

She draws a deep breath, clutches her arms across her chest, and walks to the window, her back to me. "Jay was a complicated man."

"He have any dealings with people for his book who might have violent tendencies?"

"None that he mentioned."

"What piqued his interest in that subject, do you think?"

She turns toward me. "Classwork, I guess. We learned about some very unusual aspects of the human psyche. He was fascinated with antisocial behavior."

"Why not go into that branch of work then? Lots of opportunities in the prison system for a psychologist."

"It fascinated him and scared him at the same time, I think. And he liked family therapy."

I keep my gaze on her, waiting.

"Detective, I told you Jay had a lonely childhood. It was just his father and grandfather. Both men were absorbed in their careers. Jay was kind of an afterthought. He'd listen to them talking in the kitchen late at night. He told me they spent a lot of time smoking, drinking, discussing their work."

"What type of work did they do?"

She smiles grimly. "They were detectives with the Boston Police Department."

"Huh." I'm immediately searching my memory for any cops named Bradley, but I draw a blank. Bob might know. "So, as a kid, he probably overheard some cop stories?"

"Yes. And his grandfather had some pretty gruesome tales to tell."

"How's that?"

"He worked on the Boston Strangler case."

CHAPTER 11

Molly

Kim and Josh live in a new subdivision about ten minutes from me and Jay. Kim works at Graybridge Elementary School, teaching fourth grade. Lucky for me, she's still on winter break. I park Corrine's BMW in the driveway and make my way to the front door.

Kim wraps me in her arms. "Come on in," she whispers against my shoulder.

The house, while fairly new and smelling faintly of paint, always looks lived in. Evidence of Willow is everywhere. Tiny ice skates sit dangerously at the bottom of the stairs. Toys and picture books are piled on the foyer table. We walk down the hall to the kitchen, where dishes are stacked in the sink and art supplies lie scattered on the counter. But it's a comfortable place, welcoming. We sit with mugs of tea and an open box of ginger snaps between us.

"It's so quiet," I say.

"Josh took Willow to the mall," Kim says, her dark eyes glancing out the French doors that open onto the deck. "She knows something's wrong, but we don't know quite how to explain to her what happened."

"I can imagine." If Jay and I actually had children, how could I help them through something like this? I shiver and change the subject. "Josh didn't go to work?"

Kim shakes her head. "He said he wouldn't be able to concentrate anyway, so Cal told him to stay home."

Cal got Josh a job a couple of years ago at the medical research lab he runs downtown. Josh had just left the hospital where he had been working. He's one of those guys who never seems to stay in one place too long, always looking for something new and different. That's what Jay said.

"Cal went in?" I ask.

"Laken said he told her work would help him keep his mind off things."

"What's Laken doing today?"

"At the spa. She needed to square things away there. She was just driving herself crazy at home anyway. You know how she is."

I do. Laken needs to be busy all the time. Even when we've taken vacations together, she doesn't know the meaning of "Let's just chill a while." Funny, her business is all about relaxation.

"When do you go back to school?"

"Wednesday." Kim sighs and covers my hand with hers. "Have you heard anything from the police today?"

"No. I guess I should call them." I almost don't want to. The cops are just another reminder that Jay is really gone. It's tempting to pretend, to hide at Corrine's and make believe that Jay is away at a conference or something. If only. But reality doesn't work that way. It slaps you square in the face, and you accept it or descend into la-la land.

The doorbell rings, and Kim jumps up. "Elise said she wanted to stop by and see you. I told her you were coming over. You don't mind, right? She had a gap in her schedule."

"No." Fine, I think, as long as she doesn't try to psychoanalyze me. I can't take that right now.

Kim scampers down the hall, and I take a deep breath and stand, waiting.

Elise is impeccably dressed, as usual, not a hair out of place, but her eyes are red, and there's a wad of tissues peeking from her jacket pocket. We hug, and she pats my back before letting me go.

"How are you, sweetheart?" she asks.

I nod and sniff. "Okay." We sit at the table while Kim goes to the stove. "Tea, Elise?"

"That would be lovely." She turns to me. "Tell me what you need, Molly. Anything. Scott and I are ready to help."

"Thanks. Jay thought so much of you." My voice catches in my throat, and Elise leans over and rubs my shoulder.

She and Kim talk about other things, other than me and Jay, and it's soothing to listen to their quiet conversation. It almost seems normal. I can zone out, which is about the most pleasant thing I can think of to do right now.

But with Elise here, I inevitably start to think about Jay's practice, his business. What do I do about that?

"What about his patients?" I ask Elise. It takes her a second to switch gears, from Kim's spring landscaping project that Scott's company is going to do, to me and my problems.

"I'll notify them, Molly. I can probably take on a few of his if they're so inclined, but most I'll refer to other therapists."

That's good. Jay would want them taken care of. "What about his office? It'll have to be cleaned out, right?" Eventually there will be someone else in Jay's space, taking his place as everyone inevitably moves on.

"At some point, Molly. But there's no rush."

I sigh and wipe my cheeks with my hands, pick at my sleeve, and pull it down over my wrist. I don't think I can face cleaning anything out yet.

That's where I met Jay. That very office, five years ago. I was having a rough time. I'd gotten a letter in the mail that totally upended my world. The man who ruined my life, who was safely locked away, had sneaked a letter by the prison censors and found out somehow where I was living. Even though I got an apology from the warden, and he was punished for breaking the rules, it rocked my world and sent me running back to therapy. I had to talk to someone, and that someone turned out to be Jay. He was kind, understanding, and nonjudgmental. After three sessions, he handed me a business card for another psychologist. At first, I was distraught, but he told me he was interested in seeing me socially, and the only ethical way to do that was not to see me professionally. I was thrilled and never ended up calling the other therapist. Three sessions with Jay had been enough, or so I thought at the time. Now, with Jay gone forever, I don't know how I'll carry on, how I'll keep the demons at bay.

CHAPTER 12

Rita

I hear the chief in his office, talking on the phone. I peer around the door frame. If he'd wanted privacy, he would've closed the door, right? He looks up at me from under his bushy gray eyebrows.

"I'll call you back." Bob drops the phone in its cradle. "What's up, Rita?"

"You remember any detectives named Bradley with the Boston PD?"

The chief leans back and threads his fingers together over his ample stomach. "Walt Bradley was a homicide detective. Worked the Strangler case."

"Huh. I think I did hear Walt's name."

"Yeah. He was a bit of a legend. He retired before we were there. Why?"

"Well, apparently Jay Bradley's father and grandfather were Boston PD detectives."

Bob blows out a breath. "No shit? Well, that's something." Bob scratches his head. "Walt must've been the grandfather. I don't remember his son though."

"Me neither. Dr. Bradley's partner said that Jay overheard some pretty gruesome stories when he was a kid."

"I bet."

"Think he got himself mixed up with some unsavory charac-ters? Maybe doing research for that book he was writing?"

"Could be, Reet." The chief leans forward, drops his feet to the floor. "You see Chase yet?"

"No, I just walked in."

"He's got notes from the autopsy."

I glance back at the squad room. "I'll find him."

Bob's phone rings. "Let me know," he says as he picks up the handset.

Chase is sitting at his computer, drinking a cup of black coffee that looks like mud, and he jumps when I call his name. "Sorry."

"It's okay. Just inputting my notes." He tucks his phone in his pocket, saves his file, and swivels in his chair. We head down the hall and turn into my office.

Chase sits across from my desk and draws a deep breath. "Dr. Gaines said time of death was between one and four a.m."

I hang my jacket on the back of my chair, pull out my note-book, and sit. "Okay," I say. "After the party, the wife said he was going to work out in his office after everybody left around eleven-thirty."

"Uh huh. And he was wearing the clothes he had on at the party, so somebody came along afterward and killed him a couple hours later."

"And broke into the filing cabinet, went through his desk," I add.

"Yeah."

"What else?"

Chase scrolls through his phone. "He did have some defensive wounds after all, just some small cuts on his right hand. Dr. Gaines said he might've made a grab for the knife, but she said the neck wound was pretty much instantly fatal. The guy didn't have a chance."

"So the perp came at him from behind?"

"That's what the doc said."

"Whoever did this walked up behind Dr. Bradley, slit his throat, then went through his stuff, looking for something." I lean back, drum my fingers on the desk. "Any chance it could've been the wife, you think?"

Chase shakes his head. "Dr. Gaines thinks the perp was a man, or maybe a tall, strong woman. Mrs. Bradley's not very big. And she said the angle of the cut makes it likely the perp was as tall as, if not taller than Dr. Bradley."

I'm five four, and Mrs. Bradley and I were about eye to eye. "How tall was Dr. Bradley?"

Chase thumbs through his phone. "Six two, one hundred seventy-six pounds."

"Okay. Pretty safe to say she's low on the list, unless she hired someone."

"And she seemed genuinely distraught." Chase's eyes are soft, as though he's on Mrs. Bradley's side, defending her honor.

"Yeah." I sigh. There's still tons to slog through. Talking to Bradley's patients alone will eat up hours of police work. I glance at my phone. "Let's run over and talk to the neighbor before the Pearsons get here."

According to Mrs. Bradley, Mrs. Murray is an elderly widow who has lived in the house next door for more than fifty years. And the house looks it. Long neglected, the porch sags, and the windows are dirty, not a total mess, but you don't have to look too close to see the decay. The house is an aberration in the otherwise pristine neighborhood. After we ring the bell two or three times, she answers the door, a huge German shepherd at her side.

I introduce Chase and myself, show her my badge. She peers at us through thick glasses, nods a gray head, and welcomes us inside. We sit in a dim living room that smells faintly of moth balls, mold, and dogs. The furniture is dark and worn, and the room is cluttered from years of living. She's a tiny woman, probably doesn't weigh as much as the huge dog sitting at attention next to her armchair.

"Can I get you two any coffee?" she asks.

"No, thank you, Mrs. Murray," I say. "Nice dog."

"Percy? Yes, he's a good boy."

I wonder how someone so small manages such a big animal, but the answer lies in the bric-a-brac scattered through the room. Yellowed and curling ribbons from dog shows decades in the past hang from every picture frame. Photos of, I assume, a young Mrs. Murray wearing poofy fifties skirts, holding the leads of majestic dogs, sit on every end table.

"My husband and I raised show dogs for years." She sighs. "Those were good times."

I tap my pencil against my notebook, and I can't help myself from sketching Percy's great ears. "You know about Dr. Bradley's death, Mrs. Murray?"

"Oh, yes. What an awful shame. I was at church yesterday morning, then I went to see my daughter, so I was out when the hubbub next door was going on." She shakes her head and dabs a handkerchief under her nose. "I can't believe it."

"Did you know the Bradleys well?"

"No. Not too. They haven't been here long. I waved when I saw them coming or going. He was real nice. Took my garbage to the curb a time or two. Told me to let them know if I ever needed anything. A handsome man."

"What about Mrs. Bradley?"

"I didn't see her as much. She'd wave, but she always acted like she was in a hurry. No time to chat. I thought she was a little snooty, but my daughter says she just might be shy." Mrs. Murray shrugs. "I feel bad for her. My husband and I were married fifty-two years. I was lucky."

"We need to know if you saw or heard anything Saturday night. You were home?"

"Oh, yes. I don't go out too much anymore. Just to my daughter's. I was home. I saw the cars next door after dinner. I figured they had company again."

"They entertain a lot?"

"Fairly often. There are cars over there quite often."

"What time did you go to bed Saturday night?"

"Ten-thirty. After the first half of the news."

"Did you get up at all in the night?"

"I don't usually get up until morning, five-thirty or so. I sleep pretty good for an old lady." She smiles, proud of this accomplishment, as she should be, I think with chagrin. A good night's sleep isn't as easy for me as it once was. I don't want to attribute it to age, but . . .

"Did you get up Saturday night?"

"I did actually." She scratches her chin with a thin, blue-veined hand. "Percy sleeps on the floor right by my bed, and he usually doesn't make a peep all night, but Saturday night I woke up because he was downstairs in the kitchen, barking his head off."

"What time was that?" I ask, my pencil raised.

"Just before two a.m."

Chase and I glance at one another. "What did you do?"

"Well, I went downstairs to see what the commotion was about. He was at the back door barking, so I turned on the porch light, but I didn't see anything. I said, 'Percy, you nuthatch, there's nothing out there.' I figured it was a tomcat maybe." She sniffs, swipes her nose with the hankie again. "Was it the murderer, do you think?" she asks, her voice a near whisper.

"We don't know. Would you mind walking us through the kitchen, showing us what happened?"

"No problem." She waves her hand and shuffles to her feet.

We walk slowly behind her down a short dark hall, floorboards squeaking, the smell of Vicks in her wake. The dog sticks like glue to her side as if he's part of the demonstration, which I guess he is.

The kitchen is as cluttered as the rest of the place, and the smells of a thousand meals linger in the air. The porcelain sink is faded to gray, and the yellow curtains over it are stiff and look like they've hung there for decades. The appliances are clean but aged, and the table is piled with neatly folded newspapers. I move the little curtains aside and see the tall, ivy-covered fence that separates Mrs. Murray's property from the Bradleys'. The top of the garage roof is visible, nothing else.

Mrs. Murray walks to the back door, and we follow. Percy pushes his nose in the crack between the edge of the door and its frame. "This is how I found him," she says. "But he was barking to beat the band. He wanted to get outside."

"Does he have a loud bark?" Chase asks.

She smirks. "He could raise the dead. The people who used to live behind me complained a time or two. But the officer who came out was real nice. He told me not to worry about it. Said they should be glad Percy was around to monitor the neighborhood."

"Did you open the door when you came downstairs?" I ask.

"The inside door, but not the storm door, so I didn't let him out. I didn't see anything amiss. He calmed down, and I went back up to bed."

"So you turned on the porch light and looked out back a little before two a.m.?"

"Yes."

"You didn't see or hear anything going on by the Bradleys' garage?"

"Not a thing." She places her hand over her heart. "Is that where it happened?"

I nod. "Would you open the inside door and turn on the light."

"Well, it was dark then."

"That's okay. We just want to see."

"All right."

The backyard is a tangle of overgrown bushes and rusting patio furniture. I step outside on the little stoop. A cold wind blows against my face, scattering a hank of hair that's fallen out of my bun. From here, you can't see much more than the garage's roof either. But distance-wise, the building is close, snugged up against the fence not far from Mrs. Murray's back door. I turn and look up at the porch light. It's pretty bright, and the perp probably would've noticed it as he searched the doctor's office. And it stands to reason he would've heard the dog barking. I return to the kitchen, where Chase and Mrs. Murray are discussing dog training. Percy gives me a knowing stare. His dark eyes seem to say, "See, I tried to tell her somebody was up to no good over there Saturday night."

"Thank you, Mrs. Murray," I say, and hand her my card. "Please call if you think of anything else."

She nods and places a gnarled hand on Percy's head. "What a terrible shame. *Jesus*, what's this world come to?"

Mr. and Mrs. Pearson are already sitting in the small interview room when Chase and I get back to the station. We sit opposite them in cold metal chairs. Mrs. Pearson is petite, smaller even than Mrs. Bradley, and I'm already crossing her off my mental list of suspects, but she looks nervous, uncomfortable.

Mr. Pearson is a different story. He slouches in his chair with a cocky look on his face like, *I'm here, but I'm not happy about it, so let's get it over with.* He's got short, sandy-blond hair and Paul Newman eyes. He's a real pretty boy, and I bet Mrs. Pearson needs to keep her eye on him.

After the preliminaries are through, we get down to business.

"Mrs. Pearson, I'm told you and Mrs. Bradley are good friends, go back a long way."

"Yes. Best friends. Growing up, we lived two streets apart, went to school together."

"Graybridge locals then?"

"Yes. Her family moved here when she was little."

"What about you, Mr. Pearson? Where'd you grow up?"

"Boston. Jay and I lived in the same neighborhood. He stayed local for college, but I went to college in New Hampshire, where I majored in biology. My mom and dad still live in the old neighborhood. Dad's a salesman, and Mom's a housewife. I've got two older brothers and an older sister. That help?"

Mrs. Pearson's eyes go wide, and she gives her husband a sideways glance.

Like I thought, a real wise guy. "It might. You're good friends with Dr. Bradley, Josh?" I ask, looking over my notes.

"Yeah."

"Anything either of you remember as odd at the party?"

They both shake their heads. "It was a fun evening," Mrs. Pearson says, sniffs and paws through her purse, pulls out a wad of tissues. "We can't believe someone would do this to Jay."

"He say anything to either of you in the days preceding that indicated he was worried about anything, anyone?"

"No," she says.

Mr. Pearson's gaze settles on Chase's phone as Chase types quickly. "He seemed fine to me," he adds, clears his throat.

"Okay, Mr. Pearson, walk us through the evening, if you would," I say, and sit back, observing his face as he goes through pretty much the same scenario as the others. He loses some of the attitude as he tells his story, as if he realizes he sounded like a dick when the interview began. He ends his tale with his hands folded on the table.

"Can either of you think of anything that might shed light on Dr. Bradley's death?"

"No." Mrs. Pearson wipes her nose and sticks the tissue back in her purse. "Do you think it was one of his patients? Someone who had severe mental problems?"

"Could be."

I look over my notes. "You guys live about a ten-minute drive from the Bradleys?"

"Yes. About," Mrs. Pearson says.

"You both go right home, right to bed after the party?"

"Yes," Mr. Pearson says. "We didn't know anything was wrong until Molly called the next morning."

"Uh huh." I scribble in my notebook, a quick sketch of both of them next to my observations. "Either of you have anything to add that might help us find your friend's killer?"

Neither of them does, and they leave, Mr. Pearson's hand firmly on his wife's back.

I turn on the lights in my apartment and drop my takeout bag on the coffee table. I head into my bedroom, peel off my work clothes and slip into yoga pants and an old Rolling Stones concert T-shirt. On my way through the kitchen, I pour a glass of wine and set it next to my burger and fries. I flip through my vinyl collection, place a record on the turntable and Crosby, Stills and Nash fill the apartment with heavenly harmonies. I get settled on the couch, take a sip of wine and sigh, then drag my satchel over. I put on my gloves and take out Dr. Bradley's planners. I'm just about to open the newest one, stamped with this year's date, when voices erupt from the foyer.

Mrs. Antonelli, my new neighbor, is screeching at her son or daughter. Don't know which one yet. They helped her move in last month. Apparently, they sold her house out from under her, as she put it, but she refused to move into the senior care facility they picked out. The compromise was the apartment across the foyer from mine. The daughter lives around the corner. It seems Mrs. Antonelli is unable to finish a conversation in the confines of her own place, and I'm treated to a loud dialogue practically on my doorstep whenever anyone comes or goes, and that's often.

For a tiny eighty-two-year-old, she has a strong, loud voice. The son's and daughter's voices are gentle hums between her bursts of conversation or shouting, as the case may be.

I want to enjoy my evening in peace, so I wait to open the planner until I hear the heavy front door close. A low voice that probably belongs to the son is inscrutable but prompts a rejoinder from his mother that I can definitely hear loud and clear.

"You're coming back Friday? *Leo!*"

Yup. The son. More low conversation. The outside door creaks open.

"Leo? What? Okay then, if that's the best you can do." The front door closes, and a second later, Mrs. Antonelli's door slams. Thank God.

I nibble cold fries straight from the bag and sip my wine and open the first planner. The pages are still crisp and white. Only the first week of January has any writing on it, but I flip through the other pages, just in case, but there's nothing there. No more plans. Only the sad reminder that this man's life has ended.

There are two notations. January 4: "Birthday." And Thursday, January 2: "Lunch with Hayes." I sift back through my notes, looking for anyone named Hayes, but don't see it written anywhere. He wasn't at the party, so who is he? I make a note to ask the wife tomorrow.

I set the planner aside, bite into my burger, which, thankfully isn't stone cold, and reach for the other planner. It was well used, slightly puffy, pages filled with notes in various colored ink, a stain of perhaps coffee here and there. Just by the feel of it, Dr. Bradley was a busy man. I start at the back, December. There are several notations for Christmas activities. Dinner dates with his wife and a smattering of friends' names corresponding to his birthday party guests. On December 9, he wrote, "Meet Laken at spa, 12:30." Maybe he went in for a massage. Thursday, December 19: "Pub, Josh and Cal." So he had a few beers with his buddies. Then I see something that has me sitting up straight, setting my wineglass on the coffee table.

On Monday, December 30, Dr. Bradley had noted an appointment at a prison in Connecticut. What was he doing there? I look back through the rest of the planner. There are no other appointments listed for that facility or any other prison. Everything else looks to be purely social. An ex-patient? Or was Dr. Bradley conducting interviews for his book? Another question for the Mrs., although she might not know. She doesn't appear to know much of anything of her husband's professional life. Maybe a question for Dr. Westmore instead. I tidy my notes, outline my questions for Mrs. Bradley for tomorrow, and finish my wine.

CHAPTER 13

Molly

Corrine drove me home in the morning. Detective Myers had called and told me that they were through with the house, and I could return as long as I stayed out of the garage, which is fine with me.

It feels strange to be here. Corrine arranged to have a cleaning crew come through and not only clean up the party mess but wash away the fingerprint dust as well. She's standing on the porch, paying the lead cleaning woman, while the other two load their equipment into their van. I feel swept away. Corrine managed everything in perfect Corrine style. No one's better at cleaning up messes.

I walk slowly down the hall and into the kitchen, gripping my arms across my stomach. My gaze shifts first to the coffee maker, as if it could tell me what happened to my husband, then out the back window. Yellow crime-scene tape crisscrosses the office door. I don't ever want to go in there again. In fact, when spring comes, I'll have it torn down and plant a garden there. Maybe a traditional English garden full of roses and peonies, perennials that will come up and bloom every year. I'll ask Scott about it.

"What?" Corrine is beside me.

"I didn't say anything." Or did I? Was I talking aloud to my-self? Who knows? I feel half out of my head.

"You sure you want to stay here tonight by yourself?" Corrine asks.

"Yes." I brush past her. "It's chilly in here." I walk down the hall and see that the cellar door is ajar. My heart pounds. I slam the door shut, slide the lock, and lean against it. I take a deep, slow breath. The cops must have done it—of all the doors to leave open. "You want to put the kettle on?" I call on my way back into the kitchen. Corrine is going through a stack of envelopes she col-lected from the mailbox. She's like that, more of a parent than a big sister. Maybe because she's nine years older than I am. Or maybe it's because she and our parents always treated me like a child, like I'm stuck at six years old.

"Sure." She drops the mail on the counter and puts on water for tea.

I sit at the table, the same spot where I sat and talked to Ser-geant Simmons two days ago. I watch Corrine pull mugs out of the cabinet, grab the box of tea bags. She knows her way around my kitchen. I usually resent her intrusiveness, her sense of owner-ship over my life. But now I don't care. She could've opened my mail and read it, for all I care now. Everything is different.

"I can't stay all day, Molly," Corrine says, placing a mug in front of me. "I have two meetings this afternoon."

"I didn't expect you to stay."

She puts a hand on her hip. "I don't like you here alone."

I shrug. "I'll be okay," I say, although I'm not sure I will be. "Detective Myers is stopping over later. She said they would have a police officer drive past the house the next few nights, if I want."

"Well, that's something, I guess. Why don't you call a security company? They should be able to have someone out here by to-morrow. You want me to do it?" She's already on her phone.

"Fine, sure."

My landline phone rings while Corrine is talking to the security people. It's Laken. I walk into the living room while we talk. I half-hear her but manage to make intelligent responses, then hang up. I pick up the wedding picture of me and Jay that sits on the mantel and carry it back into the kitchen.

Corrine ends her call. "A guy will be here in the morning to install the security equipment."

"Great," I say, and walk past her to the counter, set the photo down, grab the coffee maker, and stash it in a bottom cupboard.

"Gee, thanks, Corrine," my sister says.

"Sorry. Yeah, thanks. I'm grateful." I am too. I just don't have the energy to run my life right now. Just walking, breathing takes everything. "Oh, Laken and Cal are coming over later. Bringing dinner, so I won't be alone."

"That's good." She glances at her phone. "I've got to get going in a few minutes, or I'm going to hit lunchtime traffic."

I walk her to the door and look both ways at the street as Corrine pulls away from the curb. No media. Thank God. But how long will they stay away? How long before they find me, like vultures looking for carrion? I slam the door shut and shoot the dead bolt.

CHAPTER 14

Rita

I'm not the most patient person in the world. And police work has gotten so paper-heavy, so weighted down with documentation, that I sometimes have a hard time just sitting at my desk when I know bad guys are running around while I'm typing at my computer. I take a sip of coffee and keep plowing ahead.

After about ten minutes, I lean back in my chair and take a deep breath. The Bradley case is moving slowly. There's lots to dig through and few clues. It'll take a while to talk to all of the patients Dr. Bradley saw in recent months. And the lab has eliminated all of the knives removed from the Bradley residence as the murder weapon, so either the killer took it with him, or it's hidden somewhere else on the property, so we don't have that.

Officer Lauren Broderick knocks on my door frame, and I glance up from my notes.

"Got an initial report on Dr. Bradley's computer." She's our smartest cop, really. She turned down a scholarship to MIT to attend the police academy. Lucky us. Dedicated and driven, she's presently a detective-in-training; unfortunately, she's slated to be someone else's partner. But Chase has grown on me since Bob paired us up last fall. I'll just miss Lauren's help when she's a full-time detective with cases of her own.

"Come on in."

She settles on the chair across from me, flicks her long braid back over her shoulder, and reads from her laptop. "He mostly had articles copied into files. Background research, I think. Not much else on it other than pictures, e-mail, family stuff. But he's got a file titled *Book*."

"Creative," I say. "How far did he get on the manuscript?"

Lauren shrugs. "Not too. About thirty pages."

"You read it all?"

"Yup." Of course, she did. "Last night."

"And?"

"The working title is *Abnormal Psychology and the Criminal Mind*. He was writing about how lots of criminals have antisocial personality disorders."

"I could've told him that."

"And he makes the point that the more violent or perverse the crime, the more severe the disorder seems to be. And how environment, difficult home life, and other stressors might trigger criminal events."

"Give the guy a Nobel Prize," I say.

Lauren looks up, grins. Her unruly brown hair, despite its braid, has sprouted little curls around her face, which is youthful, fresh-scrubbed, and sans makeup. Lauren is a no-nonsense girl in the beauty department.

"Sorry. I'm sure Dr. Bradley had some new theories to add to that particular subject." I lean back in my chair, prop my feet on a wooden slat that runs under my desk. "He name anybody in particular?"

"No. You think one of his patients killed him? I can't see that he really rocked anybody's boat in his book so far. There's nothing really damning. He doesn't name names. And the perp probably would've taken the computer if he was worried about that."

"Hard to tell at this point. We've got one more friend to interview. A guy he had lunch with a couple days before he died.

Maybe he can throw some light on all this." I hope so. We need *something*.

Lauren bites her bottom lip and clicks the keys on her computer. I flip the pages of my notebook, which lies open on my desk, settling on the interview with Dr. Westmore in her office. I can't resist adding some bubbles to the sketch of the blue fish.

Lauren peeps over her laptop screen. "Why do you draw in your notebook, Rita?" she asks quietly, as though I might bite her head off. I don't know why these young cops think I'm so intimidating. I've explained a time or two over the years when someone's asked. No big deal.

"It helps me think when I'm questioning a subject. Slows me down. And it seems to unnerve some of them, which can be helpful." I chuckle.

"Did you always draw?"

I take a deep breath. "Yeah. Since grade school, I guess. Didn't win any art contests or anything, but it helps me make sense of things sometimes."

When I was a kid, I was a tomboy, climbing trees, running around the neighborhood, getting into fistfights with the local kids. When Ma called us in for supper, I was often sporting a split lip or scraped knees. She would look at me with a soul-weary expression, turn and whisper under her breath, "Jesus, Mary, and Joseph, I don't want to know." After raising eight other rambunctious kids, I guess she hoped that I, number nine and the last of the McMahon children (she'd had a hysterectomy after I was born, just to make sure) wouldn't drive her to an early grave. My third-grade teacher, Miss Hanson, suggested I needed a hobby. A *quiet* hobby. I was a little too rambunctious in school too. She sat me down in a corner of the classroom one day while the rest of the kids were silent reading, which I never could quite take to, and plunked down a piece of sketch paper and a handful of colored pencils and told me to draw a tree. That was the start. I could do that. Drawing was active but quiet. It took concentration, and I found I liked the process. I continued to draw at home, at school, on the bus, anywhere I needed to slow down and be quiet for a while. I never got great at it. No one was going to suggest I go to art school or think about a career in it, but I was pretty good, just the same. It's carried into my work in law enforcement, complementing my notes, giving me time to think and pauses for interviewees to stew, if need be.

"You're a visual learner," Lauren says.

I glance up at her. "Yeah, I suppose so." I've always thought in pictures. I guess that's what they call people like me nowadays when everybody's got a label or a collection of labels. Whatever.

Lauren stands, juggles her laptop in her arms.

"Oh, did you get a look at their social media?" I ask. "The Bradleys and their friends?"

Lauren leans against the door frame, a furrow between her eyebrows. "Yeah. Typical stuff for the Pearsons and the Ferrises. Scott Westmore has a website for his business, but that's all. Dr. Westmore and Dr. Bradley have no social media that I could find. Just a business website and LinkedIn. But I think that's typical for their occupations. They wouldn't want any of their patients stalking them, you know?"

I nod. "Seems prudent."

"But the funny thing is Mrs. Bradley." Lauren shifts the laptop to her other hip. "She's relatively young. Women in her age group typically have Facebook at least. Her friends have an extensive social media presence. But not her. Not a trace."

"Huh." Even I've got a Facebook page under my maiden name, although I hardly ever post anything. One of my nieces cajoled me into it a few years ago when she had her first baby and wanted me to see pictures. I guess no one actually prints them out and sends them anymore.

"Seems odd," Lauren says. "Like she's hiding from the world maybe."

Mrs. Bradley answers the door, looking thin and peaked, washed out. She's wearing an oversized pair of gray sweatpants and a man's flannel shirt that looks like it's been pulled from the bottom of a laundry basket.

She leads Chase and me down the hall and into the kitchen. The party mess has all been cleared away, I notice as we sit at the table. The house smells of lemon and bleach and seems to echo in its stillness.

"We want to bring you up to date on the investigation, Mrs. Bradley."

"Do you have any leads?"

"Not yet."

She nods. "When can I have my phone back?"

"Soon. We've got a lot to process, but it's a priority." How times have changed. Cell phones are the number one thing people want back after a crime.

I open a file folder. "The autopsy is complete, so we'll be releasing your husband's body later today." She stares at me with round, blue eyes that look like they've been bruised in a prize fight, but that look is typical too.

"I'll need to arrange a service," she says almost to herself.

"It would be appropriate to go ahead with those plans." I wonder if she's up to it. Hopefully, she's got family who can make the arrangements because this woman doesn't look like she could handle planning a trip to the grocery store.

"How are you holding up, Mrs. Bradley?" Chase asks, his eyes searching her face. "Are you staying here alone?"

"Yes," she says quietly.

"Do you want one of our officers to drive by while on patrol tonight?"

"Yes. Please. Someone told me they could do that."

"I'll make sure." Chase squeezes her hand, then inputs notes on his phone. He seems a little taken with our widow. He spent ten years as a patrol cop, and while they see lots of carnage, deal with dangerous situations, they don't tend to spend the time with the victims that detectives do. They don't have an opportunity to develop a relationship with the people they serve, and that can sometimes get tricky for a detective. Professional distance is a must, even if that means being a little distant.

That thought takes me back to when I was a young cop in Boston. One hot summer night, my partner and I were called to a nice neighborhood where someone had reported shots fired. We entered an upscale home to find a man sobbing and cradling his dying wife in his arms. Blood covered his shirt, and he mumbled about a man with a gun who had broken in the back door. I was so caught up in the husband's apparent grief that I missed obvious signs that he was, in fact, his wife's killer. Later a veteran cop sat me down for a talk, set me on the right road. People are great at projecting the emotions they want you to see. Lesson learned.

"Mrs. Bradley," I say, "the autopsy revealed that your husband was killed by a single neck wound. Otherwise, he appeared to be a healthy man. Nothing else of note was found."

Her gaze is on the table, and she makes a noise in her throat, and I'm afraid she's going to cry, but she holds it together. "Who would do that to Jay, Detective? Everybody loved him."

Not everybody, apparently, but I don't say so. I shuffle through my notes. "Was your husband talking to anyone about what he was writing? You think he might have interviewed anybody for his book?"

"I don't think so. Maybe Elise would know about that. If he talked to anybody about his work, it would be her."

I pull a planner from my satchel.

"What's that?" she asks.

"Your husband's social calendar. Last year."

Her eyes narrow. "Where did you get it?"

"His office in town." I open the notebook to December, and she leans over to look. "He, Josh, and Cal go to the pub often?"

"Once in a while."

"What about him meeting Laken Ferris at the spa on the ninth?"

She shrugs. "He might have gone in for a massage. I seem to remember that. He'd tweaked his back doing yard work about then. Why is this important?"

"May not be. Just trying to get a sense of what was going on in your husband's life leading up to his murder." I push the calendar closer to her. "What's this about?" I point to Saturday, December 28, which bears the notation "window."

"Oh. Jay drove up to our mountain house in Mountclair, New Hampshire. A little ways past Manchester. He got a call that a couple of kids were throwing snowballs and had broken one of the windows. He went up to fix it."

"Okay. What about this on December 30?" The appointment at the prison.

She leans forward again, purses her lips. "I have no idea what that's about."

"He never mentioned it to you?"

She shakes her head. "I'm sure it was work-related or had something to do with his book maybe, Detective. I have no idea."

"Okay. One more." I close the book, slide it back in the bag, and retrieve the other planner. I open it to the first page. "What about this?" I tap my finger on the square in question. "Lunch with Hayes. Who's he?"

She blinks her eyes. "My boss at the bookstore."

"You didn't know about this either?"

"No." She looks truly baffled.

"Why would your husband be talking to your boss?"

"Well, they're friends too."

"He wasn't at the birthday party?"

She shakes her head. "He couldn't make it. But we see him regularly."

"But you don't know why they were meeting last week two days before your husband was killed?"

"Maybe they were just having lunch, Detective." Her voice rises an octave. "I don't know what you want me to say." Tears gather in her eyes.

Chase heaves a deep breath. "It's okay, Mrs. Bradley. We're just trying to gather everything we can to help you."

She grabs a paper napkin from a holder on the table and presses it to her nose. I slip both planners into my satchel, give her a minute.

"Just one more thing."

She nods and grabs another napkin.

"Dr. Bradley see much of his dad?"

She clears her throat. "His father? No. He passed away last year. He was eighty-one. He and his wife had Jay when they were older."

Shit. I was hoping Dr. Bradley might have confided in his dad. Maybe there would have been something to glean there. Oh well.

She glances up at me. "He was a detective."

"We've heard that." I collect my notes and stash them in my satchel. "If you need anything, Mrs. Bradley, please call."

She stands and walks us to the foyer. "Thanks," she says, as she closes the door behind us.

A frigid wind has picked up. The mild weather of a couple of days ago is gone, and we're back to typical winter temperatures. I pull the lapels of my jacket up around my ears as we get into my van. The engine takes a minute or two to catch, and Chase throws me a look.

"We're fine," I say, as I rev the motor.

"Don't you ever worry this old thing is going to go tits up, Rita, and leave you stranded someplace?"

"I've got triple A, son."

He laughs and searches through his phone. My old van is my home away from home. I like being able to have the things I might need in the course of an investigation. Tools, waders, extra clothes. I drive it only on routine calls, knowing that if I need to chase a suspect, he'd leave me in the dust. Still, Chase has never been comfortable in my old vehicle. He's a pretty tidy guy, and my van—well, keeping it spick-and-span isn't a priority.

We stop at André's Café for a late lunch. Neither André nor Collin is here today. The counter is manned by a teenage girl with jet-black hair and a colorful sleeve full of fairies on her bare left arm. We take our trays to a round table that sits by a plate-glass window.

"So what are you thinking so far?" I ask Chase. He and Lauren are still learning, and I enjoy pushing them along. After being the baby in a big family, I get a charge out of being the older, smarter one when I can.

He shrugs and rubs his chin. He's let a little stubble grow. "Well, I don't think it was a stranger since he left the laptop sitting on the desk and the doctor's wallet was in his pocket. I think a lot depends on what his patients have to say, don't you think?"

"Yeah. If it was a patient. But maybe it was someone he met doing research for his book. Someone his wife and friends don't know about."

"Are we going out to the prison he noted in his planner?"

I nod. "Yeah. Just waiting for them to get back to me. He met with an inmate." I'd learned that much when I'd called.

"The perp couldn't've been some guy who was locked up."

"No, obviously. But maybe he knows something useful. Maybe he knows who else Dr. Bradley was talking to, someone on the outside." Maybe the prison visit will be worthwhile, maybe not. But we've got nothing to go on so far.

I sip my Coke and watch a woman jaywalk across the street,

her red scarf fluttering in the wind. "What do you think the perp was after in the office? That's the key to this whole thing."

"Don't know." Chase leans back, drums the table with his fingers. "But I was thinking . . ." His eyes meet mine. "What if one of Dr. Bradley's patients told him that he'd committed a crime. Then he had second thoughts."

"Could be." I take a bite of my tuna on rye. Watch Chase ruminate over his clam chowder.

"Psychiatrists have to report criminal behavior, don't they?" he asks.

"Dr. Bradley was a psychologist, but the same rules apply." I shake chips onto my plate. "They have to report *threats* of criminal activity. Like, if I tell my shrink I'm going to shoot my annoying new neighbor with my service weapon, he's legally bound to report it."

"What if it's an old crime. Somebody's already dead?"

I tip my head. "That's murkier territory. Doctor-client privilege still exists since no one is going to be hurt if the doc keeps it to himself."

"You think someone might've confessed a crime to Dr. Bradley, but then worried he'd tell somebody?" Chase asks. "The perp might not have wanted to trust doctor-client privilege."

"It's possible. But what was he after in the home office?"

Chase shakes his head.

My phone chimes. A text has come in from Lauren. "We need to get back," I say, "so finish your soup."

"What's the rush?" He lifts his bowl, glances around to see if anyone is looking, and slurps it down.

"Lauren said they might have something, and the chief wants to update everyone. She said to hurry along."

You can feel the electricity snap through the station as we walk in. People look up from their desks at me with anticipation. Bob's standing in his office doorway, a file folder in his hand and his cell phone tucked between his neck and jowls, where it nearly disappears. He catches my eye and motions us toward the conference room. Everyone working the case, which is half the department in one way or another, crams inside the small space.

Bob stands at the front, the whiteboard with its photos and red and blue lists and lines behind him. He pulls down a projection screen and nods to a young cop sitting with a laptop balanced on his knees.

"Connors just got surveillance footage from the Bradley neighborhood. Hit the lights, Chase." The room plunges into darkness, and the cop with the laptop starts clicking keys. "So far, this is the only pertinent video we've been able to secure. It was taken by a neighbor's home-security system the night of the incident."

"Which neighbor?" I ask, pulling out my notebook.

Bob glances at his notes on the table in front of him. "Two doors down from the Bradley residence." He draws a deep breath. "Okay, people, I want you to take a good look. Then we'll send the clip to everyone who needs a copy for further review." He nods to the kid with the laptop.

A grainy shot of the sidewalk and street comes into view in front of a wintery yard. There's a date and time stamp that counts off at the bottom of the screen. Excellent. One fifteen a.m. Nothing. One sixteen. One seventeen. And then there's a dim image. We all lean forward. A figure, tall, wearing dark clothing, a hat pulled low. Looks like a man, but that's not for sure. The video quality is too poor to really make out his features, and the light from a nearby lamppost doesn't help much. He walks quickly in long, smooth strides. His gaze is straight ahead, moving toward the Bradley residence. There's something that looks like a backpack slung over his shoulder.

The chief signals the kid working the computer, and he freezes the frame with the figure dead center.

Bob blows out a breath. "This, people, could be our killer. It fits the ME's timeline. And why would anyone be walking down that street at one a.m.? There are no other people on the tape."

"Do we see him later? On his way back?" I ask.

"No. This is it. He might've crossed the road or taken another way back out. We just don't know."

"Could've just been a guy walking home from a bar," I say, always the devil's advocate.

"Maybe. But there's not any businesses out that way that would be open that time of night. No bars or restaurants close by."

"What about the gas station on the corner?" I ask.

"We've looked at their video and didn't spot anyone who matched up with this guy."

"We have a vehicle anywhere that might be his?"

"No. This is all we've got so far."

Still, this is something. This could very well be our man. "Can the lab enhance it?" I ask.

"Hopefully," Bob says. "I'm sending it over."

CHAPTER 15

Molly

Laken and Cal sit at my kitchen table and, unlike me, look every inch in control of their lives. They are both strong and athletic. Laken, despite resembling a runway model, was a state tennis champion when she was in high school and then played on her college team. She and Cal ski, sail, skate, you name it. I sometimes envy their fortitude. I was on my high school swim team but didn't collect many medals.

Laken has a loud, funny laugh, and it feels good, but strange, to hear her. It occurs to me that I haven't heard anybody laugh since Saturday night. We've all gone along on tiptoe, whispering and sobbing quietly into wads of tissues.

Her boys run around the house, making laps from living room to foyer to dining room to kitchen. Laken grabs Liam (or is it Logan?) by the collar, and he skids to a stop.

"Enough! You guys take your dinner in the other room and watch TV, okay?" She removes slices of pepperoni pizza from one of two boxes on the table and lays them on paper plates.

"I'll get the boys settled," Cal says, going to the fridge, filling two glasses with milk.

They troop into the other room, and the TV comes on. Channels switch until landing on some loud kids' program. Laken blows out an irritated breath. "Sorry, Molly. The sitter was busy tonight."

"They're fine." They are too. A distraction.

Laken fills a paper plate with salad and adds a slice of veggie pizza next to it. I do the same and pour us each a glass of red. Cal returns and gets another beer from the fridge and joins us at the table.

"Have the cops found anything, Molly?" he asks.

"Not that they've told me."

Cal heaves a breath and takes a long sip of his beer.

"They think it was a robbery maybe?"

I shake my head. "Who knows? Jay didn't talk to you about anything, did he? Anything bothering him?"

"I really hadn't spoken much to him the past couple of weeks. I've been really busy at the lab, and Josh . . ."

Laken throws him a look.

"What?" I ask.

"Josh's been calling out a lot. And when he's there, his work is less than stellar. I've been kind of focused on that situation." Cal rubs his fingers over his eyes, making his glasses bounce precariously. "I shouldn't talk about this. Maybe something is going on with him. Maybe he discussed it with Jay."

Laken swallows, sips her wine. "What's that got to do with who killed Jay? I'm sure Josh will get things sorted out, Cal. His sister's got cancer, you know. Maybe that's weighing on him. I don't think it would be the best time to fire him."

Cal's lips thin. "I'm not going to *fire* him, Lake. It's just causing me more work, that's all. I'll talk to him." Cal clears his throat, stands, and throws his plate in the garbage. "I'll check on the boys."

"So," Laken says, "you going to be all right here by yourself?"

"Yes. I'm fine. Corrine's got a guy coming tomorrow to install a security system."

Laken nods. "That's good. Make sure you lock the doors to-night before you go to bed."

"I'll be careful. You don't think whoever killed Jay would come back for me?"

She sips her wine, looks away from me momentarily. "Of course not. I didn't mean to scare you. Whoever did this is prob-ably a thousand miles away by now."

Does she really think that, or is she just trying to make me feel better? Probably the latter, but that's okay. I don't have the en-ergy to worry about it. In some part of my brain, I think that being dead alongside Jay wouldn't be the worst thing that could happen to me.

"Hey, why don't you come into the shop tomorrow? How about a massage and a facial?"

"I don't know. Maybe."

Laken shrugs. "What'll you do all day? You've got to get out." She glances around the kitchen. "You'll go crazy if you stay in all the time."

"I'm thinking I'll go back to work in a few days."

"That's what you want to do?"

I don't want to do anything. I want to stay in the house, burrow on the sofa, and pull a blanket over my head. That's what I want to do. "What else can I do, Laken? Go back and live with my par-ents? I'd rather die."

Her dark eyes widen under her perfectly sculpted brows.

"Sorry," I say, "that was melodramatic. You know what I mean. Going back to live with my parents is not an option."

She places her hand on mine. "I read you shouldn't make any major life decisions right after a traumatic event."

I manage a thin smile. "Exactly. So going back to work might be the best thing."

Laken, Cal, and the kids left at eight. I watched them from the porch pile into their big SUV and disappear into the night. I stood outside awhile, my arms clutching my sweater around my chest, and shivered in the dark. Sleety snowflakes pinged against my face like small razors. When I turned and went into the house, I felt utterly alone, knowing that Jay was truly gone forever.

I turn on all the lights downstairs and walk from room to room, checking corners and closets, double-checking that the lock Jay put on the cellar door is fastened. There's a little room tucked behind the kitchen. Jay said it was probably a larder years ago, and I picture rows of mason jars lined up on the shelves, their chunks of onion and cucumber swimming in briny water full of floating herbs. I picture some ghostly woman in her long dress and apron lining them up there, and it makes me think of how quickly life passes. I wonder about the people who have lived in our house and how many of them are probably dead. We have no need for a larder, so we use the room for storage and the washer and dryer. I pull a chain that controls the bulb hanging overhead, and the room is filled with sickly light.

I walk down the hall to the door to the side porch. The air turns colder as I approach. The house needs new insulation. Something else on the long list of home improvements we'd had planned. The enclosed side porch with its rows of louvered windows is my favorite spot. Last spring, a couple of months after we moved in, white lilac bushes bloomed right outside this little room, providing a fragrant hiding place to read or relax. I can't wait until winter ends and I can sit there again. I try the knob to make sure the door is securely locked. It is, and I turn and head back down the hall.

In the living room, I turn on the TV and switch channels until I land on a movie, one with bright colors and chirpy dialog. I hope the sound will chase away the stillness. I glance at the pile of books on the end table. Normally, in the evening, I'd read. Losing myself in a story has been a lifelong passion and escape. I'd cuddle up with Jay and read while he watched a game. I sniff back tears. I'm so exhausted, I don't even have the energy for a novel right now. I don't think my brain could follow words on a page. So TV it is.

At midnight, after watching two movies, the names of which I couldn't tell you, I head upstairs. Standing in the doorway of the master bedroom, I see that the cleaning ladies have made the bed and folded the clothes that had been scattered throughout the room. My clothes and Jay's now sit in a neat stack, mixed together, my sweater nestled between two pairs of his Dockers.

I go through my night routine like a robot, pretending Jay is away at a conference, anything but reality. With the lights on, I slide into bed, stay on my side, and despite myself fall into a deep, murky doze.

Darkness wraps around me, and the walls of my prison reek of earth and decay. I'm on my hands and knees, crawling, feeling for the stairs, soaked in my own urine. A girl is crying, whimpering, and I can't tell if it's me or someone else. There's a monster down here in this hole. I smell his sour breath, hear his raspy breathing. I scuttle across the floor, my fingernails digging into the muck, my knees burning. But I can't get away. I can't find the stairs. My heart pounds as he leans over me and shoves me roughly face-down. My teeth hit dirt, and it lies bitter in my mouth. I can't breathe. And his fingers, sharp as talons, squeeze my flesh. He yanks my arm out from under me and pierces my tender skin. I feel the bite of the knife as I'm sinking into the earth, never to get away.

I wake, choking for air, dripping with sweat. It takes me a minute to ease my breathing into a normal rhythm. I swallow my tears, swing my feet to the floor, and pull myself out of bed. I find Jay's robe on the back of the closet door, slip my arms into the sleeves, wrap the flannel firmly around my waist, and pull the lapels to my nose, willing myself to breathe slow and steady. I wander out into the hall, my bare feet on the cold hardwood. At the top of the stairs is a small round window that overlooks the backyard. I pad over to it and wonder how many people over the years have stood here in this very spot looking out, looking for something or someone. My mind settles on the idea, anything to chase the nightmare away. Chilly air seeps around the old frame, and I lean my forehead against the cool glass.

My heartbeat kicks up. The backyard is dark, but there's a light on in the office. Did the police leave it on when they left? I peer more closely. A shadow passes the office window. I instinctively reach into the pocket of Jay's robe for my phone, but of course it isn't there. I'll have to use the landline in the kitchen. But what if I'm wrong? What if the shadow is just a trick of the light? A remnant of my nightmare? They'll think I'm crazy. My heart is thrumming, pulsing in my ears. Then I see a figure, a man in dark clothing, a hat pulled low, crouch under the yellow tape, and sprint across the yard.

CHAPTER 16

Rita

I'm dog-tired this morning after a five a.m. wake-up call. I shuffle into the station, my eyes bleary, my hair in a lopsided, messy bun. But it could've been worse; a couple of uniform cops spent the even earlier morning hours at the Bradley place after Mrs. Bradley placed a two a.m. 911 call. She claims to have seen a man wearing dark clothing come out of her husband's home office and run toward the street. The forensics team went back out, but so far, they've found nothing.

Looks like our killer didn't find what he was looking for the night of the murder, perhaps scared away by Mrs. Murray's barking dog and porch light.

Mrs. Bradley sits in the little room we use when talking to distraught family members. It's a little more comfortable than the interrogation rooms. We hope it is anyway. She sits at the little table, clutching a paper cup of tea that Chase made her in the Keurig that sits on a small counter. He laid sugar packets and a variety of little creamer cups in front of her as well. So far, she's barely sipped her tea, holding it instead like a kid with a security blanket.

Chase pulls up the surveillance video we got yesterday from her neighbor. He clicks the keys on his laptop, and the tape rolls.

"Please take a good look, Mrs. Bradley. Is this the man you saw last night?" I ask.

Her tired eyes shift to the screen, and she follows the video man's trek down the sidewalk.

"Mrs. Bradley?"

"It could be him." She shivers and grips her cup with both hands.

"What seems the same?" I ask.

"Um, he seemed tall like this man."

"What about his clothes?"

The man in the video is wearing a long coat, dark gray or black over what could be jeans. His feet are encased in boots. The hat on his head is knitted and pulled low.

"They look the same, I think." Her eyes meet mine, as though she's looking for approval.

"Are you sure?"

"The hat is the same kind. But I think he was wearing a shorter jacket maybe. Not a long coat like the man in the video."

"What about his face? What could you make out?"

She shakes her head. "I really couldn't see it. It happened so fast, and the light was behind him."

"But it could be the same man?"

She nods. "Yes." She looks over at Chase, her voice tremulous. "Why would he come back?"

"We don't know, Mrs. Bradley." Chase's gaze is on the table, as though it's his fault.

"Was he carrying anything?" I prod.

"Not that I could tell," she says, her eyes back on the video of the man. "I don't think the man I saw had a backpack."

"Okay." I lean forward in my chair. "We've got our lab guys trying to enhance the video, so we might have more to ask you about it later."

We stand, and I collect my notes. Chase opens the door. "Do you need a ride home, Mrs. Bradley?" he asks.

"No, I'm okay. I drove myself. My sister is at my house. I've got a guy there installing a security system."

"That's a good idea," Chase says.

"Will you have outside cameras?" I ask.

"Yes. My sister ordered it." She almost smiles. "Cameras inside and out, all the bells and whistles."

Chase says he'll walk her to her car, and I head back to my office. I've got my notes spread out on my desk, the video pulled up on my laptop, when Lauren walks in.

"We found something, Rita." She holds up an evidence bag with an envelope inside. She drops into the chair opposite me and lays the bag flat. "The guys found it wedged in the back of one of the filing cabinet drawers."

I grab my reading glasses from my jacket pocket and lean close to the bag. Lauren lets go an excited breath, pulls on a latex glove, and reaches inside. She lays the envelope on top of the bag.

It's a power company envelope, like the ones your bill comes in. "Okay." I glance up at her.

She pulls a folded white tissue out of the envelope, unwraps something shiny, and drapes a delicate necklace over her palm like an anxious jeweler. She runs her thumb over the round disk of a pendant. There's a chip of topaz set in the middle, with Scorpio inscribed beneath it.

"Interesting," is all I manage. "Doesn't look awfully expensive."

"It's not," Lauren gushes.

I lean back in my chair. "You think the perp was coming back for *that*?"

"He was coming back for something."

"But a fairly worthless pendant?"

"The necklace might have some meaning for him." Lauren licks her lips. "I think we ought to at least look into it. Why take the trouble to stash it in a locked filing cabinet? And here's the best part," she says, and flips the pendant over. "Initials."

I sit up. Push my reading glasses up the bridge of my nose, but, shit, I still can't see them.

"A.R.," Lauren says.

"It could've been in that drawer forever."

Lauren taps her finger against the envelope. There's a postmark. The bill was mailed two weeks ago.

"Huh." That changes things. Dr. Bradley hid the necklace recently. "Okay, I see your point. It's worth looking into."

"I think so." Lauren folds the necklace back into the tissue, replaces it in the envelope and bag, and jumps up. "I'm going to start digging."

CHAPTER 17

Molly

When I get home, the security guy is pulling away from the curb. Corrine is in the kitchen, laptop open, cycling through screens.

"How'd it go?" she asks without looking up.

"Okay. They showed me video they got from the Fergusons' security camera. It shows a guy walking past their house headed in our direction Saturday night. They wanted to know if he was the same man I saw last night."

"Was it?"

"Might've been. It happened so fast."

"Well, look." She tips her computer toward me, and I see my backyard in black and white, startlingly clear. Corrine clicks through screens, and I see the office, with its yellow tape a sickly gray, one piece fluttering in the wind. Then she switches to the backyard, fence and trees, the side yard, the driveway, and finally the front porch and street view. She clicks more keys, and all shots shrink into tiny rectangles and fill the screen.

"You can see everything at once," Corrine says. "Or one shot, or a couple at a time. She stands, runs a hand through her hair. "Same for inside. Wherever you have your phone or computer, you can see both inside and outside."

"Wow."

"Secure as Fort Knox."

"Will they bill me monthly? How does that work?"

She blows out a breath. "Rich and I are paying for it."

"I can't let you do that."

"Not an option. It's done." She picks up her Coach purse and swings the strap over her shoulder.

I appreciate her generosity but feel unsettled. This is just another thing she thinks I can't do for myself.

"Look, Molly. It's no big deal for us, okay? We want to help."

This I know. They both earn big salaries, and Rich has family money besides.

"How are you set financially?" Corrine asks. "Mom and Dad are worried, and I told them I'd talk to you."

"I'm fine. You guys don't need to be concerned about me."

"Now that Jay's income is gone . . . did he have life insurance? Savings?"

"Yes, of course." Though I'm not sure how much. I wasn't worried about making ends meet before. I turn and walk to the back door, where I can see the office.

"You could sell the mountain house," Corrine says. "You don't use it that much anyway."

The mountain house in New Hampshire. Jay inherited the property from his mother. It was all she had to leave him. It had been in her family for years, originally built as a hunting lodge. Apparently, her great-grandfather had made money in shipping, but each succeeding generation had squandered a little more until they'd sold off everything except their vacation home in the mountains. It's a beautiful place up a steep mountain road with majestic views, a couple of rivers and lakes nearby. We go up a few times a year and often invite friends.

But I was never comfortable in the house. When Jay first took me there, animal heads were mounted on the walls in odd spots, catching you unawares with their glassy eyes. And then, of course, there was the basement.

Jay loved the house though. I think it reminded him of his mother and the time they spent there together while his father hunted. She died so young that Jay didn't have much time with her. He told me about the cocoa she used to make from scratch and the jigsaw puzzles they'd worked together up there. Memories of her, I think, made the mountain house a special place for him.

To an outsider, the house looks imposing, sitting on its peak, lording over the trees and river, full of dark paneling and plaid wallpaper. I picture it as the kind of place where the gentry used to go to indulge in hunting and other vigorous winter sports to prove to themselves perhaps that they weren't all fluff and money.

So, for Jay's sake, I tried to fit in, tried to enjoy our time there. We invited friends along whenever we could. We rarely went up there on our own, just the two of us. But even with Jay beside me, the house overwhelmed me. It felt sinister, alive with the blood spilled by men who took pleasure in the hunt and the kill.

I sigh. "I can't think about that now." Dealing with real estate agents, contracts, and fussy buyers.

"Well, it's an option if you need cash."

"Yeah. I know, but I'll be all right." I walk Corrine to the door, where she gives me a quick hug and leaves.

I sit at the table, flipping through screens like a stalker. In the backyard, a squirrel tiptoes past the bird feeder. It stops, listens, looks both ways before clambering up the bare maple tree to reach the goodies suspended in the feeder. I'm afraid it'll be disappointed. I haven't refilled it in a few days. I watch the squirrel, get lost in its world until the doorbell rings, and I'm pulled back to real life.

I switch screens to see who's there. This is kind of cool if I don't think about why I need this technology. Hayes and Alice wait patiently on my porch. I close my laptop and answer the door.

"Hi, guys. Come on in." Hayes catches me in a hug, and Alice nudges him aside.

"We brought you these, Molly." She holds up a box tied with string. "Lemon poppy-seed muffins. I made them."

"Thanks, Alice." I take the box and drape my arm around her shoulders.

"How are you?" Hayes asks, unwrapping his scarf. He's wearing a black turtleneck, his dark curly hair in disarray.

"I'm okay." I set the box on the table and collect their coats. Alice pulls off her red hat with its pom-pom on top and pats it onto the pile in my arms.

We sit at the kitchen table with tea and Alice's muffins. Her long fair hair is plaited in two braids that she's wrapped around her head like a little Swiss girl. Her huge gray eyes are grave, as usual. She's eleven going on forty-five, as Hayes likes to say.

He takes my hand. "You're really all right?"

I nod. "As well as can be expected."

"Don't worry about the store. You come back whenever you're ready."

Alice frowns. "Sharon is more than happy to work your hours, Molly."

That makes me smile. Alice and Sharon have an uneasy, slightly adversarial relationship. Sharon, sixty-two years old and a self-proclaimed expert on all things child-rearing, thinks that Alice needs to get out of the bookstore, go to the mall with a gaggle of squealing preteens, and ogle boys. Alice finds the idea immature and beneath her.

"Well, I was thinking of coming in on Friday, actually," I say, although up until this moment I hadn't decided on a definite return date. "I could use the distraction." I get up from the table, retrieve my laptop, which I'd left on the foyer table.

"Have the police found anything?" Hayes asks when I return.

"Not yet, but they have video of a man walking toward the house Saturday night, and"—I swallow—"I saw a man in Jay's office last night. He ran toward the street, and I called 911."

"Oh my God, Molly. You should've called me. I would've come right over."

"It's okay. The cops came and stayed with me until morning. Then I went to the police station and gave them a statement."

"You must've been so scared!" Alice says. "What's that?" She points to the images on my screen, which I've pulled up and am clicking through like a kid with a new toy.

"My security system. Now I can see if anyone's near the house. Inside too."

Hayes sighs. "That's good." He runs his hand through his hair, which only serves to dishevel it further.

"It makes me feel better. But I'm thinking of getting a dog too."

"Yes," Alice says. "A dog would be even better."

"Hayes." I clear my throat. "The police showed me Jay's calendar, and he had lunch with you noted last Thursday. What was that about?"

He colors slightly, adjusts his dark-framed glasses. "Jay wanted to talk to me about your anniversary."

"Oh. Right. It's coming up," I say, and that thought has my heart sinking.

Jay and I got married on Valentine's Day. Kind of hokey, I know, but we decided quickly, didn't want a big wedding that involved months of planning, so we decided to have our friends and family up to the mountain house for the ceremony and reception. I wasn't crazy about getting married up there, but Jay's townhouse and my apartment were definitely not going to work, and we didn't want to go to the trouble of finding a venue at the last minute. Jay thought the mountain house was a great idea, and I was trying so hard to be like everyone else. A house, no matter its original purpose, shouldn't faze the me I was trying to be, someone for whom old structures and dark basements held no power, so I readily agreed to the plan.

"Why did he want to talk to you?" I ask, my voice hoarse.

"He wanted to surprise you with a trip. He thought I might have some ideas." Hayes is our most well-traveled friend. He and Alice have toured the world, bringing back all manner of souvenirs for me and Jay. Teacups from London. Woolen blankets from Ireland. His and hers kimonos from Japan.

"Oh." Tears start to collect in my eyes again. Jay and I liked to travel too, but we hadn't had a chance to do as much of that as we would have liked. A week in Paris two years ago was the highlight of our travel thus far. I dab my eyes with a tissue, sip my tea.

Hayes pats my hand. "We're all here for you, Molly."

CHAPTER 18

Rita

Forbidding gray buildings tower over the landscape, tucked behind concrete walls topped with razor wire. The surrounding fields are winter bare, and a steady wind tosses the skeletal branches of trees as we approach the prison.

Dr. Bradley had asked and been granted permission to talk to an inmate named Tyler White. He's twenty-six years old and has been at the facility for three years. Prior to his present incarceration, he had an extensive juvie record that included drug use and theft, but nothing violent or disturbing that anyone knew about. When he was twenty-one, his mother had him committed to a psychiatric treatment center, claiming he was delusional and had threatened her and had hit her on several occasions. He was treated for six months and released. He went back to live with her and seemed to be, according to the records, adjusting well. On a warm June day, when she returned from work, Tyler told his mother that their dog, a blind lab named Lady, had gotten out and had run off into the forest behind their house. While Louise White traipsed through the wooded acres, calling for her dog, her son tracked her until they were deep in the forest. He called her name, and when she turned to face him, he shot her with a bow and arrow, killing her. He returned to the house, where Lady was sleeping soundly in his bedroom. Tyler lived happily for six days, ordering pizza and playing video games, before police found Louise White's body resting against a pine tree, one arrow protruding from her chest, another wedged in her right eye.

It turned out that Tyler had also killed two teenage runaways who'd disappeared four months earlier and whose bodies were also found in the same woods.

I don't know that we'll get anything useful from him, but so far, we're not getting anywhere in the investigation, and that makes me antsy.

The room is built from cinder blocks and painted an institutional gray. There are no windows, just a scratched metal table with three chairs. A paunchy, blond guard escorts a handcuffed Tyler White into the room, where he sits heavily in the chair opposite us. He's thin as a rail with bony arms covered in homemade tattoos. His dull blue eyes gaze vacantly at the wall, and I figure he's medicated. One eye looks off to the side, as though it has wandered of its own accord. His hair lies thin and lank, a nondescript brown that doesn't look like it's been cut in a few months.

"Mr. White," I begin, and his good eye rolls in my direction, "thanks for meeting with us." I introduce myself and Chase. He doesn't respond, so I keep going. "You spoke with a man, Dr. Bradley, last week. Do you remember that?"

He snorts derisively. "Yeah. I'm not a retard." Spittle clings in the corners of his cracked lips.

"Didn't mean to imply anything," I say. Chase clears his throat, automatically reaches in his pocket for his phone to take notes, but quickly realizes his phone was confiscated back at the intake desk.

"Why did you agree to see him?"

Tyler shifts in his chair, stretches his back, as though he's just waking up. "He's writing a book. He asked if he could interview me for it."

"You agreed?"

"Obviously, since I talked to him." He rubs his fingertips together. Then studies them as if he'd touched something interesting. "Nothing else to do in this place."

"What did you talk about?"

Tyler takes a deep breath. "All the same stuff the other doctors want to know about. Did I decide to kill my mother because of my shitty childhood."

"What did you tell him?"

"I told him the truth." He stabs the table with his index finger. "I killed Louise in self-defense."

"How's that?"

"She beat the shit out of me my whole life. Every goddamn thing was my fault." His eye meets mine. "She had some kinda powers too."

"Powers?"

His head droops and his voice falters. "She knew things. Secret things. I can't describe it." Silence fills the room. The clock high on the wall ticks. Finally, Tyler sits up, glares at me and Chase, and whispers, "She was going to kill me. I heard her talking to someone. She was always talking to someone where I couldn't see her."

"Who was she talking to?"

His bottom lip trembles slightly. "How the hell should I know? I never saw him." Tyler makes a strange, low sound in his throat before meeting my gaze. "So it was her or me."

"So you had no choice?"

"No. I had no choice. No *choice*. That's what I keep telling them." He shakes his head like he's trying to dislodge something stuck in his brain.

"Uh huh. What else did Dr. Bradley ask you about?"

"Let me think a minute." He closes his eyes, and a slow smile spreads across his face. His good eye pops open and pins me in my seat. "He wanted to know when the switch flipped."

"What do you mean?"

"When I went from being a regular guy to a killer. What changed?" He looks off at the wall, his eyes fixed and unblinking. "Like I knew. I didn't change. I've always been the same person. I didn't know what he was getting at, if you want to know the truth. Then he asked me if I fantasized about killing my mother before I did it."

"Did you?"

He shrugs one thin shoulder. "I don't want to talk about that. I told him that was private. A person's fantasies should be private, don't you think? What goes on in your head is nobody's business."

I don't know that this is getting us anywhere. "Did he say that he'd interviewed other people for his book?"

Tyler's thin lips turn up in a smile. "He said I was the first. He picked me first."

I lean back in my chair, glance at the clock. "Did you know that someone killed Dr. Bradley last Saturday night?"

"You're shitting me." He grins, practically bounces in his chair, and his body odor wafts over me. "They know who did it?"

"No. You have any idea? He mention anything to you about someone he was afraid of maybe?" This is a long shot, but who knows?

Tyler leans back and folds his hands, cuffs jangling. He nods his head as though he's thinking. "Nope. He didn't say nothing like that." Suddenly, he's animated again, like his medicine just wore off. "That's a trip, huh? He's researching murderers, and he ends up getting murdered. That's fucking crazy. So he's dead? Well, shit."

"Yes. Ironic. What else did you two talk about?"

Tyler takes a deep breath and drums his fingers on the table, tapping a metallic melody. He's getting bored. "So I'm not going to be in his book then?"

"I don't know. Maybe his colleague will finish it," I say, hoping to regain his interest.

He nods, turns to the guard.

"Tyler?" He looks back at me. "Did he ask you about the two girls they found in the woods behind your house?"

His brow furls. "I don't want to talk about them. I had nothing to do with that."

"Okay. Anything else you can remember from your conversation with Dr. Bradley?"

He shrugs again, both shoulders this time. "It's nearly dinnertime," he says. "Pizza night."

"We're almost done. Anything at all you remember Dr. Bradley saying about other people?"

Tyler gets to his feet, and the guard walks quickly to his side. "I'm ready to go back."

"Wait, Tyler. Anything else you remember from the interview?"

He shakes his head and turns to the guard. "Chocolate pudding tonight, Tom. With sprinkles." And they're gone.

CHAPTER 19

Molly

I stayed up half the night watching the camera feeds. I didn't see anything interesting, but I couldn't seem to look away. The man didn't come back, from what I saw, so that was a relief. Hopefully, whatever he was looking for, he found or realized it wasn't there.

I pull up in front of the animal shelter on the outskirts of Graybridge. When Jay and I met, he had a chocolate lab named Winston. After we'd been dating for six months, I went with Jay to have Winston put down. He was thirteen, suffering from cancer. We cried like babies all the way home. Jay and I had been making a regular monthly donation to the shelter and talking about getting another dog, something else we'll never do together.

I never had a dog of my own. When I was growing up, my mother said we couldn't have one because she was allergic, but I eventually figured out that wasn't true. She just didn't want the trouble of caring for an animal. Everything was well ordered in our house. Everything in its place. You couldn't have a puppy running amok.

That's one reason I liked Sundays so much when I was little. We always went out to visit my Grandpa Wright. He was a widower who lived on a little farm in the middle of nowhere. He had two fat beagles named Sparky and Thumper, and I loved those dogs. My parents never wanted to stay long, and my mother always put me straight in the bathtub when we got home.

I take a deep breath and head inside the shelter. The woman at the desk is middle-aged, wears faded jeans and a sweatshirt decorated with black pawprints. Her hair is pulled back in a graying ponytail, and she wears no makeup on her moon-like face.

"I'd like to adopt a dog," I say.

"Okay." She points to a clipboard full of papers. "Fill out the forms, please." She hands me a pen with a big plastic flower taped to it. "What type of dog are you interested in?"

"Not a puppy." I'm too worn out to train one at this point. "One that's a couple years old maybe. Already housebroken."

"Okay." She stands and puts her hand on her ample hip.

"A bigger dog too. One that has an intimidating bark would be great."

"We don't adopt out guard dogs," she says, narrowing her eyes.

I look up from the forms. "Oh, no. I'm looking for a pet. He or she will get lots of love. Live in the house. I'm a good pet owner."

"Uh huh." She walks around the desk and looks over my shoulder as I flip to the next page. "You can finish those in a minute. Why don't you come on back? See if any of them is a good match." She props open the door with her hip. Barks and yips stream out.

I take a step back. "No. Why don't you pick one and bring it out here?"

She gives me another scowl. "Why?"

I bite my lips. Will I sound like a lunatic? I can't go back there without falling to pieces. "I trust your judgment. It makes me sad, that's all."

She huffs out a breath as though I'm a troublesome customer in an upscale boutique. "Well, we are pretty full right now. So you want a big dog?"

"Not like a hundred pounds or anything. Like a lab size, I guess."

"No problem with a mixed breed?"

"No, of course not."

"A couple years old, not a puppy?"

"Yes. Girl or boy, either is fine."

She doesn't say anything else, just turns and walks through the door, letting it close behind her.

A few minutes later, she comes back with a black dog on a leash. "This is Sadie. She's got shepherd and lab in her, among other things."

I reach my hand down and let her sniff, then pet her head, which she keeps low. But then she licks my arm when I stop. "She's perfect."

"She's been here a couple months."

"What's her story?"

The woman snorts. "People surrendered her when they moved. Said they couldn't take her to their new apartment."

"Why didn't they find an apartment that accepted dogs? A lot of them do."

"Typical excuse when people get tired of taking care of a pet."

Sadie looks at me and wags her tail, and I'm smitten. "I won't do that. My husband and I believe that pets are family forever."

That seems to change the woman's tune. She's smiling now. "Okay, Mrs. Bradley. Looks like Sadie here is happy. Finish up that paperwork, and if everything checks out, you and your husband have a new family member."

I don't have the heart to tell her Jay is dead. It will be just me and Sadie.

"Thanks. That would be great."

On the way home, Sadie and I stop at the pet store, where I buy a cart full of stuff she'll need: food, toys, a plush dog bed, stainless steel bowls. When we get home, she is tentative about coming in the house, and I have to coax her. I curse her former owners. She's definitely unsure, as if waiting for someone to yell at her. But she walks well on the leash, and I finally get her in the house, where she sticks close by my side. I put her stuff away, drag a thirty-pound bag of dry food into the laundry room, then wash and fill one of her bowls with water.

The landline rings, and I pick up the receiver, Sadie's food dish in my other hand.

"Mrs. Bradley?" I pause. I don't recognize the voice.

"Yes?"

"Hi, it's George Barton from Mountclair Dry Goods?"

"Oh, yes."

"That window Jay ordered has come in. You'll let him know then?"

I swallow. "Yes, of course. Thank you, Mr. Barton." I hang up before the conversation can continue. Why didn't I tell him about Jay? I'm going to have to start letting people who don't live here know. Mountclair is the little town at the foot of the mountain where our New Hampshire house is located. It's where we pick up supplies. Where we cheerfully browse the racks of canned goods and snacks, glass-fronted coolers full of beer and soft drinks. Kerosene and camping gear fill one corner of the store, everything you might need for a weekend in the mountains. I'd worked Saturday the week before Jay's birthday, so he ran up to the house alone. He told me he'd boarded up the window and ordered a new one from George. I sit on a kitchen chair. One more thing to worry about. Sadie walks to my side, her claws clicking on the wood floor, and lays her head in my lap.

CHAPTER 20

Molly

Friday morning is dim, the sun buried somewhere above the thick cloud deck so common in the Northeast in winter. Graybridge Books sits on a corner of the square, its lights glowing inside like a warm beacon. The weather has turned colder, and fat snowflakes swirl and land on the sidewalk, covering everything in white. I took a shower this morning, dressed in slim black pants and a green sweater, put on a little makeup, trying to put a little color in my cheeks and hide the dark circles under my eyes.

I need to make an effort. Jay would want me to. Going back to work is a step in the right direction. What else would I do today except sit in the house and think about the funeral scheduled for tomorrow? So I walk down the sidewalk through the falling snow, which is already gathering on my black wool coat. The flakes are perfect, yet ephemeral works of art. Sadie trots at my side, proudly displaying her red harness and leash. I plan on taking her with me wherever I go. If other people can have an emotional support animal, I surely can. To complete her ensemble, I ordered a service dog vest, which should be here in a couple of days.

I see Alice behind the plate-glass window, peering out beneath the gold script that spells out the shop's name. She opens the heavy door before I can reach for the knob.

"Molly! Dad said you'd be back today, but I wasn't sure . . ." Her voice trails off as it so often does. She's wearing a purple sweater with layered handmade beaded necklaces around her neck. Her long hair hangs behind her shoulders, and I detect a trace of pink shadow on her lids. She leans over and pets Sadie. "She's perfect, Molly. Just the dog I pictured you getting."

"She's really sweet," I say. "She hasn't left my side since I got her."

Hayes walks up behind Alice and puts his hands on her shoulders. "You sure you're up to coming back?" He reaches around and pats Sadie.

I nod. "The house was starting to close in on me. I needed to get out." I force a smile. "And I can't think of a better place to be than here."

"We're glad you're back." Hayes wraps me in a quick hug.

Two elderly women walk into the store, and we move out of the way. They head to the romance section after a quick greeting.

"I'm ready to get busy," I say, breaking our little spell.

"Great," Hayes says.

"What's been going on?" I ask, as my eyes take in the familiar stacks and displays.

"We've been a little slow. Post-holiday letdown."

"Excuse me?" one of the women calls. "I need help finding the latest Nora Roberts."

"Be right there, Mrs. Curtis." Hayes turns and heads in her direction.

"I'm starting a new social studies unit, Molly," Alice says. Hayes homeschools her, and she goes to work with him every day. She's often on the computer in the kids' section, doing her homework, or if it's busy, she retreats to the office, where she sits at Hayes's big antique desk.

"What's it about?"

"Colonial America. I'm doing a paper on the Salem witch trials."

"Wow. That should be interesting, and you're right here where it all happened."

"Well, close by anyway. No one in Graybridge was accused."

"Right." Alice is precocious. Hayes has raised her alone since his wife died when Alice was five years old.

Hayes walks back to where we stand. "There's a box of books that need to be shelved upstairs if you want to tackle that," he says.

"Will do." Sadie and I climb the wooden stairs that spiral up from the first floor. They creak delightfully, and we emerge in the children's section, which takes up half the second-floor space. The back wall is painted with fanciful murals: Beatrix Potter, Winnie-the-Pooh, Tenniel drawings from *Alice in Wonderland*, the story that Hayes's daughter was named for. In the center of the wall, in pride of place, is a portrait of Amelia Mitchell, author of middle-grade fantasy novels. Her characters, fairies and other exotic creatures, are painted around her as if frolicking in delight. Ms. Mitchell has been painted in dreamy watercolor; her fair pixie haircut frames her face, her elfin-like features making her seem like one of her own creations. Her eyes are large and gray and just Alice's color, which is no surprise since Amelia Mitchell was her mother. She'd gained a modicum of success, publishing four books in a series before her untimely death at the age of thirty-four.

I stand still for a moment and admire our lovely children's section, where I myself had spent so many hours long ago, before Hayes returned from boarding school and his wife and daughter were still years in the future.

I pull books from the box and inhale their crisp newness. The store smells of paper and lemongrass diffused from a dispenser on the upstairs counter. There's just a tinge of mold beneath it all. It's an old building. But I feel comfort here among the books. It was my hiding place, is my hiding place, after all that happened before.

Chapter 21

Rita

Saturday morning is cold as a witch's teat, as my grandmother used to say. Chase and I are in our Sunday best as we file into St. Mary's church. We stand along the back, and our eyes go over the crowd as people pass and find their seats. Redolent with incense, the church is old, with soaring stained-glass and blazing candles. I find myself examining the saints depicted in the colorful windows. It's cloudy outside, but occasionally a stray sunbeam sets a halo or red robe ablaze. It takes me back to my childhood in a not unpleasant way. When Grandma would come down from Maine for a visit, Ma would be on pins and needles, hoping for a good showing, especially at church.

Like most of the other families in our Boston neighborhood, Sunday mass was a tradition in the McMahon household. It took two hours of fighting over the one bathroom to get us all presentable. By the time we were squished into a pew in the back, my sisters were angry, my older brothers annoyed, and I was pouting, sitting between Danny and Jimmy. During the most sacred part of the mass, when the priest elevated the host, they would poke me in the ribs to try to make me laugh until Dad would smack them in the back of the head. Despite the monumental task of keeping nine kids quiet, we went to church like clockwork. Ma didn't intend to raise heathens.

Chase clears his throat, brings me back to the task at hand. We're here to pay our respects and to observe, based on the age-old cop tenet that a murderer often likes to take part in the aftermath of his deed. The trip out to see Tyler White didn't yield anything helpful except to confirm the fact that Dr. Bradley had started interviews for his book, and if what Tyler told us was true, he didn't get very far. I glance over the congregation. Maybe there's a killer in this church somewhere.

Mrs. Bradley sits in the front pew with her sister, brother-in-law, and parents. She's a thin figure in a black dress and long dark coat, her hair tied back in a ponytail. The casket rests up front and is covered with an impressive spray of white flowers. The priest and his attendants are busy, and the organ, upstairs and behind us, roars to life with heart-pounding resonance. The congregation stands. It's a big crowd. Dr. Bradley was a popular man.

The priest's deep voice echoes through the church as my eyes search the people standing before him. The Bradleys' friends, the ones we've interviewed, are all accounted for. I try to figure out who the others might be. It's just a guessing game, of course, but one that could, possibly, provide a smidgeon of insight into what appears to be a totally senseless murder.

When the service is over, the family leads the exiting mourners up the center aisle. Mrs. Bradley catches my eye, but her sister hurries her away. Chase and I remain in our seats, allowing us to observe the faces of the people leaving the church.

Once the place is empty, save the priest's attendants working up front, Chase turns to me. "You notice anything interesting?"

"No. You?"

He shakes his head.

I'm reluctant to leave and wander slowly down a side aisle past tapestries that hang between the stained-glass windows. They depict the twelve stations of the cross. While St. Mary's is a beautiful church, I remember the comfort of our parish church in our old neighborhood. It was where my siblings and I had our First Communions. Where my two oldest sisters got married and where my brother Ricky's funeral was held. I was just a kid when Ricky was killed in Vietnam. The memory sweeps over me and fills me with an aching sadness. It was an early lesson in the unfairness of life. To my child's mind, it was inconceivable that the big, strong brother who used to carry me piggyback was never coming home again. For months, I listened for the front door, for his booming voice in the hall.

I still have the last letter he wrote me from Vietnam. He was already dead by the time it arrived, so Ma grabbed it from the stack of mail. She kept it tucked in the pocket of an old cardigan she wore. Even though it was addressed to me, Ma kept it with her until she died. She'd sit at the kitchen table, drink her tea, and slip her hand into her pocket periodically and run her fingers over the envelope. It was the one thing I wanted when Ma died. My sister Maureen, the oldest girl in the family and by far the bossiest, was in charge of doling out Ma's few possessions. Maureen made a stink about it until Danny and I cornered her in Ma's kitchen and she handed it over. Maureen never liked the fact that I was the youngest and, in her eyes, a spoiled brat, but Ricky had sent the letter to me, and as Danny told her, Ma would have wanted me to have it.

I sigh, shake my head.

"Want to head back, Rita?" Chase says.

"What? Yeah, in a minute. You think the perp was coming back for that necklace?"

"Could be. Dr. Bradley hid it, and recently, for a reason."

I sigh. "Who knows? But we need something to pop." I stand still by the altar. The scent of flowers is sweet and pungent. "Let's go. See if Lauren's got anything."

Chapter 22

Molly

There's something strange about the gathering at my house after the funeral. It's almost like Jay's birthday party, but everyone is wearing black. And my sister and parents are here, along with other family members. A carful from back home made the trip across Massachusetts.

But our little group, the ones who were here a week ago to celebrate with Jay, are clustered at the kitchen table with drinks and plates of food. Corrine organized it all, the food ordered from some fancy shop in Boston. Rich is manning the drinks, and he catches me coming down the hall.

"Aunt Ellen asked for a glass of white wine, Molly."

"Um. Sure. In the cellar."

He stands still for a moment. He's rarely at my house and isn't familiar with its layout. "I'll show you." He follows me to the door, where I stand on tiptoe and slide the lock open. He gives me a quizzical look, but I'm not going there. Not today, not with him. "Downstairs. Turn right. You'll see the racks. There's a light switch to the left." I walk briskly away and into the kitchen, which is full of conversations mingling together in a subdued cacophony.

"Hayes said you went back to work yesterday," Laken says.

"Yes. It felt good to be out of the house. Doing something normal."

"Good for you," Laken replies. "You need to keep busy."

"Speaking of busy," I say, "some kids broke one of the attic windows at the mountain house. Jay went up a couple weeks ago to check on it, and he ordered the window from Mr. Barton. He called me and said it was in. I guess I'll need to go up there." Although I'd rather not, especially by myself.

Scott, who's been leaning against the kitchen door frame, holding a bottle of beer, straightens. "I can put it in for you, Molly. There's no need for you to worry about it."

"I appreciate that."

Kim takes a deep breath. "It seems like a lifetime ago that we were all there."

I half smile. Jay and I'd hosted our friends for a big Fourth of July week and my birthday celebration rolled into one.

"I can give you a hand, Scott," Cal says.

"I can handle it," Scott replies. "But either way."

Hayes gives me a look. "Don't take on too much right away, Molly. Jay said he boarded up that window." Hayes's gaze falls to the table. "He told me about it when we had lunch."

Josh, who's sitting next to Kim, his arm draped around her shoulders, says, "That road gets slick in the winter. And with the snowfall yesterday, you might want to wait."

I shrug. "I guess there's no rush." And I'd just as soon not deal with the mountain house at all.

I fill my wineglass from the bottle sitting on the counter. Alice walks into the room carrying a tray of cookies. She's wearing a lacy black dress and matching gloves that look like something out of early last century. She probably bought them at the vintage clothing store she likes so much.

"Are you going up to the mountain house, Molly?" she asks.

"At some point. I might have to."

Alice sighs. She and Hayes were there last summer as well, and she spent her time sketching on the deck and collecting wild-flowers by the river. "I could go with you if you want company."

"That would be nice. I'll let you know."

She sets the platter on the counter. "Sadie's at the back door. You want me to take her out?"

"Yes. Please."

"Molly!" My mother calls from the living room. Alice gri-maces, and we exchange a smile.

I'm pulled into the group from back home. My aunts, uncles, and a cousin who drove in from Albany. It's not a group I'm close to or am comfortable around. My mom, who's sitting on the sofa, reaches up a hand and squeezes mine. "Are you all right?" she whispers. "I haven't seen you since we got back from church."

"I'm fine. Just busy in the kitchen."

My dad gets up and grabs Uncle Jim's glass. He pats my shoul-der as he passes behind me. I sit next to my mother, feeling oblig-ated to make conversation, which I do, but I steer the conversation to the bookstore and the weather and how much I like Gray-bridge. Sadie. Anything to keep talking while I know what's run-ning through their minds. *How is she coping? Is she going to be able to hold it together after what she's been through? How could anybody?*

After catching up with everyone, I feel safe to retreat to the kitchen. It's like my friends and my Graybridge family are in one place, separate from the people from my past, and it needs to stay that way. But as I walk down the hall, I change direction and head toward the side porch. I need a minute, so I unlock the door, and cold air rushes to greet me, but I don't care. I just need a break. I sit on the glider, an old piece of furniture left by the woman from whom we bought the house. It's a relic from the past. Plastic upholstery covered with faded yellow flowers. It crackles beneath me as I sit and look out on the gray afternoon. Fat snowflakes float lazily past the windows, and I let my gaze follow one, then another on its trip to the ground.

"Molly?" Corrine stands in the doorway. "You okay?"

I swipe a tear from my cheek. "Yeah."

She moves into the room and shuts the door, takes a seat in a rattan chair across from me. "It's really cold out here."

"I'll come in in a minute."

She clears her throat, pulls on the hem of her Vera Wang dress. "I know this is hard, especially with everyone from back home here."

"They won't say anything, will they?" My heart is in my throat.

"No, Molly. You know that. They know better." Dad has made it clear for years that when they're here in Graybridge, the past is totally off-limits, but I still worry.

I take a deep breath and watch the snowflakes.

"Don't you think it would be a good idea for you to talk to someone?" Corrine says.

I know what she means by this euphemism. I've spent half my life in therapy. "Probably."

"Does Elise know?"

I shake my head. "*No one* here knows, Corrine. No one except Jay, and that's the way I want it. That was the reason we moved to Graybridge, wasn't it? So that we could live a normal life. So that no one knew who I was." I can't bring myself to say it, the moniker given to me by the media. The girl in the cellar.

"Yes, of course. But now that Jay . . ."

"I'll ask Elise for a referral. I'll tell her that I need help with Jay's death." Which I do, but I'm not convinced that therapy is going to help anymore. Like I've run out of sessions. Like I've had my share. Time to accept my life as it is. For the past five years I've had Jay to talk to, to hold me in the night when I had a bad dream, to dry my tears when something triggered a memory. But now that he's gone, I'm alone and will have to carry on by myself if I'm to survive.

Corrine takes my hands in hers. "You're freezing, Molly. Let's go inside."

I rise with her, and she puts her arm around my shoulders. She's a good big sister, really. Her past is twined with mine, and it hasn't been easy for her either.

CHAPTER 23

Rita

I didn't feel like swinging back by my apartment to change my clothes, so I show up at the station in my funeral attire. As I wend my way back to my office, I nearly bump into Doug Schmitt, the other lead detective in our department.

"Hey, Rita. Nice dress."

"Gee, thanks, Doug. I almost look as fashionable as you do." He stands like a *GQ* model in his dark tailored suit, holding a cup of coffee. Doug's big on appearances, as though his favorite part of the job is trying to look like some suave movie detective. He starts to walk with me as I make my way down the hall.

"Heard you've got a homicide cooking," he says.

"It looks that way."

He comes to a stop at his office door, sips his coffee. "Why does everything interesting happen when I'm not here?"

"Next time we'll be sure to schedule a murder for after you get back from vacation."

He smirks as though we're in on some big joke. It sticks in his craw that the chief gives me the most high-profile cases. That I've got fifteen years of experience on Schmitt doesn't seem to faze him.

"Well, good luck with that," he says, and darts inside his office.

As I power up my computer, Chase peers in.

"Lauren said they've released Mrs. Bradley's phone."

"Good. Anything pertinent?"

"Nope." Chase clears his throat. "I can run it by her place if you want me to. I was going to head out anyway. I'm supposed to be off."

"Right." I'd forgotten. "You don't mind?"

His gaze shifts to the window. "No problem. It's on my way."

I put my hand on my hip. "Maybe we should wait, you know? The funeral just ended."

"She seemed anxious to have it back. It might make her feel better."

"Yeah. I guess. Okay, go for it." When Chase leaves, I send a picture of the necklace to Mrs. Bradley's number with a message asking if she knows who it belongs to.

Lauren walks in holding her laptop. "I might have something, Rita!" She drops down on the chair facing me. Lauren doesn't usually get too excited, so her exuberance has my full attention.

"What?"

"Okay." She sets her computer on the edge of my desk. She needs two hands to relate her story, I guess. "On a hunch, I've been searching for missing persons with the initials A.R."

"And?"

She takes a big breath. "Annalise Robb. Twenty-four years old. Disappeared from a bar last summer. She and her boyfriend got into a fight, and she stormed out. Her mom filed the report the next day when she hadn't returned."

"No leads since then?"

"I couldn't find anything. The sheriff on the case is a Tom Skinner. I'll forward his number to you so you can give him a call."

"Why do you think the necklace belongs to her? Could be a lot of A.R.'s out there who lost a necklace."

"Because there might be a connection to Dr. Bradley."

I look up from my computer screen. "How's that?"

"She disappeared in Mountclair, New Hampshire."

"Huh. Thanks, Lauren. I'll give him a call then."

She grabs her laptop and bounces on her way. I look back through my notes, just to be sure. Sometimes those innocuous questions bear fruit. That's why I ask them despite people's impatience. I grab my reading glasses and skim down the page, stop where I've sketched a little house, and find what I'm looking for. The Bradleys' mountain home is definitely in a little town called Mountclair. *Holy shit.* I dial Sheriff Skinner's number.

After I speak with a woman, my call is transferred to the sheriff. He answers, voice gruff.

"Hello, Sheriff. This is Detective Rita Myers with Graybridge PD down here in Massachusetts. How are you?"

"All right, Detective. What can I do for you?"

"We're investigating a homicide and found a woman's necklace at the scene, and we're wondering if it might be connected to a case of yours."

"And why's that?"

"The necklace has the initials A.R. on it, and we've discovered that you've got a missing woman with those initials." I stretch my legs under my desk.

"What's this necklace look like?"

"Hold on. I'll send you a picture." I wait for the technical stuff to happen. Listen to the sheriff breathing on the other end. He's either a husky guy or has asthma, by the sound of it.

After a minute, he clears his throat. "Where'd you say you found this necklace?"

"In the home office of our vic. Here in Graybridge. Forty-year-old local psychologist."

He draws another labored breath, covers a cough. "How in hell did it get there?" he mumbles to himself.

"Well, that's what we'd like to know. But there is a connection. The vic owns a vacation home up there in Mountclair. What can you tell me about your missing woman?"

The line goes silent. "Wait a minute," he says at last, and I hear the clicking of what sounds like computer keys.

Certainly, he knows the details by heart. How many missing women does he have in that little place? As if reading my mind, he says, "I just sent you a file, but this is the gist of it. Annalise Robb was drinking with her boyfriend at the Mountclair Tavern on July Fourth. She and he got into an argument about one a.m., and she said she'd walk home. We have a bar full of witnesses who attested to that. It was busy, being the Fourth. Anyway, the boyfriend, Lyle Peabody, drank another beer, then left. After that, nobody saw her. Well, somebody saw her, but we just don't know who."

"The boyfriend?"

"We've had him in here half a dozen times. Says he didn't see her. Passed a polygraph. We've got nothing to connect him to her disappearance. And no leads. It's like that girl just vanished."

"This was last July Fourth?"

"Yes."

"Busy up there in the mountains during that time?"

"It sure is."

"What about the necklace?"

He draws a deep breath. "It matches the description her mom gave us."

"Could be our vic happened to find it and picked it up."

"Maybe. What's his name?"

"Dr. Jay Bradley. You know him?"

"Yup." The sheriff clears his throat. "The Bradleys have owned a big place up here for years. So he's dead? Victim of a homicide?"

"That's right."

"Jesus. We'll need to get together on this, looks like."

"Yes." I make some notes, and the sheriff and I make tentative plans. I hang up, lean back in my chair, and let go a deep breath.

It's nearly six o'clock, and I'm starting to get hungry, so I switch off my desk lamp and scrape my notes together to stuff into my satchel. I think about my dinner options. My fridge is empty, as usual, and André and Collin are downtown catering a conference, so I poke my head in at Bob's door.

"You want to grab a bite across the street?"

He looks up from the mess on his desk. "Sounds good."

Mac's is a little place, a bar really, but the food isn't bad in a pinch. It isn't busy tonight, not even any cops hanging out having a cold one after their shifts. Mac himself, the big wide-shouldered owner, who played a couple of seasons for the Patriots a million years ago, is pouring drinks. All his former muscle has morphed into fat, and his belly strains his knit shirt.

He leans on his hands, takes a raspy breath. "Bob, Rita." He nods. "How's it going?"

"Just dandy, Mac. You?" I ask.

"Couldn't be better." He grins. "Angela's pregnant. Did I tell ya that?" *About ten times.* His daughter, his only child, beams from a framed photo hanging behind the bar. "Gonna be a grand-pa this summer."

"Congrats," Bob says. "Nothing like grandkids."

Mac nods again and rubs his hands together. "Yous in for a drink or a meal?"

"I could do with both," I say. "Should we seat ourselves?"

"Yeah. Anywhere you want. As you can see, the place is packed," he says sarcastically, but with a smile.

The chief and I sit in a dark booth in the back. Mac's a great guy, but he'll talk your ear off if he's not busy, and Bob and I've got business to talk about.

I fill him in on everything Lauren and I have discovered. He takes a long pull on his bottle of Bud Light. "Jesus, Rita. You think Dr. Bradley was involved in that girl's disappearance?"

I shrug. "Who knows? But there's some reason he had her necklace locked in his filing cabinet. The most innocent reason is that he found it while out on a walk in the mountains, picked it up, and decided to keep it, but that's a stretch. Why hide it?"

Bob dips a tortilla chip in a bowl of chunky salsa. "You think that's what the perp was after when he came back?"

"Maybe." I sip my wine. "Worst case, as I can figure it, Dr. Bradley and another man were involved in Ms. Robb's disappearance. The killer was worried that the good doctor was growing a conscience and going to turn them in, and so he killed him. The necklace was what tied them to the crime, so the perp wanted it."

Bob nods. "Could be. You find anything in the doc's background that might predispose him to criminal activity?"

"Nothing official. When we ran him, he didn't even have a speeding ticket in the last ten years." Our server slides steaming plates in front of us, bubbling fajitas for Bob, a cheeseburger and fries for me. "His partner at the therapy practice said he's a good guy. Squeaky clean. And she seems to know him about as well as anybody."

"But we both know what that's worth. Some of those twisted guys go years before a whiff of anything sinister comes to light."

I nod and recall various training sessions over the years and the serial killers we'd learned about who managed to blend into society for years before their dark sides were discovered. And I've seen enough of human nature to know firsthand that people aren't always what they seem. Evil lurks, as the saying goes, sometimes in the most unexpected places.

"Yeah. I know. Chase and I are going to bring the wife back in and see if we can get anything more out of her."

CHAPTER 24

Rita

Monday morning, Chase and I sit at the little table across from Mrs. Bradley and her new dog. Emotional support animal, she says. Doesn't matter to me. I like dogs, and this one seems content enough to sit quietly while we talk. Chase jumps up and turns up the heat, offers Mrs. Bradley tea, but she says she's okay.

"I've never seen that necklace before, Detective," she says. She looks frazzled, dark red hair tied back in a lumpy ponytail, purple circles under her eyes. "Is this why you wanted to talk to me?"

"Yes. Take another look, in case the photo was hard to see," I say. Chase removes the necklace from its bag with a gloved hand. He turns it so she can see both sides.

She shakes her head. "I have no idea where it came from. You found it in my husband's filing cabinet?"

"Yes." We're almost positive the necklace belonged to Annalise Robb but want to see if Mrs. Bradley knows anything about it.

Mrs. Bradley glances from me to Chase and back again. "Maybe it belonged to a patient. I don't know. Maybe he found it in his work office and brought it home for safekeeping until he figured out who it belonged to."

"The initials are on the back. Shouldn't have been too hard to figure out if it was a patient."

Her hand finds the dog's back, where she runs her fingers through its fur. "I don't know what to say. What has this got to do with who murdered my husband?"

"Whoever killed Mr. Bradley also broke into the filing cabinet and went through his desk. They must've been looking for something."

"I have no idea what that could be, Detective."

"Well, there was some reason he came back. Maybe he didn't get what he was looking for the first time. The necklace was stuck in the back of the drawer, hard to find. But when he returned, of course, the cabinet had been removed. Let's talk about something else," I say, and she reluctantly meets my gaze.

"Okay."

"The mountain house in Mountclair."

"What about it?"

"You said your husband was there the week before he was killed."

"Yes. He went up to see about a broken window. I told you that."

"When was the last time he was there before that?"

She blinks her eyes. "Um, well. I think it was October. He and Scott Westmore spent a couple days up there fishing."

"You didn't go?"

"No. I was working that weekend, and"—she shivers—"I don't like fishing. Blood sports."

I arch my eyebrows.

"I grew up in a small town," she explains, "a rural area, and a lot of people hunted and fished. I never liked it."

"Thought you were from Graybridge."

She pulls on the neck of her sweater, her thin fingers worrying the yarn. "We moved here when I was seven, so it feels like home. It is home."

"Okay. Anyway, before that, when was your husband up at the house?"

"What does this have to do with anything?" She blinks her red-rimmed eyes, lets go a sigh.

"We'll get there. Please just answer the question."

She sniffs and meets my eyes. "We actually didn't get up there too much last fall, so I guess the time before that would be the Fourth of July. We went up for a week and had our friends up to celebrate my birthday and the holiday."

My heartbeat kicks up. I clear my throat and tap my pencil against my open notebook. "Who else was up there besides you and your husband? What friends?"

"The same ones who were at Jay's birthday party."

"The Westmores, Ferrises, and Pearsons? Anybody else?"

"Hayes Branch and his daughter."

"That's a lot of people."

"It's a big house."

This is getting interesting. "So you had a houseful that week?"

"Yes."

I lean back, blow out a breath. Now we have a job in front of us: reconstructing a week with ten people in one house and a missing woman in the vicinity. This is going to take some time and planning. "Mrs. Bradley, anything unusual happen that week? Anything happen that seemed odd or out of place?"

"No. What does this have to do with anything?"

"When did everyone leave?"

"The fifth. That Friday."

"Huh." I place my pencil on my notebook and tap my fingers on the table. "The necklace in your husband's filing cabinet we believe belonged to a woman from Mountclair."

Her mouth drops open. "That's strange. I have no idea . . ."

She doesn't either. I can tell by the look on her face that she's totally stumped and probably didn't hear anything about the disappearance of Annelise Robb.

"The woman is missing, Mrs. Bradley. She hasn't been seen since the night of July Fourth."

Chapter 25

Molly

André's Café is busy at lunchtime, and Laken, Hayes, and I huddle around a small round table penned in on all sides by other diners. Moms with kids in strollers, men and women who work nearby, block every escape route. But this is our favorite place. Convenient for Laken's spa and the bookstore.

I get a dirty look from an elderly woman at the next table as Sadie pants near her elbow. Too bad. I just don't care.

"What did the cops want?" Laken asks, flipping her hair over her shoulder.

"They found a necklace in Jay's filing cabinet, and they hinted it might've been what the killer was looking for."

"A necklace? Was it valuable?"

"I don't think so, but the weird thing is, they think it belonged to a woman from Mountclair. She went missing the night of July Fourth."

Laken shivers. "Creepy. I don't remember hearing anything about it."

"Me neither."

Hayes coughs and sips his latte. "Why would Jay have her necklace?"

"I have no idea. None of this makes sense." I stir more sugar into my tea. "Then they wanted to know when we'd been up to the mountain house."

"What does all this have to do with finding the bastard who killed Jay?" Hayes pokes at his Thai chicken salad with his fork.

I shrug. "I have no idea." I don't. Jay must've found the necklace and didn't know who it belonged to. That's the only thing that makes sense. It's too distressing to think about, so I change the subject. "Where's Alice today?"

Hayes smiles. "Working on her witch trials paper back at the store. She's in my office with the door shut, hoping Sharon won't bother her." He glances at his phone. "Speaking of Sharon, I probably should get back so she can go to lunch." He stands, grabs his half-finished salad. "See you guys later." He maneuvers past Sadie and the other diners and dumps his lunch in the trash on his way out the door. I watch him outside the café, buttoning his coat and pulling a hat on his head.

Laken blows out a big breath.

"What's wrong?" I ask.

Her dark eyes glance out the window. "Nothing. It's nothing. You've got enough on your plate."

"Hey, tell me." I'd rather listen to someone else's problems than think about my own.

She shrugs. "Cal."

"What's wrong with Cal?"

"He's been irritable." She sips her coffee. "It's fine. We'll work it out."

"His friend just died, Laken."

"No. It's not that. I mean, he's devastated about Jay, don't get me wrong. But this has been going on long before that."

"Maybe the trouble with Josh? You know."

She gets a funny look on her face. "It's nothing. Work stuff, I'm sure. I shouldn't have brought it up. All couples have rough patches."

Jay and I never did, but I guess other people do. Maybe Jay and I would've had "a rough patch" had he lived, though I can't imagine it.

I take Sadie out for a walk before the sun sets. It's dusky, but the snow on the ground lends a strange light to the late afternoon. We wander along the sidewalk past the Fergusons' house, and I think about their security camera capturing me and Sadie, like it did the man walking by the night Jay was killed. What was going through his mind? How long had he planned to kill Jay? Did Jay have any idea his life was in danger? Or maybe it was just random. A disturbed guy saw the light on in the office and wandered back there.

Sadie and I stop, look both ways, and cross the street. I love our old neighborhood. Each house is different, built long ago, with wide covered porches, multiple fireplaces, side entrances, some with porte cocheres. Our house wasn't too expensive because it needed work. Still, I hope I'll be able to afford to keep it. The thought of selling feels like losing another part of Jay. I sigh, and Sadie and I pick up the pace. It's getting really cold, the temperature dropping quickly as the evening advances.

We arrive at the corner, where the gas station bustles with people stopping on their way home from work, getting gas, buying a soda or a six-pack of beer. I watch them for a moment before we turn back toward home.

Just before Sadie and I reach our porch, my phone vibrates in my pocket. I forgot my gloves, so I grasp it with stiff fingers.

"Hello?"

Silence, then a deep muffled voice speaks. "I know who you are." It sounds like someone talking through some device.

"Who is this?" I shiver in the gloom, glancing around me as if the speaker is hidden nearby.

"The girl in the cellar. Melinda Wright. That's who you are."

My knees nearly give way, and I grab for the porch railing with my left hand.

The line goes quiet. The man has hung up. I glance at the screen. Unknown caller. My heart is thumping against my ribs. I turn and look over my shoulder into the shadows. But everything is quiet, snow-shrouded. Still. Is he here? Has he found me? I shake my head. That's not possible. He's in prison. He can't get out, or can he? *Hold it together, Molly.* It was just a crank call. Someone trying to upset me. I grip Sadie's leash tighter, and we run up the porch steps, slip inside, and I lock the heavy door behind us.

CHAPTER 26

Molly

I stayed up most of the night watching the video feeds from the outside cameras. I wrapped myself in an old quilt and sat in the living room with my computer on my lap, flipping screens. I kept all the lights on inside and out. Sadie curled up on the rug by my side. I dozed off a time or two but tried to keep vigilant. Who could've called me? Why? Why now?

I've been bothered off and on over the years by a reporter or two looking to write a story or a book about me, and I've fended them off. The last thing I ever wanted was notoriety, a book with six-year-old me plastered on the cover. Black-and-white pictures stuffed in the middle, my hometown, my parents, Corrine and I smiling, dressed in our Halloween costumes. The thought makes me tremble. But no one's ever contacted me this way, in a threatening manner.

Jay wouldn't have told anyone. Was it someone from back home? But I haven't been there in twenty-eight years. Surely no one is thinking about it anymore or would be interested enough in it to harass me. But this is what I've always feared. Someone will find out. Someone will make it public again, dig out the story like some long-slumbering beast. Make me the focus of hideous attention again. And then my Graybridge life will crumble in the dust. I will be outed and be that girl again. My friends will always see me through that lens.

I need Jay. I can't survive this alone. I start to dial Corrine but kill the call before it connects. The sun has just barely risen, and the morning is gray and damp. I get up, grab Sadie's leash, slip into my coat, and head out the front door. It's early enough that people driving to work have their headlights on, and the traffic is still fairly light. Sadie and I walk in a new direction, new for her anyway. We turn before we get to the gas station and head along a wide road. It's busier than mine, with bigger, grander, older homes.

Sadie trots along with me. Sensing my purpose, she doesn't pull to stop and sniff. Elise's house rises up from the misty morning. It's a huge place and has been designated a historical site. Some Graybridge bigwig built it nearly two centuries ago.

Her car is still in the driveway, as I'd hoped. Elise answers the door, a napkin clenched in her hand.

"Molly! What brings you by so early? Is everything okay?"

"Can I come in a minute?"

"Of course, Scott and I were just finishing breakfast. Can I get you some coffee?" she asks as Sadie and I trail her down the hardwood hallway.

I shiver. *No coffee, Elise, don't you get that?* But I guess not. People aren't going to automatically know my triggers, as Jay used to tell me.

"No, thank you."

The kitchen is small for such a big place. There's a little round table covered with a white cloth pushed against the wall. A plate of scones, toast, a coffee carafe, and mugs are set out in an orderly fashion. An open jar of jam sits in the middle, next to a knife and dribbled strawberries that look like blood against the tablecloth. Scott is standing at the sink, rinsing a dish.

"Molly. Good morning. You okay?"

He's dressed in heavy work clothes. The delicate dish with its band of little blue flowers looks out of place in his rough hand.

"Yeah, I'm fine."

"I can run up this weekend and take care of that window."

"Don't worry about it." I want him to leave so I can talk to Elise, and he seems to get the message.

"Just let me know. I've got to get to work." He kisses Elise and heads out the back door.

"Sit, please," Elise says, and resumes her spot at the table. "Are you sure you don't want anything?"

"I'm okay." My eyes sweep over their breakfast and the pleasantness of it all.

"So what brings you by so early?"

Now that I'm here, I'm unsure. Do I get into this with her? Maybe it'll just open a can of worms that is best left closed. But if Jay told anyone, it would've been Elise.

"What do you know about me?"

She swallows her toast, sips her coffee. "What do you mean?"

I take a deep breath, glance at Sadie for support. "Did Jay ever talk to you about me and my past?" It comes out almost angry.

A nervous look drifts over Elise's face. "Jay told me that you'd had a difficult childhood, traumatic."

I don't like this. Why did Jay say anything? I shake my head. "He had no business . . ."

"You were at our practice for treatment, Molly."

"Well, yeah, okay. Did he say any more than that? Did he give you details?" Tears catch in my throat.

"No. Of course not." She looks away, and I don't believe her.

"He had no right to tell you about me."

She squeezes my hand, then lets go. "He didn't. He never gave me any specifics."

I try to ratchet down my feelings, but I'm exhausted as well as angry. I work my right hand over the sleeve of my left arm.

Elise rises from the table and sets a cup of steaming water, tea bag submerged, in front of me. "Why don't you tell me what's going on?"

I dunk the tea bag and feel foolish. "It's nothing. It's just not having Jay." Do I tell her about the man who called me? What would she know about that? What would that have to do with her? It was stupid to come here.

"You've been through hell, Molly. Why don't you let me refer you to somebody?" She's at the counter, digging through her purse. "Morgan Blanton is wonderful. You'll be comfortable with her. I guarantee it." She turns to me, lifts a business card in the air. "And you know you can always talk to me. Always." Her cat has silently entered the room and twines around her legs. Sadie sits up but doesn't seem too interested.

Elise sets the card next to my cup. "Why don't you have some breakfast? I don't have to be at the office for another thirty minutes. We can talk about whatever you want. Jay or not Jay or the weather." She smiles.

I nod and sip my tea, but the man's muffled voice flutters through my mind. *I know who you are.*

CHAPTER 27

Rita

The little town of Mountclair is bisected by two main routes, two-lane highways that get a fair amount of traffic, people cutting through on their way to somewhere else. We meet Sheriff Skinner in the parking lot of the Mountclair Dry Goods store on the corner. He's a burly man, late fortyish and well fed. His eyes are dark and direct and convey a sense of let's get this done.

After introductions, Chase and I hop back in our cruiser. He insisted we drive a department vehicle, not trusting my van to make it through New Hampshire mountain country. The air is raw, damp and cold, but at least it's not snowing. We follow Sheriff Skinner. There are a few businesses on either side of the road: a car-repair place with old tires piled along an outside wall, an ice cream shop, a small pink motel, a gas station with two pumps, and a bar. We turn into the Mountclair Tavern lot and jump out.

"This is where Ms. Robb was drinking with her boyfriend the night of the Fourth," Sheriff Skinner says.

It's a small place, painted gray, reasonably new with unlit neon beer signs in the two big front windows. It's dim inside, not open this early in the morning, but we follow the sheriff through the front door.

There's a thirty-something man behind the bar stocking glasses.

"This is Sid Jenkins," the sheriff introduces us, and Sid offers a meaty hand. His bulging biceps are on display. He's wearing a T-shirt despite the cold weather.

"Annalise and Lyle were sitting in that booth." Sheriff Skinner points to a spot near one of the front windows. "The place was packed." He glances at Sid.

"We do a good business on the Fourth," he affirms. "Summers are always busy, especially on a holiday."

"Locals or weekend people?" I ask.

"Both."

"You know most of the people who come in?"

Sid tips his head, chews a toothpick. "Most."

I had read over the statements the sheriff sent me. The investigation looked pretty thorough. "You didn't see anyone who was paying undue attention to Annalise?" She was an attractive young woman. Blond wavy hair, a nice smile.

Sid shakes his head. "Annalise and Lyle used to come in once a week at least. Usually Saturday night. I didn't see anyone bothering her. Most people know her."

I glance at the sheriff. "You definitely eliminated the boyfriend?"

Sid answers, "It wasn't Lyle."

"How do you know?"

"He worshiped the ground she walked on. He wanted to get married."

"What were they fighting about?" I ask.

He shrugs. "Same old stuff. She wanted to move. See some of the country, but Lyle's a real hometown boy. He wasn't interested in that."

"So emotions ran high?"

Sid shakes his head. "Lyle wouldn't hurt a fly and especially not Annalise. He's devastated."

The sheriff clears his throat. "We're pretty sure it wasn't him, Detective."

"It wasn't a townie," Sid says. He picks up a rag and starts wiping the bar.

"What makes you say that?"

He stops his cleaning, looks up. His gaze meets mine. "Everybody loved Annalise. We all would've protected her."

You can feel the hurt this woman's disappearance has had on him and the sheriff as well, like a heavy cloud before a thunderstorm. You get the feeling that Mountclair is a tight-knit community. "She left sometime around one a.m.? Said she was going to walk home?" I ask.

"Yes. It's not too far, but the road between here and there is through the woods, not too many people out that way," Sid says. "But there's a lot of traffic in the summer. People up from the cities looking to cool off. Outsiders looking for a good time."

We follow the sheriff out the door and get in his vehicle. I'd asked to see where Annalise was abducted, so we set off along the two-lane road. We turn a corner, and I see what Sid means. There are woods on both sides of the road. There's literally nothing out here. Not a good place for a woman to be walking alone at night.

"Where's her house?" I ask Sheriff Skinner.

"Up this way about another half mile."

"What else is up this road?"

"Nothing much until you get over the mountain. There's a good bit of traffic, though, between here and Anderson, the town on the other side. There's a turnoff to another road about halfway that heads straight up the mountain."

"Who would access that road? What's up there?"

"Half-dozen houses. Weekend places mostly."

"The Bradley place?"

"Yeah. That's up there."

The sheriff told me earlier that everyone in the houses on the Bradleys' road was questioned the day after Annalise's disappearance. No one was home at the Bradley place, but the sheriff had placed a call to Dr. Bradley, who said that he and his guests had all left early and that they had all been at the house and didn't hear or see anything out of the ordinary. That sent the sheriff and his department in other directions. They literally had a lot of ground to cover. Anyone driving the busy main road could've picked her up, and that became their focus. But now, with the discovery of the necklace in Dr. Bradley's filing cabinet, that has all changed. And it also means that Dr. Bradley knew about the missing woman; either he had something to do with her disappearance, or the sheriff's call informed him of the fact. Either way, he knew.

The sheriff comes to a stop in a nondescript section of road, slides the gearshift into PARK, and we jump out. "This is where her cell phone was found," he says, "by those two pine trees."

"Anything on her phone helpful?"

"Nothing. Except a text to her mother saying she'd be home soon that we figure she placed right as she left the bar. There was also a small amount of blood on the road here and fibers that probably came from her jeans." He lifts his hat and scratches his head. "We think he knocked her down, then dragged her into his vehicle. That's our theory anyway."

"Sounds reasonable."

I glance at the trees standing silently in the snow, close my eyes, and try to get a sense of Annalise. But I feel nothing but a cold emptiness.

Chase walks past us and heads up the road, turns. "Her house up this way then?"

"Yeah. Over that rise, there's a gravel driveway on the left."

Chase cranes his neck looking through the trees.

"You can't see it from here," the sheriff says. "Sits pretty far back."

The sheriff is standing still as if this is the end of the line. It doesn't seem like there's much else to see up this way.

"You want to head back and go through all this?" I ask.

"That'd be good," he says, and leads us back to his vehicle.

CHAPTER 28

Molly

Elise dropped me and Sadie off at home on her way to work. The house is still, quiet. I flip through my security screens and then carry my laptop up to the master bathroom and set it on the sink while I shower and dress for the day.

The bookstore isn't busy on a Tuesday morning, and I settle in on the second floor with Sadie. I shelve books while she snores between the stacks. Childish laughter and women's voices trickle through to where I work behind a wall of books. Sounds like a couple of moms with their preschool-age kids. I sigh. To be one of them, a mom with a child to take care of. Jay home in the evening at the end of a workday. Dinner as a family. First steps and bed-time stories. I take a deep breath and reach for the next book to be shelved.

Eventually, the women and their children leave, off to the next stop, I guess. And the floor becomes lonely and still. I work steadily, and the morning passes quietly. I try to keep my mind off Jay, and off my caller. I play a game where I decide which book on any given shelf is my favorite.

When my parents moved us to Graybridge, I'd beg Corrine to bring me here. She was sixteen in a new town, missing her friends back home. The first few months, she was lonely and didn't mind hanging out with me. We'd both sit and read, then head to the candy shop across the square. The candy shop is long gone, replaced by a skateboard store.

When school started in the fall, Corrine's life picked up where it had left off. She made friends easily and grew to be grateful for the move, and Graybridge became home. I found Kim that year too. The harder I tried to disappear in the back row in our classroom, the more interested in me Kim became. She made it her mission to befriend the new girl—the strange, quiet new girl. She was out-going and popular, even in second grade. The other kids, who might have found something in my oddness to make fun of, didn't dare with Kim at my side. And she never asked any questions, still hasn't all these years later. Whether she ever figured out who I was, I don't really know. But as long as no one brings it to light and makes it real again, I'm okay.

At lunchtime, I head across the square to Laken's spa. Alice asked if Sadie could stay with her in the office while she did homework, so I reluctantly left her behind.

Serene Lake Spa takes up two storefronts, and inside it's like another world. The walls are painted off-white, with soft blue and green accents. The sound of gentle waves fills the dimly lit waiting room. The scent of lavender and citrus hangs in the air. Ferns and smooth stones cover the counter where the receptionist is checking in two middle-aged ladies, and I wave to her as I head to Laken's office.

I tap on her closed door, and it takes her a few minutes to answer, flipping the lock.

"Molly! Hey."

"Do you want to grab some lunch?"

She clears her throat and peers over her shoulder. "Yeah. That would be great. I was just finishing up some paperwork." She's acting oddly but swings the door open, and I see Josh sitting on a sofa near the window.

"Hey, Molly," he says cheerfully. "I was just taking a break myself and stopped to see if Laken wanted to head over to André's."

Laken runs her fingers through her disheveled hair. Two of her blouse buttons are undone, the lacy top of her bra showing. I feel as though I've walked into an improv skit. "Oh, sorry. Well, if you two had plans," I say like an idiot.

Josh jumps to his feet and tucks his shirt in his pants. "No. No. You guys go. I'll catch up with you another time," he says to Laken and practically runs out the door.

Laken and I walk across the square. I don't know what to say to her as she rambles on about business and her boys until we reach the café. We put in our orders at the counter, take a metal stand with a number attached at the top, and set it on our table.

"Josh wanted to book a massage," she says. "Things have been pretty rough for him at work."

Laken's a terrible liar, and I've lost my appetite. How could they do this to Kim and Cal? And why now, when we're all torn up over Jay? *Jesus.* What am I supposed to do about this? Then I hear Jay's voice in my head. *Not your problem, Molly. Not yours to fix.* Which is funny because all Jay ever did professionally or otherwise was try to fix people.

But it's going to be damn hard not to get involved. I can't keep this from Kim, my oldest friend. Laken came along later. Losing Laken's friendship, while it would sting, wouldn't be devastating. And Josh. Well, he was never my favorite person, but as Kim was over the moon about him, I tried. The fact that he asked Kim to marry him, after dating for just six months, surprised me and Jay at the time, but she seemed happy.

I listen as Laken prattles on about the spa and her twins and everything except Josh. I run my spoon through my soup, like I did when I was little, and leave as soon as I can without it seeming as though I'm running away from her, which I am. I need to get back to the bookstore and on even ground again.

*   *   *

Sadie and I wander the house in the encroaching evening darkness. I call Corrine since I haven't spoken to her in a few days, but my call goes to voicemail. Then I remember she has some apartment board meeting tonight, so I sit in the kitchen with a bowl of melting ice cream and my laptop, watching the video feeds from the outside cameras. The doorbell rings, and I switch to the front porch camera. A man stands there, hands jammed into the pockets of his jacket, moving from foot to foot. My heartbeat kicks up, and then I recognize Josh.

Sadie and I go to the door.

"Can I come in?" His frosted breath wafts toward the porch light.

I swing the door open, and he hurries into the foyer.

"What can I do for you, Josh?"

"I just want to talk." His gaze meets mine for a fraction of a second, then drops to the floor. I don't particularly want to talk to him, but it's a situation that has my stomach in knots, so I lead him down the hall to the kitchen.

We sit at the table, and I finish my ice cream but don't offer him anything.

"I want to explain," he says, running his hand through his sandy hair.

"Okay."

"I know you probably figured out about me and Laken." I start to respond, but he puts up a palm to stop me. "Please, just listen for a minute before you say anything."

"Fine. Explain."

He draws a deep breath. "Laken and I've been seeing each other for a couple of months. I know it's wrong. I never meant for it to happen—"

"Nobody ever does."

"Things have been pretty rough for her."

I arch my eyebrows.

"I know you're going through hell right now. I don't want to burden you with this. The rest of our problems don't seem like such a big deal next to yours."

"It's not a contest."

He looks away, wipes his mouth with his hand. "I wish Jay was here."

I get up and walk to the sink, rinse my bowl, and gather my wits. *He* wishes Jay was here.

"Sorry. That was insensitive."

"Did Jay know?" I turn to face him, lean against the counter.

"Yeah." He hangs his head. "Jay knew."

This sends a dart of pain through my chest. Why didn't Jay tell me? "How long did he know, Josh?"

"I told him a couple of weeks before Christmas. He, Cal, and I met at the pub for drinks. But Cal left early."

"How could you guys do this?"

He rubs his hands over his eyes. "Something's been bothering Cal for a while, and he's been taking it out primarily on Laken. You didn't notice?"

"No. I guess I missed all the drama."

Josh waves his hand in the air. "Doesn't matter. Anyway, we were talking and drinking at the pub, and Cal just up and leaves. Said he needed to get home. Jay and I kept drinking and talking. That's when I told him about me and Laken."

"What did he say?"

"He wasn't happy about it. Read me the riot act. Then he told me I should tell Kim and we should go to marriage counseling."

That sounds like Jay.

"Look, Molly. Laken's been upset, and I've been having trouble at work. Cal never misses an opportunity to remind me that he's my boss, that I'm not living up to the standards of the company and I'm lucky to still have a job."

"So you got even with him?"

Josh shakes his head. "No."

"Did you take Jay's advice? Did you tell Kim?" I'm thinking no. She would've told me.

"I'm going to. Soon. I just need to find a way to break it to Laken. She's having a rough time." He draws a deep breath. "Jay kept pressuring me, and that didn't help." His eyes flash with anger. He looks like a drowning man who's realized that there's no help in sight.

"Uh huh. What about Kim? How could you do this to her?" Tears start to bubble up for my friend, and I feel Jay's absence in a million different ways. He'd be able to sort this out.

Josh drops his head in his hands. "I'm an asshole, Molly. I fully get that. I never wanted to hurt Kim. She and Willow mean everything to me."

"Then why haven't you tried to fix this?"

"I was ready to. I really was. I got my courage up, even knowing that my wife would be devastated and I'd lose my job. Then Jay died, and I lost my nerve."

I wipe a tear from my cheek and fold my arms. "Well, Jay is dead and buried. Time to move on, eh?" My voice is brittle. I have no sympathy for this sorry man.

He glances up at me and shakes his head. "It'll crush Kim."

"Yeah. You should've thought of that."

He's crying now and wipes his eyes with his palms, takes a deep breath. "She's pregnant," he whispers.

I catch the side of the counter to keep myself from tumbling to the floor. Sadie walks over and nudges me with her nose.

"Kim? Kim's *pregnant*?"

He nods. "She didn't want to tell you right away. She was hoping you'd have good news too. You'd be pregnant together."

I glance at the ceiling and let my gaze linger there. What a lovely dream that would've been.

"Look. I'm so sorry, Molly. I've royally screwed up, and I know that you and Kim are really close." He jumps up from the table and moves to put his arm around my shoulders, but I step away. "You won't tell her, will you?" He grabs my arm. "I'll make it right, okay? I'll make it right. It's just . . . you remember when Willow was born seven weeks early? What if Kim delivers the new baby early? Or what if the stress causes her to lose the baby altogether? I'd never forgive myself."

God, what a mess.

His fingers are digging into my flesh, hurting.

"I'll tell her. I promise. But I need time."

"Whatever, Josh. Just break it off with Laken. You can at least do that for now."

His bloodshot eyes meet mine. "Yeah. Right. It's the right thing to do."

Oh, how I despise this man. The fact that he and Jay were friends is beyond me. But then, Jay liked everybody, saw the best in everyone. "I'm tired, Josh. You should be on your way."

I walk down the hall, Josh tagging behind me, and open the door to the dark night.

CHAPTER 29

Rita

Another cold morning, and no one has anything new to offer on the Bradley murder, except that a disgruntled patient bent on revenge hasn't surfaced. And that's okay now that the necklace has pointed us in a different direction. In the conference room, I catch the team up on our visit to Mountclair. But a certain pall lingers as everyone filters back to their desks. We need a break, something to breathe life into this investigation.

I settle in my office and place a call to Mrs. Bradley.

"Hello?"

"Detective Myers here. How are you this morning?" I flip through my notebook, phone clenched between my jaw and shoulder.

"Okay. Do you have anything new?"

She sounds pretty worn out, and I glance at the clock, wondering if I woke her. "Well, not exactly, but we would like your permission to search the house in Mountclair."

Silence, but I can hear her ragged breath. "Mrs. Bradley?"

"Why? Do you really think that's necessary?"

"Just routine. If we're going to find your husband's killer, we need to put all these pieces together."

She clears her throat. "I don't see what the necklace has to do with anything. My husband probably found it somewhere in Mountclair. Maybe he picked it up off the street."

"Could be."

"This woman is still missing?"

"Yes."

"What was her name?"

"Annalise Robb. You know her?"

"No."

"Okay. Can you meet us up at the house? We'd like to take a look around."

"I guess I could if you think it will help."

"Tell me again about your husband's last trip up there."

"He went up to fix the window. But you said this woman disappeared last *summer*."

"Yes. That's right. How was Dr. Bradley's demeanor when he returned from fixing the window?" I start drawing the necklace in the margin next to my notes from my last conversation with Mrs. Bradley.

She sniffles. "Uh, I don't know. He was fine."

I shuffle back through my notebook. "Didn't you tell me that he was preoccupied, troubled when he came back?"

"I don't remember."

I read back her statement to her. "You remember that?" Dr. Westmore had also noticed Dr. Bradley's "preoccupation."

"I guess. But I think it was just turning forty, you know? Big birthday."

"Yeah. It hits some people hard. But maybe he was troubled by something else."

"I don't know what that could be. Maybe he heard from someone in town about the missing woman and felt bad."

"Why wouldn't he have turned the necklace in to the sheriff?"

Silence. Then, "Jay wouldn't have had anything to do with a

missing woman, Detective." She's breathing hard. "Jay wouldn't ever . . . hurt anybody."

"That's not what we're saying. So can we meet you up there?"

"Yes. Of course."

We iron out the details and hang up. Her mood had swung from confused to desperate and fearful to resolved to vindicate her husband. That's fine; as long as she cooperates, things will move along.

CHAPTER 30

Molly

All morning, I wandered the house, Sadie following in my wake. What does Detective Myers think happened to Annalise Robb, and why would Jay have her necklace? It's totally got to be a fluke. A strange coincidence. But what if someone in Mountclair *thought* Jay hurt that woman and they came here and killed Jay? Could that have happened? Is that what the cops think? I searched the internet for information about the incident. I hadn't heard anything about it at the time. But we did leave early on that Friday, before anyone would have been searching for her probably and before her disappearance made the community gossip. I don't know what to think. According to what I read, it appears that the local investigation has stalled. Annalise Robb is still missing. It sends a chill down my spine. I know what it's like to be missing.

After lunch, Sadie and I drive over to Laken's house. I need to get out and think about something besides Jay. I need to talk to Laken. I don't know what I'll say to her about Josh, but this is causing me more pain than I can handle right now. It needs to be settled.

I ring the doorbell, but there's no answer. I hear children's voices from the backyard, so Sadie and I trudge through the snow around the side of the house. The twins are dressed in heavy sweatpants and jackets, helmets on their heads as they glide across Cal's man-made ice rink that runs across the expanse of his yard, hockey sticks in their hands.

Cal is sitting on the top of the picnic table, watching his boys. I call out, and he turns in my direction. Jumps down. "Hey, Molly. What are you doing here?"

"I was looking for Laken."

"She's at the spa. Amanda's out sick again, so Laken went in." Wednesdays are usually her day off.

"I left work early so I could pick up the boys from school." He glances at the twins, who've begun to race each other across the ice, hockey sticks forgotten.

"Dad!" Logan, I think, screams. "Can we go inside and get a snack?"

"Yeah. Okay. Let's go." Cal turns to me. "You want to come in?"

At first, I think no, but change my mind. "Okay."

The boys take a bag of chips into the family room and turn on the TV. Cal and I sit at the glass-top table with a can of Coke each. The kitchen is big, all stainless-steel appliances, granite counters, and cool colors. Sadie settles on the floor next to me.

"What was going on with Jay?" I blurt out. "Do you know?"

He looks startled. "What do you mean?"

"Didn't he seem a little troubled to you?"

Cal rubs his chin. "I didn't notice, Molly. Why?"

I shake my head. "Just trying to make sense of it all. Why would anyone want to kill Jay? Do you think someone was threatening him? Did Laken tell you about the necklace? The missing woman?"

"Yeah."

"Well, I'm trying to figure out how it's all connected. *If* it's connected."

"That seems like a stretch, don't you think?" Cal sips his soda. "Sorry, Molly. If something was bothering Jay, I wasn't aware of it.

But I've been preoccupied. Things have been rough between me and Laken. Did she say anything to you?"

"No," I lie.

"Jay was trying to help me out with that. You know how he was, always wanting everyone to be okay. Maybe my problems were weighing him down. I'd been leaning on him a little bit lately." Anger flits across his face, and he blinks as if to right himself.

"That's it? You and Laken not getting along?" Maybe trying to help Cal and knowing that Laken and Josh were involved. Maybe that *was* what Jay was worried about.

"That's not all," Cal says, and drops his head in his hands. "Jesus, Molly. I don't want to get into this."

"Well, okay then. I've got enough going on in my life right now anyway." I stand and pick up my purse to leave. "I'll get going."

"Wait. Wait, please." He takes off his glasses and lays them on the table, rubs his eyes.

I sit back down.

"Maybe I was a little needy. Jay had a lot of responsibilities, and I might've added too much to them, and I wasn't always too nice when he was just trying to help."

"What? What else, Cal?"

He blows out a breath. "Last spring, back when you guys were moving into the house, I got some bad news."

"What kind of bad news?"

"I got diagnosed with a hereditary eye disease." He drops his clenched hands on the table. "My mother had it. She was diagnosed in her forties and was totally blind by her late fifties."

"Oh, no. Is there anything they can do?"

"Not much. That's why I've been irritable. I've been taking it out on everybody, I guess. No one knows except Laken and Jay. I really didn't want anyone else to know. And Laken's tried to be understanding, but I haven't made it easy. I know that. I'm just having a hard time."

Good job, Laken, I think sarcastically. Go have an affair when your husband gets crushing medical news. "I understand. But don't you think you two could be there for each other? Help each other?" *You can hope.*

Something like anger flashes in his face again. "I'm just having trouble coming to terms with this. The thought of not being able to work, to support my family. Not being able to skate or ski or play tennis." He shakes his head. "I'll die, Molly." He scrubs his hands across his head as if his hair is on fire.

"I'm really sorry, Cal."

He jumps up from the table and grabs our Coke cans. "You want a drink?"

It's four in the afternoon, but his face looks so forlorn. "Yeah. Okay. Maybe one."

He goes to the fridge and pulls out a can of craft beer, sets it on the counter. "Laken's got a bottle of merlot open."

"That's fine." We sit and sip our drinks, and I'm not sure what else to say to him.

Cal clears his throat. "I don't mean to dump this on you, Molly. You've got enough to deal with." He squeezes my hand but lets go quickly. "How have you been coping?"

"I'm trying to keep busy. I'm working as many hours as I can at the bookstore."

He huffs out a breath.

"What's that for?" I ask.

"Nothing."

"No, what?" I clasp his arm.

He squeezes his mouth with his hand. "It's just that Jay always worried that Hayes had a thing for you. He wasn't jealous or anything, just kept a wary eye on him."

My breath stops. "That's crazy. Hayes and I are friends. Period. Was Jay really worried?"

Cal tips his head. "A little. But then he was super protective of you, you know that."

The thought that Hayes is interested in me for more than friendship never crossed my mind. True, he doesn't date much, but I figured he was being sensitive about Alice. It's just too out there to comprehend.

"Well, I'm fine. Hayes is fine. I'm certainly not interested in a relationship with anyone."

"Just thought you should know. Forewarned is forearmed, as the saying goes." Cal jumps up and gets another beer out of the fridge. "Have the cops found anything?" he asks.

I shake my head. I don't want to get into it. "Nothing important. They're totally distracted by that necklace."

He sighs and pops the top on his beer. His melancholy shows in his eyes, the set of his shoulders. "I still can't believe it. I wake up every morning and have to remind myself that he's gone."

"Me too."

Cal takes a long pull on his beer, looks out the back window to the ice rink. "Who's going to keep us all sane now?"

I wish I knew. "I guess we'll have to rely on each other and family too." I sip my wine. "Do you see your mother often? I've never heard you mention her."

A grimace flits over his face. "She died a few years ago." He points at my glass and stands. "You want a refill?"

"No. Thank you. I'm driving." I get up, and Sadie rises too.

Cal squeezes my shoulder. "Stay well, Molly," he says as I let myself out.

CHAPTER 31

Molly

Thursday morning, I head up to the mountain house. The road is covered in a light layer of fresh snow as I follow Detectives Myers and Fuller, who are driving a police cruiser. Coming up over the rise, I see several sheriffs' cars lined up on the side of the road next to the house. It looks like more than routine, and I wonder if I should've contacted a lawyer. Corrine thought it would be a good idea. But we're here now. If I'd said no, they would've probably gotten a warrant anyway. Besides, if this can clear up the necklace mystery and get the cops back on the trail of Jay's murderer, maybe it will be helpful.

Alice sits in the passenger's seat, and Sadie pants from the back, her head between us. It took some convincing for Hayes to let Alice come with me, but she managed to put it in educational terms. How often does one have an opportunity to witness a police search? She swayed him, as she usually does, and I'm glad to have the company. With Alice to look after, I'll be less likely to obsess about the house and think about Jay.

The house looks bigger, more forbidding in the winter, standing among the drifts, snow lining the valleys of the roof. I shiver, remembering its original purpose. A place to rest between hunts, a respite where long-dead hunters could boast to one another and relive the moments of pursuit and kill over glasses of whiskey.

Alice, Sadie, and I follow the detectives to the door, where they stand aside for me to unlock it. I want this over with as quickly and quietly as possible. The last thing I want is for the media to catch wind of it. That I couldn't bear. And for the first time, I'm angry with Jay. How could he have let this happen to me? He was my rock. The only reason I'd had to hold on to something of a normal happy life. But now . . .

"Mrs. Bradley?" Detective Myers says. "We need you to walk us through the house."

"Yes. Okay." We stop in the mudroom, and I automatically remove my boots and hang my jacket on a peg. The house is chilly, but the others follow suit.

"What do those go to?" Detective Myers asks, pointing at the key ring hanging on the wall.

"The spare keys. We keep them there for guests."

"Which doors do they open?"

"The front door, back door. The door to the deck. And the basement outside doors."

Detective Myers scribbles in her notebook.

We tread down the hall, and I point to Jay's den. They go inside the room and look around, then we proceed into the kitchen. After a brief inspection there, we step out into the large great room. The tall windows at the back of the house look over snow-covered mountains, and I momentarily lose myself in their beauty, before turning to the fireplace. It dominates the room and is made of local fieldstone and blackened by decades of use. When Jay first brought me here, there was a large deer head hanging over the mantel. He removed it and a collection of smaller heads from the den and other rooms, at my request, and they're stored away in the attic.

We wander through the downstairs. The detectives ask a question or two. Alice has a notebook out as well, making notations, of what I have no idea, but that's Alice.

"There are two bedrooms downstairs," I say, "and two up-stairs."

"Four in all then?" Detective Myers asks.

"Yes."

"Where was everyone staying, Mrs. Bradley?"

I lead her into the master bedroom first. "Jay and I were in here." It's the biggest room, has its own bath, and is the most private of all the bedrooms. We have our own fireplace and sitting area, so when you're in here you hardly notice anyone else is around.

The door to the summer porch is just beyond our room, and I point that out. "Alice and her dad slept out there. It was really hot that week."

The other bedroom on the first floor is on the other side of the house. "This is where the Westmores stayed," I say. Detective Fuller walks the perimeter of the room, peers out the window that looks out on the back lawn. I watch Detective Myers write in her notebook, and I notice that she's drawing as well.

"Okay," she says. "What about upstairs?"

I lead them to the staircase that runs halfway up, opening to the great room before turning on a landing and continuing to the upper floor. "There are two bedrooms up here, with a shared bath between them. The Pearsons stayed in the room on the right, and the Ferrises were on the left."

"Any kids here that weekend?"

"No. They were all with the grandparents. Well, except Alice."

"Convenient," she says. "*Where* were Mr. Branch and his daughter staying?"

"Downstairs," Alice says, totally at ease in the adult conversation. "We slept on the summer porch." Alice puts pencil to paper as if she's an integral part of the proceedings.

Detective Myers looks at her as though she's just noticed her. "Hmmm. Okay." She tips her head up and points to the panel on the ceiling. "Attic access?"

"Yes."

"That where your husband would've had to go to get to that window?"

"Yes."

Detective Fuller pulls the cord, and we all step aside as it creaks open and frigid air rushes out like a trapped demon. I wrap my arms around my stomach. Sadie pulls close to my side. Fuller swings the stairs down, and we're practically pinned against the walls of the hallway.

"Mind if Detective Fuller and I look around up there by ourselves?"

I shake my head. "No. Be my guest. We'll wait downstairs."

CHAPTER 32

Rita

The house is pretty cool. I can picture Teddy Roosevelt or Ernest Hemingway walking through the front door with a dead animal draped over his shoulders. Not that I'm a fan of hunting. I'm not. But the place is interesting and rustic posh. I can see Hemingway sitting on the deck, notebook in one hand, bottle in the other.

Mrs. Bradley has been pretty shaky, her voice coming out in nervous bursts as she walked us through the rooms and pointed out where everyone slept. I don't know if the nerves are the result of her husband's murder, which is understandable, or if it's her nature. But there's something about her, something deeper that makes me think there's more going on, a latent hysteria that lives just under the surface of this woman.

I've drawn a floor map and labeled each bedroom with its occupants. I want to take a closer look at the attic without the Mrs. and her entourage over my shoulder, so I sent them downstairs. As we reach the top of the folding stairs, Chase feels around for a light switch, and the room comes into focus. It's still fairly dark since there's only one bare bulb overhead and one of the two windows is boarded up. Chase puts his phone on flashlight and fans the room. He starts to walk forward when I grab his jacket.

"Wait." I stow my notebook and fish my flashlight out of my satchel, thumb it on, and bright light illuminates the attic. I sweep the beam across the wooden plank floor.

The windows would look out on either side of the house to the side yards. There are boxes and trunks, dust-covered, packed tightly in the corners. The light lands on the back wall, and I bobble my flashlight. Dark eyes shimmer, and it takes me a frightened second before my brain registers the stares of dead animal heads, dozens of them stacked like the relics of an ancient hunt.

"That's freaking scary," Chase says.

I take a deep breath. "Yeah. Creepy." I swing my light beam over the other side of the attic, where dust lies in a pretty heavy blanket. Away from the broken window. I swing the beam back. "Over here, the dust's been disturbed. You can see where Dr. Bradley worked."

When we approach the boarded-up window, chunks of glass shimmer on the floor and crunch underfoot. The plywood is neatly nailed into place, but he didn't bother to clean up. Why leave a mess?

CHAPTER 33

Molly

Alice and I sit on the sofa that faces the backyard toward the mountains. Several sheriff's deputies are trudging through the snow, back and forth.

"What do they think they'll find out there?" Alice asks, standing, hands on her hips.

I'd told her about the necklace and that the detectives think it belonged to a local woman who disappeared last summer.

"I don't know."

"They're making a mess," she says, and she's right. When we first got here, the view was like a postcard. Mountains in the background, beyond our pristine snow-covered lawn that runs downhill until meeting a stand of pine trees, where the river lies. "It was so pretty," Alice says. "So white and still. Can we go out and take a walk before they mess it all up?"

I glance toward the staircase and don't hear the detectives.

"Sure. Sadie probably could use a walk anyway."

We put our coats on. Alice pulls her red hat firmly over her ears, and we head out and around the house.

"Let's take the path to the river," I say. That way we can avoid the deputies, who seem to be concentrated closer to the house. But before we can set off, a deputy waves me over to where he stands halfway down the sloping lawn. I trudge through the snow to reach him while Alice and Sadie wait for me by the path.

"Where do these doors go to, Mrs. Bradley?" He's pointing to metal double doors that are recessed into the side of the slope. You can't see them from the house.

I shove my hands deep into my pockets. "The basement." The first time Jay brought me to the mountain house, he was eager to show me around. He asked if I was okay to go down into the basement, and I'd said, of course. I wanted to be like everyone else, be the normal woman I thought Jay deserved, so with my arm through his, we descended the wooden staircase. But when that moist, fetid air hit me, I went into a full-blown panic attack, and Jay whisked me back upstairs. I was humiliated, but Jay simply dried my tears and held me in his arms until I stopped shaking. I haven't been down there since.

"Are they locked?"

"They should be. The keys are in the house if you really need to get in there."

"I'll let the sheriff know." He nods and walks back toward the deputies.

Alice and I head off through the pines and down the path. The snow's only about three inches deep, so it's not too hard to navigate. Sadie takes the lead, tilting her head in the pine-scented air periodically and pulling in deep breaths. I'm cold, but this is a good diversion. We can hear the voices of the deputies, growing distant now, as we make our way through the woods along the winding path.

The sound of the river reaches us sooner than it does in summer. It's running faster too, as if in a hurry to get to the bottom of the mountain. And the leaves that would muffle its sound are, of course, dead and buried under the snow. We see it sooner as well through the barren trees.

"I picked wildflowers down here, remember?" Alice says.

I smile. "You put them in a vase on the kitchen table, and Laken had a sneezing fit."

We both laugh. "And then my dad got mad because I'd been down here by myself."

"He was afraid you'd fall in, Alice. It's a pretty deep river, and there are waterfalls not far from here."

"He worries about everything."

"You're his whole world, you know."

"Yeah. I know. But I'm nearly twelve. He's got to let up on me sometime."

We stand still and listen to the water rushing by, carrying a chilly breeze with it. My nose and cheeks tingle. The path has wound back closer to the house. This bend in the river isn't far from the end of the lawn. We can hear the deputies' voices again.

"Maybe we should head back. You cold?"

She shrugs. "A little. Can we walk on the bridge first?"

There's a little footbridge that allows access to the other side of the river. "Then we'll go back, okay?"

Alice nods, and we walk slowly, as the bridge is icy, and stop at the halfway point. The gray water rushes beneath us.

"There's something over there." Alice points at what looks like a branch sticking awkwardly out of the bank on the other side of the river.

We step carefully across the bridge, Sadie trying to pull ahead, and I have to use both hands on her leash to hold her back. But as we get nearer, the stray branch comes into focus. Sadie is barking now, her hackles raised and quivering. Alice grabs me around the waist and buries her head in my shoulder.

It's not a branch. It's an arm.

Chapter 34

Rita

Annalise Robb has been found, or the mostly skeletal remains of a young woman have. Sheriff Skinner and his team are pretty sure it's her, based on the blond hair and the clothing found in the riverbank as well. But, of course, a formal identification will have to wait for the medical examiner to determine.

Chase has taken Mrs. Bradley and Alice into the house, trying to keep them calm and out of the way, while I assist the sheriff and his deputies. A forensic team has just arrived, and they're carrying equipment down the hill toward the scene.

A blue tent has been erected over the site, and there's a steady stream of officers trudging up and down from the river to the road, where vehicles line up like a parade.

I'm standing with the sheriff next to his vehicle. Snow has begun to fall softly, big fat flakes that settle on our shoulders and the tops of our heads.

"Detective Fuller and I did a cursory search of the main floors and the attic, but we haven't been in the basement yet," I say.

We look down on the scene, where the deputies are busy. The sheriff removes his hat and scratches his balding scalp. "Well, you two go ahead with that then. I appreciate your help, Detective."

"You're helping us too. I think together we'll get this figured out."

His eyes are hopeful, and I see how this woman's disappearance has weighed on him. There's relief there that she's been found, but sorrow too that he couldn't bring her home alive. All we can work toward now is justice.

Chase has found a couple of cans of ginger ale somewhere, and Mrs. Bradley and Alice sit tucked up together on the couch, sodas in their hands, when I enter the living room. He looks up at me, as if to ask, What do we do now?

"Mrs. Bradley," I say, "we'd like to take a look at the basement."

Her bottom lip trembles. "Okay."

"The door would be?"

She points back toward the mudroom.

"Will you two be okay here if Detective Fuller joins me?"

She nods.

"You won't go anywhere?"

"No."

I flip a switch just inside the basement door, and dim light illuminates a wooden staircase. The air is icy as we descend. The walls are stone, and the age of the house is readily apparent as we make our way down.

"Creepy place," Chase says as we hit bottom. The floor is also made of stone, which is slick with condensation. There are a few small windows at the tops of the walls, and snow blocks them halfway up. Cobwebs hang from every corner, and what looks like old farm equipment, rusting and covered with dust, is pushed against the wall. "Doesn't look like anyone comes down here much," Chase says, wiping his hand on his jacket.

We walk forward, and I thumb on my flashlight. The smell of dirt and decay hangs in the air. But there's something else, something pungent that becomes more fetid as we move deeper into the basement.

I pivot and shine my light back toward the stairs. "Nothing

much at this end except the furnace and water heater." And they're close by the stairs. No need for anyone to access the rest of the place, I guess. I turn back toward the far end of the basement, and there's light coming from somewhere ahead. Chase and I walk on and discover a door with a small window in it, the source of the light. I open the door, and we're standing at the beginning of what looks like a long stone hallway with an arched ceiling. The floor dips and slopes down. Double metal doors are at the end.

"This is strange," I say.

Chase is behind me. "Look at this, Rita."

I turn and run my flashlight over a wooden table. Tools and knives hang neatly on a pegboard on the wall over it. There's a hammer sitting on the edge of the table, as though someone forgot to put it away. There's a sink next to the table, gray with age, stained with dark smudges, and there's a drain in the floor nearby.

Chase coughs and staggers back. "I think this is where the hunters brought their game." He holds his hand over his mouth and mumbles. "My grandfather used to hunt. We had to have venison or rabbit whenever we visited him. He had a friend who processed meat, and he took me to the guy's place once. That's why I'm such a wuss around blood. I was eight. The smell made me sick, and I puked up my lunch."

Goose bumps rise on my arms. There's something on the floor next to the table. A spilled box of nails. "Looks like Dr. Bradley might've dropped the nails when he finished with the window. Wonder why he left them all over the floor?" I get down on my hands and knees and wave the flashlight beam under the table. "Look at this, Chase."

He crouches beside me. "Is that blood?"

"Looks like it to me."

"Maybe it's from animals."

"Maybe." I sit back on my haunches and rub the back of my neck, thinking. "But what if Dr. Bradley bent down to pick up the nails and saw something that made him forget all about putting away his tools or cleaning up the glass in the attic."

"He would've needed a flashlight to look under the table to see the blood, Rita. Why would he have bothered when the nails were in plain sight?"

"Maybe he *didn't* see the blood. Maybe he saw something else."

"The necklace?"

"Could be. Then he saw the initials and put two and two together." I take a deep breath. "Let's see where those doors go."

The metal doors are rusted, and the windows are covered in grime. But when I try the lock, it gives way easily enough. The light and air feel fresh as I step out into the snow. We're a stone's throw from the river here, and across a small bridge lies the blue tent.

The forensics team has sent a couple of people to check out the basement, and Chase and I return to the living room.

Mrs. Bradley looks toward us when she hears us approach. "Is it her? The missing woman?"

"We can't say until the body's positively identified."

Mrs. Bradley nods, her mouth clenched like a child who's trying not to cry. "Why would someone bury her here? The killer must've passed the house and dropped the necklace. I bet Jay found it in the yard."

"Could be."

She jumps up from the couch and starts pacing, holding her arms across her chest. "I don't know how this could've happened, Detective, so close. We didn't hear a thing. They're sure she disappeared the night of the Fourth?"

"Yes."

Mrs. Bradley is shaking, and her nose is running, which she doesn't seem to notice. She's got that wild-eyed look that sometimes precedes hysteria. She stops walking and stands still as a pointer.

"Is the media here?" she asks.

"I don't think so. Not yet, anyway, but I expect some will be here soon. At least from Manchester, to start."

This seems to break her. She wraps her hand over her mouth and sinks down on the couch.

"You okay?" I ask. Chase sits by her side and pats her shoulder.

"I need to go home. I need to get out of here before they get here," she pleads, eyes on Chase, her hand squeezing his arm.

But he looks to me. She's in no shape to drive. "Okay, maybe we can have Detective Fuller drive you and Alice back to Graybridge in your car. Would that be okay?"

She nods, sending tears tumbling down her cheeks. "Can we go now, please?"

"Yeah. Give us a minute."

I motion Chase to follow me into the hall. "You mind?" I ask. "Can you drive her car back? I don't think she should be on the road. Call the station and have one of the guys pick you up from her house. Will that work?"

"Yeah. Sure. You don't need me here?"

"I'll catch you up when I get back. When you get to the station, you can fill the chief in, and you and the team can work on what we've got."

I peek around the corner, where Mrs. Bradley is pacing again and wiping her eyes with her sleeve. "See if you can get something out of her on the drive."

"She's really freaked out," Chase says. "But I guess that's normal given there's a body in her yard."

Yeah, I think, but there's something more here. Something else going on with Mrs. Bradley. I can feel it.

CHAPTER 35

Molly

I'm finally home. Relief spilled off my shoulders as I walked through the front door. I don't ever want to see the mountain house again.

Detective Fuller dropped Alice off first, and now he's waiting for Corrine to show up before he leaves for the station. I've switched on all the lights and turned on my laptop to check my security cameras. I can't seem to settle. At least we beat the media. We passed a white satellite truck going toward the mountain house as we left, and I breathed a sigh of relief that we'd missed it.

"Are you sure I can't make you a cup of tea, Mrs. Bradley?" Detective Fuller stands by the counter, as if waiting for instructions, his brown eyes full of concern.

"No. Thank you. I'm fine." But I'm not fine, and he knows it. All the way back, he asked me questions about myself, but I deflected the best I could. I hope that doesn't make me look as though I'm hiding something, which I am, but nothing to do with that woman's murder. I tried instead to talk to Alice, reassure her. She was awfully quiet on the way back, and Hayes was upset when I spoke to him on the phone. But Alice rallied when we got

168 / TERRI PARLATO

close to her house and told me she was fine. She seemed pretty much back to normal. I hope so.

With Detective Fuller gone, Corrine sits with me at the kitchen table. Although I'm not hungry, she brought takeout Chinese and drinks since I haven't eaten all day.

"What happened, Molly?"

"They think that missing woman was probably killed the night she disappeared and buried by the river just down from the house while we were asleep inside!" I take a deep breath. Talk myself down, look to Corrine. "Jay might've found the necklace in the yard when he went up to fix the window. That's what I think." I glance away from my laptop, the camera feed on Jay's office on the screen. "It was terrifying, Corrine. What Alice and I saw." I'd already described it to her on the phone and don't want to think about it again.

Corrine rubs my arm. "Try to eat something. Did you ever call that therapist Elise referred you to?"

I swallow, poke at my lo mein. "I will. I definitely will." I try to hold them back, but tears slip down my cheeks.

"Hey, I'm here. It's going to be okay."

I sniff. "What if they think Jay killed that woman? It's not possible, but I get the feeling they think he was involved."

"That's crazy. Jay wasn't a killer."

"What if someone back in Mountclair *thinks* he did it and that's who killed him? Why else would someone kill Jay? There has to be a connection, Corrine."

"Didn't you say the woman had a boyfriend and they were fighting before she disappeared? It's usually the husband or the boyfriend, right?"

"Yeah. That could be, and then maybe he thought that Jay *saw* him, and that's why he killed Jay." This is the scenario that makes the most sense. I know my husband wasn't a killer.

"I let Mom and Dad know what happened."

"Great."

Corrine pauses, chopsticks in her hand. "What was I supposed to do, let them see it on the news?"

"No. That's fine."

"They wanted to rush over, but I put them off. I told them I'd be here with you."

"Thanks. I'll call Mom later."

Corrine and I finish our dinner. Well, I did the best I could to force a few mouthfuls down. She wanted me to go back to her place for the night, but I didn't want to. I walked with her through the house, checking that all the doors were locked and lights on. Sadie stuck right by my side. Finally, Corrine left, and I set myself up on the sofa with my computer on my lap, flipping screens, monitoring the house.

The doorbell rings, and I go back to the porch feed. A young woman with long dark hair is standing there with a cameraman next to her. She leans on the doorbell again, and Sadie runs down the hall to see who's there.

I don't move. Maybe she'll go away.

"Mrs. Bradley?" I hear through the door. More bell ringing. "Mrs. Bradley? It's Ashlyn Davis from Channel 2 News. May I speak with you for a minute?"

Go the fuck away. Please. I say under my breath. *Please. Please. Please.*

"Mrs. Bradley?"

I watch her take a couple of steps back. Then she walks toward the living room window, leans, and shades her eyes. I go cold, sitting still as a statue, and pray she can't see me. Eventually, she leaves, and I can breathe again. I set my laptop on the coffee table, pull the throw over me, and burrow into the sofa.

My phone jolts me awake. It's dark outside, and I must've dozed off. The clock on the mantel says one-thirty a.m. Who would be calling at this hour? Sadie jumps up from where she's been lying on the floor next to me.

"Hello?"

"Melinda Wright?" I shiver. Another reporter? But then the voice continues, muffled, the same caller from before.

"I know who you are, Melinda Wright. The girl in the cellar. I heard they found a dead woman near your house. You better take care, Melinda. You escaped once—"

I throw my phone on the floor, jump up from the sofa, and run for the laundry room. Sadie trots after me, and I close us both inside the room. I slide down onto the floor. Sadie lies next to me, and I sob, my hand on her bristly back.

CHAPTER 36

Rita

I didn't get home until midnight last night, and then I couldn't sleep. It had been a busy day, full of revelations and just plain hard work. After tossing and turning for an hour, worrying about not getting enough rest to tackle a busy day today, I got up and ran a hot bath. I threw in one of those bath bombs that foam up and smell nice. André and Collin gave me a huge basket of expensive bath products for Christmas, and I figured I might as well start using some of the stuff. I sank into the tub with a glass of wine, had the Moody Blues playing softly on my phone in the corner. After methodically working through what I think happened at the mountain house and a good soak, I finally felt sleepy and went back to bed.

I woke up with the sunrise, swung by Dunkin' for a large coffee, and met the chief as I was walking into the station. It's early yet, and not everybody's in. Lauren is here, of course, all bright-eyed and bushy-tailed. I don't think she ever goes home. Her latest boyfriend just broke up with her, and she doesn't seem to understand why they never hang around for more than a month or two. But working 24/7 will do that, as I well know. My own romantic life is nothing to write home about.

The chief has rounded up the team, or at least everybody who's here, and we head to the conference room. This is my show, so I walk to the whiteboard, set my notes on the table. I run through everything we discovered yesterday at the Bradleys' mountain house.

When I finish, I ask Lauren to follow me to my office. Just as we're getting settled, Chase arrives, coffee in hand. Lauren has already taken the chair, so Chase moves my dead philodendron from a low filing cabinet and sits there.

"What are you thinking, Rita?" Lauren asks.

I draw a deep breath. "If the blood turns out to be Ms. Robb's, she was probably killed there in the basement, and the killer missed the blood under the table, and he may have missed the necklace too when he cleaned up. When Dr. Bradley went to return his tools, he dropped the box of nails. When he bent down to pick it up, he found the necklace, so I think either Dr. Bradley is the killer and needed to remove the necklace from the scene, or he's not the killer, but knows about the missing woman because the sheriff called him when it happened last summer. He brings the necklace back to Graybridge and locks it in his filing cabinet. But then who killed him? They were obviously looking for something in the office. If it was the necklace, how did the perp know it was in there unless Dr. Bradley told him? One way or another, Dr. Bradley knew Ms. Robb was missing. He would've deduced that the necklace was probably hers. Either he killed her, or he knew who did and let the killer know he had the necklace in the office."

Chase clears his throat. "If the doctor was innocent, why wouldn't he call the police when he found the necklace?"

"Think. If the necklace was found inside his house, and he had guests there the night Annalise disappeared, who could the murderer be?"

I lean back in my chair, prop up my feet.

"Dr. Bradley," I say, "didn't call the police because he knew who the murderer was. It could only be someone who was in that house the night of July Fourth."

Lauren's mouth pops open. "It was one of his friends."

I pick up a legal pad and list their names: Dr. Bradley, Mrs. Bradley, Elise Westmore, Scott Westmore, Cal Ferris, Laken Ferris, Josh Pearson, Kim Pearson, Hayes Branch, Alice Branch. "It all depends on the blood belonging to Ms. Robb, but if it does, I believe one of these people killed her." I drop my pen and pad on the desk. "When Dr. Bradley found the necklace, he put two and two together. He probably didn't see the blood. He would've had to get down on the floor and use a flashlight. Annalise was only missing at that point. I think he figured out one of his friends was involved, and when the doctor confronted him, he killed the doctor." I take a deep breath. "Who can I eliminate?"

"Alice," Lauren says.

I draw a line through her name. "Okay, it's highly unlikely an eleven-year-old was involved in a double homicide. Anybody else?"

"It could be any one of them," Chase says.

"No." Lauren leans forward. "I don't think it was any of the women. Women don't usually kill women they don't know. It's highly unlikely that one of them killed and buried Ms. Robb."

I draw a line through their names. "I agree. Possible, but not likely."

"What if it's just animal blood under the table?" Chase asks. "What if he found the necklace out on the road maybe?"

"Then we're back to square one. But why wouldn't he have taken it straight to the sheriff? Why keep it if not to protect somebody?"

CHAPTER 37

Molly

Hayes is upset. I can tell as soon as I walk through the bookstore door. He's sorting a box next to the front register, and there's a line between his eyebrows that he gets when he's thinking or brooding over something.

"Hey," I say. He looks up, gives me something between a smirk and a smile.

"You're early," he says.

"Yeah. I couldn't sleep. So I decided to get ready for the day and come in."

He nods. "Are you okay, Molly?"

"Yes. I'm fine," I say with as much conviction as I can muster. "How's Alice?"

"She says she's fine." He slams a book on the HOLD shelf behind him. "I never should've let her go yesterday."

My heart hammers. My fault. "I didn't know anything like that was going to happen, Hayes. I wouldn't have taken her up there if I'd thought . . . It was supposed to be just routine. Detective Myers said they just wanted to look through the house. Nothing bad was supposed to happen."

Hayes straightens, looks at me, his eyes soften. "Sorry. I know this has got to be hard on you." He comes out from behind the counter and wraps me in his arms. I relax against his shoulder.

I take a deep breath and sniff back tears. "I'm so sorry," I mumble.

"Look, I don't blame you. How would you know they were going to find that woman buried by the river?"

I pull away and wipe my eyes on a tissue. "It's all so surreal."

"Do they have any theories?"

"I have no idea, but I think Jay is a suspect." I manage a disgusted laugh. "But what are they going to do, arrest a dead man?" Tears start to flow again at my own flippant words. Hayes rubs my back.

"Why don't you go check on Alice. She's in my office doing her schoolwork."

"Yeah. Okay. I'll go dry my face first." I glance around the store. "Then I'll get busy."

The bookstore closes at eight o'clock on Friday in the winter, and I usually work until six. Hayes has left to take Alice to the hobby store to get supplies for a school project and is coming back to close, so Sharon and I are the only ones here. It has been slow all day. We've had a steady snowfall, and all the shops on the square have been quiet.

Just as darkness descends like a heavy blanket, we finally have a customer. A tall man, thirty-something, with a shaved head and a three-day stubble, asks Sharon for help finding a book in the literature section. I'm standing at the register, still lost in thoughts of Jay and Annalise Robb, and trying not to think of my caller.

Sharon, her thick red cardigan gaping around her middle, huffs back to the counter. "Can you go help him?" She glances toward the back of the store. "I left my reading glasses at home, and I'm having a devil of a time." She leans heavily on the counter, bends over, and searches through the odds and ends on a shelf below it. "I thought I had another pair here someplace."

I head back to where the man peruses the stacks. "May I help you?"

He straightens and smiles. "Just found it," he says. I notice a paperback copy of Mary Shelley's *Frankenstein* in his hand. "I haven't read it since senior year high school." He holds the book up. "Didn't finish it back then, so thought I'd give it another go."

I nod. "It's a good one," I say, and turn to head back to the register.

"Wait. This is a quaint little place." He glances around.

"Yes. It is." For some reason, I feel unnerved here behind the shelves with this stranger. Lately, I'm assessing every man I see, wondering if he's my caller. Is he lurking nearby, following me, not content to torment me over the phone? I shiver and step away, but the stranger steps with me.

"I'm from out of town," he says. "Do you have a children's section?"

"Yes. Of course. Second floor." I wrap my arms around my stomach, desperate to get away, yet not wanting to seem rude or paranoid.

"I'm visiting my brother, and I didn't think to bring my niece a gift. What kind of uncle would I be if I showed up empty-handed?" He smiles again. Friendly, almost flirting.

He has a backpack slung over his shoulder, wears a leather jacket and skinny jeans. For some reason, I get a reporter vibe, and I can't bring myself to escort him upstairs. I just want to get back to the relative safety of the counter.

"We have a great selection of kids' books. Let me know if you need help," I say, and walk away.

Sharon has taken a pair of reading glasses off a display stand near the front and has them perched on her nose, tag and all. "That's better," she says. "Oh, Molly. Would you go down to the basement?" She holds out a list. "Hayes said these came in, and he put them down there out of the way. He wanted me to sort them out, but . . ." She twists her leg back and forth. "My knee's killing me." She blows out a breath. "I can't take those stairs today. You mind?"

I don't want to go down there. She and Hayes know that. They think I'm claustrophobic. That's what I've told them, and my excuse has worked since the basement is a small space with a low ceiling. Hayes always goes himself or has Sharon go down there. Now I'm stuck.

"Oh, come on," Sharon says. "Leave the door open and the lights on, Molly. I'd do it myself, but my knee . . ."

I grab the list. "Fine." At least I'll put some space between me and the man.

"When you finish, why don't you go ahead and go home?" she calls after me. "We both don't need to be here."

I make my way to the basement door. It's old, like everything else in the building, and creaks as I open it. I flip the light on and shiver as cold musty air floats up and surrounds me.

You've got this, Molly. It's only the bookstore.

I start down and hear the man talking with Sharon behind me in the distance. My footfalls echo on the wooden stairs, and I take them slowly, one at a time. There are no windows down here, just boxes stacked everywhere and a large table in the center of the room. *It's just the bookstore*, I repeat in a whisper. I square my shoulders and make my way to the books piled on the table and set the list down. I get to work, concentrating on the task at hand, keeping my mind on the books.

I'm nearly through the pile when suddenly the lights go out and the basement plunges into darkness. Fear ripples through my chest, and I grab the edge of the table, holding on in a death grip. The basement door slams shut, and the floor above me creaks as someone walks overhead. Why would Sharon turn the lights out on me? Maybe we lost power. Maybe the snowfall.

My heart starts to hammer, and my palms perspire. I take a deep, wavering breath and try to feel my way slowly to where the staircase should be, sweat gathering under my arms, my breath catching in my throat. I never should have come down here.

Just when I'm starting to panic that I'll never find the stairs, I bang my shin painfully against the first step.

"Sharon!" I climb on my hands and knees up the stairs, my pulse beating in my ears, fear coursing through my veins. I can't breathe. I think I hear him behind me. I hear him scuttling in the darkness. A gust of cold air hits the back of my neck as I rush up the stairs.

I reach the top step, clamber to standing, and grab the door-knob, twist, but it holds fast. It's locked. I choke on my tears and beat against the door with my fists. It's like a flashback, a nightmare. I'm locked in, and there's no escape.

Finally, the door flies open, and Hayes is standing silhouetted against the light behind him.

"Molly!"

I nearly jump into his arms, shaking.

"What the hell happened?" He brushes my damp hair off my face. "What were you doing down there? Sharon said you went home." He walks me to the counter and hands me his water bottle.

Alice comes out of the office. "What happened?"

My pulse eases down, and I feel foolish. They're both looking at me, concern all over their faces. "I don't know. I got locked down there somehow." I try to stifle my tears. "Panic attack, I guess."

Hayes hugs me, and I take a deep breath against his sweater.

"After all you've been through," he says, "no wonder you got scared."

I peep over his shoulder and out the plate-glass front window. The man with the *Frankenstein* book is standing across the road under a streetlight looking up at the store.

CHAPTER 38

Molly

When I wake up, it's nearly eleven a.m. Hayes drove me home last night and sat up with me until midnight. We shared a bottle of pinot noir and talked about books and movies, our favorite topics during normal times, while Alice watched a documentary on the rain forest on TV. Finally, I felt sleepy, like a child who'd cried herself out, and they went home.

The afternoon is gray, with thick winter clouds, but no snow other than what's already on the ground. I plug in the Christmas tree, and the white lights and colorful ornaments twinkle. I really should take it down, but I can't. Not yet. It'll seem like another way of putting Jay away, wrapping him up and moving on.

My doorbell chimes, and I rush to my laptop to check the camera. Kim. *Shit.* I haven't seen her since before I discovered Josh and Laken at the spa. We've spoken a few times on the phone, but I made the conversations short.

We sit in the kitchen after hugs at the door. She seems okay. Josh must not have told her yet. Damn him.

"I wanted to make sure you were all right after what happened at the mountain house," Kim says.

"I'm fine. I feel sorry for Alice, though. She was pretty shaken up. I never would've taken her with me if I'd thought anything like that would've happened." I take a deep breath.

"It's not your fault. How could you have possibly known that missing woman would be found on your property?"

I shake my head. "It's all been a nightmare, Kim. I just want it to stop." I try to smile at her. "Josh told me you're pregnant."

Her face flushes. "He did?" She lets go an irritated breath. "I wanted to tell you, eventually."

"I'm happy for you, really."

"Well, nothing other than the baby has turned out right lately."

"That's not your fault. Have you told Willow?"

"Not yet. We wanted to wait until I'm further along after what happened last time."

I think back to Willow's birth, seeing her through the glass in the NICU. She was in an incubator, covered in tubes, her eyes shielded with a cloth mask. It was painful to see her so little, fighting for her life. "Is everything all right so far?" I ask.

Kim nods. "My doctor says all is well, so hopefully I'll carry to term this time."

Anger starts to bubble up in my chest when I think about Josh and Laken. I push it down as best I can. Not the time and not for me to tell. But I have no compunction about putting pressure on Josh, just as Jay was doing before he died.

"When are you due?"

"The end of June."

"Well, that's something good to look forward to," I say, and squeeze her hand. "We need something good to happen."

"Thanks, Molly. I'm just sorry for the timing."

I shrug. "Life happens. I'll be okay."

We talk about mindless things, school, the bookstore. Things that seemed so important a few weeks ago. It's nice to talk to my friend and pretend for a little while that everything is normal.

Kim checks her phone. It's getting toward dinnertime. I stand on the porch and wave as she starts her car. Just after she pulls away from the curb, a dark sedan slides to a stop in front of the house. A man with a backpack gets out. Is it the same guy from the bookstore? I head inside, slam the door quickly, and shoot the dead bolt.

Sadie and I hide in the laundry room, computer on my lap. I watch the man stride up the walkway. I peer closely at the black-and-white screen. I can't tell if it's the same man. Don't know if he's a reporter. But now that a body has been found on our property, they will come. People seeking me out by any means necessary. The coverage will escalate. There's a sensational story here. Murdered psychologist. A missing woman found dead and some connection between them.

I hold my breath as I watch him lean on the doorbell. My phone rings, and I pick it up without taking my eyes off my laptop.

"Molly?"

"Mom, hi."

"Are you all right?"

"Yes. Fine." The man looks like he's giving up. I watch him turn and head down the porch steps. I strain to see if he has a phone in his hand. Will he try to call me? Is he the one who's harassing me, or is he just a reporter looking for a story?

"Molly?"

"What?"

"Do you want Dad and me to come over?" I hear *please say no* in her voice.

"I'm okay, really." I can just see the man's car at the curb. He's pulling away. I draw a deep breath. "I'm keeping busy around the house today. Maybe tomorrow would be better."

We say our goodbyes, and I heave a sigh of relief.

My parents have been their usual perplexed selves. Mom calls daily to "check on me," but they rely on Corrine to do the heavy lifting. That's been their way from the start. Why not leverage that much older sibling, especially when the youngest wasn't planned? When I was little, not long after we'd moved to Graybridge, my mother's aunts came for a visit, and I heard my Aunt Ellen tell our neighbor that I'd been an oops baby. I thought that meant I was clumsy, which my mother was always saying was the case. But then I asked Corrine, and she told me I hadn't been expected, whatever that meant. It was only years later that I realized why there was such a gap between me and Corrine and what the expression really meant.

My dad is an accountant and mom a math professor. Their lives were planned and ordered, and having me had been an aberration. Something they never quite figured out. Mom was working on her doctorate that fateful summer. She was up at the college when she entrusted me to our neighbor, Mrs. Arndt, on the day that would change all our lives. I'd been missing for hours before she got home and found out. I've never been able to quite rid myself of the feeling that I'd let them all down, ruined their lives. No one ever said that, of course, but people don't have to say everything for you to feel it.

And now, just when they were comfortable that I'd married a man who would keep me from sinking back into the abyss, everything has gone to hell again, and I'm right in the center of it, dragging them down with me.

I need to take Sadie for her evening walk, so I check my camera feeds, look out the windows to make sure there's no one around. The coast looks clear, and since it's almost dark, I need to get going.

Sadie walks obediently at my side as we head down the sidewalk. I fidget with my phone, nestled in my coat pocket, fearful the man will call again. My gaze lands on every shrub, every tree, every place someone could possibly hide. I glance over my shoulder periodically. I've got to stay vigilant. I wonder why he's bothering me. What could he possibly want?

Sadie and I cross the street and head home. Snow starts to fall, and I try to concentrate on the white flakes falling through the light of the lampposts. I love snow. I love how it deadens sound and covers up all the gray. It's the opposite of the oppressive summer sun that burns and smothers.

I stop at our mailbox before going in and grab a handful of envelopes and sales flyers and tuck the bundle under my arm.

Inside, I fill Sadie's bowl and refresh her water. The mail lies splayed on the countertop, and I weed through it. An envelope catches my eye. The return address is marked OSSINING, NEW YORK. SING SING CORRECTIONAL FACILITY. My heart feels like it's going to beat out of my chest. The letter is addressed to Dr. Jay Bradley.

I sink into a kitchen chair and tear it open.

> Dear Dr. Bradley,
> Thank you so much for your letter. I'm flattered that you would consider me for your book. I would be very interested in talking to you in person. So many lies were spread about the incident that got me here. I would like a chance to explain what really happened.
> It was a long time ago but I remember it pretty vividly. All the details of that sad event. I can give those to you in hopes that your book will shed light on the truth which hasn't been what was reported in the media.
> Please arrange for a visit and I'll be glad to answer all your questions.
> Very truly yours,
> Keith Russell

I'm trembling. I can't breathe. Sadie whimpers as she nudges me with her nose. This can't be real. It can't be right. I drop the letter as though it's on fire. I don't want to touch anything that he touched. Why can't this ever be over? How can he still, all these years later, intrude on my life?

Then it dawns on me. Jay had written to him. That can't be. Even if he wanted to interview prisoners for his book. Why would he reach out to Keith Russell? How could he do that to me?

I pace through the house, wrapping my arms around my stomach to try to still my shaking, but I can't.

When I couldn't settle down, I called Corrine, and she came over.

"What's going on, Molly?" she asks. I hadn't told her anything on the phone, just that I needed her.

I drop the letter in front of her. She reads quickly. "Oh my God." Her eyes meet mine. "Why would Jay want to talk to *Keith Russell*?" She spits out his name like it's poison. "Couldn't he find enough demented killers for his fucking book without talking to that asshole?"

I shake my head. How could my husband have betrayed me this way? "What if . . ." I can't bring myself to meet Corrine's gaze, and my breath catches in my throat as I try to speak. "What if Jay only wanted to marry me because of who I am? Maybe I was just an interesting study for him. Maybe he just wanted to write a book about me and my sorry life . . ."

Corrine wraps me in her arms. "No. Molly. Jay loved you. He just made a huge mistake. Huge. But he loved you."

I cry in her arms, and she cries too. I agree to go back to her place for the night. Somehow my house has lost its luster, so Sadie and I pack up and leave.

On the drive, I tell Corrine about the phone calls I've gotten.

"Why didn't you tell me before?"

"They're just crank calls, don't you think?" I don't want her to think I'm paranoid, hysterical.

She slams her hand on the steering wheel. "After all this time? I don't like it, Moll. Why now, all these years later?"

"I don't know." I lean my head against the passenger window, pick at my sleeve.

Corrine drives quickly, making sharp turns until we get on the highway headed downtown. She cruises along in the fast lane, her brow furled.

"We're going to the police station tomorrow morning and telling Detective Myers about those phone calls," she says.

"I'll have to tell her about me, Corrine."

"Well, you'll just have to. It's not like she's going to tell anybody or call the newspaper. Maybe they can find out who's harassing you and why. Maybe they can talk to somebody at the prison. Check that that bastard isn't causing any trouble."

I've always been haunted by the possibility. Could he still hurt me somehow? Would a prison cell really hold him?

By the time we reach the apartment, it's snowing again, not the big fluffy flakes that have fallen lately, but small, hard pellets. I curl up on the guest room bed and listen to the sleet ping against the window. Too much has happened in recent days for me to process, one disaster after another, and I'm too weak, too beaten down to keep the nightmares at bay. Despite my best efforts, my mind goes back to that day.

On July third, a day after my sixth birthday, the sun blazed unimpeded in a blue sky. I was playing in the neighbors' backyard with their four-year-old, Indie. Short for India. She was a little young for me, but we were the only two kids in the neighborhood under ten, so we made the best of it. Her mom was watching us or was supposed to be. She'd walk out on the patio every so often, but quickly retreat into the house to watch her soaps and sip vodka from a coffee cup.

My mom was at the college, working on a paper in the media center before it closed for the holiday. Corrine had gone to the mall with a friend, and my dad was at work, so I was left with the neighbors.

Summers in upstate New York can be cool or mercilessly hot. That summer was the latter. So hot your hair stuck to your neck where sweat bees menacingly buzzed by your ears, where your skin sizzled if you forgot your sunscreen. Indie and I had been on the swing set, pumping our plump legs and soaring to the metallic music of the chains as we swung back and forth. Tiring of that, we moved to the back of the yard, where a faded plastic playhouse sat among tall weeds that Indie's dad's mower couldn't reach. Something my mother often grumbled about. "He needs to get in there with a weed whacker," she'd say. "He's drawing ticks."

Indie and I knew less than nothing about ticks and tromped through the thick overgrowth, picking the wildflowers that fought their way through the tangle of vegetation, looking for the sun. With a sticky handful of Queen Anne's lace and blue daisies, I saw someone moving through the thin line of trees that ran behind the houses. At first, I stood still like a rabbit who'd spotted a hawk, but relaxed when he came from behind an oak tree.

Keith Russell, Indie's cousin from Poughkeepsie, was eighteen and was spending the summer with his aunt and uncle. He was really tall, or he seemed so to me at the time, and thin, with a bulging pointed Adam's apple that bobbed when he talked. His hair was thick and brown and hung over his bushy eyebrows. His teeth were too big for his mouth, and shiny red spots covered his chin. But he was nice to me and Indie. He liked to play with us in the yard, pushing us on the swings or chasing us in a game of tag. When he'd catch us, he'd grab us from behind and lift us high in the air. It was strange that he was coming through the woods. I'd heard him tell his aunt that he was going to the movies when I showed up at their door earlier. Maybe he changed his mind, I thought, and we were glad to see him as we had run through all our usual routines and were looking for something to do. Keith beckoned to us from the trees, and we eagerly climbed through the hole in the chain-link fence.

"Let's go get ice cream," he'd said, and led us through the woods to his car, which was parked on the next street. The lure of adventure and ice cream trumped all worry about running off without letting anybody know. And it was Keith. He must've told Indie's mom.

I remember everything clearly as we rode through the street in Keith's rusted blue car, the windows rolled down and hot, dusty air blowing over us. He gave us each a warm bottle of orange soda, and we drank eagerly. He had the radio on, and the song that was playing is forever the backdrop of that fateful ride. A ride into a new life, something that could never be undone. But, at the time, I anticipated a strawberry sundae topped with lots of whipped cream. I remember looking back over my shoulder as the ice cream parlor faded into the distance.

"You missed it, Keith," Indie said. "It's back there." She'd stood up on tiptoe and was pointing. We were both crowded onto the passenger's seat up front. He yanked her top to get her to sit back down but kept his eyes on the road.

"Keith!" Indie shouted, her long dark hair sweaty and tangled.

"I'll turn around in a minute. Sit still. Drink your soda." His voice had become strange, so we sat, our little thighs sticking together in the heat, and wondered what we'd done wrong. Obediently, we sipped our drinks, and the hot day began to grow woozy around me.

I don't want to tell this story to Detective Myers or to anyone else for that matter. But maybe she already knows. Maybe she's already dug into my past. People do that. They pick and dig and peer into our most private lives as if it is their privilege to unearth our secrets.

As always when I think of that day, I'm filled with anger. What right had Keith Russell to do this to me? What right did he have to destroy my life before it had barely started? Afterward, therapists had all pointed out that I was in control of my own life. How I *responded* and chose to live the rest of it was what was important. But I don't think that's entirely true. Like every other child who's been the victim of an abuser, your life is different, altered, and there's nothing you can do about that.

I finally grow drowsy, with Sadie stretched out on the floor next to me, where I can reach my hand down and touch her back, feel her even breathing.

My phone vibrates on my pillow. Unknown caller. I want to kill the bastard.

"Hello!"

"Hello, Melinda Wright."

"What the fuck do you want from me?"

Big raspy breath. "I'm the one who knows, and I won't be happy until you're back in that cellar for good."

CHAPTER 39

Rita

I'm supposed to be off today, but I was just driving myself crazy at home, so I came in. We need to get our suspects in for questioning, but better to wait until Sheriff Skinner gets back to me with what his forensics team found. That report will be key in our questioning. But I'm antsy as hell waiting. I've worked through files on my other cases, made a few phone calls, but the Bradley case intrudes on my thoughts, scenarios running around and around, squirrels in a cage.

My phone rings. An unfamiliar number pops up on the screen.

"Rita?" At first, I don't recognize the voice.

"Yes."

"Joe Thorne."

I break into a smile. Joe and I go back a ways, but I haven't heard from him in a couple of years. He's an FBI agent I'd worked with on a case five or six years ago. And the memories of that case—or, more especially, what happened afterward—bring a flutter to my heart and a blush to my cheeks. He'd reached out a few times in the subsequent years, but I, coward that I am when it comes to relationships, had let things drop. Now here he is again, stepping back into my world, and I'm both excited and troubled at the prospect, but above everything else, I'm a professional. I can handle this.

"Great to hear from you, Joe. It's been a while. How are you?"

"Fine. Getting old." I laugh with him. He doesn't sound old. "Looks like we'll be working together on this Annalise Robb case."

"Sheriff Skinner turning the hard work over to you guys?"

"Yeah. Since it looks like our focus is turning to several people of interest in Graybridge, he reached out, asked for our help."

"Has Sheriff Skinner told you guys anything new?"

"Yeah." He clears his throat. "The initial lab report on the blood found in the Bradley basement has come back. It's been identified as Ms. Robb's."

I blow out a breath, sink back in my chair. "So she *was* killed in the Bradley basement?"

"Looks that way."

"Then we have a lot to talk about, Agent Thorne."

"We do," he says.

Is he implying more than police work? I take a deep breath, drop my feet to the floor. "Alrighty then, Joe. Let's get to it." After arranging the particulars, I hang up. Chase is standing in my doorway.

"What did you hear?" I ask, hoping that the blush on my cheeks has dissipated.

"Not much? Who's Agent Thorne?"

"FBI. They'll be here Monday."

I hear voices in the hall and loud footsteps. Someone's in a hurry. Mrs. Bradley and her sister burst into my office, Chase in their wake.

"We need some help here," Corrine Alworth says, slamming an envelope on my desk.

"What's this?" I ask.

"It was in my sister's mail yesterday."

Mrs. Bradley has dropped into the chair across from me, pulled up her legs, and practically rolled herself into a ball like a scared kid might. Her dog pants at her side, lolling tongue, perky ears. Emotion radiates from all three of them,

I inspect the return address. Hmmm. Sing Sing. Read through the letter. "This was sent to Dr. Bradley?"

Mrs. Alworth nods. She's standing behind her sister, a hand on her shoulder.

I drop the letter on the desk. "Just another subject for his book, right?" I ask tentatively, but something's up.

Mrs. Bradley chokes out a sob and covers her eyes with her hands. Something is very strange here.

Mrs. Alworth draws a deep angry breath. "Keith Russell is in prison for assaulting my sister when she was just a child."

"I'm sorry to hear that." I get it. That sucks that the doctor would be interested in talking to him then.

"*Detective.*" Mrs. Alworth is leaning over my desk, teeth bared. "My sister is *Melinda Wright.*"

Okay, that name rings a bell. *Think, Rita.* I know this case. It comes back. Bits and pieces. It was a very long time ago. But it was a national sensation. Two little girls abducted and held in the cellar of an old farmhouse for three days. It was an ugly story.

The realization hits me right between the eyes. "I'm so sorry, Mrs. Bradley," I say, afraid we haven't been sensitive enough. Afraid we've added to her pain. *Jesus, she's a misery magnet.* No wonder she needs a therapy dog. "Why didn't you tell us?" I ask quietly.

Mrs. Bradley's bloodshot eyes meet mine. "I don't want anyone to *know.* I don't want this. Any of it."

"Why tell me now?"

Mrs. Alworth clenches her fists. "She's been getting crank calls since her husband was killed."

I dig for my notebook. "What kind of calls?"

Mrs. Alworth describes them, stopping occasionally to get corroboration from her sister that she's got it right.

"The caller is threatening you, Mrs. Bradley?"

"*Yes*," the sister answers.

"Why?" It doesn't really make sense. How does it fit in with her husband's murder? Maybe it doesn't. The perp had at least two opportunities to assault Mrs. Bradley, but he didn't. She was asleep upstairs when her husband was killed. And then when the perp came back, he went into the garage but made no attempt to get into the house, where Mrs. Bradley was alone and vulnerable.

"I don't know," she chokes out.

"Okay. We'll see what we can do." I tap my notebook with my pencil.

Chase steps forward. "I can handle it, Rita. I'll take Mrs. Bradley's statement and see if we can trace the calls."

The three of them exit my office, dog in tow, and I take a deep breath. This case is getting more complicated by the minute.

CHAPTER 40

Molly

I'm curled up on my bed at Corrine's. She asked me if I wanted to come out and eat dinner, but I don't. My stomach is in knots. When we drove up to the apartment, several news vans were parked at the curb. Have they finally started putting the pieces together? Thank God, there's a gated parking lot, and they couldn't follow us.

I flip on the TV just to block out the hum of Corrine and Rich's conversation in the other room.

An entertainment news show starts. After upbeat bumper music plays, the news anchor comes on. She's smiling broadly, and her slick blond bob glistens under studio lights. *My picture*, a small square in the upper right-hand corner of the screen, appears, and my heart pounds. There has been coverage on the local news of Jay's murder and the woman found at the mountain house, but nothing national so far that I've seen until now.

The anchor's red lips part.

"Melinda Wright Bradley is no stranger to tragedy. On Sunday, January fifth, someone broke into her Massachusetts home and brutally murdered her husband, psychologist Jay Bradley, while Melinda slept upstairs. But that's not the first catastrophe to befall this hard-luck beauty. In 1991, the nation fell in love with little red-haired Melinda when she, along with neighbor India Arndt, disappeared from the Arndt backyard in upstate New York. After a three-day search, the girls were located in the cellar of an abandoned farmhouse, where they had been brutally assaulted by a disturbed teenager. Unfortunately, little India did not survive her ordeal.

"And now, if things weren't bad enough for Melinda, the body of a missing New Hampshire woman has been found on property owned by her late husband. Authorities are working to establish a connection between the woman's murder and that of Dr. Bradley—"

Corrine strides into the room and turns off the TV.

I'm stunned and lie on the bed like a dead thing, feeling nothing. My phone is ringing, texts chiming. Everybody knows now, and I've got nowhere to hide.

Chapter 41

Molly

I stayed in my room at Corrine's all day yesterday with my phone turned off. But today, Monday morning, I figure I'll face the fire. Either that or never leave this apartment again. I've got dozens of texts, and I hit delete without even looking at who they're from. As I'm clearing out my phone, it rings, and Kim's name pops up. I take a deep breath and answer.

"Hi, Kim."

"Molly! Are you all right?"

"I'm fine. I'm at Corrine's." Silence. She doesn't know what to say. I don't either.

"We're all worried about you. We saw the news," she adds quietly.

"I guess everyone's seen it by now, and I don't want to talk about it."

"I understand." But I can hear the hurt in her voice. We're best friends, and I didn't tell her who I was. I had years to do it, and I didn't. I understand her feelings, but no one seems to understand mine. Not any of the therapists I've seen over the years. Not until Jay anyway. Tears fill my eyes. I guess I was wrong about him too.

"Molly?"

"Yes. Sorry. I'm fine."

"We're all concerned about you."

"Please tell them I'm okay. I just don't want to talk right now. Maybe sometime, just not now."

"I'm here if you need me."

"Thanks, Kim." I hang up and toss the phone beside me on the bed and think back to my last days as Melinda.

We stayed in New York the year after I was found. Hiding in our house, reporters camped out on the lawn. My dad's Aunt Martha was a retired teacher, and she moved in with us to home-school me and help keep me entertained since I rarely went anywhere. My parents eventually went back to work, walking the gauntlet of snapping cameras and microphones. Corrine insisted on going back to high school that fall, and I've always been in awe of her strength and resilience. The reporters began to fade away until the following spring when the trial commenced. The media attention ramped up again. I remember peering through the curtains of the living room, frightened, feeling like a prisoner. Mom had asked her hairdresser to come over and cut off my long hair. She bought me new clothes in drab, nondescript colors. I remember feeling like they were trying to make Melinda go away, as if my parents wanted another little girl in my place. They started calling me Molly then too.

After Keith was convicted, the reporters started leaving, packing up their equipment and moving on to the next shiny thing. My parents huddled in the kitchen in the evenings, talking, planning. Corrine told me later, I don't remember it myself, that Mom and Dad decided we needed to move, to start over. My dad opened the phone book in the middle and stuck his finger on a random name, and we became the Morgans. The paperwork was filed, and the name change was official. Then Dad got a job in Graybridge, and we moved to Massachusetts. I do remember the drive to the new house, Mom turning around to where Corrine and I sat in the back seat. "Remember, Molly, your last name is Morgan, and we're from Pennsylvania. Don't forget. If you tell people our other name and where we're from, those reporters will come back, and you'll never be able to go outside or to school again." I was, of course, terrified and managed to bury our secrets deep inside myself until I no longer thought about Melinda Wright or New York unless I was very tired or upset. Then memories would flood back, and I'd retreat to my room and lie on my bed, crying until I could put Melinda in her place.

And, of course, the therapy sessions continued. My parents hoped they would save me from debilitating anxiety and acting out, which our pediatrician back in New York warned them about. Mom dutifully drove me to see a therapist once a week in Providence. She didn't want me to see anyone locally. She didn't want to take a chance that someone would figure out who we were. I kept busy in the back seat on those long rides by reading. I lost myself in hefty chapter books while Mom listened to talk radio.

I sigh and bury my face in my pillow. Then I hear the doorbell ring, female voices in the hall. Elise. *Shit.*

"Molly?" Corrine knocks on my door.

"I'm coming." Might as well face her too.

Elise is sitting in the living room, dressed in neat khakis, a blue scarf over her white blouse. The harbor lies behind her like an enormous beast. "How are you, Molly?"

She stands and embraces me, but I don't return the hug. "I'm okay. Why are you here?"

Corrine shoots me a look. "I called her. I told her what was going on, including the letter. I thought she could help."

"I don't need anyone's help," I snap. "The cops are handling it. So if you're here to tell me what a great guy Jay was, Elise, you can save it, okay? I can't think about him right now." I pace the room in little circles. "I can't think about my husband right now. I need to take care of myself."

"I understand."

I stand still in front of her, shake my head. This woman doesn't *understand.* No one can possibly understand. "I'm sure you know all about me *now*, right?"

"Yes." But she doesn't meet my eyes.

"Jay told you, didn't he? You didn't just hear it on TV."

"No. I didn't hear it on TV. I knew all along, Molly."

I clap my hands together. "*Great.* I knew it."

"Jay didn't tell me," she says. I tip my head, wait for her explanation. "I read your file when you were at the office for treatment. Before you and Jay were a couple."

"What? *Why?* That was confidential. I wasn't your patient!"

Elise raises a palm. "I'm sorry. It was an accident. I picked up a file from Candace's desk. I thought it was one of mine. One I'd just handed her a moment earlier. I didn't read it all, Molly. When I realized my mistake, I put it down."

"Oh, *Christ*, Elise. Really?" I nearly laugh. "But you didn't put it down before you read all the good stuff, right?"

"I'm being honest here. I never told a soul. I didn't even tell Jay I knew. I wanted to respect your privacy."

"Well, that's just great. So, now that Jay's gone, you think you can help me?"

Her eyes meet mine. "You went through hell, Molly. Most children need ongoing care after something like that."

"I've been in therapy off and on for years." I think back to my first psychologist, Dr. Sommers. She was an older lady who wore long skirts and sandals, had short gray hair and bug-like glasses. She kept a basket of puppets in her office, along with crayons and paper, props to get kids to reveal the monsters that peopled their lives. She worked with the police, and they taped my testimony, I was told. I don't remember it. But I remember feeling tricked. I don't remember her as a nice lady, but that's probably not fair. A child's view.

"I'd like to help if I can." She shoots a look at Corrine.

"Yeah. Well, I don't need your help, Elise."

"Are you sure?"

I squeeze the sides of my head with my hands. "Don't you get it? No one can help me." No one can remove the demon and the memories, snippets though they are, from my brain. I drop my hands to my sides. "Only I can."

"Can what?" Corrine asks.

"Only I can fix this."

She walks to my side. "What do you mean, Molly?"

"Him. He's still there, taunting me. I need to stop him."

"Those calls couldn't be from . . ." Corrine says, and glances at Elise. "Molly's been getting crank calls from someone who knows who she is and what happened."

Elise shakes her head. "They monitor calls in prisons. They wouldn't allow it."

"Whatever," I say. "I'm exhausted. I'm going back to bed. I don't want to talk about this."

I slam the guest room door behind me. I meant what I said. I need to fix this. That or be lost forever. Jay's gone, and I'm utterly alone. But maybe that's where I need to be.

CHAPTER 42

Rita

After lunch, FBI special agents Joe Thorne and Alison Metz arrive. I've had just enough time to finish my tacos when Chase comes to get me. I pop a breath mint in my mouth as I walk down the hall. They're already seated in the conference room when I get there.

Joe stands and shakes my hand, which feels strange, awkward. But it's great to see him. Our eyes meet, and I look away first, clear my throat. Agent Metz is nearer Chase's age, light brown hair slicked back in a bun, a face full of freckles.

After introductions, we take our seats at the table. All of our notes and photos pertaining to Dr. Bradley's murder remain on the front-facing whiteboard, but we've started another board on the side for Annalise Robb. Her murder is the first order of business. Get a solve there and hopefully Dr. Bradley's murder will fall into place.

Agent Thorne opens a file folder while Agent Metz hands around a folder to each of us.

"A copy of the autopsy is on top," Joe says. "Let's start there."

We all open our folders, and the iconic diagram greets us. "Ms. Robb was twenty-four years old. Five feet, three inches tall, approximately a hundred twenty pounds." He meets my eyes.

"Luckily, considering the state of the body, we have a probable cause of death." The room goes quiet. "Blunt-force trauma to the back of the head, which the ME said was probably not fatal but could've knocked her out. Then she was probably killed by strangulation, based on the damage in the neck area, ligature intact there as well."

"Sheriff Skinner thought that the perp may have knocked her to the pavement as she walked home," I say.

"Yeah. Her clothes were recovered buried next to her. Her jeans were ripped and bloodied at the knees, matching the fibers and blood found in the road."

I squeeze my chin with my hand. "He saw her walking. Maybe he followed her in his vehicle. Then knocked her down . . ."

"And might've struck her in the head there as well. That way she didn't fight him as he put her in his vehicle," Joe finishes. "That's what we're thinking."

Chase asks, "She was definitely killed in the Bradley basement?"

"Yes," Agent Metz answers. "Forensics has identified it as the scene. If you look at page three, you'll see their report." We all turn over pages and read silently.

"And no DNA?" I ask.

"Just hers. This guy knew what he was doing. The lab is still looking, however. They may still turn up something." Joe continues, "The body was buried in the riverbank, partially wrapped in a blue tarp."

"Like you put on a leaky roof?" Chase asks.

"Yes."

I lean back in my chair, eyes staring vacantly at the report. There's little doubt in my mind that Dr. Bradley or one of his guests was the perpetrator. Unless an unknown person had gotten into the basement. But why would a stranger bring her back there with a houseful of people, cars in the driveway? But someone who was intimately acquainted with the house would know how distant the basement area near the double doors was. It was a great place to get an unconscious Annalise out of sight and have your way with her. And the riverbank wasn't far, just over the footbridge, where the path wraps back around the property. And if a stranger had kept her someplace, then waited for the Bradleys and their friends to leave, there would've been some evidence of forced entry, and there wasn't. And why wouldn't the perp have taken her someplace farther away from town if he was going to keep her alive for a while? That just seems too far-fetched.

I stand and stretch my legs. I direct the agents' attention to the whiteboard, where Annalise's picture is taped, the names of the men in the house that night neatly printed beneath it. The women's names were listed in a separate column.

"We've done an initial search into the men's backgrounds," I say. Chase stands and distributes our folders on the suspects.

"These are the men who were in the Bradley house that night. Let's start with Dr. Bradley," I say. "He was a hometown boy, born and raised in Boston. Forty years old." I give them all the basics, including his father's and grandfather's backgrounds, which, of course, piques their interest. "He was currently doing research and starting interviews for a book he was writing on abnormal psychology and the criminal mind. It seems the doctor was particularly interested in homicide." I go on to give them Mrs. Bradley's newly discovered background, which intrigues them as well.

Joe leans forward. "Any criminal activity in the doctor's background?"

"None. Just testimonials from friends and acquaintances that he was a good guy."

We move on to Josh Pearson. "He and the doctor were friends from childhood. Now, Josh Pearson does have an arrest in his past. When he was twenty-three, he got into a bar fight and was arrested for assault and battery."

Agent Metz shrugs. "Just a young guy thing?"

I draw a deep breath. "One of the injured was a woman. She claimed that Pearson choked her and wouldn't let her leave the bar."

Agent Metz grimaces. "How'd that turn out?"

"He pleaded down and paid a fine. No jail time. He was a first-time offender and hasn't been in trouble since."

We flip pages and come to Calvin Ferris. "Mr. Ferris is originally from Hartford, went to college here in Boston. He and the doctor became friends through a men's hockey league. The only thing interesting in his background is that there was a restraining order taken out against him."

"By whom?" Joe asks.

I smirk. "His mother."

"Huh. What did she say when you talked to her?"

"She's deceased. This was six years ago. Next up is Scott Westmore. He's married to the doctor's business partner. He and Doctor Bradley were fishing buddies and occasionally went up to the Mountclair house. He's a landscaper. There wasn't much in his background. No arrests. No one seems to know much about him. He did go to MIT for two years but dropped out."

Joe taps the table with his pen. "That leaves Hayes Branch. He one of the Boston Branches?"

"Yes. He's Phyllis Branch's son. Owns a local bookstore. Mrs. Bradley works for him."

"Anything in his background?"

"Nothing much. Went to boarding school, then Harvard. Typical pedigree. Only unusual thing we could find is his wife's death. He found her dead in their home seven years ago. She was thirty-four. The death certificate states she died of natural causes. No autopsy."

Agent Metz huffs out a breath. "Natural causes at thirty-four?"

"So the paperwork says." I stand and go to the whiteboard, point to the list of names. "These, then, would be my people of interest, Agents, unless you've got another theory."

Joe is skimming back through his folder, shakes his head. "It seems unlikely that someone outside of that house would've abducted Ms. Robb, then brought her to the Bradley home's basement."

Agent Metz pipes up. "But how did he manage to murder her in the basement while everybody else slept upstairs oblivious?"

"Have you seen that basement?" I ask.

"Alison hasn't been to the scene yet," Joe says. "I did a walkthrough with Sheriff Skinner yesterday." He looks at his partner. "You'll understand when you see it."

"Can't wait," she says.

Joe looks at me. "How much do these guys know?"

"Just that Ms. Robb's body was found buried in the riverbank. The wife, and I assume the others, know that Dr. Bradley found her necklace, but they don't know where. *We're* not sure where. They don't know that the murder took place in the Bradley home. For all they know, the murderer was some local who carried her body past the house or through the woods." I look at the faces around the table. "It's crucial no one goes public with that information."

Joe nods. "I think we need to get these guys in here and find out what they have to say."

CHAPTER 43

Molly

Elise finally leaves. I hear her and Corrine whispering at the front door before it opens and closes. I lie on the bed, on my side, petting Sadie. I feel totally exposed here in the Boston area. It had been my refuge since I was a little girl, someplace new and pristine, where Melinda didn't exist. And now this life is over too. Molly has been outed.

Anger seeps up through my pores, builds in my chest, threatening to overwhelm me. What right did Keith Russell have to ruin my life? To haunt my dreams? This won't be over until I confront him. That's what has been nibbling at the edges of my conscience all my life. But therapists told me it wasn't necessary. I didn't have to confront my tormenter to heal. But what did they know? Nothing, it turns out. I'm in a worse place now than I was years ago.

I burrow under a pillow, moan into the mattress.

If only I'd said no. If only I'd gone into the house and told Indie's mother. If only I'd told Keith to go away.

"Molly?" Corrine calls through the door. "Would you like a cup of tea?"

I sit up, wipe the tears from my cheeks. I've got to end this. I've got to pull myself together. "Sure. I'll be out in a minute." I walk over to the window and look down on the street below. A couple of news vans are parked at the curb, but no one is standing out-side. It's too cold, too gray. A woman carrying shopping bags walks by. She ducks her head, and the wind whips her scarf be-hind her like a flag.

I can't go out the front of the building or they might see me. But the back entrance, where Corrine takes the trash down, that might be clear. I smooth my hair back, eye my overnight bag. I'll drink my tea, reassure Corrine that I'm okay. Then later, when they're asleep, Sadie and I will slip away.

CHAPTER 44

Rita

As dusk edges out the winter light, we wrap up for the day. Chase has left for home, and Agent Metz has gone to meet up with friends, so Joe and I head across the street to Mac's. The lights are comfortably low, and no cops are sitting at the bar. We take a seat in a booth in the corner. Joe slips out of his leather jacket and tosses it beside him.

The case we'd worked on together was only a few years ago, and while at first Joe and I had stayed in touch, that contact diminished over the last couple of years. We both got busy, but I remember the case clearly. A man had killed his wife in Maine and fled to Graybridge, where his grandmother lived. He'd left a trail of crimes in his wake, and Joe came in to help us. We got the collar, and Joe and I celebrated at Mac's with a couple bottles of chardonnay.

Our server comes over and drops menus on the table, takes our drink order.

I search my mind for small talk, which isn't my specialty. "You still running?"

"Yeah. Not so much anymore, but enough to keep me in some kind of shape." He looks good. Definitely in shape. I remember he used to hit the gym regularly too, and it looks like that's still part of his routine. Joe's tall, but not too. Six feet maybe. His hair is still thick, mostly gray, but it suits him. His eyes are the same as I remember. He's got the kind of eyes with irises so dark they meld with the pupils, giving him an intense look that's eked confessions out of hundreds of bad guys. His cheeks are slightly sunken, though—too much work and worry as well as years, I guess. A thin scar runs from his ear to nearly the corner of his mouth. He mentioned last time we were together something about a knife fight years ago, but he didn't seem to want to elaborate. Still, he's a handsome man.

At the time of our last meeting, he'd been divorced about six months. Ed and I'd split up years earlier. Joe and I'd spent the evening drinking, and I'd spent the night in his hotel room. Not professional, I admit, but things sometimes happen. The memory brings another blush to my face, and I'm glad it's dark in here.

Our drinks arrive, which is timely, a pinot noir for me and a draft for Joe. I lower my eyes and sip. "How are your kids?" I ask.

"Great. My daughter got married last summer." He smiles. "She's a nurse. They live in Stowe. Both big-time skiers. She's happy."

"Great." I remember him talking about his daughter.

"My son's a finance executive in New York." Joe raises his eyebrows. "Neither kid was interested in law enforcement."

"I wonder why?" I smirk and take another big sip of my wine.

Joe scratches the back of his neck. Sighs. He'd seldom been home when his kids were little, and his wife had finally had it, a common enough story in our line of work. "It's been a whirlwind, hasn't it?" he says. "When I started as a rookie cop almost forty years ago, I could never have imagined lasting this long."

"Me neither," I say. But that's not true. From the moment I put on the uniform, I knew I'd found my home. My brother Jimmy had wanted to be a cop. He, Danny, and I were the youngest of the McMahon kids and spent a lot of time playing together. Cops and robbers was one of our favorite pastimes. They always made me be the robber, and I've probably been arrested more times than your average real criminal. Anyway, Jimmy died before he was old enough for the dream to become a reality, and I kind of picked up the mantle. I sometimes feel as if I'm living life for both of us.

"I'll be sixty-two in August," Joe says, as though he's amazed such a thing could happen. I know how he feels.

"I was sixty last November."

He reaches over and squeezes my hand. "You look great, Rita," he says, and smiles. "Any thoughts of retiring?"

"No," I say quickly. "What would I do with my time?"

"No man in your life?"

"Not presently." It's been a while, but I don't tell him that. Despite Collin's efforts to find me a date, I've been in a lull lately. Don't know why exactly. I fiddle with my collar and change the subject. "Besides, Joe. I like what I do. I don't feel sixty, do you?"

He shakes his head, takes a long sip of his beer. "Not most days."

I stretch my legs under the table and feel a small ache in my hip. "I had a big case last fall. I had to kick in a door. Hostage situation."

He grins. "No shit?"

"Well, the door was pretty well rotted, but I kicked the fucker in."

We laugh. He salutes me with his beer. I pick up my wine and drain my glass.

When I get back to my place, enter the foyer, Collin is just about to head upstairs, a small Tupperware in his hand.

"Hey, Rita." He looks guilty, of what I have no idea.

"What you got there?" Usually he's coming *down* the stairs with a Tupperware full of food for me.

"Oh, this. Uh, Mrs. Antonelli invited me for dinner. André's out of town this week, that convention I was telling you about."

"Thought you were going with him? Catch some rays in Miami?"

He sighs. "I was, but Margo got the flu."

She's their café manager. "Huh, so you had to stay behind."

"Yeah. Anyway, Mrs. A's son canceled on her, and she had all this gnocchi." He raises the container.

"Good?" I feel a dart of jealousy. Never had kids, and since Collin and André have lived upstairs, Collin and I have gotten close.

"Yes. Amazing. I asked her for her recipe, but she *yelled* at me. I guess old Italian ladies don't use recipes." He smiles. "She told me she'd teach me to make it, though."

"Well, that's nice. But I've had your gnocchi. I don't think she can teach you anything."

He tips his head. "It's *better* than mine, Rita. I was so bummed." His brow furls. "Where were you? Working late on that psychologist case?"

I fish my keys out of my purse, turn to my door. "Yeah. It's gotten pretty complicated."

"It's really late. I keep telling you, you work too hard. Oh, I met Mrs. Antonelli's son, Leo, the other day. He's about your age. Pretty handsome, Rita, and he's divorced."

I try not to laugh. "I don't need you and André fixing me up, Collin. I told you that."

"Everybody can use some help now and then."

I glance back at him. "We'll see."

"Hey, André made a lemon cream cake before he left. You want me to run some down?"

I take a deep breath. I could use a little dessert to absorb the wine. "Yeah. That would be great."

"Be right back," he says, and runs up the stairs.

Chapter 45

Molly

In the gray of dawn, just as the sun starts to come up, Sadie and I head down the apartment building's back stairs. The Uber I'd called, a small black sedan, is idling at the curb. Sadie and I jump in, and the young man at the wheel mumbles a "Good morning." My stomach is in knots as we head to the highway. We're going home.

The house looks forlorn as Sadie and I make our way inside. It's chilly and echoes with emptiness. I usually feel a sense of calm when I walk through my front door, but not now. The letter from Keith Russell has soiled it, soiled Jay. Everything I'd held on to is broken.

Upstairs I pack a suitcase, stow my toiletries in a small bag. Glance around to see that I've got everything I need from up here. Downstairs, I gather Sadie's stuff, wrap her service dog vest around her as she stands patiently. Then I slip my laptop in its carry bag, and we're ready.

I've been driving Jay's Mercedes lately, but I decide to take my Subaru instead. As I back down the driveway, I call Corrine, put the phone on speaker.

"*Where* are you?" she asks. "I just went in to check on you."

"I'm home, or I was home. I'm on the road now." Sadie is

panting quietly, sitting in the passenger's seat. I reach over and lower the heat. "Look, Corrine. I need to get away for a while."

"What do you mean?"

"I'm going to go stay in a hotel and relax someplace where the media can't find me."

"Where?"

"I don't know." But I do, and I don't want her to worry. "I'm just going to drive out of town a ways and find a hotel. I'll call and keep in touch."

"Are you sure that's a good idea? I don't like this, Molly. Don't you think it would be better to stay with me and Rich? You're safe here."

"I appreciate your help, really. I just need some time. I'll be fine. I promise."

I hear her take a deep breath. "You'll call me?"

"Yes. I'll stay in touch."

"You'll keep your phone on and nearby?"

"Yes. Yes. It'll be fine. I'll be back in a couple of days."

"We were supposed to go to the police station this morning."

"Tell Detective Myers I'll be back soon. She can wait."

We hang up, and I feel guilty just a little to be lying to my sister, but I know she wouldn't approve. Big sister Corrine would come out. The one who doesn't think I can run my own life. She doesn't mean to be overbearing. I know that. It's what Keith Russell did to her too.

CHAPTER 46

Rita

Joe and I are in an interview room, drinking coffee, waiting for Mrs. Bradley. I take out my phone to check the time and see if she's texted that she's running late. It's ten minutes past nine o'clock. Joe is on his third cup. We've been working awhile.

Finally, the door opens, and Chase shows Corrine Alworth into the room. She looks a little haggard, a navy cardigan thrown over a T-shirt, blond hair clipped up on top of her head, a few hanks dropping to her shoulders.

"Where's Mrs. Bradley?" I ask.

She sits across from us and drapes her purse strap on the back of her chair. "She's not coming."

"Why not?"

"She left town for a few days." Mrs. Alworth sets her phone on the table.

Great. Not sure I like this development. Mrs. Bradley seems like an emotional loose cannon to me. I liked it better when she was here in town, where we could keep an eye on her. I clear my throat. "Okay. This is Special Agent Joe Thorne." He clasps her hand. "Mrs. Alworth is Mrs. Bradley's sister."

"FBI?"

"Yes," Joe says. "We're helping out." He opens his file folder and retrieves his reading glasses from his shirt pocket. "You weren't at the Mountclair house the night of the incident?"

"No. But I wanted to come in and check on how things were progressing."

"Where did your sister go?" I ask.

"I don't know." Mrs. Alworth glances at her phone as if she expects a call at any moment. "But she said she'd be back soon. She needed a break from the press."

"You're worried about her?"

"Of course. The man who's been calling *threatened* her last time."

"What did he say?" Joe asks.

Mrs. Alworth's eyes meet Joe's. "He said that he wanted her back in the cellar. Did you have any luck tracing the phone?" she asks me.

I lean back in my chair. "It's a burner, so we don't know who owns it, but Detective Fuller's been working on locating the area the calls were placed from." I text Chase, let him know that Mrs. Alworth is here.

"Like the ones drug dealers use?"

"Yes. We did check on Keith Russell. He's right where he's supposed to be—at Sing Sing. They even searched his cell and didn't find any contraband, phone or otherwise."

She drops her head in her hand, rubs her forehead. "Why would someone want to harass my sister?"

"We're doing everything we can to sort this out. Hopefully, it's just an idiot wanting to cause trouble." But even as I say the words, my gut clenches. Someone went to a lot of trouble to scare Mrs. Bradley.

Chase walks in, greets Mrs. Alworth. "We were able to figure out a location on the calls to your sister."

"And?"

"Graybridge area."

"Where in Graybridge?"

"Near the highway."

Mrs. Alworth blows out a breath. "Definitely not Keith Russell then. But who? Who would do this to Molly?" She looks at me with red-rimmed eyes. "All my sister ever wanted, Detective, was an ordinary life. A good husband, a couple of kids, a house, and a golden retriever. That's it. That's all Molly wanted. Me? I wanted the powerful career, travel the world. Big house. Family. I wanted it all, and I got it. Why not Molly? Why has she had to suffer so? She never hurt a soul."

"Life doesn't always work out the way we want it to," Joe says. "I went into law enforcement to help people whose lives went sideways through no fault of their own."

Well said, Joe. Mrs. Alworth half smiles at him.

"We'll do everything we can to help your sister," Chase says.

"Is she safe wherever she's gone?" I ask.

"I think so. She's got her dog with her. She said she was just going to drive a ways, then stay a couple days in a hotel. She said she'd keep in touch."

I take a deep breath. "I was hoping to ask Mrs. Bradley about the night of July Fourth."

"That woman's murder?"

"Yes. Maybe she heard something." Maybe somebody in that house heard or saw something that seemed unimportant at the time, but now, given what we know, might make all the difference.

"What about Jay, *his* death?"

"We're working that alongside Ms. Robb's murder."

"I'm sorry, but I'm concerned about my sister, her husband. I'm sorry about that woman, but you understand?"

"Of course," Joe says. "Dr. Bradley's case is getting our full attention."

She nods, checks her phone, then drops it in her purse. "Anything else, Detectives?"

"That should do it for now." I stand. "You'll call if you need us?"

Mrs. Alworth slings her purse strap over her shoulder. "Yes. Thank you."

Chase walks Mrs. Alworth out. I finish my notes, anxious to question Mrs. Bradley's friends.

CHAPTER 47

Molly

I'm on Interstate 84, heading southwest. The traffic is fairly light and the road clear. Snow in small banks lines the sides, and I glance up at the sky, hoping for a clear day. I didn't think to check the weather before I left, but that's what all-wheel drive is for, right? Most of my driving will be highway anyway, so I should be fine.

It's only a three-hour trip, and Sadie and I make good time. It's not quite eleven a.m., and we're already here. I guess I was more anxious to get going than I thought. Once I'd made up my mind, nothing was going to stop me, not snow, not my family or friends. I'm in a desperate search to save myself. I can no longer hide or depend on someone else to do it for me.

Sadie and I sit in the parking lot of the hotel I'd booked online last night, and I call the front desk to see if we can do an early check-in. The woman tells me to come on in. They've got a room available. I adjust Sadie's service-dog vest and take her for a walk first.

Inside the lobby, I pick up our card keys and head upstairs. The room is chain-hotel nice, knobby carpet, white puffy duvet on the king-size bed, faux granite in the bath with a glass-enclosed walk-in shower. Perfect for a place to disappear, leave my life behind for a few days. And a perfect place to gather my strength and take a stand.

I turn on the large flat-screen and switch to a news station. I take a deep, slow breath as I listen to the latest political wrangling, but anything is preferable to my story.

I search my tote bag and pull out a bag of Oreos and a bottle of water. Sadie stretches out on the floor and promptly goes to sleep. I pile up the pillows and get settled on the bed, switch channels, and find an old movie. *The Creature from the Black Lagoon*, black-and-white and suitably dramatic. No thinking, no worrying, just me and an old classic with pseudo-scary music and no connection to reality. I want to relax awhile, clear my head before getting down to the reason for my trip.

CHAPTER 48

Rita

Kim Pearson squirms in the chair facing me and Joe. Chase and Agent Metz are taping all the interviews and are in the little room next door watching on-screen. As each couple comes in, we are talking to the women first, while the husbands wait their turn.

"Mrs. Pearson, we're interested in the night of July Fourth, last summer. You and your husband were at the Bradleys' Mountclair home, correct?" I ask.

"Yes. Is this about the woman they found by the river?"

"Part of that investigation," Joe says.

She seems to settle some, smooths the front of her sweater.

I open my notebook. "Can you run through that visit for us, please?"

"Yes. Sure. We were there since Monday. Molly invited us up to celebrate the Fourth and her birthday on the second. We'd had a fun week—"

"What did you do?" Joe asks. "All week?"

"We barbequed. Walked in the woods. Had drinks. Watched movies."

"Anything out of the ordinary?" He peers at her, his dark eyes unblinking.

"No."

I sketch her face, the frown lines on her forehead. "What about the Fourth itself?"

"We grilled hamburgers and hot dogs outside."

"You go out to see fireworks?" Joe asks. He and I have slipped easily into our previous pattern. Taking turns asking questions, quickly tossing the reins back and forth, hoping to keep our interviewee on her back foot.

"No. Molly doesn't like them."

"Why not?"

She shrugs. "She's, I don't know, anxious. Loud noises bother her. We stayed at the house."

"So it was a quiet evening?" I ask.

"Yes. We ate and drank. Watched a Fourth of July show on TV."

"What time did everyone go to bed?"

"I don't know."

"Who went first?"

Mrs. Pearson blows out a breath. "Molly, I think. She had a headache."

Chase and I had pinned a diagram of the house on an easel in the corner. I stand and point to the first floor. "Mrs. Bradley went to the master bedroom here? What time?"

"Gee, I don't know. Maybe around ten?"

"What about Dr. Bradley?"

"I'm not sure. I went to bed shortly after Molly did, so I guess I was next."

"Pretty early, huh?" Joe says. "Where did you sleep?"

"Show us on the diagram, please," I say.

She gets up and walks to the easel. It takes her a minute to orient herself. "Here. This upstairs bedroom."

"You go right to sleep?" Joe asks.

"No. I read for a while."

"When did your husband come up?"

"I think it was around eleven."

"Were you still awake?"

"Yes."

"You or he leave the bedroom all night?"

Her eyes open wide. "No. We went to sleep."

"You hear anything in the night? Anything at all?" I tap my pencil against my notebook.

"Oh, wait. I did get up. I heard cars driving by the house."

"What time was that?" Joe leans forward.

"Um, around midnight, I think. The people up the road had a big party. People were coming and going all day." She puts a hand to her mouth. "Do you think someone from the party killed that woman?"

"Maybe," I say. "You hear anything else?"

"No. I went downstairs for a glass of water."

"At midnight?"

"Yes."

"Was anyone else up downstairs?" Joe clicks the top of his pen.

"Jay was. I saw the light on in the den, so I peeked in. Jay was drinking coffee, working on his laptop."

My heart starts to pound. "Did you speak with Dr. Bradley?"

"A little. He said he was just finishing up. He was going to bed shortly."

"Then what happened?"

She shakes her head. "I got my drink and went back upstairs."

"Was anyone else awake?"

"Not that I noticed. The house was dark."

I add to my notes and sketch of the mountain house. "Did you hear any more cars go by?"

"Maybe. I don't remember."

Joe leans forward. "Did you fall back asleep right away?"

"I think so. I don't remember lying awake too long."

"In the morning, was everyone there?" I ask.

She frowns like where else would they be? "Yes. We all left at around eight. Everybody wanted to get back. Pick up our kids."

"Everything seem normal in the morning?" Joe asks. "Anything odd that you remember?"

"No. Nothing."

Joe and I exchange a glance. "Okay, Mrs. Pearson. Thank you." I walk her out to the waiting room and beckon to Mr. Pearson before they can talk to each other and compare notes.

Pearson is back to his obnoxious self as he runs through the week at the Mountclair house. His rendition doesn't vary from his wife's. He slept soundly through the night of the Fourth, so he says. Didn't mention his wife getting up for that drink of water.

"What about this bar incident when you were twenty-three?" I ask, glancing through a file folder.

His face goes blank, and he blinks his eyes. "What?"

"You were arrested for a bar fight, right?" I hold up the report.

"Jesus Christ. Yes. Okay? I was a dumbass kid, for crying out loud. It was no big deal."

Joe clears his throat, stabs the table with his index finger. "You choked a woman. Wouldn't let her leave."

Pearson wipes a hand over his mouth. "My ex-girlfriend. She was a fatal attraction and a freaking liar. She came into the bar just to pick a fight with me. She made a big scene. Some jerk got involved, and we threw a few punches. That's it. The bouncer called 911."

"You never touched her?" Joe asks, raises his eyebrows.

Pearson shrugs. "She attacked me."

"She went to the ER. There are pictures." Joe's voice is throaty. He's a whisper away from angry.

Pearson hits the table with his fist. "I just tried to get her off me, that's all. It was no big deal." He looks at me. "What does this have to do with anything? I paid a fine. That's it."

"We're just looking at everything." I make some notes. "Got a bit of a temper, do we?"

His face reddens. "For fuck's sake," he says under his breath.

"What was that?" Joe asks.

"Nothing. Okay? I didn't kill that girl in Mountclair if that's what you're getting at. And I sure as hell never hurt Jay. Are we done here?"

"You sure you never left the house that night?" I ask. "Went looking for a little fun. Seems like a pretty dull time at the house. You didn't decide to ride into town for a drink maybe?"

"No. I didn't fucking leave the house that night."

"Just one more thing. You want to give us a DNA sample?" He has no idea we don't have DNA from the scene to compare his to, but hopefully we will soon.

He jumps to his feet. "No, I don't want to give you a DNA sample. Can I go?"

Joe and I exchange glances. "Okay, Mr. Pearson. We'll be talking to you again."

"Do whatever the fuck you want."

When he leaves, Joe and I huddle. "He doesn't do himself any favors," Joe says.

"Obnoxious twit," I say. "But Mrs. Pearson's information is interesting. We've got something of a timeline." I tap my notebook with my pencil.

"If what Mrs. Pearson says is accurate, yeah. If the doctor was awake at twelve, he could've waited for her to go back up to bed, given her a few minutes to fall asleep, and slipped out the door. She'd been hearing cars on the road all night, so if the doctor took off, she might not have been able to distinguish his car from the others if she'd been listening."

Laken Ferris is a bundle of nerves. She looks tired, not as glamorous as she had at the beginning of the investigation. Her story meshes with Mrs. Pearson's. She says she had another drink after Mrs. Pearson went up for the night, then she and her husband followed suit. She estimates they were in bed by eleven-thirty, as far as she remembers.

Mr. Ferris is red-eyed, but otherwise, he looks composed. He sits calmly, hands folded in his lap. His story matches his wife's. They went to bed, didn't hear a thing.

"Mr. Ferris," I say, "we've been looking through a lot of information and discovered that you had a restraining order taken out against you six years ago."

His face blanches. "What?"

"A restraining order, Mr. Ferris."

He drops his head and rubs his eyes under his glasses. "My mother took that out," he says quietly.

"Your *mother*?" Joe says, feigning surprise.

He nods. "It was no big deal. My mother was a bit . . . disturbed. My father had died and left me some things."

"What kind of things?"

"Baseball cards. Other sports memorabilia mostly. Nothing my mother had any interest in. And it was my stuff. Anyway, my mother was ill. She died shortly afterward. She wasn't in her right mind. When I went to see her, I asked for the boxes, and she told me I couldn't have them. I went up into the attic anyway. She freaked out, and when I came down with the first load, she pushed me and scratched my arms."

"You push her back?" Joe asks, leaning forward.

Ferris shrugs. "A little, okay? She had a hold of my arm. I didn't hurt her."

"Then what happened?" I ask.

"I put the first load in the trunk of my car, but when I went back to get the rest, she'd locked the door."

I look over the paper. "She says she was scared of you and that you'd harassed her with phone calls after that and tried to break into the house."

"I didn't harass her." He grimaces.

"Did you try to get back into the house?"

"Once, but then she got the order, and I gave up."

"You said she was ill, died not long after. Why not just wait?" Joe asks, eyebrows raised.

"The stuff was mine. It belonged to me, and I wanted it. I didn't realize she'd get so worked up about it. Once she took out the order, I let it go, okay? That was the end of it."

I tap my pencil against my notebook. "You sure you never left the mountain house on July Fourth?"

His eyes open wide behind his glasses. "No. We all stayed at the house that night. Someone suggested we drive over to some local fireworks, but we decided not to go." He shakes his head. "I had nothing to do with that woman's death, if that's what you're getting at." His gaze meets mine.

"I heard there was a lot of drinking. You didn't get a little inebriated? Didn't go out looking for a little excitement after everyone was asleep?" I stand and lean against the door. "Maybe you met Annalise and things got out of hand?"

Mr. Ferris's eyes flash. "No. No fucking way are you going to pin this on me." His face reddens. "It wasn't one of us. Just because she was found nearby doesn't mean anything. Anybody could've dragged her down that hill." He turns to Joe. "Somebody could've buried her there just to make it look as though one of us did it."

"Maybe," Joe says mildly, shrugs, goes back to his notes, then drops his pen on the table. "You hear anything that night?" His gaze meets Ferris's. "Maybe you heard or saw something that could help us find the real killer."

"I don't know anything. I didn't *do* anything."

"Then you won't mind giving us a DNA sample? Just to eliminate you."

Mr. Ferris's mouth falls open. "I think I need to talk to my lawyer before this gets out of hand."

"Of course," Joe says.

"You sure?" I ask. "It's quick and easy. Then we won't have to bother you again. Come on, Mr. Ferris. What are you afraid of?"

He jumps to his feet, perspiration running down the sides of his face. "I'll get back to you. I need to get home to my family."

He leaves, and we wrap up for the day. Joe asks if I want to grab a drink, but I'm tired, so I tell him we'll do it another time and hurry through the dark parking lot to my van.

At home, I put on my oldest, rattiest T-shirt and a pair of faded gym shorts. I stand in front of the bathroom mirror and pull out the elastic from the top of my head. My hair falls down over my shoulders, and I paw through it. There are definitely more grays than there were last time I really looked, whenever that was.

A box of dark brown hair color sits on the edge of the tub, and I eye it suspiciously. When I was young, my mother and her friends used to dye their hair every six weeks like clockwork. They'd sit in the kitchen on a Saturday afternoon with coffee and cigarettes, shoo us kids outside, and perform the ritual. They'd sit like statues, heads glistening with stinky goo.

I want to think I'm not that vain, but maybe I am. When my mom was my age, she looked old. By then, she'd let the grays win and cut off her hair, wearing it in a neat, curled cap like all the other old ladies she knew. Like you had no choice. The calendar said you were old, so fall in line.

I've kept my hair long, still enjoy wearing makeup, but I've been distracted lately and have let myself go a little. My exercise bike sits in the corner, covered with clothes like an extension of my closet. I usually use it three or four times a week and lift hand weights besides to stay slim and toned. But I've slacked off lately. I pick up the box, peruse the directions. I can probably pedal while the dye is doing its thing on my head.

My doorbell rings. *Shit.* I've got ten minutes left before it's time to rinse. The bell rings again, and I jump off my bike, sweat running down my chest, soaking my sports bra.

I look through the peephole. "What d'you want, Collin?" I ask through the door.

"Reet? Open the door. I've got dinner."

"Leave it on the mat. I'll get it in a minute."

"Why? Do you have a man in there?"

"*No.*"

"It's eggplant parm."

I flip the lock. "Okay, fine. Come in."

He gives me a sideways glance as he walks past me. "Why didn't you call my stylist? I gave you his card. Those box colors are really harsh, Rita."

I draw a deep breath. "This was quicker."

He wiggles his eyebrows. "Have you talked to Leo? He's been visiting his mother quite a bit lately."

"No. I was just getting tired of looking at myself, Collin." My phone timer goes off. "I gotta get in the shower."

"Say no more. I'll preheat the oven for you and put this in the fridge."

"You're a pal, Collin." I smile as I head to the bathroom.

CHAPTER 49

Molly

When the movie ends, I get up and run a brush through my hair and grab Sadie's leash. We head to the hotel's restaurant, and I order dinner. There's hardly anyone here since it's January. The holidays are over. It's the dead of winter. It suits me.

A couple of businessmen sit at a table in the center of the room, and that's it. Sadie and I are snugged into a corner table. She sits patiently next to me while I eat grilled salmon and string beans, a healthy meal to make up for the bag of cookies. Afterward, Sadie and I go for a quick walk, and I'm freezing since I forgot to bring my jacket with me when I came down for dinner.

When we get back to the room, I close the curtains as the town's lights flicker below. I look at my phone. No messages. Corrine is respecting my need to disappear, but I call her anyway.

"How are you, Molly?" I hear concern in her voice, barely tamped below her words.

"I'm fine, really. Sadie and I just went for a walk. Now I'm going to stretch out on the bed and watch another movie." I feel prickles of guilt.

Corrine blows out a breath. "Good. Relax. When are you coming back?"

"Probably Thursday. Not sure."

"Okay. Stay safe."

"I will."

"You're feeling okay, right?"

"Yes. I'm fine. Don't worry. I'll be back soon."

"You'll call me if you need to talk?"

"Promise."

I hear the reluctance to let go in her voice as we say our good-byes and end the call.

I go through my suitcase and hang up my clothes for tomor-row. I should've done it sooner. If the wrinkles don't fall out, I'll have to drag out the iron. The online instructions listed a dress code to make sure people don't show up looking like hookers, I guess. No chance of that for me. I brought my most business-like clothes, not exactly a power suit, but the closest I have—gray pants, a white cotton blouse, and a black blazer.

I double-check that the door is locked. Take a look around the room and bathroom, open the closet door. I put on my pajamas and get into bed. Thoughts, scenarios of what tomorrow might bring, swirl through my brain, and it's difficult to shut them off. One of my therapists when I was in college was big on relaxation exercises. Close your eyes, clear your mind, and imagine each part of your body, each muscle tensing, then letting go. I dutifully tried her techniques every night before going to sleep, with little suc-cess in actually relaxing, but I still do them sometimes. I try now, hoping to banish thoughts of tomorrow as I work from one mus-cle to the next.

My phone vibrates next to me and startles me awake. The room is dark, and my phone's screen seems to pulse in the night. UNKNOWN CALLER. I glance at Sadie, but she's sleeping content-edly, no bad guys lurking, I hope. Just some sicko who's getting a thrill out of scaring me. I turn off the phone, shudder, and stick it under a pillow.

CHAPTER 50

Rita

In the morning, I run into Lauren on my way back to my office.

"How's it going, Rita?" she asks.

"Making some progress." I feel guilty that she's been shut out. After the FBI became involved, Detective Schmitt went to Bob and complained that he needed Lauren's undivided attention to help him with his cases, and wasn't she his partner in training anyway? Bob concurred and pulled Lauren, even though she'd been crucial in our investigation so far. But that's the way things sometimes happen.

"Hey, why don't we head over to Mac's later? I'll fill you in," I say.

She nods. "That would be great."

Doug sticks his head out his door. "Morning, Rita. Running late?"

Go fuck yourself, Doug, I mumble under my breath.

Joe, Chase, Agent Metz, and I meet in the conference room. Chase sets down a cardboard tray of coffees he picked up on the way in, and I place a tin of André's cookies next to it. We're all a little tired and need the caffeine and sugar.

We review everything we've got so far on Annalise Robb, the

autopsy report, the forensics, and what we've gleaned from our interviews. "What are you thinking, Chase?" I ask.

He runs his hand through his dark hair. "It was planned. The guy must've had the ligature and the tarp ready to go."

I nod. "But what about the victim. How did he know she'd be there if he was someone from the Bradley house?"

Agent Metz clears her throat. "What if it was chance? He was out driving around, looking for a victim. Anybody. And he ran into her."

"Could be," Joe says. "Maybe our guy was thinking about this for a while. He was prepared for when the opportunity arose."

"Dr. Bradley," Chase says, "was researching serial killers. His grandfather worked the Strangler case. He definitely had an interest. Maybe he wanted a firsthand experience."

Joe sips his coffee. "Maybe after Mrs. Pearson spoke to him at midnight and then went back up to bed, the doctor left. Got in his car and went out looking for a victim."

"Might've happened that way," I say. But I'm not so sure. It doesn't feel right, and I think we're missing something, but I'm damned if I know what.

Chase rubs his hand over his mouth. "You think he had a murder kit ready to go?"

"Maybe." I drop my pencil on my notebook.

Joe checks his watch. "The Westmores coming in soon?"

"Yeah. Let's wrap this up." But it bugs me. If Dr. Bradley killed Annalise, who then came along and killed *him* months after she was murdered in his basement?

Elise Westmore, like everyone else we've interviewed lately, looks as though she could use a week on a beach somewhere. Her hair and clothes are perfect, but her eyes are puffy, and her makeup doesn't cover the circles beneath them.

Joe and I sit across from her as she runs through the same scenario as the others, adding that she and her husband went to bed at around eleven-thirty. The same time as the Ferrises. Their bedroom was on the first floor on the side of the house where the perpetrator probably walked with an unconscious Ms. Robb—if he didn't bring her through the house. But she says she heard nothing. Slept straight through.

"What about Dr. Bradley?" I ask. "What time did he go to bed?"

"I don't know. After we did. He said he was going to work on his book for a while. Jay didn't sleep much."

"Why was that?" Joe asks.

She shrugs. "That was just him. Some people don't."

"Was he troubled, Doctor?" I ask. Time to do a little probing of Dr. Bradley's psyche, at least from a close friend's perspective.

Her eyes meet mine. "What do you mean?"

"Well, both you and Mrs. Bradley said he was 'quiet, preoccupied' the week before his death, but maybe he was troubled long before that."

She shakes her head. "No. Jay and I talked about a lot of things. He worried some about his wife. He never told me the details of her ordeal, just that she had a traumatic event in her childhood. But I understand you know all about that."

I nod. "But what about him? He have any demons?" I watch her face carefully, the worry in her eyes, the tilt of her head. She cared about this guy, and his memory is precious to her.

"No. I don't think so. He was very well adjusted. As part of our training, we had to undergo therapy ourselves. Jay seemed to fly right through, while the rest of our class had varying levels of anxiety over it." Dr. Westmore smiles slightly, as if thoughts of school and the past bring back brighter days.

"He didn't have any strange thoughts, obsessions, after all he'd heard as a kid?" Joe asks.

She clears her throat. "If you're thinking Jay killed that woman, you're wrong. He was a kind, gentle man. He wasn't having serial killer fantasies." She's adamant, like a defense attorney in a court-room.

"How do you know?" I sit back, tap the arm of my chair with my pencil.

She blows out an irritated breath. "I just know."

"Lots of serial killers fool their friends and families for years," Joe says quietly.

She looks at him with something akin to anger. "I don't think any of those individuals you're referring to had a trained psychologist as a close friend."

"Maybe not," he agrees.

This isn't getting us anywhere, so we wrap up with Dr. Westmore and bring in her husband.

Scott Westmore is wearing one of his landscaper shirts, light denim with his company logo stitched in the upper corner. His jeans are worn and dirt-stained. He runs us quickly through the night of the Fourth, nothing new.

"Mr. Westmore," I say, "we're looking at everything here." I flip through my notes. "We didn't find a whole lot in your background." He remains our man of mystery. Does a killer lurk beneath that stoic exterior?

He doesn't respond, a man of few words, annoyance on his weather-worn face.

"I see that you went to MIT for a couple semesters," I say, perusing my notebook.

"That's right." His gaze is steady, and I break away first.

"Why didn't you finish?"

"It wasn't for me."

"What was your major?" I add to my sketch of him, wrinkles fanning out from his eyes.

"Pre-med."

"Huh. Went from that to landscaping?" Joe meets his gaze.

"Yes. Elise and I met as undergrads. We got married. Then I started my business while she finished school."

"Okay. You didn't hear *anything* the night of the Fourth? That woman was buried not a quarter mile from the house." Joe stabs the table with his index finger.

"No." His jaw tightens.

"You know the river pretty well, don't you?" I ask.

"I told you before that Jay and I fished there."

"You're quite an outdoorsman," I say, and lay my pencil down.

"I like to be outside." His roughened hands twitch slightly, and I picture them around Annalise's slim neck.

Joe glances at his notes, pen poised. "What vehicle did you drive up there that week?"

"My truck."

"You carry any tools for work in your truck?" Joe asks as though he's ready to make a list.

"Of course." There's a slight shrug of his shoulders.

"What kinds of items did you have in the truck the week of the Fourth?"

"I don't know exactly. A lot of junk."

"A shovel?" Joe deadpans.

"I'm a landscaper," he says by way of explanation, anger in the set of his teeth. "If you think I had anything to do with that woman's death, you're sadly mistaken." He gets to his feet, leans toward us. "I've got to get to work, Detectives. If you have any more questions, call my lawyer." He strides out of the room, leaving the door open.

"Well, that went well," Joe says under his breath. He gets up and closes the door. "Strange guy."

I smirk. "There's something strange about the whole pack of them." I straighten my notes. "Well, almost done. We've got the Branches later."

CHAPTER 51

Molly

The letter helped push me over the edge, into action that had been only a fantasy years in the making. I feel if I don't do this now, I'll fall completely, irreparably apart. I have no expectations, only an overwhelming desire to end the power this monster has had over my life. That has supplied the adrenaline that has carried me to Sing Sing Correctional Facility. My childhood was stolen; a sense of peace and security is an unknown thing. Even the husband who lifted me out of the mud is gone. And he wasn't the man I thought he was. I can fall no lower. I'm prepared to face the beast in the lowest ring of hell, and the spoils go to the victor.

I walk with a strong stride behind the guard, a short man with a thick, blotchy neck. He escorts me through the doors, deeper into the prison. I will meet my attacker face-to-face across a small metal table, no plexiglass, no phones. Metal jangles as the guard opens the final door, and I'm shown into a gray cinder-block room. I stop in my tracks, waver for a moment, fearing I might turn and run, but I don't. My escort leaves, and I glance at the guard standing in the corner, the man who has charge of Keith Russell. He nods slightly. This guard is a big man, six two or three, I'd guess. Muscled arms and an erect stature. I find reassurance in his gaze and take a seat across from the man who ruined my life.

My heart is pounding, and the pulsing of it is all I hear. Sweat breaks out on my upper lip and under my arms as I sit in a cold metal chair. Then he smiles at me. Keith Russell, or what's become of him, smiles and says my name.

"Melinda."

My adrenaline rushes back, flushes my face, and I sit up straight. I know the conversation must be civil. Any shouting or emotional outbursts will bring the visit to an end, so I swallow and take a deep breath.

"Keith," I say. His eyes are sunken and rheumy. His face as thin and lined as that of a man in his eighties, although he's only forty-seven. His body a shrunken shell. The Keith Russell who has haunted my dreams for twenty-nine years is young, tall, lanky, and strong, a monster with protruding eyes and sharp teeth. But this man has become something else.

Child killers don't fare well in prison. As the lowest of the low, they are often attacked by other inmates, sometimes killed. Keith's mottled, skinny arms are scarred, and near his neck is something that looks like a healed knife wound. He's been diminished physically over the years, and I stretch myself up taller in my seat as my pulse slowly eases down.

"It's nice to see you." He smiles again, his mouth a dark hole of missing teeth.

I draw a breath. My voice wavers. "It's not nice to see you, Keith."

"Then why did you come?" His voice grates. "No one comes to see me, now that my mother's dead, except my miserable brother when the mood strikes him." A shadow passes across his face, and he shakes his head like a dog might.

"It's not a social call."

His eyes—a light amber brown, all that remains of his physical self that hasn't changed—bore into mine. Then he drops his gaze to my left arm, and I instinctively cover the spot under my sleeve with my right hand. I hear him chuckle and curse myself for falling into his trap. He's looking for his mark, the brand he carved into my tender flesh with his pocketknife all those years ago. KR. He marked me as his possession.

When I was a teenager, Corrine took me to a dermatologist, whose laser treatments reduced the scar to a few faint ripples on my skin. But both Keith and I know it was there. I feel my breath flutter, catch in my chest.

"They might let me out, one day," he says, nibbles a fingernail.

"I doubt that." He'd been given life without the possibility of parole.

He only nods. Then leans forward. "I didn't kill Indie," he whispers. "I didn't kill anybody."

I grip the edge of the table, and the room swirls around me. I feel his sour breath on the back of my neck, the pain from thick strong fingers, pinching, shoving me into the dirt of the cellar floor. The burn of the knife on my flesh. The guard coughs, and I'm back to the present. My eyes settle on Keith's hands, locked together by the handcuffs at his wrists. They're not the same. They are thin and knotted, as if arthritis has rendered them useless. I take a deep breath and look him in the eyes.

"Tell all the lies you want," I say quietly. "No one will believe you, and no one will ever hear you."

He leans back slightly. "Someday, Melinda."

My breath catches again, and I clear my throat. "My husband is dead, Keith, so any thoughts you had about speaking to him, being in his book, that's all gone. He'll never write to you again. He'll never speak to you." My voice is rising, and the guard gives me a look. I settle back into my chair. "You can't hurt me anymore. You took away my childhood, Keith. You hurt me down to my soul, but I'm here to tell you that you've . . . lost. I've won. I'm not only surviving, but I'm flourishing. I'm living a good life." Maybe not yet, not completely, but I will. When I walk out of here. I will live a good life. I clench my hands into fists.

"You're a nothing, Keith Russell. You're in here behind these walls for life, and I'm going to walk away. I'm going to get into my car and drive back to my wonderful life."

He shrugs and glances at the guard. "But the past can never be changed, Melinda. And I might just write a book about those three days. I can't profit off it, that's the law, but I can write it. Tell the truth."

My heartbeat kicks up again, and I fight to catch my breath. "My husband won't help you!" The guard makes a move toward the table, but I sit back, fold my hands, and he retreats.

Keith shakes his head. "What husband? I don't know what in hell you're talking about."

I blink my eyes. "He wrote to you. My husband. He's writing a book, and you said you'd talk to him."

"You're crazy, Melinda. You know that?" His lips curl, and he leans forward. "You come in here, all high and mighty, but you're still a little girl who likes to tell tales." His sour breath wafts over me.

"You wrote to him! I read the letter."

He snorts. "I haven't written a letter in years. I got my hand broke in a fight. Can't even hold a pen." He flexes his right hand as if to prove his story. I watch the gnarled fingers stretch and then shrink back into a useless claw.

My breath stops. "You didn't write to my husband?"

"Shit, Melinda. I didn't even know you had a husband. Why would I?"

The letter had been handwritten, the writing neat and completely legible. My heart pounds. He's telling the truth. Jay never wrote to him. Never asked to interview him. I let go a long breath, lean back in my chair.

The room goes silent, and I close my eyes. I hear the clock, which sits high on the wall, softly ticking. I look at the guard, and he nods slightly, as though he's on my side. "I'm done here," I say to him. He unlocks the door, and the other guard is standing there to walk me out.

I sit in my car in the parking lot and look at the winter sky. It's gray, but the sun is up there somewhere. I feel weak in a good way, like you feel after a workout. Jay never contacted Keith. My heart swells. And Keith Russell can't hurt me anymore. He's paid a steep price, as he should have, for what he'd done to me and Indie, and he'll never get out.

I start my car and drive out onto the street. The only thing that still lingers in a dark place in my being is the fact that someone out there, some unknown person, is trying to scare me. Would go to the trouble of calling me, harassing me, wrote me that letter. Someone who knows me well. Knows what was going on in my life, and that Jay was writing a book.

But I feel stronger than I have in a very long time. I can do this.

CHAPTER 52

Rita

M̲r. Branch comes in first, leaving his eleven-year-old daughter in the waiting room. His curly hair is in disarray, as if he needs a good haircut, and his glasses are smudged. He's wearing a slightly rumpled tweed sport coat, like a harried professor.

The questions about the Fourth of July week have gotten routine by now, and his replies are the same as everyone else's, and we hope for something more when we turn to his past.

"Mr. Branch, we've done a bit of poking around and discovered your wife died a few years ago."

"Yes."

"She was only thirty-four?"

"That's right." He clears his throat. His eyes flicker.

"That must've been tough," Joe says.

He lets go a deep breath. "It was. It was awful."

I lift a sheet of paper from a file folder. "It says here in her obit that she died of natural causes." My eyes meet his.

He glances away. "Yes. She had a heart condition. I found her at home on the bathroom floor."

"That must've been traumatic."

He nods.

"There wasn't an autopsy?" I ask.

"No."

"Huh." I make a note.

"Her cardiologist verified her cause of death," he adds, his jaw muscles tense. Beads of perspiration gather at his temples.

"Okay. An autopsy is usually standard procedure in one so young."

"Well, it wasn't necessary—everyone agreed at the time." He glances at Joe, then back to me. "Why is this important?"

"Didn't say it was," I reply.

"Look, I don't have anything to add to your investigation. I don't know anything about that Mountclair woman, and I have no idea what happened to Jay." He runs a hand through his hair, setting his curls at odd angles. "This has all been really upsetting for my daughter and Molly."

"That's why we're trying to get it all sorted out, Mr. Branch," Joe says, leaning back in his chair.

He nods, bites his lips. "Well, I'm glad to help if I can, but I've told you everything I know, which is next to nothing."

"So you didn't leave the mountain house that night?" I ask.

"No, of course not."

"Maybe you didn't feel sleepy and decided to go for a drive?"

"No."

"How about giving us a DNA sample, Mr. Branch?" I ask.

His mouth hangs open. "Yes. Of course."

"We can do it right now." Joe starts to stand, but Branch looks suddenly panicky.

"My daughter's here. Right outside. I don't want her upset. Can I come back alone another time?"

"Why is this such a big deal?" I ask, leaning toward him. "Your daughter's a bright girl. She surely would understand that this is just routine."

He shakes his head. "No. I'll come back another time. I don't want Alice involved."

Now I'm worried he won't let us talk to her, so I back off.

"Okay. That's fine." I go out and bring Alice in. Since she's a minor, her father gets to stay while we question her.

Her long blond hair is neatly combed and held back with a black headband. She's wearing a white blouse with a navy cardigan and looks like a teenager from the fifties on her way to boarding school.

"Hello, Alice," I say.

She smiles slightly and nods.

"You know why we're here?"

"Yes. You're trying to find out what happened to the lady in the riverbank." She glances at her dad.

"Yes. And we know you were the one who found her."

Alice's cheeks flush.

"That must've been upsetting."

"I didn't know what it was at first, but when Molly and I got closer, I knew it was something bad."

I look over my notes. "We want to go back to the night of July Fourth. You remember that?"

"Yes."

"You and your dad were sleeping on the summer porch, is that right?"

"Yes. It was hot, so we decided to sleep out there instead of on the living room couches."

"Did you hear anything at all in the night?"

"No. It was quiet."

The porch is on the side of the house farthest from the riverbank, so despite the screens, it might've been hard to hear anything.

"Did you get up at all during the night?" Joe seems content to let me question Alice. He settles back with his notebook, and I get it. We don't want her intimidated or uncomfortable. She knows me at least a little.

"No."

"What about your dad?"

She glances at him again. "I don't think so." Mr. Branch puts an arm around her shoulders.

"So you both slept straight through the night then?"

Alice purses her lips as though she's thinking. "Yes. But I got up really early."

"What time?" I ask quietly.

She draws a deep breath. "Well, I set my phone alarm because I wanted to sketch the sunrise. I like to draw out on the deck, so I set it for five o'clock. It was still dark when I got up, but I didn't want to miss it. I wanted time to make a cup of tea and get my materials together."

"Did you hear anything? See anyone at that hour?"

"No. Everything was quiet."

"Was your dad still asleep?"

"Yes. He was snoring."

"So what did you do?"

"I went into the kitchen and turned on the little light over the stove. I made tea. I was careful not to let the kettle whistle because I didn't want to wake anyone up. While the tea bag steeped, I went into the mudroom to get the key ring because Molly locks up all the doors at night and I needed to get out on the deck."

"Okay. Then what?"

Alice shrugs. "It wasn't there."

"What wasn't there?" I ask, pencil poised.

"The key ring."

My heartbeat kicks up. "Was it there the night before?"

"I think so. It's always there."

"Then what happened?"

She sighs. "I went back to bed. There wasn't any sense in staying up if I couldn't get out on the deck."

"Did you go back to sleep?"

"Yes. I fell back asleep until seven or so when my dad woke me up."

"Was the key ring back? Did you notice?"

"I saw it there when we left."

"What time was that?"

She looks at her dad.

"We left a little after eight, I think," Mr. Branch says. "Is that all, Detectives? I've got a store to run."

Joe and I exchange looks. "I think we're done here. Alice, thank you very much for your help."

CHAPTER 53

Molly

I'm back at the hotel, and Sadie greets me at our door. I'd locked her in with the do not disturb flag hanging from the outside knob when I left for the prison. She's all wagging tail when I come in. I clip on her leash, and we head back out.

We walk down the sloping hotel driveway and start down the sidewalk. Traffic streams by, people on their way to the grocery store or to school to pick up kids maybe, oblivious to me and my dog. Unaware of the enormous lightness I feel as I stride along beside them. I'm just some woman walking her pet.

I'm jittery too as emotions bubble through my body. I never thought I'd see my attacker again. Confronting him had been a strange dream, an idea that never seemed possible, discouraged by the professionals I'd talked to over the years. But the power I felt when the meeting concluded reaffirmed my belief that, for me, this was a necessary step, one a long time in the making.

And Jay, he didn't betray me. Tears slip down my cheeks as the cold, gusty wind tosses my hair back over my shoulders. With one hand, I tug my knitted hat more firmly over my ears. I miss my husband so much it sends shudders of pain through my chest. I want to tell him what I did today like a proud child. That's the worst thing about death: you want to tell your loved one things, both trivial and life-altering. You start to form in your mind what you're going to say, anticipate his or her reaction, feel that warm glow of experiences shared between you. Death severs that most primal connection, and that leaves maybe the biggest hole of all. Still, I whisper to Jay and close my eyes a moment. I imagine his voice in the wind. *Well done, Molly!*

Back in the room, Sadie and I relax. I need to decompress, let today's events settle through me, then I'll go home. Tomorrow.

I peruse the plastic menu that sits on the credenza and order room service. After Sadie and I eat, I watch TV, read a magazine, although my mind skims the words without them sticking. It's full dark now, but I'm not sleepy. I'm full of energy.

I rifle through my suitcase and pull out my swimsuit, cap, and goggles. When I first started seeing Jay as his patient, he asked me what I did for exercise. At the time, I was working at the bookstore and basically going home at night, where I would watch TV, eat a microwaved frozen meal, and go to bed depressed and exhausted. But Jay, a great believer in the mind-body connection, encouraged me to exercise. In high school, I'd been on the swim team, so I rediscovered an old love. Since Jay and I'd been married, I'd gradually given up my trips to the Y, secure and happy with my husband, my mind on other things.

The hotel pool is empty and the lights low, the blue-green water deep and enticing. The sharp chemical smell is welcoming. I slip into the shallow end, stand still a moment, and touch the scar on my arm. After I'd been rescued and taken to the hospital, I recall the doctor probing the cuts, which were infected and suppurating. I remember the pain and my tears as he cleaned and bandaged Keith's initials. My mother took care of the wound the next couple of weeks until it healed. She'd yank off the old bandage and clean it with cotton balls soaked in stinging alcohol. Then she'd apply ointment from a special tube and put on a new bandage. She never said anything while this process occurred, except "Be a big girl, Melinda. It's not that bad." As though it was a scraped knee, an ordinary childhood mishap. I clear my throat. Seeing Keith today helped put that behind me as well. The scar is a battle wound. And I've finally won the war.

I pull my goggles down over my eyes, feel the familiar suction as they cling to my face, and kick off from the wall. The water is perfectly cool, like silk, and I glide slowly, doing an easy crawl. It's quiet underwater, like being in another world. My muscles warm as my arms reach and my legs propel me across the pool. My mind clears as I turn and start back, lap after lap, one flowing into the next until time slips by and I'm ready for sleep.

CHAPTER 54

Rita

"Okay, Alison, start walking," Joe says.

He and I stand in the cold morning air in the Mountclair Tavern's parking lot. Agent Metz takes a couple of steps, her phone in her hand counting the minutes. She turns and walks backward.

"Shouldn't I drink a couple of beers first for accuracy's sake?"

Joe smiles, and she turns back around and keeps walking along the side of the road.

"Maybe later," Joe yells after her. "Work first."

She waves at him over her shoulder. We want to see about how long it took Annalise Robb to walk from the bar to where she was abducted. Agent Metz is closest in age and size to our vic, so she got volunteered. Chase stands at the side road, where Annalise would've turned the corner, to direct Alison.

Joe and I drive up to the end spot where Annalise disappeared and wait for Agent Metz to arrive.

We sit in his vehicle, heater cranking, coffees in hand.

"Whoever did this had to leave the Bradley house sometime after midnight," Joe says, "or Mrs. Pearson probably would've noticed. Annalise left the bar anywhere from one o'clock to one-twenty, according to witnesses." When we reread the statements gathered by the sheriff's department, there was some discrepancy as to when Annalise actually left. Still, it's a pretty good timeline.

"And the deed was probably done by five a.m.," I add.

"Key ring wasn't back, according to Alice." Joe raises his eyebrows.

"True. But wouldn't she have heard something? I'm thinking the perp replaced the ring later. Realized it was still in his pocket maybe. I think he was finished by then and back in bed. It would've been risky to have been prowling around the house in the early-morning hours. I think he got the job done overnight when he was sure everyone was asleep."

We'd gone over all this since we interviewed Alice yesterday, but talking through possible scenarios is always ongoing. You never know when something you hadn't thought of before might pop up.

"And," I say, "I don't think it was the doctor." I had lain awake half the night thinking about this case, and I'm growing more convinced Jay Bradley wasn't a killer. Maybe it's just my gut talking, but it's getting louder. Ma always said the McMahons could feel things that not everyone else could. She used to visit an old woman who lived over Corrigan's Bar on the corner who claimed to be a psychic, much to Father O'Brien's chagrin. I don't necessarily buy into that sort of thing, but you never know.

Joe tips his head. "Maybe not, Rita."

"I still think he would've used his own keys. Why bother with the ring in the mudroom?"

"Maybe it was handy."

We sit in silence. The car is facing down the road so we can see Agent Metz coming. She eventually appears, walking at a moderate pace, trying to embody a tipsy Annalise. When she gets close, Joe and I exit the vehicle.

Alison takes a big breath and points over her shoulder. "That incline is steeper than it looks."

Chase appears headed our way, having walked a little behind her. We stand in a huddle.

"Okay, how did you do?" Joe asks, and Agent Metz hands him her phone, leans over, and puts her hands on her thighs.

"Asthma," she says to me.

When I raise my eyebrows, she adds. "Cold weather does it. It's not normally a problem."

Joe writes in his notebook. "That took you twenty-two minutes." He looks at me.

"So Annalise arrived at this spot anywhere from one twenty-two to one forty-two, give or take."

"Yeah. Looks like."

Chase arrives, also a little winded. "What now?"

Joe stows his notepad in his pocket. "We drive from here to the Bradley place. Hop in."

We drive in silence, the bare winter trees skimming by. I've got my phone timing us as Joe drives. He'd been to the scene before he'd arrived in Graybridge, but together, armed with the statements from our people of interest, we hope to find some answers. Joe pulls up on the side of the road. The old hunting lodge looks dark, dreary in the snow, like a huge dead beast. "How long did that take?" he asks me.

"Six minutes." We get out, and he pulls a tarp out of the back of the car.

"I don't have to get in that, right?" Agent Metz says. We'd run through our plan back in Graybridge and decided we weren't going to go that far, but we all laugh.

"No, although it would help." Joe cocks an eyebrow. She snorts and steps back. "Okay. We know that whether he took her around the house from the outside or went through the house entrance to the basement, he had to carry her quite a ways."

"All of our suspects are big men," I say. "Mr. Westmore carries heavy objects in the course of his work. Mr. Ferris plays hockey and tennis. Mr. Pearson isn't any wimp."

"Hayes Branch?" Chase says.

"Okay. He's not Goliath, but he's not a hundred-pound weakling either, and with adrenaline pumping . . ."

"The doctor was also a fairly big guy, and Ms. Robb was petite," Agent Metz says.

"Right," Joe adds. "Anyway, let's walk around the outside of the house first." He lays three cinder blocks in the tarp and wraps it up, and we head down the sloping lawn. The blocks aren't quite the same as a full-grown woman, but Joe wanted something to approximate an unwieldy load. The snow isn't too deep, thank God, but we slip a little anyway. We're on the side of the house where the Westmores' bedroom had been, but no windows. The other side of the house would've presented more difficulties. Much steeper, more trees, windows, the side porch where the Branches were sleeping. If the perp carried Ms. Robb outside, it would stand to reason it was on this side.

We make our way slowly down the hill, perspiration dotting Joe's forehead, his muscles straining. We finally reach the metal double doors of the basement. Wearing a latex glove, I remove the key ring from an evidence bag and find the basement key among several hanging together. The lock clicks open easily enough with little sound, and I swing the door open.

The musty, pungent smell hits us. It has probably been here for decades, adding a little to the stench after the years and animal carcasses had their turn. Mrs. Bradley said that no one went down here much anymore. No one has actually hunted here since Dr. Bradley's father, more than twenty years ago. And when the doctor and Mr. Westmore came up here to fish, they usually threw back their catch. They didn't clean the fish down here.

I flip on the overhead light, a dim, sickly fluorescent tube suspended on the low arched ceiling. It hums overhead, adding eerie background noise. The table, with its wall-mounted pegboard over it, sits just as we'd found it last time we were here. But forensics has been through, and tiny, yellow, numbered tents mark the areas where the spilled nails and box were found on the floor, as well as the drops of blood under the table.

"Creepy place," Agent Metz says.

"Yeah. But a perfect place to . . ." Chase says, coughs.

Because of the state of the body, it was impossible to tell if Ms. Robb had been raped, but there was some reason he brought her here. Maybe just to finish what he started in the road. Maybe she started to stir from the head injury. We'll never know unless he decides to tell us. But the important thing is that we find justice for her and her family by putting the bastard away for good.

Joe has finished looking around and rejoins us by the doors. "Let's walk over to the burial site." He picks up his bundle where he's laid it on the concrete floor next to the drain.

Outside the air is cold but fresh, and I draw a deep breath. We walk down the lawn, slipping in the snow. The footbridge is slick with a thin layer of ice, and we've got to hold on to the handrail to keep from falling. The river below is gray and, as it's late January, running fast with melted snow. The sound of the current makes conversation nearly impossible, so we silently press ahead and make our way to the spot where Ms. Robb's body spent the last six months.

Crime-scene tape marks off a rough rectangle. Agent Metz wipes the sleeve of her jacket across her mouth and nose. "Why bury her so close? Pretty sloppy, huh? Why didn't he go farther into the woods? It didn't take much erosion here to expose her."

I shake my head. "He might've been worried about time. He needed to get back inside, clean up, and slip back into bed before anyone noticed. The whole operation was pretty risky."

"Maybe that's what he liked," Chase says. "Doing this right under his friends' noses."

"Maybe," Joe says.

The area has been pretty well canvassed by the forensics team, so we head back across the bridge and up the sloping lawn to our vehicle.

Joe drops his weighted tarp, takes a deep breath, and wipes his hands on his jeans. "Okay, let's try this through the house this time."

We head down the driveway, and I unlock the door. I pause in the mudroom and point to the peg where the key ring would usually hang.

"Convenient," Joe says.

"Yeah. Mrs. Bradley said it was there for whoever needed it."

"Like a serial killer?" Agent Metz chuckles. "Here you go. Take the keys, and go find a victim, and end her life in our basement. The perfect host." We all groan. She's young, but she's got the gallows humor down pat.

"The first door on the right after the mudroom leads to the basement."

"The perp wouldn't have had to go through much of the house if he brought her through this way," Joe says. "Let's take a look."

We head down the basement steps. The light switch is easily accessible on the wall at the top. I'm in the lead, so I flick it on. The staircase isn't terribly steep or hard to maneuver. It looks like it was probably replaced in the last twenty or thirty years. Not original to the house. At the bottom, the light peters out, and we're in darkness.

Joe drops his tarp, and the cinder blocks make a scraping sound. He points to the faint light coming from the door at the far end. "So when he had her in the house and down here," Joe says, "I doubt anyone could've heard him once he got through the door to the tunnel." We follow as he leads us deeper into the basement and through the door. That ubiquitous smell increases as we approach the table and sink area. Cobwebs line the arched ceiling, and a constant drip echoes from somewhere. We stand silently, each wondering, I suspect, about Annalise Robb's last minutes in this dim cellar.

CHAPTER 55

Molly

It feels good to be home. Sadie and I walk through the house, and I open curtains and let in the sunshine. The Christmas tree still stands in the corner, and I head to the laundry room, where I've stashed the packing bins.

Before I get started on the tree, I sit cross-legged on the floor and reach for the basket on the hearth where I'd placed Christmas cards as they came in. I sift through until I find the one I'm looking for, a white card with a red barn on the front, next to a tree with a cardinal perched in its branches. Clear glitter falls from it as I peek inside. It wishes me a peaceful Christmas, full of love and joy, and is signed simply in a shaky hand: Sincerely, John and Margaret Castleberry.

Twenty-nine years ago, John Castleberry, a middle-aged farmer, had been out on an ATV, checking his crops, when he saw a blue car parked behind the abandoned house next to his fields. He'd written the town every year for ten years asking for the house to be torn down, as it was a hazard, but some official would write him back and say that they were trying to locate the owner, who'd moved to Florida years earlier. That was all Mr. Castleberry would hear about it until he wrote again the next year. But that hot July day, he saw a young man leave through the back door and climb into the vehicle. After the man had pulled away, John, fearful that teenagers were causing trouble inside the dilapidated house again, decided to investigate. Mr. Castleberry returned to his house and got his car and went back. He didn't find any teenagers, but instead heard a child's whimper coming from the cellar. Despite the state-wide search that had been ongoing for me and Indie, Mr. Castleberry was shocked when he found two little girls locked below. That was how I heard the story.

But I remember how the sunshine blinded my eyes when he carried me out, and the smell of his work shirt—dirt and sweat and tobacco. I clung to him and buried my face in his shoulder. I was tired and hungry and frightened.

He deposited me on his wife Margaret's ample lap in the passenger seat of their old Dodge and drove me to the police station. I didn't know why he left Indie behind, and I tried to tell him that she was still down there, but the words wouldn't come. Mrs. Castleberry hugged me tight and murmured that I was safe now.

Every year I send them a Christmas card and get one from them. They are the only people from back home, besides family, who know where I am. Their yearly Christmas card is all I hear from them, just enough to let me know they're still there, still thinking about me, and it makes me feel safe somehow. They must be well into their eighties, and I dread the time that will come when the cards stop.

Chapter 56

Rita

After conferring with Sheriff Skinner, we head to the Mountclair Tavern to catch a bite before heading back to Graybridge. The place isn't busy, a little early for dinner or drinks, but there are a couple of guys at the bar, drafts in front of them, engaged in conversation with Sid the bartender.

The waitress comes over, a smile on her face, probably grateful for something to do. She's young, a messy bun atop her head. She asks us for our drink order, all the while glancing at "FBI" printed on Joe's and Agent Metz's jackets. Her round blue eyes then wander to my badge and service weapon as I stand and strip off my coat. She scurries away but returns promptly with a New England IPA for each of us.

"What can I get you guys to eat?" she asks, a slight tremble in her voice. After writing down our orders on her notepad, she starts to walk away, but spins back around.

"Are you here about Annalise?" she asks Joe.

"Yes. Did you know her?"

"Everybody knew her." She puts a hand on her hip, glances over her shoulder. "I don't know if I should say anything. I mean, I don't want to overreact or get anybody in trouble."

Chase fumbles his phone out of his pocket.

"You know something that might help us?" I ask.

"Probably not." She blows out a breath, scattering her bangs. "I wasn't here. I wasn't working the night she disappeared, but something kinda strange happened before that."

I take out my notebook. "Why don't you tell us anyway."

"Okay."

Chase says, "You mind if I record you?" He holds up his phone.

She glances at Joe then back at me. "No. I guess not."

We have her state her name, which is Melissa Haskins, the date, yada, yada.

"Well, a couple of days before Annalise went missing—"

"What day was that?" Joe asks.

"Um. The second, I guess."

"You sure?"

She nods. "Yes. I went for a run after work."

"What time?"

"Just before dark. My mom told me not to go because it was getting late. But I said I'd hurry. I try to run four times a week. Well, I ran my usual route from my house to the dry goods store and back. It's about three and a half miles."

"Where's your house?" Joe asks.

She tilts her chin. "If you turn right out of the parking lot, opposite direction of Annalise's, go about three quarters of a mile and turn right again on Midline Road, that's where I live."

"Okay. You're running. When did it actually get dark? How far into your run?"

"By the time I got to the store and turned around, it was getting pretty dark."

"How dark?" I ask.

"Not quite all the way, but getting there." She bites her lips. "Well, I was on my road when I heard a car. Someone was behind me, driving really slow."

I lean forward. "Did he stop?"

"No. But he was definitely following me, going super slow." Her eyes start to tear up.

"Then what happened, Melissa?"

"I jumped off the asphalt and ran on the dirt and picked up the pace."

"Did you look back at the vehicle?"

"Just briefly. I was scared."

"What kind of vehicle was it?" I ask.

She takes a deep breath. "I don't know. The headlights were blinding me."

Joe leans toward her. "Was it a car?"

She shakes her head. "No. It was bigger. A truck maybe or an SUV."

"What color?"

"I couldn't really tell."

"Your best guess?"

"Black or dark blue?"

"Could it have been silver?" I ask.

"No. It was definitely a dark color."

I feel my pulse kick up. "How about the driver? Was he alone?"

"Yes. It looked like it. I only saw one guy."

"Did he get out of the vehicle?"

"No."

"Can you describe him at all? Anything?"

She shakes her head. "It was getting too dark, and the headlights were in my eyes."

"Then what happened?"

She sniffs. "I started running really fast and thinking I would head out through the woods if he stopped. But then another car came down the road behind him, and he sped off." She draws another deep breath.

"Did you tell Sheriff Skinner or anyone at the sheriff's department?"

"No." Her lips quiver. "Working here, I sometimes get guys hitting on me. No one local that I need to worry about, but sometimes guys from out of town get a little creepy. I guess I should've reported it."

Joe smiles a kind fatherly smile. "You're telling us now, Melissa."

"Does that help?"

"It does indeed," I say.

"I'm glad. I was starting to worry about it, and I was afraid Sherriff Skinner would be mad I didn't say anything at the time." She glances out the front window. "Is that all?"

"Yeah. For now," Joe says.

She smiles, relieved. "I'll go put your orders in."

I'm flipping quickly through my notes.

"Rita?" Joe asks.

I hold up my index finger until I find what I'm looking for and read aloud. "Mr. Westmore drives a black pickup. The Ferrises, a dark blue SUV, the Pearsons, a dark gray truck, Mr. Branch, a black SUV." I smile at Joe.

"Dr. Bradley?"

"A silver sedan."

CHAPTER 57

Molly

I'm feeling a rush of optimism after my trip to the prison. I definitely feel stronger in a real physical sense, and my mystery caller hasn't bothered me since I got back. I almost wish he would. I'm spoiling for a fight, as my Aunt Ellen would say.

I finished my lunch, and I'm cleaning up when my doorbell rings. I check my computer screen and see Josh standing on my porch. *Great.* I throw the dishes in the sink and let him in.

"Hey, Molly. Can we talk a minute?"

"Fine, Josh. What's up?"

He tips his head toward the kitchen, so I shut the door behind him and walk down the hall. We sit at the kitchen table.

He rubs his chin, glances toward the window. "I'm really sorry, you know, about what happened to you."

My spine stiffens. "I don't want to talk about that. It's behind me, okay?"

"Yeah, sure."

"What do you want?"

"I'm, uh, having a small birthday party for Kim on Saturday afternoon."

"Really? I guess you still haven't told her about you and Laken, right?"

He closes his eyes. "Hear me out, please."

I fold my arms. In the past, we've held a joint celebration for Kim and Jay, but this year, since Jay's birthday was a big one, I decided he needed his own special day.

"I know the timing's bad, but I don't want to just blow it off. Kim deserves something."

"Yeah, Josh, she does. When do you plan on telling her?"

"I'm just worried about the baby, Molly, okay?"

"She's past her first trimester. Doctor says everything's fine. You *have* broken it off with Laken, right?"

"Yes. Of course."

"So when are you going to talk to Kim?"

"Next Saturday. We'll have the party *this* Saturday. Give it a week, and I'll talk to her the following weekend. I don't want to spoil her birthday. My parents can take Willow, and I'll, I'll do it then."

I lean back in my chair. Shake my head. "I still can't believe this, Josh. How could you?"

He drops his head in his hands.

"Did you find a marriage counselor?" I ask. "Have a name anyway?"

"I'll ask Elise. She doesn't need to know the particulars, but she'll know somebody."

"Okay. But . . . ." I squeeze his arm, and his eyes meet mine. "If you don't tell Kim by next Saturday, I'll tell her myself."

Anger flashes in his eyes, and he shakes his arm free from my grip. "I'll do it, okay? I don't need your threats, Molly."

I stand and pace the kitchen. "So who are you inviting? *Laken and Cal?*"

"Just a few people. But I have to invite them. It'll seem strange if I don't. Laken's cool with everything. She actually took it better than I thought."

I lean against the counter and let go a disgusted breath. "So she wasn't destroyed by you dumping her. Go figure."

"Okay, I deserve your attitude. I get it. But just ease up. I'll do the right thing. Just give me a goddamn minute."

I don't dignify this with a response. "Who else is coming?"

"The usual, plus her parents and my sister. That's all probably."

"Okay, Josh. But if she doesn't know by next weekend . . ." I shake my finger at him.

He stands, nods. "Loud and clear, Molly. I'll see you around." There's a glint in his eye that sends a shiver down my spine. There's no doubt in my mind that we've gone from friends to enemies in the course of a week's time.

CHAPTER 58

Rita

When I pull up in front of my building, I see Collin sitting on the stoop, smoking a cigarette. He said he was quitting for the new year, but it didn't last. Hard to, I guess, when André is a smoker with no plans to give it up. Collin stubs his cigarette out quickly when he sees me coming up the walkway, as if I would scold him. I don't want him smoking, of course, since it's bad for his health, but he's a grown man, young, but grown, and I understand that we all have our little weaknesses. We all find ways to survive.

I remember Ma and Dad when Ricky died in Vietnam. The extended family descended like locusts, and the house was full of the smells of brewing coffee and the sounds of whispered conversations. The bottle of whiskey Dad kept on a high shelf in a kitchen cupboard was quickly emptied, and one relative or another would slip out to the liquor store for reinforcements. The first couple of weeks went by in a blur, with a houseful of people shedding tears, laughing even, as they talked about Ricky. But then after the funeral, it was as though a dark blanket covered everything. The house was deadly quiet, the relatives gone. We all went back to school. My sisters made excuses to stay out late, part-time jobs, friends' houses. But Danny, Jimmy, and I were too young for that, so we sat in their room and played Battleship for some reason, over and over again, until we were tired and cranky. My brothers would end up in a fight, wrestling on the floor, but at least fighting kept our minds off Ricky at least for a little while.

What we didn't know in the weeks after Ricky died was that another tragedy was on the horizon. Another blow to the McMahon family, one that waited like a greedy beast not content with one brother. In the spring, Jimmy started to feel tired all the time, and after a trip to old Dr. Doyle, nothing would be the same.

"Hey, Rita." Collin jumps up and holds the door for me. "How was work?"

"Fine. Busy."

He follows me into the foyer. "You want to come in?" I ask.

"Yeah. I guess. For a minute."

"So what's new?" I drop my satchel on the couch and shrug out of my jacket. "Haven't seen you around for a couple days."

"Yeah. I've been busy at the café, and we've got a couple big catering jobs this weekend, so we've been slammed." He moves a stack of newspapers and deposits himself in the armchair in the living room.

I lean over and unlace my boots. "You want something to drink?"

"Only if you do."

I slip my feet into my slippers, pad into the kitchen, and pour us each a glass of red.

"How is your case going?" he asks as I hand him his wine.

"Slow." I sigh. With Joe here, I'd hoped to get a solve quickly, but the lack of DNA and other clues is dragging things out.

"That's too bad. I feel sorry for Mrs. Bradley." He sets his glass on the end table and leans forward. "I saw a story about her on the news. Did you guys know who she was?"

"Not until recently. She's been keeping a low profile."

Collin shudders. "It's horrible what happened to her. Now this."

"Yeah. Trouble just seems to follow some people." It makes me uncomfortable to talk about Mrs. Bradley. Knowing her background just makes me feel more pressure to catch her husband's killer quickly. She's been through enough. "So what have you been doing besides work?" I ask.

Collin's gaze shifts to the door and back. "Mrs. Antonelli had me down to make gnocchi."

"Right. How did that go?"

"Awkward."

"Why's that?"

"She invited her granddaughter. A nurse from New York who just moved to town. I guess her longtime boyfriend dumped her."

"Oooh."

"Yeah. She was really sweet, though. I complimented her shoes. She was wearing these really cute Christian Louboutin pumps. Later, she cornered me in the hall and said, 'Sorry about my nonnie. She's clueless.' "

I smile. Collin's sensitive and yearning, it seems to me. Like most of us, I guess. I worry about him and André sometimes. While Collin is twenty-nine, André is in his mid-thirties, born in Paris to an American mother, an actress who pops up occasionally in old made-for-TV movies. André's traveled the world, speaks three languages, and is constantly on the go. Sometimes in the warm weather, I open my kitchen window, and I smell André's cigarette, hear him on the fire escape talking on his phone, switching from French to English to Spanish on the turn of a dime. He's a nice man, but there's a certain carelessness about him, and I can't help but worry that Collin's going to be hurt someday.

Collin and I have a second glass of wine and laugh about Mrs. Antonelli and her numerous extended family members. Nothing mean, but snarky enough to get us giggling like fools, just blowing off steam.

CHAPTER 59

Molly

Saturday afternoon, Willow and two of her older cousins greet me at the door. I don't want to be here. It's difficult to look into my friend's eyes, knowing what I know about her husband. Not to mention that everyone at the party, thanks to the media, knows who I am now. Knows Melinda Wright.

The girls are all smiles; the oldest, a middle schooler with long brown hair, offers to place my present on the table. I reluctantly give it up, feeling more exposed without the brightly wrapped box to hide behind. And I'd left Sadie at home since Willow is allergic, and that makes me feel exposed as well. Willow slips her small, sweaty hand into mine and peers up at me with Kim's large brown eyes. It's as if she knows my fears, as though we're kindred souls; maybe we are. Her short life has been marked by challenges, and crowds are tough for her too, even if they are friends and relatives. I take a deep breath. If she can be brave, I can too.

The family room is alive with laughter and movement. Kim's parents sit side by side on the sofa. I haven't seen them since Jay's funeral. So much has happened since then. Kim's dad relates a story with arms waving, his audience captive. They're a happy family. Growing up, I spent a lot of time at their house and always felt envious. The solid ordinariness of them. Strong, supportive, joking. There were no skeletons in their many closets. No therapy appointments noted on the kitchen calendar, no walking on eggshells while talking around the dinner table. They were the family I'd always wanted us to be.

Josh is rushing drinks to and from the kitchen. Kim jumps up from her chair and moves to my side. She looks beautiful, her long dark hair falling in waves over her shoulders, her eyes shining. She's totally oblivious to her husband's treachery, and I feel guilt throb in my stomach as she squeezes me in her arms and whispers in my ear.

"I'm so glad you're here." She takes me by the hand. "Let's get you a glass of wine."

I wave and nod to everyone as we head for the other room.

Cal and Hayes are sitting at the kitchen table drinking beer. They both look at me with unsure smiles, not knowing what to do or say, I guess, but I'm not going to talk about Melinda Wright. Not here, not now.

The wine is perfect, tangy and rich. I take another sip. "I need to run to the restroom." I say, taking my glass with me. I walk down the hallway to the powder room and run into Josh.

He pastes a smile on his face. "Glad you're here, Molly."

I bet. I noticed that Laken and her boys weren't among the throng in the family room. "Where's Laken?" I can't resist asking.

Josh frowns, lowers his voice. "Cal said she took the boys and went to her parents' house on the Cape for the weekend."

I raise my eyebrows. "Huh, well, I guess that makes today a little easier for you."

Josh clears his throat. "I promise, okay? Let's just enjoy Kim's party." He brushes past me, nearly spilling my wine. I take another big sip.

When I leave the powder room, Hayes is waiting just outside. "Hey," I say. "Where's Alice?"

"Um, upstairs with some of the kids." He places a hand on my arm. "I'm so sorry, Molly. I wish you'd told me. Maybe I could've helped."

People are naïve, and I shake my head. "No, you couldn't have, Hayes. It's my business, and I didn't want anyone to know, you understand?"

I see the hurt in his eyes and know I'm being an ass, but I can't help it. The only thing I wanted from Graybridge, from my friends, was anonymity. I didn't want to be defined by my victimhood. Now that's over. I never wanted to be seen through that lens, yet I can't seem to escape it. Confronting my abuser helped in some primal way, made me feel stronger, more in control, but now I'm faced with the other part of the equation, moving forward, facing my friends, and I'm not sure yet how to do that.

He drops his hand. "I care about you, Molly. I'm here like always."

I take a breath and nod. "Thanks, Hayes. I don't mean to be rude. Maybe we'll talk about it someday. But right now, I'm just trying to figure things out." I walk back down the hall and join the group in the family room. No time like the present to put on a brave face. I listen to Kim's dad relate another story and laugh with the rest. I drain my wineglass and head to the kitchen for a refill.

Cal is standing before the open fridge, selecting another beer. He sees me out of the corner of his eye. "Hey, you want more wine?" He closes the door and picks up the bottle from the counter.

"Sure." I hold out my glass, and he fills it nearly to the rim.

Scott walks in. "Got another beer in there?" he asks Cal, who hands him a colorful can. Elise appears behind him, a gold and silver gift bag in her hands. They must've just gotten here. She lays the present on the table. "Molly, glad you're here. Corrine said you'd gone out of town for a couple days."

"Yes. I had to get away." Her eyes run over me, assessing. "It was just what I needed," I add.

"That's good. Rest is vital."

"How's the case coming along?" Scott asks. "The cops find anything new?"

I shake my head. "Not that they've told me."

"They talked to all of us. Did you know that?" Cal says, eyes narrowing. He leans against the counter.

"About what?"

"Last summer. The night of the Fourth when that woman was killed."

"Huh."

Scott sips his beer. "You still need that window replaced?"

"Yes. At some point. I'll let you know."

Kim walks in, with Willow behind her. "Juice, Mommy," Willow says.

"Yes, sweetie. I'll get it." While Kim pours Willow's drink, Josh comes in.

"Time for cake?" he asks, his eyes glancing at the clock. Kim nods and starts getting out the plates and flatware.

It all seems reminiscent of Jay's party, and it's hard to believe that was only a few weeks ago. So much has changed.

Josh carries the cake into the dining room, and we all gather around and sing. Kim bends over, eyes shining, and blows out the candles. I wonder if she made a wish. I would have.

The afternoon bleeds into evening, and I've had a little too much wine while dodging everyone who tried to maneuver me into an uncomfortable conversation.

I give Kim a hug. "I have to get going. I need to walk Sadie."

She whispers, "Call me any time if you need to talk."

"I will." I scurry outside and take a deep breath, hoping the cold air sobers me up. I'm glad to be out of there and on my way back to my house and my dog.

* * *

Sadie and I hurry down the sidewalk. It's dark, and I don't want to be out here too long. At least the media hasn't realized I'm back yet, but that will probably change. Corrine said they were camped in front of her building for a couple days after I left, until they figured out that I wasn't there or at least wasn't coming out. The traffic is light. It's dinnertime, and most people are home or out at a restaurant. We approach the gas station, and I stand still for a couple of minutes. Maybe I ought to go in and pick up some snacks for the night. My pantry is just about bare. Two young men exit the building and glance in my direction. They're muffled up in coats and gloves, hats pulled low. They light cigarettes, smoke tendrils wafting into the night, and jump into a pickup truck.

I hesitate a moment longer, then Sadie and I go inside the store. It's warm and a little busy. I wend my way to the snack aisle and select a bag of Oreos and a couple of giant-size Milky Way bars. Might as well go whole hog while I'm at it. I pay for my treats, and Sadie and I head outside.

I hear a woman shriek behind me, and I freeze, but she's laughing, I realize. Sadie and I start back down the sidewalk, away from the lights of the gas station. There's an alley, then a vacant commercial building, before the houses start up.

It's full dark, and there are places between the streetlights, lengths of sidewalk completely in the shadow. I hurry Sadie along when I hear footsteps behind me. I pick up the pace, but the person behind me matches my stride. My heart drums loudly, and I walk more quickly. He's too close. I hear his heavy breath. Then a strong arm circles my waist and a gloved hand crushes my mouth. I try to scream, but my breath is trapped, my heart racing. Is he my caller or someone else? I drop Sadie's leash and struggle to pull away. I kick, but his grip only tightens, and he's pulling me into the alley.

No, no, no! I won't let anyone hurt me. Not again. I make a sound like a rabid animal and reach back and tear at the man's face, but my gloves shield my fingernails. He rips my jacket away, and I take a step to run, but then I feel a sharp jab in my arm. Cold waves surge through my veins, and I know I'm sinking. I stagger a step or two, but he pulls me close against his chest. I slip through his grasp and tumble face-first to the ground, unable to right myself, unable to move. I taste dirt. Just like before.

CHAPTER 60

Rita

I was in court yesterday and anxious to get back to the station and get back to work on the Bradley case. Unfortunately, I got tangled up in one thing after another, as sometimes happens, and Friday was a bust. So I came in this morning, hoping to make up for my unfruitful day yesterday.

Joe came in after noon and worked in the conference room for a while. We all feel a sense of urgency over the Robb-Bradley case, but a certain malaise too—looking at each other for something, anything that'll move the investigation along. Nothing much has happened all day, and I collect my things to go home.

Joe pops his head in my office. "Want to go for a drink, Rita? Saturday night, after all."

"Sounds good. Let me clean up my desk first." I've got papers everywhere, my notebook open. Joe walks in and peruses my work, runs a finger over a sketch of Mrs. Bradley.

"What's with all the drawings?"

"I like to doodle. Helps me think." Seems to me he asked me that the last time we worked together.

Noise comes from the squad room, and we head out in the hall to investigate. Chase is leading a man toward the interview rooms. Joe and I follow.

Chase meets us in the hall, having deposited the man inside. "Who's that?" I ask.

"I found him lurking around Mrs. Bradley's house."

"And you were there why?"

He shrugs. "I was in the neighborhood and thought I'd drive by. I've been doing that on occasion," he adds quietly.

"So who is he?"

"You want to talk to him with me?"

"Sure." I glance at Joe.

"I'll let you two handle it, unless you need me."

"We've got it," I say.

The man is thirty-something, shaved head, skinny jeans, and a leather jacket. He slouches in his chair as though we're a big pain in his ass.

I introduce myself and we sit. "And you are?"

"Brian Fleck."

Chase says, "I found Mr. Fleck standing across the street from the Bradley residence. Then I saw him on her porch, looking in the windows."

"I told you I was trying to contact Mrs. Bradley."

"For what purpose?" I ask.

"Look, I didn't do anything illegal, okay? I agreed to come in and talk so we can clear this up."

"All right. Good deal. So answer the question."

He sits up and purses his lips. "I would like to ask Mrs. Bradley if she'd be interested in collaborating on a book."

"You're a writer then?"

He sets his backpack on the floor and fishes out his wallet, hands me a business card. It's decorated with red splotches that are supposed to look like blood. He apparently writes for a crime e-magazine.

"Yes. I write articles on current crimes and old interesting cases. But I think Mrs. Bradley's story warrants a book, and I thought I'd be a good candidate to write it."

"Okay." I glance at Chase.

"He said he's been in the area for a couple of weeks."

"Have you called Mrs. Bradley?" I ask.

"I tried a couple of times, but she hasn't answered. That's why I've been trying to catch her at home."

Chase huffs out a breath. "Haven't been harassing her, have you?"

"No, of course not."

"She might not see it that way," I say.

He leans toward us, the eager reporter. "Someone's going to write a book about her, and I think I'm the best person to do that. I feel for the woman. She's been through hell—"

"You got that right," Chase says.

"She could make some big-time money on this too." He slouches back in his chair. "She might need it, now that she's a widow."

"Okay."

"Look, I haven't done anything illegal. I'm trying to do the decent thing by talking to you guys. I don't want to be bothered again for doing my job."

"Then don't bother Mrs. Bradley," Chase says, voice slightly raised. I nudge him with my knee.

"Just don't push her, Mr. Fleck," I say. "Stay within the letter of the law. If she wants to talk to you, she will. If not, leave her alone, and we'll leave you alone. But if your attention turns to harassment, that's a different beast."

He stands, slings his backpack over his shoulder. "Fair enough."

Chase heads home, and I walk into the conference room where Joe works, bent over his laptop. I scoop my freshly dyed hair over my shoulders and take a deep breath. Joe being here, us working together again, has brought some of those old feelings to the surface. But damn, I like my life the way it is. I sigh. Maybe I'm just being a coward. In any case, I can't think about my personal life right now. Lauren walks by, and I tap her shoulder. "Want to head over to Mac's with Joe and me?"

CHAPTER 61

Molly

The smell of decay wakes me from a deep slumber. I feel wretched, hungover. Then I remember the alley and the man. I shudder. Where am I? There's little light, and I'm shaking, freezing, my nose running. On my right wrist, there's a handcuff attached to a chain. I follow the metal with my left hand. The chain is anchored around a pipe that runs along a cement wall. I struggle to my feet and pull like a wild animal caught in a trap, but I can't get away. Tears slip down my cheeks, and I clear my raw throat to scream, but my voice only echoes, bounces off the walls. I feel faint. My legs are like rubber, so I slide back down to the floor and take a couple of deep, fetid breaths.

There's dim light coming from a small window high on the wall across the room. It must be morning. My clothes are undisturbed, so I wasn't raped. I shut my eyes and swallow grateful tears. So why am I here? My caller's words come back to me.

I won't be happy until you're back in that cellar for good.

That's where I am, in a cellar. The mustiness and mold, water dripping somewhere in the distance. I'm shivering, and there are a couple of thick blankets on the floor next to me, as though my captor was somewhat afraid I'd freeze to death.

A wave of nausea flutters through my stomach, and I swallow down bile. Where is Sadie? I hope she's okay. Thoughts of something bad happening to my dog send more tears down my cheeks.

I sniff, clear my throat, and try to do an inventory. I don't have anything with me. No keys, no wallet, no phone. There's an old toilet and sink near where I'm chained. I pull myself up on the sink and turn the faucet handle. It screeches, but nothing comes out, and in the dim light I see rusty stains in the basin. The toilet bowl has water in it, but it's dark, as though it's been there twenty years.

I walk in the other direction, as far as I can away from the toilet and sink, until I reach the end of my chain tether. There doesn't seem to be anything else down here. Through the gloom, I look for the stairs, but don't see any, only an open door high up where the stairs should be. The end of a ladder protrudes from the floor above. I'm trapped. Even if I can get the handcuff off, I can't get out.

My stomach pitches. I feel sick and collapse back down to the floor. I'm woozy. Like before. Like when I was six years old. Then I remember when the man grabbed me, he stuck me in my arm with something. I wonder what it was and hope it isn't something terrible. I rub my face with stiff cold fingers. What am I going to do?

This place is old, but not as old as the farmhouse was, at least as much as I can remember. There was no bathroom there, and the floor was dirt. Indie and I had peed our pants. That I remember, and that had made him angry, but we were just little girls. This place is different. I have a bathroom, such as it is, and that almost makes me laugh. The caller said he wanted me back in the cellar. So here I am. A new cellar but trapped just the same.

CHAPTER 62

Rita

Chase is off this morning, but Joe and Agent Metz meet me at the station. I've got hazelnut muffins that André made, and Joe brought coffees. Work sometimes feels awfully civil even when we're dealing with the worst of humanity. It's a strange balance that ultimately unnerves some people and sends them skittering for work outside of law enforcement, like my ex-husband, Ed. Four and a half years on the force, and he was done.

We sit in the conference room, where we can spread out. I've drawn a red line through Dr. Bradley's name on the Robb suspect list. Don't know that everyone agrees with me, but I'm making a statement by eliminating him. We need to do a deeper dive on the four remaining suspects. We're still hopeful that there's DNA somewhere that will point the finger at one of them, but until then, all we have is old-fashioned police work.

My phone vibrates, dances across the table, drawing my concentration from the notes I was rereading. I don't recognize the number but answer anyway. "Detective Myers."

"Is this Detective Myers?" a weak voice asks. *Didn't I just say that?*

"Speaking. How can I help you?"

"This is Gladys Murray, Detective."

"Yes." The old lady who lives next door to the Bradleys.

"I think something might be wrong here." I put my phone on speaker, glance at Joe, whose dark eyes meet mine.

"What's happened?"

"Well, Percy went to our front door and started scratching a while ago, and he never does that. When I opened the door, Sadie was standing there."

"Who's Sadie?"

"Mrs. Bradley's dog. She had her leash on, and I thought she got away from Mrs. Bradley. She walks her by the house a couple times a day, but it was really early, not when she usually goes by. Anyway, Percy and I took Sadie over to the house. Mrs. Bradley's car's in the driveway. I rang the bell several times, knocked, but no one answered. She seems to take good care of her dog, Detective. I don't think she'd let her loose like that on purpose. You suppose something's not right?"

"We're on the way, Mrs. Murray." Joe and Agent Metz start to gather their things.

"I've got Sadie here with me."

"That's great. We'll be there shortly." I disconnect the call. Throw my phone in my satchel.

Joe drives, and I call Corrine Alworth on the way over.

"You don't know where she is?" I ask.

"She should be home," Mrs. Alworth says. "The neighbor found her dog *wandering*?"

"That's what she said, and no one answered the door when she knocked."

Mrs. Alworth blows out a ragged breath. "I talked to her yesterday. She was going to a party at her friend's house, then she was staying home for the night. Where could she be?" Her frustration and fear burst through in her words.

"Whose party?"

"Kim Pearson's."

"Who else was there?"

"Her regular group, I think."

"Okay. We're on our way to her house now to check it out. Call if you hear from her." Now I'm starting to sweat. Did we take the harassing phone calls seriously enough, especially with all that's gone on? *Shit.* I direct Joe to turn at the light, and we're heading down the Bradleys' street.

I try Mrs. Bradley's cell and landline again, but no answer again.

Mrs. Murray, flanked by the two dogs, stands on her porch, leans over the rail to watch us as we knock on Mrs. Bradley's door. Agent Metz and Joe circle the house, but soon return to the front.

"Anything?" I ask.

"Looks locked up, undisturbed," Joe says.

"Christ." We turn and look up the street as if Mrs. Bradley might come walking down the road. Maybe she will, but my gut tells me otherwise. There's an emptiness at the house, as though it's been abandoned. We walk over to talk to Mrs. Murray, and she verifies that Mrs. Bradley walks her dog no earlier than nine a.m., and it's barely seven-thirty. We also see that the dog is gentle, easily handled; it's not likely she would've pulled away from Mrs. Bradley and run off.

Joe drops down on his haunches, pets the dog, and examines her paws. "Looks like she might've been out a while," he says, standing. "Her feet are pretty muddy, and"—he runs a hand over her back—"her coat's pretty wet, like she might've been lying in the snow. How long has the dog been here?"

Mrs. Murray looks at her watch. "I called right away after we got back from Mrs. Bradley's place, so not long. Do you think something's happened to her?"

I shake my head. "We don't know. Where does she walk when she goes by your house? Which direction?"

"Well." Mrs. Murray wrings her hands, anxious to help. "She

walks up toward the corner, most days. That's what I've noticed anyway."

"Toward the gas station?"

"Yes." She points a skinny, knotted hand. "Up that way, toward the intersection."

"When does she usually walk the dog?"

"I see her morning and evening most days when I'm around."

"What time in the evenings?"

"About dinnertime, I guess."

"Did you see her last evening?"

"I'm afraid I didn't. I'm not always in the front room where I can see her, Detective," Mrs. Murray says, as if she's failed in her duties somehow

"That's fine. We appreciate your help." We start down the stairs.

"I'll keep Sadie here with me if that's all right," she calls behind us.

"That would be a big help," I say. We take off at a brisk pace, following the path we hope Mrs. Bradley took.

"Alison, would you see if the Fergusons are home?" I point to the gray house next to Mrs. Murray's. "They have a security camera. See if they've got Mrs. Bradley on tape walking by."

"Sure." Agent Metz peels off and heads up the porch steps.

Joe and I continue up the sidewalk. Traffic is picking up, horns honking in the distance, engines rumbling as cars file past, leaving exhaust in their wake. The traffic light up ahead cycles through yellow to red to green. A moist bitter wind picks up, and I wish I'd remembered my gloves.

The gas station is busy, people streaming in and out. Dirty snow lies in piles along the edges of the parking lot. The young man at the counter is wearing a reflective vest over a lumpy hoodie and a knit cap pulled low over his ears.

I show him my badge and identify us. "When did you start your shift?" I ask.

"Five. Is there a problem?" His lips are chapped, nose runny from the cold.

"No. Just looking for a woman walking a dog." I take out Mrs. Bradley's picture and show it to the kid. He takes a good look.

"I don't remember seeing her."

"She'd have had a black dog with her."

He shakes his head.

"Can we take a look at your video?"

"Boss is in the office." He tips his head. We walk down a short hall past stacked cases of soda and rap on a half-open door.

Mr. Armini is a short man with dark hair sprouting from the sides of his head, nothing on top. His forehead is a mass of horizontal wrinkles. He listens and pulls up the tape.

Luckily, he's agreeable. We've helped him out a time or two with unruly customers. We view the tape quickly. Nothing this morning, so we back it up to last night, and there she is, perusing the snack aisle. At six thirty-four, she's paying for her items at the counter. She looks fine, not like anything is amiss. The dog sits placidly at her side. Then they leave and head across the parking lot toward home.

We canvass the outside of the store. There's a bit of an alley behind it, but we don't find anything but some debris, Styrofoam cups, and a few plastic bags blown against the back wall of the gas station.

I stomp around, trying to collect my thoughts, shiver in the cold. I reach into my satchel, pull out my phone, and call Mrs. Bradley again—and bingo!

We hear it. Joe and I march steadily toward the sound, pull up at a dumpster.

"*Shit.*"

I call the station and request a forensics team.

After two hours of searching, Mrs. Bradley's phone and wallet are found, but no trace of the woman herself. So Joe and I head back to the station to regroup while the team completes their work.

Bob meets us in the conference room, and we brief him on our findings.

"Shit," he says, and rubs his face with a big meaty hand.

That about sums it up, I think to myself.

Agent Metz has returned from talking to the Fergusons. Their surveillance tape shows Mrs. Bradley walking by last evening, but nothing after that, which confirms what we suspected. She disappeared on her way home from her walk.

Corrine Alworth comes tearing into the station and bursts into the conference room, leaving the officer who was escorting her in her wake.

"Did you find anything?" she asks, her face taut with worry.

We run through everything we've got so far, not a reassuring list.

"What are you doing to find her?" Mrs. Alworth yells.

Bob comes through the door and puts a hand on her shoulder. "Why don't you come down to my office? We'll talk."

She looks at me, then Joe, but finally acquiesces.

CHAPTER 63

Rita

After the chief returns, he calls everyone together and runs through a strategy for finding Mrs. Bradley. Lauren and even Detective Schmitt are involved. They've been tasked with organizing the search, dividing the area around the gas station into quadrants and assigning teams.

Joe and I head out to question Mrs. Bradley's friends. They might have been the last people to see her at the party yesterday, and four of them are murder suspects besides.

Mr. Ferris answers the door, looking bleary-eyed, dark hair disheveled.

"To what do I owe the pleasure?" He smiles grimly at me and Joe.

"We'd like to ask you a few questions if you have a minute," I say.

He looks back over his shoulder as if seeking permission from someone inside. He doesn't saying anything, just opens the door wider and walks away. We follow him into the living room, where he flops on the couch.

"What can I do for you, Detectives? Or is it Agents?"

"Either's fine," Joe says, keeping his voice even despite

Mr. Ferris's obnoxious tone. "We need to know where you were yesterday."

Mr. Ferris sits up and squeezes his eyes under his glasses. "Yesterday? Why?"

"Just run through it for us," I say.

He blows out a breath. "Okay. I hung around the house all morning. Went to Kim Pearson's birthday party in the afternoon."

The house seems eerily quiet. "Where's your wife?" I ask.

"She's not here." Mr. Ferris rubs his chin like he can't quite figure out what happened to her. But then his eyes meet mine. "She's visiting her parents on the Cape. The boys wanted to see their grandparents."

"Huh. They go to the Pearsons' party before they left?"

"No. They left Friday night."

"You went alone?"

"*Yes.*" He looks worn out, and his voice and body language tell me there might be trouble between him and the Mrs.

"Lots of January birthdays in your little group," I say.

"Just the two."

"Was Mrs. Bradley at the party?"

"Yes. She was there."

"What time did you leave?"

He lets go a deep breath. "I don't know. Five maybe? A little after? Why? What's this all about?"

"You go straight home after you left the Pearsons' house?" Joe asks, his low-timbred voice stern.

"Yes."

"Then what did you do?"

He shrugs. "Watched TV. ESPN. Had a beer and a snack. Went to bed around eleven." He tosses his glasses on the coffee table. "*Why?*"

"Mrs. Bradley is missing," I say, watching his expression closely.

His gaze settles on the floor between his feet. "Seriously? Like no one knows where she is?"

"That appears to be the case. You wouldn't have any ideas, would you?"

"No. Did you check with her sister? She's probably with her."

"Been there. Done that, Mr. Ferris." I sketch his glasses in my notebook. "Can anybody verify you were home all night?"

He spreads out his hands as though he's showing us they're empty, nothing here. "No. I was home watching TV."

"No phone calls?"

He shakes his head.

"Didn't call your wife to say good night?"

His jaw tightens. "No."

The Pearsons' place is next on our list, and Joe and I drive the ten minutes in silence, both of us locked in on the task at hand.

Mrs. Pearson answers the door, a smile on her pixie face. "Yes?" Her mouth turns down quickly when she realizes who's standing on her porch. "Has something happened?"

"You might say that," I reply. Joe gives me a sideways glance. "May we come in?"

We stand in the kitchen, where kids' toys are scattered around the floor. Straggly dolls rest in a heap by the back door. Some colorful plastic items of unknown purpose are under the table. There's half a cake sitting on the counter, with pink frosting smeared on the white cabinet below. Outside the French doors, Mr. Pearson and a little girl are building a snowman.

"Mrs. Pearson, when was the last time you saw or spoke to Mrs. Bradley?" Joe asks.

Her delicate hand reaches for her throat. "What happened?"

"We don't know," Joe says. "No one has seen her or spoken to her since yesterday evening."

"Maybe she went out of town again, but she didn't say anything to me." Mrs. Pearson's eyes glisten with tears. "Corrine doesn't know where she is?"

I shake my head.

"Do you think something . . . happened to her?"

"We don't know," Joe reiterates. "What was the last contact you had with her?"

Mrs. Pearson paces by the counter. "She was here yesterday at my party. She was fine."

"What time did she leave?"

"I'm not sure. She had to walk her dog. She needed to get home."

"That was the last you heard from her?"

"Yes." Mrs. Pearson stands still as a pointer. "Oh my God. You don't think whoever killed Jay . . ."

"We don't have any reason to think that," I say. "She might've just needed to get away, like you said." There's no sense in scaring the bejesus out of Mrs. Pearson. That won't help anyone. "Did you leave the house yesterday after your party?"

"No. We stayed right here. We cleaned up, and I gave Willow her bath."

"What about your husband? He go anywhere last night?" I ask.

She looks out the back door, where Mr. Pearson is holding his little girl up so she can place an old baseball cap on the snowman's head. "Just to take my parents home. My dad likes to have a few drinks, and we don't like them driving."

"What time was that?"

She glances at a decorative clock on the wall above the table. "I'm not sure. Five-thirty?"

"Where do they live?"

"About a fifteen-minute drive, not far."

"He come right back?"

Mrs. Pearson hesitates, one hand gripping the back of a chair. "No. He said he might run some errands while he was out."

"What time did he return?"

"I'm really not sure. It was a busy day. Chaotic. Lots of kids over running around. You know how that is."

"Uh huh."

She puts her hands on the sides of her forehead momentarily, as though she needs to organize her thoughts. "I was bathing Willow. Then I put her to bed."

"He still wasn't home?" Joe asks, an eyebrow raised. He walks the length of the kitchen, stops to peer out the back door.

"It wasn't that late," she says. "Willow was worn out. Parties are tough on her." She clasps her hand over her mouth, mumbles, "You don't think my husband . . ."

Joe steps aside, and Mr. Pearson and his daughter come through the back door, red-cheeked and smiling until they see us.

"Mr. Pearson," I say, "your wife was telling us that you ran your in-laws home after the party yesterday."

"Yeah." He stands still while the little girl starts peeling off her coat and mittens, dropping them on the floor. "Why?"

"You come straight home?"

He glances at his wife. "No. I had some running around to do." His gaze shifts between me and Joe, not settling on either of us.

"Where did you go?" Joe asks, folding his arms and leaning against the counter.

Pearson walks over to his wife, stands beside her. "What's this all about?"

"Molly's missing," she says, her voice catching in her throat.

"What? Really?"

"So," I say, "where did you go after your wife's party?"

He drops down on a kitchen chair and pulls off his gloves, chucks them in the middle of the table. "I didn't see Molly, if that's what you want to know." His obnoxious tone is in full force.

"So where were you?"

"Walmart." He smiles. "But they didn't have what I was looking for, so I went to Lowe's."

"What were you looking for?" I tap my pencil against my notebook. This guy is lying through his teeth.

"Tools." His gaze shifts to his wife.

"Okay. What time did you get home?"

He rubs his hand over his mouth. "I don't know, Detective."

"You buy anything?" Joe asks.

"They didn't have what I wanted."

"So you don't have a receipt?"

"No."

"Which stores did you go to, Mr. Pearson?" I ask. "We'll take a look at their security footage."

He slams his chair back and jumps up. "I don't give a good goddamn if you believe me or not. If Molly's missing, I didn't have anything to do with it. She's probably just out of town again. Jesus." He stomps out of the room. Mrs. Pearson's little girl has buried her face against her mother's stomach.

No one is home at the Westmores' place, so I call Dr. Westmore as we sit in her driveway, looking up at her grand house.

"Detective? What can I do for you?"

"We're looking into a new development here. Where were you and your husband yesterday?"

"Yesterday? We were at Kim Pearson's house in the afternoon. Then home. Why?"

"You go straight home after the party? Stay in all night?"

"Yes, Detective. What's this about?"

"Mrs. Bradley is missing." I hear her breath catch.

"Her sister doesn't know where she is?"

"No."

Dr. Westmore's voice wavers. "Oh my God."

"Do you know something that might help us locate her?"

"No. No, I don't. Do you think something's happened to her?"

"We don't know. Can you and your husband meet us at the police station? We'd like to talk to you."

"Yes. Of course, but I'm a couple hours away at my sister's house. And Scott, he was called out on a job. One of his client's had an emergency. A retaining wall collapsed or something. I'll call him and let him know."

"This is urgent, Doctor."

"I'm on my way."

I end the call, and Joe backs down the long driveway.

That just leaves Hayes Branch on our list of suspects in the Robb murder. Maybe Mrs. Bradley's disappearance is unrelated, but we need to make sure. Something tells me, though, that all of this mess is connected.

Joe and I drive out of Graybridge and take the highway two exits west of town. The Branches own multiple properties in the Boston metro area, but Hayes and his daughter live in the old family estate. His illustrious mother prefers a Manhattan apartment most of the year.

Mr. Branch greets us at the door. His face is pale, and his hair is a tangled nest, as though he tossed and turned all night and didn't bother with a comb this morning. He's wearing a faded gray Harvard sweatshirt and well-worn jeans. He escorts us to a fancy living room with soaring ceilings and large oil paintings on the walls. Embers glow in a huge fireplace that sits at one end of the room.

We ask him the same questions we've asked the others, and he says nothing that helps, other than he doesn't have an alibi. He says that, after the party, he dropped Alice off at a friend's house for a sleepover, then came home. He was home by himself the rest of the night.

He drops his head in his hands. "Do you think she's all right?" His voice is tight and teary.

"We hope so."

Media trucks are lined up like soldiers in formation in front of the police station when we return. Joe and I drive around the building and go in through the back entrance. The place is buzzing like a hive, alive with anxiety and the smell of bad coffee. Bob stands in his office doorway, phone clenched between his jaw and shoulder. He motions us inside, closes the door, and throws his phone on his desk.

"Find anything?" he asks, settling in his chair.

"We can't eliminate Pearson, Ferris, or Branch. We've still got to talk to Mr. Westmore," I say. "But the wife says they were home last night. He's out on a job now." My eyes meet Joe's. "She's calling him, and hopefully he'll be here soon so we can question him."

Bob's face falls as though he was hoping, praying maybe, that we'd be back with the answers we need to find Mrs. Bradley.

I shake my head. "After the Pearson party, none of them has a solid alibi for last night."

Joe leans forward. "They all had opportunity."

"For Chrissake," Bob says. "You guys sure that one of those men abducted Mrs. Bradley?"

I sigh. "We're not sure of anything, Chief."

He rubs his face with his hand while his landline phone rings.

"Anything here?" I ask. "Any developments."

"Not a damn thing." Bob stands, his breath coming in deep, worrisome gasps. "Okay, just keep at it." We leave as he answers his phone.

CHAPTER 64

Molly

"Melinda?"

My eyes slit open. I've been sitting here all day, huddled in the blankets, watching the faint light in the far window dim until it disappeared, thinking, crying, trying to figure out how to get out of here.

"Melinda?"

Keith? My stomach drops. How can that be? He's in prison. He can't get out. It's my imagination. Thoughts of Keith Russell have flitted through my mind all day, despite my efforts to keep them at bay. It's as though he inhabits the mold and decay in this basement, caught here like a demon spirit.

"Answer me, little girl." His voice sing-songs.

I stay quiet in the dark, leaning against the wall. My heart thumps so heavily my body shakes with each pulse.

"Melinda?"

I hear the ladder scrape against the floor above.

"I just want to talk. For now," he says.

It sounds like Keith, but not. Someone else. Someone familiar. I hear his footfalls slap against the ladder steps. I hear him advance toward me across the cement floor. A flashlight beam sweeps the basement, blinding me, then he switches it off. Despite the cold, sweat drips down my back.

He's next to me now, breathing heavily, sitting beside me like two people just hanging out. I want to tear at him, fight my way out, but what will that get me? I close my eyes to push back tears and hope I don't have a heart attack from sheer terror. Does that really happen?

"Let's talk," he whispers. "But don't scream. It's not worth the effort. Have you tried that already? I bet you did, and no one came, did they? Just like before. This whole street is deserted. This is an old row house. The whole neighborhood is going to be demolished soon. But it's perfect for us."

His voice. I know him. He's sitting so close to me my shoulder touches his arm. I start to hyperventilate and have to talk myself down. I can do this. I can survive—again.

He clutches my chin and turns my face toward him. Through the darkness, my eyes meet his, and my heart seems to drop out of my chest. My captor is my friend.

CHAPTER 65

Rita

It's early evening by the time Dr. Westmore arrives at the station. We have her escorted to an interview room, and Joe and I join her. This is as frazzled as I've seen the doctor. Her hair looks like it needs a good brushing, her clothes are wrinkled, and she smells distinctly of cigarettes.

"Any news?" she asks.

"No," I say. "Where's your husband?"

She pulls her phone from her purse, scans the screen. There's a furrow between her eyebrows as she types. "I've left him several messages." Her red-rimmed eyes meet mine. "He's not always where he has a signal, but he'll get back to me as soon as he can, Detective." She sticks her phone in her jacket pocket. Her fingers twitch as if yearning for a cigarette.

I ask her again where they were after the party last night, and she insists they were at home. That's it. She's his alibi.

Dr. Westmore clears her throat. "You must know something by now." Her voice escalates. "Corrine's frantic."

"We're doing everything we can," Joe says, his dark eyes intently assessing her.

"Well, I can't imagine where Molly could be." She wrings her shaking hands. "I need to go," she says, and stands abruptly. "I can leave, can't I?"

"Yes. But call as soon as you hear from your husband," I say.

She nods. From the lines on her face to her body language, she looks about a whisper from a breakdown.

"I'll be at Molly's house," she says. "I told Corrine I'd meet her there."

"She could probably use the company," Joe says.

Dr. Westmore nods and hurries down the hall.

CHAPTER 66

Molly

"Why are you doing this to me?" I ask in a strangled whisper. "Why, Cal?"

He shakes his head. "You'll understand, Melinda, eventually."

I clear my throat, gather my wits. "Where's Sadie?"

"Who?"

"My dog." My stomach is in knots. How can this be real? How can my captor be our friend? None of this makes sense.

"I have no idea."

"If you hurt her, I'll kill you," I cry.

He brushes my hair away from my face, and his fingers lightly linger on my cheek. "I didn't touch her, Melinda. I wouldn't hurt an animal."

I shudder and take a deep breath, trying to pull it deep into my chest, trying to clear my head of this craziness. "Did you kill Jay?" It comes out in a hoarse whisper.

Cal straightens up, lets go a deep sigh. "He gave me no choice. He found the necklace. He was going to go to the police."

Why, Jay, didn't you go straight there? I ask myself. As if Cal could read my thoughts he continues.

"He wasn't sure, of course. He found the necklace on the basement floor when he went up to fix the window. It was dark when

I cleaned up in July, and I missed it. Jay told me he'd found it when he came back from Mountclair. He said he wanted to talk to me, so I knew. I told him I'd meet him in his office, later, after the party."

I clench my cold fingers into fists. "Why would you *kill* him, Cal?" I'm sobbing. "He was your *friend*. And what did that woman ever do to you?"

"It all runs much deeper than that. Everything goes way back, Melinda."

"Stop calling me that!" My voice comes out high and childlike. He chuckles.

I clear my throat, brush away tears with cold, rigid fingers. "Tell me then." Anything to keep him talking. Give myself time to figure this out. And hopefully, the police are looking for me by now. I need to give them time to find me.

"All right. Might as well since it's run its course. It's all at an end now." He settles back, runs his fingers under his glasses. "When I was thirteen, living in Hartford with my mother and father, I started getting interested in true crime. My mother, a vicious bitch, took out all her frustrations on me. My brother had been her target, but then he left, and she turned on me. She liked to humiliate me, make me feel small, like a nothing, like dog shit on the bottom of her shoe. She told me I was a nobody. Would always be a nobody. Anyway, I used to hide in our basement, which my dad had finished with thin carpet and paneled walls, a TV. I started watching true crime stories, and I found my way. I found something that spoke to me. Women bound and dominated. Then killed. It was . . . satisfying. Anyway, I followed your story, and I was enthralled. I researched you, cut out every article, and found out you'd moved to Boston. When the time came for me to go to college, I followed you here."

"This was about *me*?" I shudder. My mouth falls open.

"Oh, yes." His voice shakes. "All for you, Melinda. I tried to forget you. I met Laken in college, and we hit it off. She was the only woman who could beat me at tennis." He smiles. "I decided that I needed to let you go. End my obsession. It wasn't healthy. Lake and I graduated, got married. Her family's pretty wealthy, as you know. It was a different life. A good life, far from my dark basement in Hartford. Laken and I spent time skating, skiing, sailing. We were always active, busy, and I was happy enough. Then the boys came along, and I thought, I can do this. I can leave my depraved thoughts and fantasies in the past. But," he sighs, "the shine kind of wore off. Work got busy and full of stress. I looked you up one day." He grins at me. "Wasn't easy since you have no social media. Smart, Melinda, but people don't realize that they still have an internet presence. Anyway, I discovered you were living in Graybridge, just a few miles from where Laken and I were living. What luck, huh?

"Well, it got even better. I began stopping off at different local bars after work, and eventually, I saw you, having a drink with a man, who I *recognized*. Jay and I were in the same hockey league. Different teams, but I definitely had met him a time or two. Well, it was all easy after that. I made a point of getting to know him. After games, guys often went out for drinks. Jay and I got to be friends. I hesitated when I found out that he was a psychologist. Didn't want him looking into *my* psyche, but it was a challenge too. Made things a little more interesting actually. One night, he let slip that his grandfather had been a detective on the Boston Strangler case. I was fascinated. He didn't like to talk about it too much, but after a few drinks, and some coaxing, he'd tell us stuff. He insisted he only described what had been released to the public. Jay was such a boy scout. Anyway, in no time, Jay and I were buds. You weren't married yet, but I remember the first time I met you, I was blown away. This is Melinda Wright, I kept thinking. Wow. Anyway, you hit it off with Laken, and the rest is history."

"Why did you kill that woman?"

He rubs his temples. "I don't feel like talking about that right now."

"How did Jay know it was you?"

"Later, maybe."

"Were you calling me?"

"That was me."

"Why did you bring me here?"

"Enough for now." He stands and reaches inside a bag. "Drink before you dehydrate." He twists the cap on a water bottle. "Oh, I've got cookies too. Oreos. Your favorite."

He sets the bottle on the floor. Suddenly, I'm filled with rage and hit him as hard as I can with my left fist, but I only clip the side of his leg. He grabs me by the shoulders and knocks my head against the wall and bursts of light float before my eyes.

"Don't do that again, Melinda." He kicks the water over, and I grab for it before it all spills out. "I'll be back later."

CHAPTER 67

Rita

Joe and I are gathering our notes when Josh Pearson is escorted into the room. His eyes are wild, and he's biting his lips. "I wanted to tell you that I lied earlier," he blurts out. "Don't bother going to Walmart and Lowe's. I wasn't there."

Just as I suspected. "Okay. Have a seat."

He flops into a chair, runs his hand through his neat sandy hair. I pull my phone back out and hit record. "Say that again, Mr. Pearson."

He does.

"You want to tell us where you were last night?" Joe asks, his hands clenched, his anger barely tamped below his words. Pearson has wasted our time, and that doesn't sit well.

He heaves a deep breath. "I was driving out to the Cape to meet somebody."

"Who?" Joe leans toward him.

"Laken Ferris."

Interesting. "Why was that, Mr. Pearson?" I ask.

He hangs his head. "I was having an affair with her." He glances up, meets my eyes. "But I broke it off."

"Then why were you going to meet her?"

"She called me. She was upset. We just met at a coffee shop to talk. That's it. But I couldn't say that in front of my wife." His eyes dart between Joe and me, begging us to believe him.

"What time was that?" I ask.

He shakes his head. "I left right after I dropped off my in-laws. Five-thirty, six maybe."

Not long before Mrs. Bradley went missing. "What did she want to talk about?"

"Her husband." He blows out a breath and drops his head in his hands.

"What about him?"

"They were having problems. That's why she took the kids and left." His gaze rests on the floor. "Cal's been a bit of a bastard lately."

"But you didn't see or talk to Mrs. Bradley?"

"No." His eyes widen. "I have no idea where she is. I swear."

"Will Mrs. Ferris corroborate your story?" I ask.

"Yes. Call her, please. I'm not guilty of anything except being a cheating asshole."

He's more believable now than he's been up to this point. "Okay. Cheating asshole it is. You mind waiting here with Agent Thorne while I give Mrs. Ferris a ring?"

"No." He hangs his head, his gaze on the table.

Mrs. Ferris tearfully details the meeting at the coffee shop. So Pearson was on the Cape, over an hour away, when Mrs. Bradley went missing. We cut him loose, and Joe and I sit in my office away from the noise and bustle of the rest of the station.

"We can cross Mr. Pearson off our list," I say.

"Yeah. That leaves us Mr. Ferris, Mr. Branch, and Mr. Westmore."

I draw a deep breath, flip back through my notes. "Let's put a tail on those guys. What do you think?"

"Good idea," Joe says. "I'll take care of it." He heads out the door.

I make my way to the conference room and peruse the map on the wall where Lauren and Detective Schmitt are busy ex-ing off quadrants that have been cleared. Teams of officers have been searching in an ever-widening circle around the gas station, coordinating with FBI agents that Joe has called in to help.

Everything in here is under control, and I'm just stepping on toes, so I wander out to the small station lobby. It's dark out. News trucks huddle under the streetlights. The reporters will want an update, and I hope the chief holds them off until we have some concrete news. As it is, phones are ringing nonstop throughout the building, adding to the chaos.

I walk back through the squad room, looking for Joe, but I don't see him. Everyone is hard at work, heads down, and I feel unnerved at my own uselessness, so I go back to my office to read through my notes for the thousandth time.

I settle into my chair, drum the desk with my fingers as I shuffle through my notebook, adding random doodles, trying to think, trying to elicit some overlooked fact that might help. My phone rings on my blotter, startling me. Unknown caller. My heart starts to pound as I answer, "Detective Myers."

"I've got Melinda." The voice is gravelly, distorted. "She's back in the cellar where she belongs." He ends the call, and I jump up from my desk and run down the hall.

CHAPTER 68

Molly

I drain the water bottle but leave the cookies. The water sloshes in my stomach, making me feel slightly seasick. My head still throbs, but anger keeps me focused.

I won't pee myself like I had to when I was six years old, so I use the ancient toilet. It doesn't flush, so I remove the tank lid and peer inside. There's a tangle of metal parts, but it doesn't look as though any of it works. Doesn't really matter if my urine sits in the bowl. Who cares? At least I'm dry.

I've been digging my fingers into the wall along the pipe all day, looking for a weak spot. Luckily, the concrete is old and crumbly. There's a loose fitting on the pipe, and if I can pull it far enough away from the wall, I might be able to work it free and slip the chain off. My fingertips throb, and my nails have broken off at the quick; blood trickles down my left hand, and I have to keep wiping it on my jeans. But at least my fingers are going numb, and the pain is subsiding.

Then I hear a door from somewhere up above and the creak of floorboards overhead. My heart hammers. He's back. I sit and slide over so that my back rests against the spot I've been digging, and wait.

The ladder scrapes from above, and he's climbing down.

"Melinda?" he calls, although with less gusto than before. Maybe he's getting tired. I hope so. Somehow, I've got to get the upper hand. It's just Cal, I say to myself, trying to pump up my courage.

He makes his way across the basement floor. "How's my girl?" He sits against the wall, a little farther from me than before, as if he's afraid I'll punch him again. "I brought you more to drink." I hear him chuckle in the darkness. He rolls a bottle toward me. It thunks against my leg. "Go on, take a sip. You've got to be thirsty."

I grab the plastic bottle, twist the cap and suck eagerly on the contents, but turn my head and spit. Orange soda. Bile rises in my throat, and Cal laughs.

"Oh, come on, Melinda. You know you like it."

"What's the point?" I ask, my throat scratchy with dried tears.

"Just a little joke between friends." He rubs his hands over his face, and his voice changes timbre, angry now. "Just be fucking grateful I brought you anything, okay? Drink. There's nothing in it. No sleeping pills. I've already got you down here. I didn't have to resort to anything so prosaic. I'm better than he was."

"Is that the point, Cal? Be better than my last captor?"

"I've always been better. Smarter, that's for sure."

"So how did Jay figure out you killed Annalise Robb?"

"He found the necklace. I told you that. But, well, I got the feeling last year that Jay was uncomfortable around me. Like he was analyzing me. After I got diagnosed last spring, all that rage that I'd kept locked away came back. It was all that fucking bitch's fault."

"Whose?"

"My lovely mother. She tormented me for years because she was unhappy. Her first husband left her. My brother was gone. My dad apparently cheated on her, and it was all my fault. But then I got away from her. Went to college. Got married. Had a family, career. Everything's great. Then *bam!*"

I jump as he smacks the floor with his palm. "Her fucking genes get me." He tips his head back against the wall and laughs. "She got me in the end. Just like she said she would. Well, Jay noticed I'd changed. He kept asking me if I wanted a referral—you know, after I found out I was going blind. He said it might help to talk to somebody." He laughs again. "Like a goddamn therapist was going to stop me from losing my sight." He's quiet, head down, looking at his hands. "They didn't help you, did they, Melinda? All those eager therapists prodding you to give up your secrets."

I shiver and inch farther away from him.

"But I know all about what happened in that cellar."

"No. You don't," I whisper. I don't even know what happened, not all of it. I've blocked it out, Jay said. I was so little and drugged besides. Keith had stolen his aunt's sleeping pills, crushed them, and put them in our orange soda.

"You killed little India, didn't you?" Cal says quietly. "Smothered her when she wouldn't stop crying."

My breath flies from my chest, as though it's being sucked out by a demon. "No. That's a lie," I mumble, barely able to form words.

"Is it?"

How does he know that Keith tried to blame me? Only the police and our lawyers knew about the accusation when Keith's lawyer tried to get him out of the murder charge. Thankfully, it didn't work, and no one ever leaked it to the press, so Corrine told me years later when I heard my parents whispering about it at the kitchen table. But I worried. What if? I was bigger. I was scared. That has been the most hideous monster always lurking in the back of my mind, all these years, all this time.

I choke on my tears. "Who told you that?"

"I have my sources."

"Did *he* tell you? Have you spoken to him?"

"Yeah. I have actually."

My skin crawls, and I wrap my untethered arm around my stomach. "You wrote the letter. The letter to Jay that was supposed to be from him."

"I did."

Tears start to run down my cheeks. "You hate me that much, Cal?"

He huffs out a breath. "It's not about you. Why do you think the world revolves around little Melinda? So high and mighty, Molly. You thought you could outrun your past. But you can't. Nobody can. What's done is done." He leans over, so close I can smell the alcohol on his breath. His lips are near my ear, and I shudder. "I'll be back, sweet Melinda." He scrambles to his feet.

"Where are you going?"

"To see my cheating bitch of a wife," he says nonchalantly, as though they're meeting for coffee. His hand reaches behind his back, and he pulls out something that glints in a stray beam of the streetlight. A gun. He tilts it back and forth—to be sure, I guess, that I see it. "Unfortunately, I might need this. Laken's not a tiny little thing like my mother or the others. She might actually be able to put up a fight."

He walks to the ladder, turns to face me. "After I see Laken, I'll come back here to the cellar. This is where it will all end. It's only appropriate to end this where it started." He plants one foot on the ladder. "Too bad Jay's dead. I'd get star billing in his book, don't you think?"

Chapter 69

Rita

After briefing everyone on the caller's message, Joe and I head to Mrs. Bradley's house. Her sister is there and has been calling non-stop for an update. We can't hold her off any longer.

Corrine Alworth meets us on the porch. "Have you found anything?" she asks, her blond hair blowing in the frigid breeze. We follow her inside.

"No. Nothing yet. But we're pulling out all the stops," I say with as much hopefulness as I can muster. Her parents, neatly dressed and befuddled, stand silently in the kitchen, looking to us, eyes begging for answers. Dr. Westmore leans against the counter, a cup of untouched coffee in her hand. My eyes meet hers.

"Scott's on his way," she says, then clears her throat.

"Okay, everyone, please sit." Joe and I catch them up on all we know.

Mrs. Alworth chokes out a sob. "Someone's got her?"

"We believe so."

She slams the table with her fist. "How could this have happened? You knew she was being harassed!"

"I'm sorry." I feel about two feet tall. "We're doing everything we can to find her."

"That's what you said about Jay's killer, what, *three weeks* ago!" Tears of rage and fear tremble on her cheeks.

My stomach burns. She's right. This investigation has moved entirely too slowly for my liking, and perhaps we should've done more to protect Mrs. Bradley. I just don't know what. There didn't seem to be any reason for the killer to have his sights on her. If that is indeed who has her.

Joe clears his throat. "We've got all of the resources of the Graybridge Police Department and the FBI looking for her."

Cold comfort, I know, when it's your loved one, but it's the best we've got.

Mrs. Bradley's parents wander into the dim living room as if they don't want to be near us, while Mrs. Alworth paces the kitchen. Dr. Westmore murmurs words of comfort.

The doorbell rings, and Hayes and Alice Branch follow Mrs. Alworth into the kitchen.

"I called him," Mrs. Alworth says. "He wanted to be here."

Mr. Branch has cleaned up a little bit from earlier. He's wearing fresh clothes, but his hair is still wild. Alice's hair is in two braids, making her look even younger than she is. When she hears that the dog is next door, she and her father walk over to Mrs. Murray's to claim her.

When they get back, Joe and I question Mr. Branch again. Although he doesn't have an alibi for last night, he seems distraught and sincere in his answers and desire to help. My gut tells me we can eliminate him.

Scott Westmore strides into the kitchen, his hands covered in dirt. "Sorry," he says. "I was on a job site. Any news?" His wife walks to his side and fills him in.

"We need to ask you a few questions," I say. "Let's step into the other room." I flip on the dining room light, and Mr. Westmore drops into a chair, perching on the edge as if afraid his dirty clothes will soil the seat. He leans over his clasped hands, his gray bangs shielding his eyes.

"Where were you last night?" Joe asks.

"Home with my wife."

"What about this afternoon?"

He blows out a breath. "I was on a job site, like I said."

Joe leans toward him. "Anyone confirm that?"

Mr. Westmore pulls his phone from his pocket and hands it to me. "My client. Bill Harris. Here's his number."

Before I can make the call, Joe's phone rings, and he peeks at the screen. "I need to take this," he says. "You go ahead and take care of him." He points his chin at Mr. Westmore.

Joe wanders down the hall. In the meantime, I ring Mr. Harris, who abruptly verifies Mr. Westmore's story while giving me an earful about the troublesome retaining wall.

When Joe returns, he motions for me to follow him out of earshot of the others.

"Anything?" I ask.

He whispers, "My agents on Mr. Ferris can't find him. They're outside his house, but he's not home, and his vehicle is gone."

"I'll call Mrs. Ferris again." I fish my phone out of my pocket.

Her voice is husky with tears. "I told you, Detective, I have no idea where Molly is—or my husband, for that matter."

"Tell me about your husband."

She draws a deep breath. "He and I have been having trouble lately."

"How lately?"

"The last year or so."

"Why? What's been going on?"

"He's been upset over some medical stuff. He's changed."

"Sorry to hear that."

She sniffs. "He's not dying or anything."

"That's good. How has that changed him?"

"He's angry, irritable. Drinking too much." She goes quiet. "He choked me," she whispers.

"When?"

"Last summer. Just one time. Our son walked in, and he stopped. I told him if he touched me again, I'd kill him. And he hasn't. But things haven't been the same after that. I don't know what to do. Leave, I guess. But the boys worship him."

"Does your husband have anything against Mrs. Bradley?"

"No. I don't think so." But there's a tremble in her voice. "I don't know what to think anymore, Detective. I really don't."

"Uh huh. You sure you have no idea where he is? We just want to talk to him." I glance up and meet Joe's gaze.

"I don't. I'd tell you if I did. As far as I know, he's home."

"Are you still at your parents' house?"

"Yes. I had planned to come home tomorrow."

"Are your parents there?"

"No. They left this morning for Florida. It's just me and the boys."

"Okay. Be sure to let us know if you hear from your husband." She says that she will.

Joe and I huddle as I tell him what I learned from Mrs. Ferris.

"He's our man," Joe says. "I'd bet on it."

The kitchen is full of people and the dog, quietly tripping over one another. Afraid to speak as if it would shatter a spell. Sniffles, shoes brushing the floor are the only sounds. I break the silence and reassure Mrs. Bradley's family and friends that we'll keep them informed. Then Joe and I head out into the cold and drive back to the station. News vans nearly clog the road as we approach, and all the lights are on in the building. No one's going home tonight.

There's no news on Ferris and nothing on the search as the big wall clock in the squad room passes midnight. I pour myself a sludgy cup of breakroom coffee and head to my office.

At four a.m., sitting in my office chair, I'm startled out of a light doze. My phone, clenched in my hand, is ringing and vibrating. I nearly drop it in my hurry to answer.

"He's here," a woman whispers. "He's got a gun."

I recognize her voice, sit up straight, instantly awake, adrenaline spiking. "Mrs. Ferris? Where is the house located?" She gives me the address before the call ends abruptly.

I rocket out of my chair, reciting the address under my breath, my heart thumping wildly. I blink my eyes in the glare of the squad room light. Joe has commandeered someone's desk and is working on his laptop. He jumps up when he sees me. "What?"

"Let's go! Ferris is at his wife's parents' place on the Cape." I swing by Bob's office and tell him what's going on as we hurry by.

Inside a cruiser, I hit the GPS while Joe pulls into the street. It'll take about an hour and twenty minutes to get there. I call for backup from local PD. They'll arrive a lot quicker than we will, and we head to I-495 south.

The huge, gray clapboard house comes into view under a fancy streetlight. It's right on the beach and got to be worth several millions. Cop cars are parked along the sandy road, their lights strobing through the morning darkness.

Joe and I exit our vehicle and are hit with damp, salty, frigid air. The crashing of waves in the distance lends an eerie backdrop to the scene. We hurry up the steps and enter through the unlocked front door. All the lights are on as we make our way to the kitchen. Several local uniformed officers are clustered there. One young female cop sits at the table with the Ferris boys, sleepy-eyed and scared, bowls of untouched cereal in front of them.

A sergeant peels off from the crowd and leads us into a living room filled with furniture covered in off-white canvas slipcovers. Blue and green knickknacks cover the end tables, and magazines are fanned on the coffee table.

"We haven't found them," the sergeant says. "When we got here, the kids were still in bed, the front door was wide open."

"No Ferris or his wife?"

"No. We've got officers combing the area, but so far no luck. We did spot tracks in the sand."

"His or hers?"

"Both, we think. But they peter out pretty quick."

I glance at Joe. "They couldn't have gotten too far on foot." I turn back to the sergeant. "What about his vehicle?"

"Gone. Hers is still here, but his isn't."

Shit. "You think he could've taken her?"

"Possibly."

"We've got a BOLO on him and his vehicle, so hopefully someone will spot him, and hopefully Mrs. Ferris is okay," I say, my eyes sweeping the room as if clues might be hidden among the bric-a-brac. "You get anything out of the kids?"

"Nope. They were asleep. Didn't hear anything. Their bedroom is upstairs in the back, so it stands to reason. And they haven't seen or heard from their father since Friday night is what they told us."

"Did they see their mom this morning? Her call came in just after four a.m."

"No. Last they saw her, she kissed them good night about ten."

So Ferris has an hour and a half lead on us. He could've gone back to Boston. He could've gone anywhere. I call and update the chief, and he tells me there've been no sightings of Ferris or Mrs. Bradley there, but they are working with the phone company, pinging his cell.

But I can feel it in this quiet house, as though an evil presence has been here and gone. Mrs. Ferris's fear is nearly palpable, and I know we're running out of time. Joe and I get in our vehicle and head back toward Graybridge.

* * *

We ride in silence, each lost in the puzzle at hand. Where would Ferris go? Where would he take his wife? Where would he stash Mrs. Bradley? There are thousands of basements in and around Boston if that's where he is. But for all we know, he's taken both women on a twisted road trip. Or, my stomach clenches, we're already too late. Neither woman is alive.

I shake that thought from my head. *Get a grip, Rita.*

We near Boston. The city lights blink in the gray early dawn. My phone rings. Lauren.

"We've got it, the location of his cell phone."

"Where?"

"Downtown." She gives me the coordinates.

"We're close." I turn to Joe and instruct him to get off two exits from where we are now.

"Boston PD's got SWAT on the way," Lauren says.

"Do we know where he is exactly?"

"Just the intersection I gave you. It's a neighborhood of old row houses, empty and slated for demolition. Should be lots of basements."

"All right. We'll be there shortly. Good work, Lauren."

The area has been cordoned off. Police and SWAT vehicles line the deserted streets. The area is depressed and ugly as it rises through the early-morning light. Joe and I trot toward a table set up as a command center. A tall man in a SWAT jacket leans over a map that has been weighted down with cop radios, which crackle with chatter.

He introduces himself quickly and outlines the search quadrants where officers are currently scouring. I look down the street. Houses that one hundred years ago would have been filled with families, children on their way to school, men and women on their way to work. The few spindly trees are winter bare and forlorn as they fight to survive in front of the abandoned homes.

Joe and I join up with a team and head down the broken sidewalk. We'd rather take part than stand still and wait. There are blocks of empty houses. We've got a lot of ground to cover.

We clear several decrepit basements, empty save for rats and debris, broken household items, and other remnants of lives lived long ago. I'm working up a sweat despite the cold temperatures and falling snow. And I'm feeling more despondent with every cleared building. *Where are you, Molly Bradley?*

CHAPTER 70

Molly

It's morning. Dim light from the lone window illuminates the basement in dull gray. My fingers throb; the numbness has worn off, and I'm in a lot of pain. I wonder when Cal will be back, and if Laken is okay. If only there were a way I could warn her, but that's impossible. All I can do is prepare for Cal to come back for me.

I think about Jay. How it would hurt him to see me like this. Fresh tears slip down my cheeks. He was a good person, and he probably wondered about Cal, worried about him, but wanted to talk to him first before going to the police. He would've wanted to be sure. He probably held out hope that Cal hadn't hurt anybody. Annalise was still just a missing person at that point. I heave a deep breath.

My thoughts travel back to my family, too. My parents and how totally ineffectual they were at handling a crisis, how they drew back into their routines and careers, even as my life crashed down around me. I think about Corrine and how she was the only one who really had my back, and I start to cry again. I haven't always been a good sister.

I glance up at the window and see snowflakes, fat and delicate, riding the air currents slowly to the ground through the gray dawn. This brings up a memory as well. My Grandpa Wright. Back before Keith Russell, we used to drive out to his farm on Sundays for dinner he cooked himself. Grandma had died years earlier. My parents were always in a rush to go home when we were out there. They didn't like his little house, which smelled of animals and pipe tobacco. But Corrine and I used to like it there. I don't remember much about Grandpa, but I do remember one thing he used to say. When Dad would ask him if he was going to clean up the place, or if he'd agree to move into town, he'd always say, "If I winter." When I asked what he meant, Dad frowned and said that was Grandpa's way of saying if he lives until spring. Now I understand. There are no guarantees in this life. Who knows if any of us will survive?

I draw a deep breath and think about my trip to see Keith Russell. Talking to him at Sing Sing was part of the puzzle that I had to solve, on my own. I came away a stronger person. It's that strength I tap into now. I'll put up a fight, just as Cal said about Laken. I won't go quietly.

I hear a door upstairs, the creak of the floorboards overhead. I bite my bottom lip and say a quick prayer.

Here we go, Molly.

"Melinda?" he calls, his voice hoarse.

A shiver runs through me. The ladder scrapes against the floor above and thumps as the bottom lands on the concrete. And he climbs down. His clothes are disheveled, and I can get a better look at him today in the daylight.

"Melinda." He's standing before me, his glasses bent and hanging precariously on his nose. His bottom lip is swollen, and there's blood dried on the side of his face.

My heart thumps wildly. "Did you hurt her?"

"Don't worry about my sweet wife. Today's the day, Melinda. The end." He sits next to me. Cal's a big man, athletic, and his bulk makes me feel even smaller than I am. He smells sweaty and salty, as if he's been swimming.

I swallow, my throat thick and scratchy. I want to keep him talking. Give the cops more time. "How did you know about me, Cal, really?"

He takes a deep breath, winces, and clutches his side. Then his big hands work over his head, stop to finger the blood dried at his temple. "I told you, I talked to Keith. He told me the whole story."

"Why would he do that?"

Cal turns toward me, his eyes red and glassy behind his twisted glasses. A slow smile spreads across his face. "Because, dear Melinda, blood is thicker than water, as the old saying goes. Keith is my big brother."

I choke on a breath. My heart pounds. *Oh my God.* I pull my stiff fingers into fists. Why didn't I know? Why couldn't I have felt it, seen it in his face?

"We don't look much alike, do we? Half-brothers. We had different dads. I'm better looking, though, right? Smarter too. Much smarter."

"You're Keith's *brother*?" My brain tries to make sense of it all. "I didn't know he had a brother." But what did I know at six years old about Keith's family?

This seems to anger Cal. "I know. All the focus was on Keith. He was some sort of celebrity. But I hated his fucking guts. He used to torment me when we were little, and I was glad as hell when my mom sent him to Albany that summer." Cal snorts. "But then she turned on me. Told me I'd never measure up to Keith." Cal shakes his head. "That idiot? I thought. Even as a kid, I knew he was dumb as a box of rocks. But all she talked about was her sweet oldest son. I guess her first husband was the love of her life, and so his spawn was like a god."

Cal gets slowly to his feet and begins to pace. "They'll write a book about me, Melinda. That'll show Keith. I'll be the most famous brother." He stops walking and looks at me. "At first, I wanted to be in Jay's book, but of course that didn't happen. Jay figured out something was going on with me way too soon." He grimaces and runs his hand through his dark hair. "He was a better shrink than I gave him credit for. Of course, he didn't know that I had *killed* anybody, but he was getting too damn close. Asking too many questions about my *feelings*." Cal huffs out a derisive breath.

"Were Jay and Annalise your only victims?" I ask, my voice quivering.

He heaves a deep breath, shrugs. "Maybe I'm not as accomplished as some, but with all this." He opens his arms, sweeps the basement. "The girl in the cellar connection. Now *that'll* warrant a book, maybe a couple, not just a chapter in Jay's. I'll be more famous than my idiot big brother ever was. Too bad my mother isn't around to see it."

"And that's important?"

His feverish eyes meet mine. "It's everything. Being *acknowledged*. That's what matters, Molly. That's *all* that matters. That's why I couldn't understand you. Why would you try to hide from the world? You were somebody. At least for a little while. If I were you, I would've written a book, a big shiny hardcover. Gone on talk shows. Made lots of money."

"You won't make any money, Cal. It's against the law."

Aggravation flits across his face. "I know that," he snaps. "For me, it's not about the money."

His phone chimes, a melodious aberration in this decaying cellar, and that throws him off-kilter. He pulls his phone from his pocket and peeks at it like a kid trying to hide from a teacher. The name that has popped up sends a cloud across his face, something vaguely akin to remorse.

"I've got to take this," Cal says, as though we're two people in the midst of a business meeting, and he heads for the ladder, pausing on the first step. "I won't be long, Melinda." His gaze flickers up to the high window, where snow continues to whirl. "Then we'll end this." He pulls the gun from his waistband, stares at it a moment, then tucks it in his jacket pocket.

I hear floorboards creaking, and I picture Cal pacing. That's what it sounds like, around and around, right over my head. He's talking in a loud voice, but I can't make out the words. Then he laughs, a deep throaty chuckle that sends shivers down my back. Who could he be talking to? And I'm amazed at his dexterity, swinging from multiple murderer to nice guy like the opening and shutting of a door. But then, he'd fooled us for years, until Jay.

I take a deep breath and reach behind my back to the cement wall. I've got to be ready. He'll kill me when his call ends. My frozen fingers run along the chain and the loose pipe fitting. I work my fingers until I stir up some warmth, enough to do what I have to do when the moment comes. I'll fight him. I'm not a helpless child anymore. I'm not six-year-old Melinda crying in a dark cellar, soaked in my own urine.

I sigh, clear my throat, and think about Jay, try to capture that feeling of being together to keep forever. For the five years he was part of my life, I felt totally loved and protected. If I survive this, what will my new life be like? Jay would want me to be happy, to fight for that happiness. I wipe a tear from my cheek as memories of Jay flood my mind. His laugh, his arms around me, my hand in his as we walked the streets of Paris.

The creaking stops. Everything's quiet. Maybe Cal left. Maybe whoever called changed his mind. But then the floorboards creak again, the sound moving toward the door above the ladder. He's coming.

My teeth chatter with cold and fear and with such force that my head bobs. He's at the open door, looking down on me.

"My sons," Cal says. "It was sweet of them to call." He sighs. "But they're better off without me. You know? This is better." He closes his eyes momentarily, as if reliving a last lovely memory of family life.

Cal turns his back to me and starts down the ladder. He walks quickly, like a man on a mission, to where I huddle against the cold, damp wall. "Little Melinda, you thought you'd escaped the cellar all those years ago." He chuckles. "But my big brother couldn't do anything right. Couldn't finish what he started. But not me." He shakes his head.

I take a deep raspy breath. "Don't you want to live for your kids, Cal?"

He paces away from me, then back again. Beads of sweat cling to his upper lip, despite the cold. The blood, which had started to dry on his temple, now begins to drip along his cheek.

I work my fingers behind my back, furiously trying to keep the feeling in them.

"Oh, I plan on living, Melinda. How else will I get to appreciate my handiwork?"

"But your boys?"

He walks away again. "I'll make them famous, and they *can* visit me if they want to. They'll write a book about their dad, what it was like to grow up in the perfect family. How no one had a clue what depraved thoughts swirled through the mind of their handsome, successful, athletic dad." He turns in my direction, his gaze seeking mine. "All the best serial killers led normal, even exemplary lives, Melinda. That's the beauty of it, being smarter than everyone else." He pulls the gun from his pocket and sets it on the floor, too far away for me to reach it.

Then he slips his hand into his other pocket and pulls out a knife, clicks a hinge to open it, and I catch my breath. Cal slides down next to me and places the tip against my throat. I go completely still, swallow, sweat dripping along the sides of my face. He lowers the knife, slides back the sleeve on my left arm. I feel the roughness of his fingers as they work their way over my scar.

"My brother's work. His brand," Cal says and snorts. "Terrible work, as usual." His eyes meet mine. "But you've probably had something done. Laser treatments to try to erase it all?"

I can't move. I can't breathe.

Cal drops my arm and stands. "I had a chance to examine it closely when I first brought you here, unconscious. Really, Melinda, you were always wearing long sleeves, and I'd been dying to get a look at it. Keith told me he'd put his mark on you. Claimed you as his own." He waves the knife in front of my face. But I'll do him one better, afterward." He leans over and places the tip of the blade against my chest. "Right here, over your heart. You'll be mine at last."

My pulse is beating in thick, heavy thumps as Cal places the knife on the floor next to the gun and grabs the dirty blankets lying next to me. He spreads them out and stands, legs apart, so close I can smell him. He pats the front of his pants. "Let's do this."

I swallow and clench my trembling jaw. Snot drips down my upper lip. "Please, Cal, don't."

"Sorry, Melinda. It's part of it. I need to possess you. Make little Melinda, the girl in the cellar, all mine. So a little interlude before the end."

I glance up at the window and see the pantlegs of people as they stride by. Cops? My heart hammers. Please let them find me. *Hurry. Hurry.* I open my mouth to scream, but Cal is bending over me, so close he could easily break my neck with his hands before the cops could get down here, so I stay quiet and hope to hold him off until they find me.

He pulls a small key from his pocket, reaches for the handcuff. I pull a great breath, as though I'm getting ready to dive into the deep end. This is it. I gather my strength, think of Jay, and bolt to my feet.

CHAPTER 71

Rita

We've just cleared another basement with no luck. With each house, we've entered the front door anxious and on alert, only to be let down. My ankle is throbbing. I'd turned it maneuvering through debris, catching my foot on a kid's rusted bicycle, but I suck it up. I'm going to see this through. I'll find Mrs. Bradley or break my leg trying.

Outside, the air's frigid, and the smells of the city surround us in the early-morning haze. Joe and I huddle against a wall as the team leader reports back on his radio. We've got one more house to search to clear this block. I try to push away the doubts that threaten to crawl into my mind.

But I can't help whispering to Joe, "What do you think? What if she's not here?" As if he's got a better plan.

He shakes his head. "We keep moving, Rita." He rubs his large hand over his chin, the scar disappearing underneath his fingers. "We keep going until we find her, wherever she is."

I glance across the street, one that's already been cleared, and hope that we've got this right. What if Ferris dumped his cell phone in the area and took off? What if we've just wasted the last hour climbing through abandoned homes, across rotted floor-boards, searching trash-filled basements for nothing? The officer leading our team looks up and motions us forward. I fall into line behind Joe, and we move out along the broken sidewalk and advance up the next set of stairs and into another decaying foyer. We fan out, clearing the first-floor rooms. Then we gather up in the back hallway, listen. There's noise, movement below, and my heartbeat ratchets up. Our team leader raises a hand and signals for quiet. A man's voice. He's here. We creep forward toward the basement door, weapons raised.

CHAPTER 72

Molly

I pull the chain from behind my back. Cal's eyes open wide in surprise and confusion. I use both hands to wrap it around his neck and push him backward. His glasses tumble to the floor. He trips and falls, and I fall on top of him.

"What the fuck?" He mumbles and grabs my hands, freeing himself from the chain. I've managed to cut his neck superficially, but nothing more. He rolls over and pins me underneath him. "You fucking bitch." He nearly laughs. "Thought you were pretty smart, huh? You been working on that the whole time?" He grabs my hand, eyes my bloody fingers. Saliva drips from his mouth onto my cheek, and his gasping, sour breath blows against my face. "Fine. You want it rough? I'm game."

I can't breathe with him on top of me. I squirm and kick, but he's too strong. I reach out with my right hand, searching for the knife or the gun, but they're too far away. His hands circle my neck. His fingers tighten on my throat. I feel woozy. I'm sinking into a swamp, dark and dreamlike. His hands loosen just before I go under, and I pull a choppy breath down into my chest. He's yanking on my jeans. *No, no, no.*

I'll fight with everything I've got. Keith and Cal meld into one before my eyes. With anger spreading through my body, filling me with purpose, I thrust my hand under my back and work my fingers down to my waist band. I slide out the metal piece I'd pulled from the toilet tank, and with all my strength stab it into the side of his neck.

He howls and rolls away as I scramble to my feet. The floorboards overhead creak. And I hear people shouting.

"Police!" They're standing at the open door, looking down, guns raised.

Cal grabs my leg, and I fall flat on my face on the crumbled cement floor. I look back at him. Blood is bubbling from the wound in his neck. He's trying to stop it with one hand and hold on to my leg with the other. I kick and thrash, finally breaking free.

Cops are descending the ladder as I run toward them. An older cop lowers his gun and pulls me to his side.

Detective Myers, her weapon raised, strides toward Cal. His face is a sickly white, and he grins at me. "Look, Melinda. They're here. The media can't be far behind."

CHAPTER 73

Rita

It has been a day so busy, no one's had a minute to eat, so when Joe and I found ourselves at the station at seven twenty-two p.m., we were ravenous.

Cal Ferris is in the hospital, uniformed officers guarding his door. Mrs. Ferris was found bleeding and unconscious on the beach and is currently in a hospital on the coast. She managed to break a couple of her husband's ribs and give him a pretty good blow to the head before he shot her twice. Luckily, his aim was off, and she'll survive.

Bob just finished a press conference in which Joe and I participated. The media, starved for information, could barely control themselves and jostled for room on the sidewalk in front of the station. Then they scurried away to file their stories or wait for their on-air cues.

Mrs. Bradley was checked out at the hospital and released to her family after giving her statement from her bedside. There'll be more questions later, but for now, we've got plenty to do.

Agent Metz left to grab dinner with her parents, and Chase is on his way home to his wife and son. Lauren is busy in the squad room, head bent over her keyboard, a half-finished ham and cheese deli sandwich next to her.

Joe and I head over to Mac's. I'm limping slightly on my sore ankle but hope a couple glasses of wine will help soothe the pain. There are a few of the guys from the station hanging over the bar, laughing and blowing off steam. We're all relieved that Mrs. Bradley was found relatively unhurt and our man is in custody. No one looks up or notices as Joe and I slide into the last booth in the corner.

We order mozzarella sticks, a large pepperoni and black olive pizza, a couple of salads, and a bottle of wine. I sip, and the alcohol hits my depleted blood stream quickly, filling my veins, making me feel tingly and light-headed. I grab up a slice of pizza and take a huge bite. I'm starving.

Joe leans back and laughs.

"What?"

"Nothing. I'd just forgotten how nice it is to work with you, Rita." His smile reaches his dark eyes.

I swallow. My hair has fallen out of its bun and hangs in a tangled mess over my shoulders. At least the gray is gone. But I'm sure my mascara is smudged, and the sleeve of my white blouse definitely has a smear of Mrs. Bradley's blood from her injured fingers. I sit up and smooth my hair back.

"Yeah. It's nice to have you here." I sip my wine. "I guess you'll be wrapping up and moving on to your next assignment."

"Pretty soon, I'm sure."

Is he thinking about what happened after we finished our last case together? I feel heat rush to my face. As much as I don't regret what happened between us, I feel like I'm past that kind of recklessness now. It's not what I want. But I don't want him to disappear for another six years either. I huff out a breath. You'd think by now I'd have my life figured out.

"What?"

I shake my head. "Just thinking. Some case, huh?"

He smiles. "It was a wild ride. But the outcome was right."

He picks up a mozzarella stick, bites into it, and leaves a long string of cheese trailing down his chin. I resist the urge to lean over and wipe it off.

"Remember when we questioned Arthur Knoll?" he asks. Knoll was the perp in our last case. "And he said that he didn't kill his wife, that she killed herself?"

"Yeah. What an idiot. He was covered in her blood, and she'd been shot in the back three times."

"Then he said the dog shot her, and he had some elaborate explanation of how that happened."

"Yeah. The dog hated her guts apparently."

We both laugh, and I'm feeling the effects of the wine and the letdown of the stress. Tears wet both our cheeks as we can't stop laughing, and even the cops at the bar turn around to look.

CHAPTER 74

Molly

One week later

The sun is shining for the first time in days. Corrine and I sit at my kitchen table, mugs of tea and brownies that Alice made in front of us. Physically, I'm back to normal, but the rest of me will take a while. Cal was released from the hospital a few days ago and is now in custody, with no bond, so that gives me some comfort.

"How's Laken?" Corrine asks.

"Better. She called me yesterday. She's at her parents' house with the boys. She wanted to apologize again and to let me know that she's not coming back to Graybridge."

"That's probably for the best. She's lucky to be alive," Corrine says. "What's happening with Kim and Josh?"

I take a breath. The last week has been tumultuous for my best friend. "She insisted that Josh move out. She's not sure how things are going to go with them. Josh called her yesterday with the name of a marriage counselor and begged her to go with him."

"What did she say?"

"She told him to fuck off. She said if she wanted to talk to him, she'd call him, but he shouldn't hold his breath."

Corrine smiles. "I always liked Kim. For a tiny little cheer-leader, she was always tough."

"She is," I agree.

Corrine sips her tea, drops her hand to Sadie's head, and pats her. "How are you feeling?"

I shrug. "Still a little numb, I guess." Corrine had been the first to rush to the hospital when the cops brought me out of the base-ment, and she'd been the first to hug me years ago, back home, when I huddled on Margaret Castleberry's lap at the police sta-tion. I clearly recall her long, permed hair brushing my cheek and the smell of her Electric Youth perfume and the sight of her stonewashed jeans as she knelt in front of me. My parents were there, of course, but I don't remember them saying much. This time they were there too, trailing behind Corrine, wringing their hands.

I pick up the business card Elise gave me, the one with Morgan Blanton's name on it.

"Are you going to give her a call?" Corrine asks.

I tap the table with the side of the card. "Yes. That's what Jay would want."

"What do you want?"

"I don't honestly know. But I'm willing to talk to her and see if it helps."

"A lot's changed, Molly."

"Yes. It has." The sound of heavy equipment draws my gaze out the back window. "Scott's men must be here," I say, and Cor-rine and I watch as two men in work clothes begin the process of tearing down the old garage.

"I want to tell you something," Corrine says. "Something that's been on my mind for a long time, but I've been too much of a coward to ever talk to you about it before."

My eyes meet hers. "What?"

"That day. The day you were abducted, the *first* time." Corrine stands and paces the kitchen. She comes to a stop by the sink and leans against the counter. "Mom asked me to watch you." Her hand goes to her mouth, and her breath catches. "But I said no. I said that Julia Wentworth's mom was going to drive us to Albany to go to the mall."

"I *know* you went to the mall, Corrine."

"But," she sniffs back tears, "if I hadn't gone to the mall, if I'd done what Mom had asked, nothing bad would've ever happened to you."

"You don't know that. He would've just looked for another opportunity. Besides," I stand and go to her, "maybe Mom and Dad shouldn't have left me with our alcoholic neighbor. Maybe they should've found someone else to watch me, or, God forbid, maybe one of them could've stayed home that day. Anyway, it wasn't your fault. You were a kid yourself. It was no one's fault but his." I hug my sister, and we stand there together. "You were always there when I needed you."

"I'll always be here, Molly." We draw apart, and Corrine wipes her cheeks. "Sorry if I'm an overbearing pain in the ass sometimes."

I smile. "That's what I like best about you."

CHAPTER 75

Rita

Lauren walks into my office with Hayes Branch behind her.

"He wanted to speak with you," Lauren says.

I drop my pencil on my blotter. "Sure. Mr. Branch, have a seat."

He turns and watches Lauren leave and shuts the door behind her before taking a chair.

"What can I do for you?"

He runs a hand through his hair. He's had it cut short, and the wild curls are gone.

"I want to confess."

I raise my eyebrows. "Okay." I reach for my phone. I have no idea what he's about to say, but the way things have been going, I don't want to take a chance. "Mind if I record you?"

"No." He shakes his head. "That's fine."

"What's this about?"

He takes a deep breath. "I lied before."

"About?"

"My wife's death."

I lean forward, grab my notebook.

His eyes widen. "I didn't kill her. It's nothing like that. I miss Amelia every day."

I sit back in my chair. "What then?"

"She didn't die from her heart condition. She had one, and it might've killed her one day, but not that day."

"What happened then?"

He rubs his eyes under his glasses and blows out a breath. "She killed herself. Suicide. She battled depression her whole life. She was in treatment and took medicine, but she overdosed. On purpose. She left me a goodbye letter on the kitchen table. I still have it locked in my desk drawer."

"Why not come clean at the time?"

He lays his glasses on my desk and blinks. "My daughter. Alice was only five years old." He smiles slightly. "Five going on fifteen. I didn't want her to know that her mother chose to leave her. I didn't want her to have to live with that."

"I understand." I do too. Suicide of a loved one is hard enough for a grown person to handle, let alone a child.

Mr. Branch continues, "And if it got out, I wouldn't have been able to keep it out of the media, and Alice was already reading at a sixth-grade level by then. I couldn't have shielded my daughter from the fallout, Detective. Amelia was a well-known author and . . ."

"And a Branch."

"Yes."

"Why tell me now?"

He draws a deep breath. "I figured you guys didn't believe me, and I didn't want to worry about being surprised by cops on my doorstep."

"What about your daughter?"

He sighs. "She's old enough to hear the truth, I guess." His eyes don't look convinced.

"How'd you get the paperwork falsified?"

"Branch money." His gaze meets mine. "I'm not proud of that."

I tap my pencil against my notebook. He leans forward and takes a pen out of my cup holder and scribbles something on the back of a business card he pulled from his wallet.

"What's this?" I ask.

"That's Amelia's sister's phone number. Anna was actually the one who found her that day. She called me at the store, hysterical. She had talked to Amelia that morning and was worried about her, so she came over." Mr. Branch clears his throat and sits up. "Anyway, please give her a call if you need confirmation."

I nod, glance at the sketches in my notebook, one of Alice with her braids. "Where did your wife die? Where did it happen?"

He tells me, and I sit back and pick up my phone. Sometimes the humane thing isn't necessarily the right thing, but you've got to make a decision.

"Hmmm. Not our jurisdiction then, Mr. Branch. This department won't be interested in looking into the matter." I delete the recording from my phone.

His eyes meet mine. "Thank you, Detective. These last few weeks have been . . . I don't have any words."

"Sometimes there aren't any."

He stands, shakes my hand, and leaves. I wander to the window and watch the snow fall.

I eat lunch at my desk, a turkey sandwich and an apple. Time to get back to a healthy diet, but I can't help but eye the tin on the corner of my desk. Maybe one of André's oatmeal raisin cookies wouldn't be too bad. Oatmeal's good for you. I'm prying up the lid when Chase peeks in at my door and holds up a file folder.

"Mrs. Bradley's here. I've got that report she requested." Chase's dark eyes meet mine for a second, then his gaze drops to the floor.

"Aren't you supposed to be off today?"

"Yeah. I'm leaving shortly."

I stand, walk over to the window, and peer between the slats of the blinds. "Fresh snow. Why don't you let me talk to Mrs. Bradley so you can get on your way? Looks like a great day to go sledding. Didn't you tell me that Santa brought Charlie a new sled? Why don't you and Sarah take him to try it out?" I turn toward him. "You've been spending too much time on the job, Chase. It'll burn you out. I'll take care of Mrs. Bradley."

Chase hesitates for just a moment. Then hands me the folder. "Yeah. Right. Good idea." He stops in the doorway. "See you tomorrow, Rita."

When he's gone, I open the folder. The little Arndt girl's autopsy results. I say her name aloud, as I do all victims that I come across.

"India Marie Arndt."

Four years and ten months old forever. But she existed. She was here.

I sigh and head down the hall.

Chapter 76

Molly

I squirm in my chair and tell myself I'm ready. My last secret fear, so far hidden in my brain, I never told anyone, not any of my therapists, not even Jay. But I'm strong enough now.

If Indie was smothered, as Keith said, I need to know. That doesn't mean that he didn't do it himself. Certainly, no one believed at the time that I was responsible. And I pray with my whole being that I wasn't. But I feel like I owe it to Indie to know the truth, as much as possible, of what happened to her. I have no recollection of it, and that hurts as well. I don't remember what happened to my little friend.

I hope Detective Fuller gets here soon before I lose my nerve. The door opens, and Detective Myers walks in.

"Hi, Mrs. Bradley. Sorry to keep you waiting. Detective Fuller needed to get home. Hope you don't mind."

"No. That's fine," I say, although I'd rather have had him here now. She intimidates me.

Detective Myers lays the file folder on the table in front of me, and I reach for it with a shaking hand.

"Mrs. Bradley," she says. "It's okay."

I find strength in her icy blue eyes, nod, and open the folder.

The page blurs in front of me, and I blink to clear my tears. I skim the notes, searching for the answer I need. Pain rises in my chest, like a heart attack, as I see it in the conclusion section. Keith was lying.

Indie died from an overdose of the sleeping pills he put in our soda.

I choke out a sob and lean my head in my hands. The room is quiet, and I clear my throat and peep up at Detective Myers. There are tears in her eyes too.

CHAPTER 77

Rita

The evening comes in dark, quiet like the snow on the trees outside my office window. There's still paperwork to clear up on the Bradley case, but the heavy lifting is done for now, and everyone in the department is working silently, heads down, computer keys clicking.

I take a deep breath. Check my phone. My brother Danny's left me a message. I haven't talked to him since I got caught up in the Bradley case, and we usually talk once a week at least. Of all my family, he and I are the closest. I make a mental note to give him a call. Maybe I'll drop by his place on my way home.

Joe raps on my open door. "I'm going to head out," he says.

"Thanks for your help, Joe. It's been great having you here every day."

He nods and walks over to where I stand near the window. "Newburyport isn't that far, Rita." He brushes my hair back over my shoulder. "Why don't you come up some weekend."

I take a deep breath. I'd really like that, but then what? "Cold place in the winter."

"Sea air will do you good. There's a really nice pub in town, historic. Great wine list." Joe and I'd made plans to get together after that first case, but something always came up until the plans faded away and we got lost in our separate lives.

I smile. "I've been to Newburyport once. A long time ago. A friend and I stopped there on the way to Maine."

"Well, you haven't been there with me."

"Okay, maybe."

"I'll take maybe." He draws me into a hug, and I can't help but relax against him. This case has taken more out of me than I'd like to admit. "Let's not let six years go by, Rita. Life's short, as the cliché goes."

"That's the truth."

He lets me go and heads out the door.

I turn on the little radio I keep on the windowsill. The young cops think it's quaint and hilarious that anyone would still listen to the radio, and *on* a radio no less. True, there aren't many good stations left, but I like my classic rock station. I sing quietly along with the Doors' "L.A. Woman," a song that always makes me feel blue. I stand at the window and watch Joe throw his backpack in the passenger's side of his truck. I stay put until his taillights fade into the night.

CHAPTER 78

Molly

September

Fall is in the air. The first crisp days are upon us. Sadie and I sit on the back porch. She pants at my side, while I snuggle under a quilt and sip tea out of one of the old cups from Grandpa Wright's house, one of the few things my parents didn't throw away.

I started seeing Dr. Blanton in February, with low expectations. My first impression of her wasn't good. Young, sleek blond ponytail, perfect makeup, and a designer dress with matching stilettos, a two-carat diamond on her left ring finger. My first thought was this pampered princess can't help me. I should've known better than to judge people.

All my previous therapists had declined to tell me anything about themselves, saying that their experiences were irrelevant. That always made me suspicious. How could they empathize with me? But Dr. Blanton had no such reticence. She told me that she'd grown up in Philadelphia in a poor rundown neighborhood. Her mother was a junkie, and she had no idea who her father was. When she was eleven years old, walking home from school, she was gang-raped by some local thugs. After that, her mother gave up her parental rights, just gave her away. She ended up in foster care, where she aged out without being adopted. Her mother had died, and Dr. Blanton applied for scholarships and put herself through college. She swore to live a better life than her mother had. There's nothing so horrible that you can't pull yourself past it, she said. Survive and flourish, that's her mantra. I believe her, and our sessions have been going well.

I've kept my job at the bookstore. Hayes and Alice have been wonderful, Kim too. Her baby, a boy, was born at the end of June, full term. Kim and Josh are working on their marriage, and he was there to support her through her delivery. Elise and Scott have also made a point of checking on me without seeming to.

And of course, Corrine.

I sold the mountain house. I thought it would be difficult with what had happened there, but I received an offer right away. I have enough in the bank, along with Jay's life insurance, so that I can keep our house and not worry about paying the bills.

I stand and lean my hands on the porch railing, inhale the autumn air. In the spring, where the garage used to stand, my new flower garden will be ripe with pink peonies, my favorite. I have a lot to look forward to. I think about Jay every day, and that gives me strength. I place my hand on my growing belly and smile. His daughter will be born in January. That will help me through the anniversary of his death. In March, the fertility clinic called me and asked if I wanted to go through another IVF cycle. We had two embryos left. I never hesitated. There are no guarantees in this life, but that's no reason not to try. After a positive pregnancy test, Corrine held my hand at the ultrasound. Sadly, one embryo didn't implant, but one did, one little girl held on, and sometimes that's all it takes.

In this riveting thriller from a new master of suspense, a young dancer's homecoming is marred by a grisly discovery—and the realization that nothing in her past may be quite what she believed.

When Esmé Foster left the Boston suburbs to become a professional ballerina, the future shimmered with promise. Eleven years later, her career has been derailed by an injury, and Esmé knows it's time to come back to Graybridge to help her brother care for their ailing father. But her return coincides with an unthinkable crime. Kara Cunningham, one of Esmé's high school friends, is found dead in the woods behind the Fosters' house.

Esmé is shocked and grieving, but also uneasy. In her dreams, she still sees the man who showed up at the scene of the car accident that killed her mother—and told Esmé he was going to kill her too. Family and friends insisted the figure a product of Esmé's imagination, that she was concussed after the crash. But she and Kara looked alike, sharing the same petite build, the same hair color. Could Kara's murder have been a case of mistaken identity?

Detective Rita Myers is familiar with close-knit communities like Graybridge, where, beneath the friendliness, there are whispers and secrets. The town has seen other tragedies too, including the long-ago drowning of a young girl in a pond, deep in the woods. Even within the once-close circle of friends that included Kara and Esmé, Rita discerns a ripple of mistrust.

Day by day, Esmé discovers more about the place she left behind—and the friends and family she thought she knew. Soon, shining a light into the darkness to learn what really happened the night Kara died is the only way she can bring the nightmare to an end . . .

Please turn the page for an exciting sneak peek of
Terri Parlato's next novel of domestic suspense,
WHAT LIES IN THE WOODS,
coming soon wherever print and e-books are sold!

CHAPTER 1

Esmé

Sometimes, the only thing you can do is leave. That was my mindset when I was eighteen. There was no thought of staying put and duking it out, fighting to make things better. I didn't have the slightest inkling of how to do that.

But eleven years later, teetering on the edge of thirty, the world looks a lot different. So I'm going home. The thruway is gray and damp, and my ancient car thumps along at fifty-five; any faster and it makes a noise that drowns out the radio. I'm not in any hurry to get to Graybridge anyway. I'm sort of liking the road between Syracuse and my Boston suburban hometown. I'm alone with my thoughts, boyfriend—ex, actually—in the rearview mirror, my family, or what's left of it, at the other end of my journey. Here, on the road, I'm in a dreamland of my own.

It's early. The weak October sun is just rising, and the dying leaves look gray, their brilliant colors hidden in the morning mist. Kevin is still asleep, most likely. He'll get up in another hour and find my note on the kitchen table; such a cliché, but I couldn't face him, see that look in his eyes, the folds in his forehead when something unpleasant and out of his control happens. I need all my strength for my brother and dad and whatever else I have waiting for me at home. I have nothing to spend on Kevin. It's been over for months, although he's refused to even consider that our relationship has ended. Six years of fighting and making up is all I had in me. I'm ready for the fighting to be over. That's why I'm going home. For one last stand maybe, to settle things there. And, besides, I have nowhere else to go.

My coffee has grown cold, sitting in the cupholder, forgotten. I sip, and the taste is bitter in my mouth, and I wonder again why I bothered to sit in the long line at the drive-thru to purchase it. Habit, I guess. Black coffee, and lots of it, has been my mainstay for years. Zero calories and a good jolt of energy. What more can a dancer ask for? I glance at the paper grocery bag sitting in the passenger seat like an old friend, or a relative who fills me with pain and disappointment. But I can't part with the contents. In some ways, they are my world. Pointe shoes, scuffed and worn, fit only for the dumpster, but their pale pink satin peeks through the grime, belies the hours of work, and I can't let go.

I'm going home a failure, never an easy prospect. The end of my dance career, which, at one time, had seemed so promising, has left me adrift, my painful hip sending shock waves when I move my foot from the gas to the brake pedal. *Ha*, it taunts. Thought you could stretch me and plié me to death? I'll show you!

I wipe a tear from my cheek. I don't know what home has to offer me. A father who's desperately ill, a brother whose phone calls have only gotten colder as the years have gone by. A mother in her grave since I was sixteen, and a man who threatened to kill me the night of my mother's accident. My phantom. Is he still lurking, waiting for my return? Or is he a figment of my imagination, like everyone said?

I sigh and turn up the radio and let the strains of Tchaikovsky lead me into a mindless numbness as a cold rain begins to fall from the dark sky.

CHAPTER 2

Rita

The body is lying in the weeds at the edge of the woods, the woman's red sweater a beacon in the gray day. From the kitchen window, the scene outside looks like a far-off movie. Crime-scene investigators and cops circle the corpse, like wrestlers trying to find a way to wrap their arms around what's happened here. The ME walks through the crowd, which parts respectfully to let her through.

I look up from my notebook at the young man, dark brown hair feathering his forehead, sweat dotting his stubbled upper lip.

"So, Mr. Foster. You knew the victim?"

"Yes," he mumbles.

"How did you know Kara Cunningham?"

He heaves a great sigh. "We went to school together. High school."

"You've seen her since?"

He scrubs his hand over his eyes. "Yes. Uh, some. It's a small town."

He's already told me that he works as a nurse, hospital night shift. When he got home at around seven-thirty this morning, his father told him that he'd heard a scream from outside.

"When was the last time you saw her?"

"Last Saturday, I guess."

"You know or you guess?"

"I know."

"Okay. We'll get back to that. I need to speak with your father. He's still here?"

Byron Foster blinks his eyes. "He lives here. I moved back in a year ago to take care of him. He doesn't leave the house."

"What's wrong with him?" I ask, which comes out a little insensitive, but that's me. I don't always get the PC phrasing right. Force of habit.

"He's an alcoholic."

I nod. Lots of people are alcoholics. My mind drifts unwittingly to my brother Danny, and I have to pull it back. *Stay on task, Rita.* Think of Danny later.

Byron continues. "He's in the last stage of cirrhosis."

"Sorry. Okay."

"He's dying, Detective," he adds matter-of-factly.

"He told you he heard a scream coming from the backyard?"

"Yes. So I went out to look around. I really didn't think I'd find anything. My father is so out of it, it's hard to believe anything he says." Mr. Foster's gaze shifts to the window, where a stretcher is being pushed through the tall grass. It gets stuck, bogged down in the mud, and two guys drop to their haunches to try to free it. "I think his mind is caught in the past. He hears things, sees things that aren't there."

"You can't get him any help?" I bite my tongue the minute this leaves my mouth. I've tried for years to help my brother, but he insists he doesn't have a problem and, if I push, tells me it's none of my goddamn business, which has me backing off. Being on the outs with Danny isn't something I'm willing to live with. He and I are the youngest and the closest siblings in a big family.

Mr. Foster's eyes find mine, and they're filled with not grief exactly, anger maybe. "You can't help people who don't want help."

I nod again. Swallow. "Okay. I still need to talk to him."

We rise from the table, and I follow him down the hall and up a dark and squeaky staircase. As we near the top, a slight sour smell, vomit and alcohol, wafts over me. My partner, Chase, picked a great week to take vacation.

Inside the dim room, a tall man, thin as a skeleton, sits shriveled into a ratty recliner. His breaths come in ragged gasps. Young Mr. Foster flips on the overhead light, and the room is thrown into garish brightness. The old man blinks his eyes like a young pup. He's wearing a flannel shirt in a cheerful red and blue plaid, unbuttoned at the neck, where white hair peeps over the top of a gray undershirt. His wrinkled hands shake, and the smell of alcohol leaches from his pores.

I glance around for a place to sit. The son moves a yellow plastic and chrome kitchen chair from the corner and places it in front of his father.

"Mr. Foster, I'm Detective Rita Myers, Graybridge Police Department," I say, settling in the chair. The old man nods, but I'm not sure if he understands what I've said. I pull out my notebook and turn to a fresh page.

"I'd like to ask you a few questions." He looks over at his son, who has seated himself on the edge of the double bed. "You told your son you heard a scream last night." He nods absently. "What time did you hear the scream?" His dark eyes cloud over like I've just asked him to explain nuclear fission. His left hand twitches and digs at a spot on his arm. "Mr. Foster?"

He shakes his head and glances out the window. "I don't know," he says finally in a trembling voice.

"Where were you when you heard it?"

"In the living room, watching TV." He stretches his mouth wide, and the wrinkles in his cheeks gather. "I heard a scream." He points to the window. "I heard someone scream out back somewhere."

"You don't know what time it was?"

He shakes his head.

"Can you guess?"

He shakes his head again.

"What were you watching?"

"The news was on."

"The six o'clock news or the ten o'clock news?" I sketch his troubled, rheumy eyes in my notebook, give him time to search through the cobwebs of his brain. Drawing helps me think, slows me down. It's something I've done since I was a kid, and it has followed me into my long career in law enforcement. My notebooks are filled with pictures of suspects and victims and crime scenes. And sometimes the visuals help lead me to answers.

"I don't know," he says at last. His voice is stronger than before.

"What time did you go upstairs to bed?" I just get a vacant stare. "You have anything to drink before you went to bed, Mr. Foster?" I hear the son huff out a breath.

The old man nods.

Young Mr. Foster says, "When I got home from work, I went upstairs to check on him, and he was agitated. He told me about the scream, so I went outside to look."

"Did he say anything to you this morning about when he heard the scream?"

"No." He shakes his head. "I really don't think he knows. His concept of time is pretty skewed."

I turn back to the old man. "Did you go outside, look around?"

"No. I stayed right here."

"Is there anything you can tell me about last night besides the scream? Did you hear any other noises? Did anyone knock on the door? Did you hear any cars stop by the house?"

He cringes in his chair as if my questions were punches. I sigh. This is getting me nowhere. "Okay, Mr. Foster. If you think of anything, please give me a call, or have your son call me," I say, standing, stashing my notebook under my arm.

We head downstairs and back into the kitchen. The body is still on the ground, the crime-scene investigators still hard at work. When I arrived on scene, I'd had a quick conversation with the first responders before heading inside. But I need to get out there and talk with the ME when I'm through here.

"Mr. Foster, you said you saw Kara on Saturday night, correct?"

"Yes."

"Where was that?"

"At Hartshorn's Brewpub. She was having drinks with a friend."

"So, you weren't with her?"

"No. I was there with a buddy from work. Kara was at another table."

"Did you speak with her?"

"No. I don't think she saw me. We weren't sitting near each other. I just noticed her on my way out."

"You didn't stop to say hello?"

"No."

"Who was she with?"

"Christy Bowers."

"Who's that?"

"She's a friend of Kara's."

"Okay. I'll need to talk with you again." I hand Mr. Foster my card. "I'll be in touch, but don't hesitate to call me if your father remembers anything."

CHAPTER 3

Esmé

It's just after ten when I exit the highway. I haven't been back to Graybridge in two and a half years. I'm a coward. I know that. I was here last to see my brother's new baby and stayed just long enough to be able to tell myself that I hadn't abandoned my family. But that's exactly what I did. I knew then that my father was in awful shape, but I told myself that Byron was the best person to take care of him. He's a nurse, and besides, they were closer. I wasn't close to anyone, not after my mother died. Her death signaled the end of the family as we knew it. Some families draw closer together after a death. But some don't. Some go the other way. My mother, tall, elegant, beautiful, was the leader, the maypole that we all danced around. When she died, we retreated into ourselves, and all thoughts of family dissipated like a dream.

I turn down Hogsworth Road. The house where I grew up is in the country, at the edge of woods and fields, the outskirts of Graybridge. I follow the curvy road, pass our few neighbors, drawing closer to our house. Past the Grady barn; I see it in the distance.

Cop cars line the road, and my heart hammers. *What happened?* My thoughts race, and I dig for my phone, which I'd silenced. I glance at the screen. Five missed calls, all from Byron.

I swing my car into the crowded driveway and run for the front door.

The familiar smells hit me as I step over the threshold. Voices buzz in the kitchen, and I nearly run headlong into a slim older woman with a leather bag over her shoulder. She stops short.

"You are?" she asks.

"Esmé Foster," I manage. "What happened?"

Byron appears behind her. "Ez, what are you doing here?"

"Is Dad okay?"

"He's fine. Well, you know. I left you a ton of messages."

"What happened?"

"Let's sit back down in the kitchen," the woman says. She introduces herself, and we get settled. My heart is pounding as I take in the scene out the window, a clutch of cops circling something on the ground.

Detective Myers pulls out a notebook and looks at me expectantly. "So, Esmé Foster, who are you?"

"His sister." I glance at Byron. He's still in his scrubs, his eyes fuzzy with fatigue.

"Do you live here?" Her eyes are a serious, piercing blue, her dark hair pulled up in a messy bun.

"No. I live in Syracuse. I was coming home." My gaze meets Byron's. "What happened?"

"We got a call this morning of a body found," the detective says, her eyes on her notebook.

"I don't understand." All I see is a group of cops and an empty stretcher at the edge of the woods.

Byron takes a deep breath, his gaze on his hands, which are folded and tapping nervously against the table.

"We don't know what happened," Detective Myers says. "That's what we're trying to figure out. When did you leave Syracuse?"

"This morning. Early."

"Why were you coming back?" She glances sidelong at Byron. "Sounds like your brother wasn't expecting you."

"No. I didn't tell anyone."

"When was the last time you were in Graybridge?"

"A little over two years ago," I whisper.

"Coming for a visit?"

This twists my stomach. "No," I say softly. "I was coming home to stay."

She raises her eyebrows, scribbles in her notebook. "Helluva homecoming."

Byron clears his throat. "Really, Ez?" He smirks. "When did you decide this?"

I don't want to fight with him. Not now. Not when I'm so off-kilter. Not when there's a *body* in our backyard. "Dad's okay then?"

"As okay as he can be with barely any liver function." My brother's eyes are like two dark stones. "Good thing you're here. You'll get to see him before he dies. I wasn't sure that was going to happen."

Detective Myers raises her gaze from her notes, like a teacher facing an unruly class. "Okay, then." She digs a business card out of her satchel and places it in front of me. "I'll need to talk to you all again." She and I rise from the table.

"Wait," I say. "You have no idea why there's a body in our yard?"

"Not at the moment."

"Who is it? Do they know?"

Byron stands so suddenly his chair scrapes halfway across the floor. "It's Kara," he says, his eyes meeting mine. "Kara Cunningham."

I drop back down in my chair.

"Do you know her?" Detective Myers asks.

I nod, my chin trembling. I glance out the window and see a flash of light brown hair splayed on the ground between two cops. "She's my best friend."

CHAPTER 4

Rita

A sharp chill penetrates my leather jacket as I tread across the yard through the tall grass to where the victim lies, near the woods. I greet the techs and cops as I make my way to Kara Cunningham's body. Byron Foster ID'd her before I arrived, and the driver's license in her purse confirmed it.

She's lying on her side, a mane of long hair draped over her face. She's fully clothed in black pants and a red sweater and looks like she could be sleeping. That is, until you walk around behind her and see the dark blood clotted against her skull.

Cops are walking the woods, eyes on the forest floor.

"They find anything?" I ask the ME. Susan Gaines and I are of an age, veterans among the mostly younger cops and techs. She readjusts the sunglasses atop her head, which function more to keep her hair out of her eyes than anything else. There's no sun out today.

"Just the purse, so far."

I shiver in the cold and pull up the zipper of my jacket. "No coat?"

"Nope. At least, we haven't found one."

I drop down on my haunches, close to the young woman's head. "Blunt-force trauma?"

"Looks like it, but you know I can't say until the postmortem."

"Anything that might be a weapon?" I stand and brush the wrinkles from my pants. There are numerous branches and rocks lying around that could've done in Kara Cunningham.

Susan shrugs. "The guys have bagged up a few possibilities."

I walk slowly around the body but don't see anything significant. She was a small woman, and I can't help but think she resembles a bird, tiny and small-boned and forgotten out here near the woods. I inhale deeply of the chill autumn air and close my eyes, trying to get a feel for this young woman's last moments. What was she doing out here? Who was here with her, and why would they leave her here to die alone? What emotion drove them to end her life? I sigh. My gut isn't giving me any help.

"No sign of another person?" I ask Susan.

She shakes her head. "Not that I noticed, but somebody was out here with her."

"I guess she couldn't have just fallen?"

The ME smirks. "No."

"Time of death?"

She gives me that look like, *Really, Rita?*

"Just a wild guess, Susan. Mr. Foster heard a scream last night but has no idea what time it was."

"I'll let you know." She turns and starts barking out instructions. I trudge back to my van and set off down the road. The nearest neighbor is less than a quarter mile away. It's a good place to start.

The farmhouse looks like it's been here at least a hundred years. The clapboards were painted white once. Now they're a dull, peeling gray. The porch steps sag and sway slightly as I make my way up to the front door. But there's a shiny new truck in the driveway, so hopefully someone's home. I rap on the wooden door, and a man opens it right away, as if he'd watched me pull into the driveway.

He's tall, thirty-something, with long, wavy brown hair and crooked teeth. The smell of weed envelopes him like a cloud.

"Can I help you?" he asks.

"I hope so. Detective Rita Myers, Graybridge Police Department." I show him my identification.

He nods like he's considering whether to believe me or not.

"I'd like to ask you a few questions."

He swings the door wide, and I follow him through the hall and into a fairly bare front room. There's a couch with a stained brown throw cover over it and a big flat-screen against a wall that was painted pink sometime in the distant past. There's an end table that he pulls around and sits on, leaving me the couch. I sink into its springless depths and pull out my notebook.

"This about all the cop cars over at the Fosters?"

"Yes. What's your name?" I ask, pencil poised.

"Ray. Raymond Ridley Junior."

"You live here alone, Mr. Ridley?"

"With my sister." An image slowly forms in my mind. A little girl with a tangle of white-blond hair. And the name Ridley. I joined the Graybridge PD nearly twenty years ago, after years as a cop in Boston. A few months before I got here, there'd been a drowning in a pond on the Ridley property. There were two little girls in a rowboat. The girls had gotten into an argument, and the older girl had knocked her little sister out of the boat. It was an ugly, tragic story that made the Boston papers. I remember the picture of the girl, the one who died. She was a little thing, almost angelic-looking, and the community was taking it hard, still taking it badly when I moved out here. I remember hearing that the older girl was charged in the case but ultimately went to a psychiatric facility. Since she was convicted as a juvenile and so long ago, she's probably been released by now. Is she the sister who lives with Ray Ridley?

"What's your sister's name?" I ask.

"Cynthia." He smirks. "I'm sure you know who she is."

I nod. "Is she home? I'd like to talk with her."

"No. She's at a doctor's appointment."

"Was she home last night?"

"Yeah." He stretches his arms over his head, and his T-shirt rises, revealing a slack, white, hairy stomach.

"Will she be back soon?" A worn armchair is squeezed into a corner near the window. A huge orange cat sits in it like a sphinx and eyes me suspiciously. Yarn is heaped in a basket on the floor. Two long knitting needles are thrust into a bright yellow skein.

"Not for a couple hours."

I'll need to talk to her another time. "Okay, Ray, you hear anything last evening?"

"No. What happened?" He tips his head in the Fosters' direction.

"Were you home yesterday?"

"Most of the day."

"Where did you go?"

"Ran out to the grocery store."

"Time?"

He shrugs. "Afternoon, I guess."

"Can you be more specific?"

"Somewhere around five, I think."

"What time did you get home?"

"About six maybe. I'm not sure."

"When you left or returned home, you see anything strange, out of place? A car parked around here you didn't recognize?"

"No." He jumps up from the end table and walks to the window that looks out on the road. The Fosters' place is visible in the distance.

"What the hell happened?" He chews his bottom lip.

"What time did you go to bed?"

He digs at his nose. "Uh, I can't remember. Late. I watched some TV and fell asleep on the couch."

"What time did you wake up?"

He snorts. "A while ago. Don't remember."

"So, you slept straight through? Didn't hear anything?"

"Nope. What happened? Byron's old man okay?"

"Yes. Mr. Foster is alive and well." Although well is a stretch.

"What happened then?" Ray bounces on his heels and walks over to the chair in the corner, lifts a knitting needle from its nest, then pushes it back into place. The cat has disappeared, annoyed by my presence maybe.

"We've got a body by the woods behind the Fosters' house."

Ray's eyes glance up and catch mine. "No shit?" He swallows and licks his lips; his eyelids twitch. "Who is it?"

"We can't say yet."

He nears the window again. "In Byron's backyard?"

"Yes. You been out in those woods lately?"

He shrugs. "Yeah. I go for nature walks now and then."

I suppress a smirk. He doesn't exactly look the nature-walking type. But who knows? He reminds me of a couple of old hippies who lived in my Boston neighborhood when I was a kid. They'd sit in the park across the street, legs folded, listening to an old radio, communing with nature. Ma warned us to steer clear of them, which only fueled my curiosity. I would sneak into the park with my trusty notebook and spy on them from the bushes, always the nosy Nancy, as my big sisters used to call me.

I clear my throat. "When was the last time you were out there?"

He draws a deep breath, looks at the ceiling. "Yesterday."

"What time yesterday?"

"Afternoon."

"See anything unusual?"

"Nope."

"You know the Fosters?"

"Yeah. I grew up in this house. They grew up over there. I went to school with Esmé. Well, she was two years behind me."

"What about Byron?"

"He was two years behind Esmé, so I didn't know him that good. When I graduated, he was still in middle school." He turns toward the window, interested in the commotion.

"You see much of him these days?"

Mr. Ridley turns back toward me, his hands in the pockets of his dirty jeans. "Not much. He works nights. We were never really friends, you know?"

"What do you do for a living?"

"I used to do construction." He sucks on his teeth. "But mostly now I take care of my sister."

Huh. "Why does she need you to take care of her?"

He shrugs. "She's got a lot of issues. She was in a group home for a while, but she kept running away, coming back here, so my mother told me I could stay in the house and take care of her. She'd pay me to do it."

"Where's your mother?"

"In Florida, in a senior apartment place. You can't live there if you're not fifty-five, so my mom couldn't take Cynthia with her." He snorts. "Not that she wanted to anyway."

"So, what exactly is wrong with Cynthia?" I need to know what to expect when I question her.

Ray lets go a deep breath. "When she was little, about two years old . . . I was just a baby, so I don't remember it. Anyway, my dad told me that while he was at work, Mom fell asleep on the couch, and Cynthia fell down the cellar stairs. She hit her head and had brain damage. She was in the hospital in Boston for a long time. She has trouble thinking straight and remembering things. She can't live on her own."

Okay. Not exactly a diagnosis, but I guess it's the best Ray can do. The injury might make Cynthia an unreliable witness. But we'll see. Maybe she saw or heard something last night, maybe not. Or maybe . . . I'll need to take a look at her records.

"Who's with Cynthia now, at the doctor?"

"A lady, a home health aide. She comes once a week to
Itake her."

"Okay, Ray. Here's my card if you think of anything, notice
anything that might help. And give me a call when your sister's
home. I'll need to speak with her."

He takes the card and shoves it in his back pocket. "You can't
tell me whose body they found?"

"Nope." I walk toward the front door, Ray on my heels.

"Did Byron do it?"

I stand still, look back over my shoulder. "What makes you
think he did it?"

Ray reaches his arm past me, grabs the doorknob. "Just wondering. Body was found by his woods, right?"

"It was."

"Well, then." He shrugs. "I wouldn't put it past him."

CHAPTER 5

Esmé

"So, you're really moving back?" Byron asks.

"Yes," I whisper, my mind awhirl, trying to comprehend that my friend is dead in our backyard. I clutch my brother's arm. "What happened to Kara?"

"I have no idea. When was the last time you talked to her?"

I walk toward the window. "Not in a long time, years."

Byron snorts. "And she's your best friend?"

"She was. You know that."

"Back in high school. Before you ditched us all for your career."

I wheel on him. "Is that how you saw it? Me taking off to dance?"

"That's what you did, didn't you?"

It's more complicated than that, and I don't want to talk about it now. Tears gather in my eyes, and my stomach knots up. Kara and I had been friends since kindergarten. Growing up, we did everything together. And because her single mom worked, I convinced my mom to pick Kara up after school and take her home with us so that she didn't have to go to day care. We played every day in the house when rain pattered on the roof or outside in those same woods when the weather was warm. We stayed friends right through high school, and it was Kara I confided in when I decided to leave Graybridge and start a new life as a dancer in another state. She was heartbroken. We were more like sisters at that point. I told her we'd keep in touch. But I didn't. I'd cut her off, like I did all my friends after I left. I just wanted to get away from Graybridge and all the painful memories here. I was young and selfish, and now it's too late to make things right. How could I have let Kara down that way?

Guilt floods over me as Kara's body is lifted from the ground and placed on the stretcher by uniformed strangers. Byron joins me at the window, and we watch, helpless and confused. The stretcher gets stuck a time or two in the muck and tall grass. Finally, the men wheel her around the house and out of sight. There are still cops out by the woods, eyes on the ground, searching.

"What was she doing out there, Byron? I don't understand. What could've happened to her?" I cover my eyes with my hands. "Her mother must be devastated. Oh, my God." I sink down in a chair, emotions rippling through me thinking of Mrs. Cunningham. Kara was her only child, all she had. More memories of my friend flit through my mind, her high-pitched giggle that never changed as she grew older. Her pixie face that grew into real beauty as we became teenagers. A sob bursts though my lips.

"I have no idea." Byron scrubs his hands over his face. "It's surreal. I found her at the end of the path like she was coming out of the woods. When Dad told me he heard a scream, I walked out there and saw her lying in the grass. I checked her right away, called her name. But it was no use. She was dead. Had been for a while. There was nothing I could do except call 911."

My brother looks exhausted, not just his usual coming-off-his-shift tired. He shakes his head and clears his throat. "Someone killed her, Ez."

"How do you know?"

"The back of her head was covered with blood."

"Maybe she fell."

"No. I've seen my share of falls when I worked in the ER. Someone crushed her skull."

I shiver, cover my mouth with my hands, and look back at the woods.

"I better make Dad's breakfast," Byron says. "He should've eaten hours ago."

"Is he still upstairs?"

"Yeah." Byron turns and heads to the kitchen counter.

The hall leading to Dad's bedroom is dark. I have to pass my old room to get to his, so I stop, turn the knob, and go into my room first. I'm drawn to the window that looks out on the backyard. The forest stretches for acres behind our house; paths lead through it from various points and converge at the pond. It was our magical playground when we were kids, filled with wonder and then danger too. Thrilling and scary at the same time. Then, as teenagers, it became our rebellious haunt, a place to get away where we could drink stolen beer and pretend we were grown-up and so much smarter than the adults in our lives.

Thoughts of Kara and our friends fill my mind. Our little group that made up my world before I moved away. When we were five years old, Kara and I started ballet lessons together. My mom signed me up, and I, of course, asked for Kara to sign up too. At the Graybridge Dance Academy, we met and befriended two other little girls in the class, Laney Morelli and Christy French. Soon, my mother was the designated driver for the four of us. The other moms were busy with work or multiple children, and they were only too happy to have my mom take charge. That's where we bonded, in dance class, as little, bun-headed, pink-clad girls. Friendships that would only deepen as the years went by. I wonder where Laney and Christy are now. Do they know yet about Kara? Are they still as close as we all used to be? The thought of facing them sends shivers down my spine. Do they hate me now for cutting them out of my life? Tears spring anew, and I quickly wipe them away. I need to see my dad. I'll have to think about Kara later.

My father's room is even more depressing than it was when I was home last. The bed has been pushed into the corner, with its old quilt dangling to the floor. The rest of the room is nearly bare. But my mother's picture still sits on the bedside table, the sole decoration in the spartan room. She smiles her radiant smile, blond hair lying in curls over her shoulders. The photo was taken at one of the backyard parties she liked to throw in the summer in the sunshine, the last summer before she died.

I sniff back tears as I near my father. He's looking out the window and doesn't hear me as I cross the floor.

"Dad?"

He doesn't move, his eyes transfixed on the backyard, where cops search the woods like busy ants.

"Dad?" He slowly turns his head. His sunken eyes meet mine.

"Esmé?" His voice is scratchy.

"Hi. I thought I'd come home and see you." I reach down and grab his hand. It's thin and feels like old paper.

He nods like he's trying to process what I just said. He places his other hand over mine, and tears gather in his eyes. I feel a stab of guilt for staying away so long. He looks worse than I ever imagined. I inhale a ragged breath as he drops my hand and points to the window.

"Something bad happened, Esmé," he says, his voice close to normal.

"I know, Dad. But it's okay. The cops are going to figure it out."

Tears spill over his cheeks. "She's not coming back . . ."

I know he's not talking about Kara. This is another reason home is so hard. My father's grief is still raw, even all these years later. Byron pushes the door open. He's carrying a tray, sets it on the bed, and tucks an old striped dish towel over Dad's shirt. He places a half-full cup of black coffee in Dad's trembling hand.

"Drink, Dad. You'll feel better." I stand back and watch as Byron efficiently helps our father eat a piece of toast, drink a cup of coffee, a routine that I'm not a part of, a life I've left behind.

Dad shakes his head. "I'm done, By. No more."

My father seems as helpless as a child. I follow Byron out of the room. "He looks terrible," I whisper.

"He's dying, Ez. I told you that. I've been telling you that for the last six months."

Byron and I talk on the phone about once a week, and he did tell me that Dad was going downhill. But I didn't want to believe it.

"He's only fifty-eight. He looks eighty-eight."

"With as much as he drinks, I'm surprised he looks as good as he does."

Back in the kitchen, my eyes are drawn to the window again. The cops are still there, still searching. Byron places the dishes in the sink.

"Why do you buy it for him? He can't go get it himself, can he?"

My brother turns to face me, his eyes flashing, and I step back. "I don't buy it for him. He hasn't driven since last spring, when he ended up in the ditch in front of Ray's place. Irene buys it."

"She's still coming over?" Irene and her husband were friends of Mom and Dad. They seemed to always be around, sitting at the kitchen table, playing cards with my parents, bringing over casseroles for dinners shared on the picnic table in our backyard. Then Mom died and Irene's husband left, leaving my father and Irene to carry on.

"Same as always. She's here most days when I'm at work. But you'd know that if you were here."

I drop down in a kitchen chair. "Well, I'm here now. I'll help."

Byron leans against the counter. "Why? Why bother now? You and Kevin finished finally?"

I'm too tired, too upset about Kara to rise to the bait. "Yes."

He nods and runs water over Dad's dishes.

"You need to get to bed?" I ask.

Byron turns to face me. "Normally, I'd take a shower and try to get some sleep, but . . ." He points out the window. "I can't sleep now." He rubs his hand over his mouth.

"What was Kara doing out there, Byron?" I haven't been out there in years and can't think of any reason Kara would've been back there now.

Byron shrugs. "I have no idea. I need to get in the shower. Then I'll be back down," he says and leaves the kitchen. I sit at the table and watch the cops work.

CHAPTER 6

Rita

As I drive back to the station, Ray Ridley's statement tumbles through my mind. Why would he suspect Byron Foster? When I pressed him on it, he offered nothing but that he thought young Mr. Foster was a dick. That might be, but that doesn't make him a killer.

And old Mr. Foster has me shaken. Is this what's in store for my brother? Wasting away, mind gone? But they're nothing alike. Danny's an English professor at a local college. He's the smartest one of all nine of us, the only one who made it all the way through college and then some. He works, shops, socializes, lives a normal life, sort of. Most people don't even suspect he has a drinking problem. But I know. I see the glass that's always in his hand when he's at home. I know there's a stockpile of booze in the kitchen cupboard. I know his mind floats too often to Ricky and Jimmy, our brothers who should be here but died long ago.

A lady in the car behind me lays on her horn as the light turns green. *Yeah, yeah, I'm going.*

I called ahead and had Detective Broderick do a background search on all parties involved so far. Lauren, young and eager, reminding me too much of myself sometimes, is waiting for me in my office when I get there.

"Didn't find much, Rita," she says as I hang my jacket on the back of my chair.

"Let's hear it." I settle behind my desk.

"Byron Foster, twenty-seven years old. Works at Graybridge General hospital. He and his wife divorced a year ago. They share custody of a two-year-old daughter." She glances up at me. "No criminal record. Thomas Foster. Fifty-eight. Was cited for drunk driving twice in the last ten years. His wife was killed in a car accident thirteen years ago. He was driving."

"Was he intoxicated that time?"

"No. Just an accident on an icy road. He wasn't charged."

"Okay. Anything else on him?"

"Nothing." She clears her throat, flips her long and often troublesome braid back over her shoulder.

"What about the daughter, Esmé?"

"A couple of traffic tickets. That's it. I did find a bunch of articles about her going way back."

"What kind of articles?"

"She was a ballerina of some note. She danced locally as a kid. Got parts in the annual professional production of *The Nutcracker.* Then she went to Syracuse and got a job with a ballet company out there."

"Huh." I can see that. She definitely had that dancer look. Skinny, light brown hair pulled up in a tight bun. "Anything else? Any run-ins with the law?"

"Just the speeding tickets."

"What about Raymond Ridley, the neighbor?" He certainly seemed nervous.

Lauren juggles her laptop, takes a deep breath. "He's got quite a rap sheet. Mostly misdemeanors. Minor drug charges. One B and E when he was seventeen."

"He do any time?"

"Doesn't look like it."

I'm fumbling with my bootlaces. Must've tied them too tight this morning, and they're pinching the tops of my feet.

"I found articles about his sister," Lauren says quietly.

"Yeah. I remembered the incident when I started questioning him. It happened right before I moved out here, but I remember the coverage. His older sister lives with him."

Lauren's gaze meets mine. "I saw that she'd been released from a psychiatric facility about a year and a half ago. Did you talk to her?"

I shake my head, wiggle my toes. "She wasn't home."

"I read some of the articles. I was just a kid when it happened, but I remember overhearing my mother and her friends talking about it. I remember them saying that the Ridleys were odd, and that Mrs. Ridley was an unfit mother. I wasn't sure exactly what they meant by that. I just remember that people were really upset." Lauren tips her laptop in my direction. She's got one of the old articles from the *Graybridge Gazette* pulled up. There's a black-and-white photo at the top. Two little girls in ballet costumes. I lean in to read the caption: *Wendy Ridley and Esmé Foster ready for the Graybridge Dance Academy annual recital one month before Wendy was killed.* Huh.

"People were still talking about it when I started here." I sniff and bend down to retie my boots. Graybridge, like many small towns, has a strong sense of community. When a kid dies, it hits everyone. Kind of like my old neighborhood in Boston. When my brother Jimmy died of leukemia when he was eleven, everyone rallied around my parents. They stopped by the house with casseroles and money. Back in those days, you gave money to grieving families. "Just in case," they'd say. Maybe a leftover tradition from long-ago days in Ireland when money was scarce and death a whisper from everyone's doorstep. I sigh, thinking of Jimmy. Clear my throat.

"Dig up our files on Wendy Ridley's death. And see if you can track down Cynthia's files from when she was incarcerated."

"You think she might've been involved in Kara's murder?" Lauren asks.

"Let's cover our bases. I hope they wouldn't have let her out if she's still a danger to society." I snort. "But we all know how that goes."

Lauren clicks the keys of her computer. "Will do."

"What about our victim? What about Kara?"

Lauren looks up over her laptop screen. "A couple of traffic tickets is all I found so far."

"You guys get anywhere with her phone, social media?"

"I finished the paperwork for her phone records. Working on the social media now."

"Chief back yet?"

She shakes her head.

Bob Murphy and I go back years. And while we're nearly the same age, he's counting the days to retirement. Bob's looking forward to leaving all this excitement behind and dividing his time between Graybridge and his little place in Florida. He muses about spending his summer days at Fenway and playing cards with his buddies, who include my ex-husband, Ed, and fishing in the Gulf. I'm happy for Bob. He's earned his retirement more than most people. When Kara was identified, Bob took it hard. He knows her mother. They were neighbors for a number of years before Bob bought his condo. He remembered Kara, an only child, growing up with her single mom. He said he helped Cathy out once in a while with minor repairs and the like. She took care of his dog when he was gone. When the ID came in, Bob sighed, put on his coat, and trudged out of the station. He said he'd break the news to Cathy himself.

That's the worst part of this job, bar none. Over the years, I've done my share of shattering parents' worlds. Those days are the worst, and in those moments, I'm always glad I never had kids.

"Thanks, Lauren. Let me know what else you come up with."

"Will do, Rita." She leaves, holding her laptop and somehow clicking keys as she walks.

Bob is back in his office, door closed. No one dares disturb him, and everyone looks to me as his old friend and contemporary. Well, I've got to know what he learned from Kara's mom, so I take a deep breath, knock, and walk in without waiting for an invitation. Bob's sitting behind his big, messy desk, his head in his hands. He's gone nearly all gray, and his face droops like an old bulldog's. He glances up as I sit in the chair opposite him.

"You okay?" I ask.

"I'm too old for this, Rita." Everything about Bob sags. "What the hell's wrong with the world?"

I don't know what to say. I've asked myself that same question over the years, and so far, I haven't come up with an answer.

He huffs out a tired breath. "She was just a kid, Reet. Younger than my own daughter."

"It's tragic," I agree.

"I remember when she was little, riding a scooter in her driveway." He points a meaty finger at me. "I yelled at her one day because she was getting too goddamn close to the street."

"I'll do everything I can to find the bastard who did this to her."

He nods and fishes his old notebook out of his coat pocket and drops it on the desk. The leather cover is scarred and battered. It's the same one, paper replaced as needed, that he carried years ago as a detective.

"Let me give you what I've got."

I open my own notebook and wait.

"Kara was twenty-nine years old, living with her mother because she couldn't afford rent on her own. She worked as a junior insurance agent." Bob spells out the name of the company. "Her mom says she was fine. No trouble. Acting completely normal in the days leading up. Mom was a little worried that she hadn't come home last night but figured she stayed with a friend, which she did occasionally. The last time Cathy spoke to her was yesterday about lunchtime. She called her mom every day at the same time."

"Anything unusual in the conversation yesterday?"

Bob shakes his head. "No."

"When was the last time her mom actually saw her?"

"Yesterday morning, when they were both getting ready for work." Bob blows out a breath.

"How's Mrs. Cunningham taking it?"

"Not good. Kara was all she had. Her sister's with her. I called her on the way over, and she got there before I did. Thank God. But Cathy's barely hanging on. The sister called her doctor, and he called in something for her." Bob takes a deep breath, runs his massive hands through his gray hair. "Jesus. Let's get everyone together and meet in the conference room in fifteen minutes."

"All right."

"This is your investigation, Rita."

"What about Doug?" He's the other lead detective in our small department and has been champing at the bit for a big case.

Bob shakes his head. "Not this time. It's yours. Besides, you've already done the initial work. Doug and Lauren will help out, but you're the lead."

The room is chilly. Bob has gone quiet, his mind somewhere else. I only hope he's thinking of his place in Florida and not all the misery he's witnessed over the years. He pushes his notebook over to me. "The names of Kara's friends," he says.

I start to copy them into my notebook.

"No, Rita. Just take it. Take the whole goddamned thing." He shuffles to his feet and walks out.